MRAC

Hall Pass

By

Award winning Author

Breanna J

This book is a work of fiction. Names, characters, places and incidents are either the product of the author's imagination or are used fictionally. Any resemblance to actual persons, living or dead, or to actual events or locales is entirely coincidental.

This book is licensed for your personal enjoyment only. This book may not be re-sold or given away to other people. If you like to share this book with another person, please purchase an additional copy for each person you share it with.

Copyright © 2024 Epic Dynasty Publishing All rights reserved. Including the right to reproduce this book or portions thereof, in any form. No part of this text may be reproduced in any form without the express written permission of the author.

Join Our Email List!

Stay in the loop! Sign up on our website for exclusive discounts, exciting prizes, contests, and more.

Visit us at: (http://www.authorbreannaj.com)

Don't miss out!

DEDICATIONS

To those who dare to chase their dreams and embrace the unexpected,

may you always find the courage to break free from the ordinary.

For the dreamers, the lovers, and the risk-takers—

this journey is for you.

With all my love,

Breanna J.

ACKNOWLEDGMENTS

I would like to extend my heartfelt gratitude to everyone who has been part of this journey with me since 2017. To my readers, thank you for your unwavering support and enthusiasm; your passion truly fuels my creativity.

To my family and friends, your encouragement and belief in me have been my guiding light. A special thank you to my editor, whose invaluable insights transformed my ideas into a polished story.

And to my daughter, Kahiya, I pick up my pen and write so that you will always know that living your dreams is possible.

With deepest appreciation,
Breanna J

Breanna J.

ONE

Dior

"Damn, I look good," I murmured to myself, admiring my reflection in the mirror. The red lace of my bra and panty set hugged my curves just right, and the black heels I slipped on added an extra edge. I had spent all day pampering myself, which wasn't something I did often because I was into saving money when I could and handling my womanly maintenance at home. I had decided to dye my hair to go with the fall season that was starting. I had a fresh red gel pedicure and a fresh set of red acrylic nails. My lash tech had gotten my lashes perfect, and my wax lady made sure I was smooth like silk. I was preparing for dinner with my best friend, but a part of me secretly hoped to catch my husband's eye.

After five years of marriage, I never expected us to already be in a dry spell. I had signed up for a marriage like the one my parents had. They were madly in love with each other. They adored each other. Even now, in their 50s, they still looked at each other with so much love. They gave me so much to inspire me and base my marriage on.

Just then, the bedroom door swung open, and I spun around, flashing a smile. "Hey babe," I greeted him, my heart fluttering with anticipation. "Hey D"," he said as he walked straight past me into the bathroom, barely acknowledging my presence.

"Dior, don't trip," I whispered to myself, trying to shake off the disappointment and anger. Damn it I looked good, smelled good and I felt good. How the hell did he just ignore me like I was a fly on the wall. "Maybe he had a long day at work and needed a moment." I walked over to my dresser, clasping on my favorite jewelry—a delicate gold chain Sergio gave me when we first started dating and some sparkling earrings that caught the light. I spritzed on my favorite perfume, a sweet yet sultry scent that paired perfectly with the body glaze I had applied earlier.

When the bathroom door finally creaked open, I plastered on my best smile, ready for a redo. "Hey," I said, my voice dripping with seduction, hoping to capture his attention. This time, he looked at me, though his enthusiasm was still lacking.

"Where are you going?" he asked, tone flat.

"Getting ready to go out with Destiny," I replied, stepping closer. "But I wanted to see you before I left." I wrapped my arms around his neck, leaning in for a kiss, hoping to ignite some spark.

"Oh really?" he replied, the lack of excitement still evident in his voice.

"Yeah, I missed you today," I said, my words laced with sincerity as I pressed my lips against his. I felt his hands begin to wander, rubbing up and down my sides as he licked his lips, and I couldn't help but bite my bottom lip, nodding slightly as if to coax him into my world.

"Is that right?" He finally met my gaze, the fire in his eyes flickering to life as he began to respond to my unspoken invitation. I could feel the tension shift, and for a moment, the weight of the day melted away, leaving just the two of us, caught in an electrifying moment that promised more than just a simple goodbye.

He walked me over to the bed, a spark of electricity crackling in the air between us, and then he gently pushed me down onto the soft sheets. He pulled his shirt off, revealing that sexy body of his—muscles taut and perfectly defined, a work of art that made my heart race.

But there it was, the one flaw I couldn't ignore, and that should have been a red flag not to marry him: his ex's name tattooed on the left side of his chest, a stark reminder of a love that once was. I knew the story all too well—she was his first love, and tragically, she'd died in a car accident. He refused to get rid of the tattoo, claiming it was a tribute to someone who'd meant so much to him. It still confused me. I was his wife and was supposed to mean the most to him. So, removing it shouldn't have even been an argument we had to have. But after expressing my feelings on it so many times and him not changing his stance about it. I swallowed my discomfort and did my best to look past it, focusing instead on the warmth of his skin and the way his eyes locked onto mine, igniting a fiery passion that pulled me in deeper.

I leaned back, inviting him closer, determined to create our memories.

He pulled down his pants and unleashed his third leg. Just like love and basketball, he gave me a smirk. "He slid in, and my body formed into him. "Damn this pussy feels so good." he said to me. "It's all yours, Daddy. Fuck me! Fuck me real good please." I told him. We were only about six strokes in, and I could feel his body tensing up. "Not yet, baby not yet." I moaned out. "Fuck…. fuck… fuck…" he moaned out before I felt his dick jump and knew that he was done. It was always like this done before it even got started.

Had I not known him better, I would have sworn he was cheating, splitting his time between me and some other woman. It was a familiar pattern: morning, noon, or night, he'd give it his all—well, sort of. Ten strokes, and it was over. Every damn time. No matter how I tried to spice things up, role play, sexy lingerie that hugged my curves just right, positions that would make a seasoned couple blush. But it never mattered. Ten strokes and he was done, leaving me to finish the job myself. I used to think I had the kind of "good pussy" that could bring a man to his knees, but what was the point if I wasn't getting my nut off as well?

Honestly, at this point, I could practically hear my rose toy sighing in frustration, tired of being my only reliable partner. I wanted fireworks, a passion that lingered long after the sheets had cooled, but instead, I was stuck in a loop that felt more like a chore than a thrill.

Sergio laid next to me, breathing heavily, while I stared at the ceiling, my annoyance simmering just below the surface. I should've just used my toy, got my nut off, gotten my ass dressed, and left, I thought, rolling my eyes in frustration. Sure, Sergio was fine as hell, his body sculpted like a damn statue, and yeah, he was packing down below, but when it came to the bedroom, he was a complete letdown. He swore he was beating the pussy up, but honestly, he wasn't even scratching the surface and his pride made him unteachable. He swore up and down he knew everything about pussy. But he didn't know how to eat it or fuck it. At this point, he was just a waste of good dick.

I sat up, adjusting my panties, trying to shake off the irritation. "Bae, can I drive your car tonight? Mine's been making this weird noise, and I'm not sure why," I asked, hoping for some sympathy.

"Nah, take an Uber and call your dad to come look at your car tomorrow," he replied dismissively, not even bothering to meet my gaze.

"I'm a married woman; I shouldn't have to call my daddy every time I have issues," I shot back, my tone sharper than I intended.

"Man, I said what I said. Figure it out," he retorted, grabbing the covers with a casual arrogance that made my blood boil. That's when I glanced down at his hand, and my heart sank.

"Sergio, where the fuck is your wedding ring?" I demanded, my voice rising. Hitting him with a pillow.

"I took it off; my finger was itching after work. It's in the car," he said boldly as if it was the most casual thing in the world.

"Your finger was itching?" I said my eyes were twitching as I looked at him.

"yeah"

I couldn't believe it. Here we were, wrapped up in our little mess, and he was acting like it was no big deal. My head spun with frustration. How could he just shrug off something so important? I sighed, knowing this wasn't the end of our problems, just another layer of the chaos that seemed to define us.

"You really got me…" I stopped myself realizing that going off at this moment wasn't going to change or help anything. So I got out of bed.

I couldn't believe the level of disrespect he was throwing my way, right to my face. It was like a slap that stung deep, igniting a fire in my chest. My blood was boiling, and before I completely fucked up my night, I needed to get the hell out of there. I threw on some clothes—nothing fancy, just a pair of jeans and a fitted top that hugged my curves—and snatched my car keys off the counter.

As I bolted for my car, my heart raced faster than the engine roaring to life. I peeled out of the driveway, tires screeching as I left all that drama behind for now. The cool night air rushed through the open window, mingling with my frustration and making me feel a little more alive.

The city lights blurred together as I sped down the street, the neon signs flickering like a heartbeat. I couldn't let him get to me, but damn if he didn't know how to push my buttons. I needed to clear my head and find a place where I could breathe without feeling his shadow looming over me. Maybe this drink with Destiny was right. On time. She always knew how to lift my spirits—or at least drown them in something strong. As I navigated the familiar streets, I vowed to reclaim my night, no matter what it took.

When I pulled up to the bar, the neon lights flickered like a heartbeat, and there, at our usual spot, was Destiny, already perched at the table and waiting for me. "Hey Ladies, Welcome back. What can I get you ladies?" the waitress asked as soon as I slid into the seat. "Surprise me. Just make sure it's something strong," I replied, my voice sharper than usual. "Whatever you bring her, bring me" Destiny added, her eyes dancing with mischief.

As soon as the waitress disappeared, Destiny leaned in, her expression shifting to concern. "What happened?"

"It's Sergio," I sighed, sinking into my chair.

"When is it not fucking Sergio?" she replied, rolling her eyes so dramatically I half expected them to get stuck that way. "I love my husband; God knows I do. But the shit he pulls? Like tonight, he took off his wedding ring because his finger was itching, and didn't bother to put it back on before coming home."

"What the fuck?" Destiny's brows shot up; disbelief etched across her face like a bad tattoo.

"Exactly," I said, my frustration bubbling over like a pot left on the stove too long.

"And you just let that shit slide?" she pressed, disbelief turning into indignation.

"I just left the house, yelling and screaming wasn't going to solve anything." I told her, feeling the weight of my own indecision.

"Fuck that. You should've told that nigga the fuck off or went upside his head. Clearly, he's got you twisted. Playing in your damn face like that? Only a sneaky nigga takes his ring off. But he's a sneaky but bold nigga, too. Took it off and didn't even bother to put it back on, then had the nerve to give you some Wack ass excuse. Man, friend, I'm telling you, stop letting his ass play in your face. You know I'd fuck him up for messing with you."

I had to admit, I loved how Destiny could go from zero to a hundred about me. It was like she had a fire in her soul, ready to defend me against the world, and it was comforting in a way I didn't expect.

Just then, the waitress returned, setting down our drinks with a flourish. "I also brought shots on the house; looks like you ladies could use them," she said with a smile.

"Thank you!" Destiny beamed slightly flirting with the waitress, like she did every time we came here; and the waitress walked off, leaving us to our conversation.

"You're always flirting with her." I said. "It's all fun but back to you. Do you think he's cheating?" Destiny asked, her tone serious now.

"I hope he's not out here embarrassing me like that. I can't even deal with it," I replied, my heart sinking.

"If he is, don't be embarrassed, friend. These niggas ain't shit," she said, trying to comfort me, but it barely scratched the surface of my anxiety.

"Shit, I don't need anyone else knowing that he's got all that dick and doesn't know what to do with it. His ass only lasts about ten strokes. Can you imagine the laughs I'd get? They'd be cackling at me for settling for that, not because they fucked my husband," I vented, downing my shot in one go.

"Bitch, I know you're lying," Destiny said, bursting into laughter. But the look I shot her let her know I wasn't playing. My heart was heavy, and this was no joke. We both knew this was just the beginning of a long night of pouring out our frustrations and drowning them in liquor.

"bestie I say this with all love, stop letting Sergio fuck you over especially when he can't fuck you. You letting that nigga get away with too much. Stand on business with his ass. At this point, if you got to fuck yourself to get off you need to focus on yourself and put yourself first. Husband or not. I need you to remember who you are and how fucking beautiful you look.

I don't even know how many drinks I'd had by then, but the Lord knows I had poured my heart out to Destiny. But that's what best friends were for. At least I was feeling better, the weight of the night beginning to lift. We were deep in conversation, laughing and sharing stories when suddenly a shadow loomed over our table, and the smell of Creed cologne that I knew all too well filled my nose. Both of us looked up, and my breath caught in my throat.

"Hello there, Dior," he said, his voice sounding like a growl of authority, smiling at me, and I felt a rush of emotions flood in. It had been years since I'd seen Armand, but time had been kind to him. He was a perfect mix of Morris Chestnut and Method Man, his presence commanding attention without even trying.

"Hello, Armand," I replied slowly, trying to play it cool but feeling my heart race.

"Girl, stop acting like a stranger, give me a hug! It's been way too long," he said. I stood up, and as he wrapped his arms around me, I did everything I could to resist melting into him. The familiar scent of him—Creed mixed with something uniquely him—wrapped around me like a warm blanket, and memories I thought I had buried came rushing back.

I remembered my first year of college when he got into some trouble and was sent up north. No one ever spoke about what he had gotten caught up in, but I suffered through the silence, missing him more than I could express. He refused to call anyone or let anyone see him other than his brothers, saying he didn't want anyone's life to stop just because he was doing time. I respected that, but it didn't make the ache of his absence any easier to bear.

With time, I eventually moved on and met Sergio, but seeing Armand again stirred something deep inside me. The feel of his strong arms around me and the intoxicating smell of him was enough to send my heart racing and my mind spinning. I could feel the walls I'd built around my heart starting to crack, and I knew this night was about to take a turn I hadn't expected.

"So, how have you been? When did you get back?" I asked, trying to sound casual, but my heart was racing like it had been shot out of a cannon.

"Good. Real good. Can't complain—been back for a while now," he replied, a hint of warmth flickering in his eyes that sent my stomach into a delightful somersault.

"And how are Ahmad and Armani?" I inquired, leaning in a little closer, desperate to catch every detail.

"My brothers are really good. They're both living life to the fullest. Armani actually has twin boys that look just like him," he told me, a proud smile spreading across his face.

"Really? You're an uncle? That's crazy," I said, lost in a wave of nostalgia. I couldn't help but think back to our younger years when every girl in the neighborhood was head over heels for one of the Riggins brothers. They were fine, no doubt, with charisma that set them apart from any guy around. I had been lucky enough to snag the baby brother. Ahmad was the oldest—when Armand and I were freshmen, he was already a senior, playing the dad role for them. Armani was just a year younger than Ahmad. But he and Armand were inseparable. If you saw one, the other wasn't too far behind. The only real difference was that Armani had a reputation as a player, always charming his way into hearts and trouble.

"How's your mom? I haven't seen Ms. Pam in years" I asked. The moment the words left my lips, I could see his expression shift, a shadow crossing his face that made my heart clench. The weight of his past settled between us like a thick fog, heavy and unyielding. "She passed," he replied, the words tumbling out quickly as if he were trying to shield himself from the pain. I wished I had known to steer clear of this moment, but a part of me was instantly saddened I hadn't been able to pay my respects. His mom had always treated me like a daughter, even when Armand was locked up. Back then, she was my rock, always offering me a warm meal and a listening ear whenever. But when I **started** dating Sergio, she backed away, I think just to respect Sergio's feelings.

"Oh my god, I'm so sorry," I said, my heart sinking for him.

"It's cool. Just glad I was home when it happened," he said, his voice steady but laced with a quiet sorrow. "She could really rest peacefully, you know? Not leave this world worrying about me."

I nodded, feeling the bittersweet comfort in his words. It was a harsh reality, losing someone you loved, yet finding solace in knowing they weren't suffering anymore. I could see the flicker of vulnerability in his eyes, a glimpse of the boy he once was, and it made my heart ache for him. In that moment, I wanted to reach out, to bridge the gap between our worlds, to let him know that even in the darkest times, he wasn't alone.

"How has life been treating you? You look good. Real good," he said changing the subject, his eyes sweeping over me, making me feel like I was the only person in the room.

"I've been okay. Got my degree like I always told you I wanted to, and I'm doing interior decorating now," I said, a smile creeping onto my face as pride bubbled up inside me.

"Good for you," he said, his smile genuine, and it felt like a warm hug.

Destiny, my ever-curious best friend, cleared her throat, breaking the moment. "I'm sorry, Destiny, this is Armand. Armand, this is my best friend from college, Destiny," I introduced them, feeling a mix of nervousness and excitement.

"Nice to meet you," Armand said, extending his hand to Destiny, his charm evident.

"Same to you," she replied, her eyes narrowing suspiciously.

"Well, I'm gonna let you get back to your night. I saw you and just couldn't pass up speaking," he said, his tone casual yet somehow heavy with unspoken words.

"Okay. Maybe we can grab lunch sometime?" I suggested, reaching into my purse and pulling out a business card, the gesture feeling both bold and scary.

"Yes, I will definitely hit you up," he said, glancing at the card before tucking it into his pocket. He leaned in, giving me another hug and a soft kiss on the cheek, sending my heart into a flurry as he turned to walk away with the smoothest walk.

I sank back down into my seat, my mind swirling with thoughts. Destiny leaned closer, a teasing smile on her lips. "Who the hell was that fine ass man? And do them brothers of his y'all were talking about look as good as he does. Because if so, I want one." she asked, her curiosity piqued, as we both watched him walk away.

"A blast from the past, and yes they do" I replied, a mix of nostalgia and anxiety flooding my chest.

"Mhmm, what type of blast from the past?" she pressed, arching an eyebrow.

Hall Pass

"One I damn sure wasn't ready for. He was my first everything, first real boyfriend, first boy my parents let into the house, the first man I had sex with—my first love," I confessed, the weight of those words hanging heavily in the air between us.

"So that's why you didn't tell him you were married," she said, my eyes widening as realization hit me like a ton of bricks. In that brief moment, I had completely forgotten about Sergio.

"Damn," I muttered, the truth settling uncomfortably in my gut.

"Girl, don't beat yourself up. Telling him about your husband who doesn't fuck good and makes you pay 80% of the bills? That's not that damn important," she said, her laughter breaking the tension.

I couldn't help but laugh too, but beneath it all, I knew this encounter with Armand would linger in my mind long after the night was over.

The night rolled on, filled with laughter and teasing, the kind of easy banter that made time slip away. But soon enough, reality crept in, and we realized it was time to go. We slipped into our cars, promising to send a text when we got home. The hum of the engines a bittersweet reminder of our separate lives. As I drove halfway home, a sudden flashing red light appeared on my dashboard, and panic flared. My car was overheating.

I pulled over to the side of the road, cursing under my breath. Reaching for my phone, I hesitated, but I knew I had to call Sergio. I dialed his number three times, each ring feeling heavier than the last. Finally, he answered, his voice slurred, half-asleep.

"Bae, can you come get me? The car overheated," I said, my voice tinged with urgency.

"No," he shot back, his tone cold.

"No?" I echoed. "What do you mean, no?"

"I told you to take an Uber. You decided to drive that car, so now you can call AAA and wait for them to come help," he replied, irritation creeping into his voice.

I stared at the phone in disbelief. "So you're just going to leave your wife out here?" I started to speak, but he interrupted me.

"Dior, I'm going back to sleep. I've got work in the morning."

"Fuck that car detailing job! Your wife is stuck, and you—" But before I could finish, the line went dead.

"Did this nigga just fucking hang up on me?"

Hall Pass

I was pissed and my hands were shaking too much from my anger for me to even call him back.

Hot tears started to roll down my cheeks, frustration and sadness mixing into a bitter brew. I calmed down and unlocked my phone ready to call the one person I knew always came through for me, my dad. Just then, a tap on my window made me jump. My heart raced until I saw who it was.

"What are you doing here?" I asked, rolling down the window to let in the cool night air.

"I was heading to the hotel where I have a room and saw you. Are you good?" Armand asked concern etched across his face.

"It said it was overheating on my dash," I replied, trying to sound casual, but I could hear the quiver in my voice.

"Pop the hood," he instructed, and I did as he said, feeling a flicker of hope.

He examined the engine for a while, his brow furrowed in concentration. When he returned to my window, he looked serious. "It's dark out, and I can't really see what's wrong. But I have a friend that's a mechanic with a tow truck also. I'm gonna call him and have him come get it and bring it to his shop for you."

"You don't have to do that. If he can get it to my house, my dad will look at it. I just need time to call an Uber," I insisted, wanting to spare him the trouble.

"First off, Dior, don't play me like that. I will take you home. And secondly, your dad is in his 50s; he doesn't need to be messing with cars. My friend will look at it. He won't treat you like some mechanic trying to pull a fast one on a woman," he said, his voice firm yet reassuring.

There was something about his words that wrapped around me like a warm blanket, easing my tension. "Umm, okay," I finally said, feeling a little more at ease.

As he moved to make the call, I couldn't help but feel a spark of gratitude, mixed with something deeper I couldn't quite place. Tonight had taken an unexpected turn, and somehow, I felt safer with him there.

Armand opened my door, his strong hand steadying me as I climbed out of my car. The night air was cool against my skin, and I felt a mix of relief and warmth being so close to him. He guided me over to his sleek Cadillac Escalade, its polished exterior gleaming under the streetlights.

"Here, let me help you in," he said, his voice smooth and reassuring. He held the door open, handling me so gently and I slid into the plush leather seat, sinking into its comfort. Once I was secure, he gently closed the door, his eyes lingering on mine for a brief moment, as if checking to see if I was okay.

Hall Pass

I watched him pull out his phone, the light illuminating his face as he made a call. There was something about the way he moved—confident yet careful—that made me feel safe in a way I hadn't in a long time. The sound of his voice was deep and commanding as he spoke, his tone professional, yet I could hear the underlying warmth.

As he finished the call, he slid into the driver's seat, the engine purring to life. "All set, he'll be here soon." he said, casting a quick smile that sent a flutter through my chest.

I must have dozed off while we waited for his friend because when I finally felt Armand's hand on my knee, my eyes popped open in surprise. The first thing I noticed was that the car was gone.

"Where am I taking you?" he asked, his voice warm and inviting.

"Can you take me to get something to eat?" I replied, my stomach rumbling at the thought.

"Sure, greedy," he laughed, a playful glint in his eyes.

"Not greedy. Just need something to soak up some of this liquor. I don't have an early day tomorrow, but I still don't want to be hungover," I shot back, smiling at his teasing.

"anywhere specific you want to go?' he asked,

"Nah it's up to you," I answered.

"Okay, no problem. I got you," he said, shifting the car into drive, the engine humming smoothly as we pulled away.

After a little while, we arrived at a diner that looked like it had seen better days, but something about it felt cozy. I shot him a side-eye as we parked. "Before you say anything, this food is good. Don't judge by what the building looks like," he warned, half-joking.

He chuckled and got out, striding around to my side. I had already opened the door and was halfway out when he reached me. "Damn, you don't know how to let a nigga `help you," he said, laughter in his voice.

"Sorry, just not used to that," I replied, feeling a little embarrassed.

"Damn, your husband is not opening doors and helping you in and out of the car?" he asked, his tone light but his eyes searching mine. "My husband?"

His question caught me off guard. "I mean, it's little, but I definitely peeped the ring on your finger," he continued, a hint of concern creeping into his voice.

I looked down at my hand, my heart sinking at the reminder. It was something about these moments that I was with Armand that wiped Sergio and his shit from my mind.

"Oh," I murmured, feeling the weight of that simple word hanging between us. It was a small gesture, but it made me realize how much I missed those little things, the kind of care that felt so effortless yet so vital.

Armand lifted my chin, his gaze steady and warm. "Whatever is going on isn't my business so pick your head up. Let's get something to eat," he said, taking my hand and leading me inside the cozy diner, the familiar scent of fried food and coffee wrapping around us like a comforting blanket. We snagged a booth in the corner, and just as I settled in, Armand flashed me a quick smile before standing up. "I'll be right back," he promised.

I picked up the menu, my mind still buzzing from the night out, when an older waitress ambled over with a friendly smile. "Good evening! What can I get for you?" she asked, her voice soothing amidst the chatter.

"Um, can I wait a moment? I'm waiting for my friend to come back," I said, glancing around for Armand.

"Who? Armand?" she chuckled knowingly. "Baby, don't worry about him; he always gets the same thing—black coffee and our biscuits and gravy meal." Her smile was infectious, making me feel a little lighter.

"That sounds good. I'll have that too, but with orange juice, please," I replied, feeling a little more at ease.

"Sure thing!" With a nod, she turned and headed back to the kitchen just as Armand reappeared, placing a Gatorade and a pack of BC powder on the table.

"To make sure you don't have a hangover in the morning," he said with a smirk, and I couldn't help but smile back. It felt nice to be heard, to have someone anticipate my needs without me having to ask. It just sucked that Sergio wasn't the one doing it for me.

"So how many girls you bring here for them to know your order by heart."

"None, I was put on to this place by Ahmad when I first was released then after my mom passed, I ate here a lot because I didn't really know anything about cooking."

I was silent.

"So, tell me about life, Dior," Armand prompted as we dug into our food.

We fell into easy conversation, sharing laughter and stories like no time had passed at all. I looked at Armand from across the table still feeling butterflies in my stomach like I did when we were kids. By the time we were done, I felt a bittersweet pang in my chest, wishing this moment could stretch on forever. But reality loomed; it was time for him to take me to the cold place I called home.

Hall Pass

We hopped into his car, and I gave him my address. The familiar streets whipped by as we talked, but soon we were pulling up in front of my place. Armand glanced at my house, admiration lighting up his features. "You really did good for yourself, Dior. I'm proud of you," he said, his voice sincere as he helped me out of the car.

I felt a swell of gratitude as we walked to my door. "Thank you for everything, Armand," I said, my heart full.

"It was no problem at all. I'll hit you up tomorrow and let you know what my friend says about your car," he replied, his eyes lingering on mine.

"Okay," I nodded, feeling a warmth spread through me.

"It was really nice seeing you, Dior, don't let this be the last time," he said softly before leaning down to give me a gentle kiss on the forehead. I savored the moment, feeling cherished.

I unlocked the door and stepped inside, glancing back as Armand pulled away. I lingered in the doorway, watching his taillights fade into the night, a mix of happiness and longing swirling inside me. It felt like something had shifted like the city outside held a million possibilities just waiting for us.

Breanna J

TWO

Armand

"Yo," I mumbled as I answered the phone on my nightstand, my eyes still heavy with sleep. "Nigga, where you at?" Armani's voice shot through the fog of my grogginess. I blinked, squinting at the screen, and realized the time. Shit—I was supposed to meet him this morning, and here I was, buried under the covers.

"Damn, I overslept. I'm at the hotel," I admitted, looking around the unfamiliar room. How the hell had I ended up here? I had a house that I'd spent thousands on, yet I was waking up in some hotel, feeling more lost than ever.

"The hotel?" Armani echoed his tone, a mix of curiosity and concern.

"It's a long story. Let's meet up later for lunch, though. I was already planning to see Ahmad, so we can make it a brother thing," I suggested, trying to keep it light.

"Cool, but your ass better tell us why you're staying in a damn hotel too," he shot back, always ready to dig deeper.

It was crazy—here I was, a grown-ass man, and my brothers still had a knack for treating me like I was some kid who needed looking after. "I'd rather tell you about my run-in with Dior," I replied, a smirk creeping onto my face.

"Dior! Oh shit. Yeah I got to hear that." he exclaimed, the surprise evident in his voice.

Hall Pass

"Hell yeah, and man, she's still so damn fine," I told him, the memory of her flooding back like a sweet, intoxicating scent.

"Alright, I'll see you and Ahmad this afternoon. I gotta go make some moves. Just wanted to check on you, 'cause it's not like you to miss a meet-up," he said, his voice softer now, more brotherly.

We exchanged goodbyes, and I hung up, the weight of the conversation lingering. I got up and headed to the shower to start my day. I didn't want to spill the reason I was holed up in a hotel; I was trying not to be pissed off about it. Instead, I wanted to focus on the fact that I was a free man, living life on my own terms. The hotel room felt like a little slice of rebellion, a reminder to be grateful for my independence—especially with Dior dancing around in my mind.

Damn, I knew she was married, but I couldn't shake the thought of her. Even after all this time, she was just as stunning as I remembered. Back in the day, I used to tell her she reminded me of Ciara, but now? She was like a more sophisticated, grown-up version of that vision, radiating confidence and allure that pulled me in like a moth to a flame. I had so many questions swirling in my mind. What kind of husband did Dior have who didn't value her enough to come get her when she was in distress? Not even a single call while she was out with me? That nigga wasn't even waiting at the door when I dropped her off. I could feel the weight of her loneliness in the air, and that's why I slid in a gentle kiss on her forehead. It was something so pure, so tender; I wanted it to linger in her mind, a quiet reminder that she deserved more.

The look on her face when I mentioned him last night told me everything I needed to know—she wasn't happy, not even close. There was a spark of frustration in her eyes, a flicker of something deeper, and a piece of me ached for her. I wished life was different, wished I could be the one stepping up, going above and beyond to make her smile, to chase away the shadows of her discontent. I wanted to be the kind of man who made her feel cherished like she was the only one in the room. But here I was, just a temporary escape from reality.

I stepped out of the shower, steam clinging to my skin, and turned around, only to be blindsided. "What the fuck are you doing here?" I blurted out, my heart racing.

My wife, Shanny, stood there, arms crossed, eyes blazing looking like Eve the rapper. Short hair, almond tone, and breast tattoos showing. "What the fuck do you mean? I'm your wife. I can be anywhere you are. And clearly you not coming home last night meant you wanted me to come to you."

"Wife?" I shot back, disbelief dripping from my tone. "Really? One fight and you just bail? You don't come home, Armand?"

"How the hell did you even know I was here?" I asked, still reeling.

Shanny rolled her eyes like I was the biggest idiot alive. "We own this motherfucker. I'm not stupid and neither are you. You are too loyal to cheat and be at another bitch house and you're not going to spend money on something you can get for free. So I knew the only place you'd go is here."

"Okay, fine. What do you want? Why the hell are you here?" I asked, exasperated.

"Because I don't understand how one little fight sends you running off like this.

"It wasn't just one damn fight, Shanny. You act like you don't want to be a wife, so why are you here?" I snapped back, frustration boiling over.

"I married you, so why would you say that?" she shot at me, her voice rising.

"Yeah, you got the ring, but you never changed your last name and you damn sure don't act like a wife. You don't even wear that damn ring I spent all that money on. The only time I feel like we're married is when you're spending my cash."

"Here you go again! Why is it so damn important for me to have your last name or wear that ring? People know I'm married. I told you you didn't even have to buy me a ring, that's why I didn't buy you one. Keeping my ties to my family matters to me. My father had no son, and I refuse to let his name die."

Her words hung in the air, heavy like the tension between us. I could see it clearly now: a marriage caught between loyalty and independence, love and resentment.

"Shanny, then why the hell are you with me? Last time I checked, I'm the one handling everything for your ass, not your daddy. If you're so damn concerned about keeping his name alive like you're his son, then do that without me. I refuse to keep getting fucking disrespected while I'm out here making shit happen."

Her expression softened for a moment, but I could still see the fire in her eyes. "And I'm thankful for that, Armand. I love you for that."

"So, you just love me for the life I provide you?" I shot back, feeling the anger bubbling inside.

"That's not what I said!" she barked; her voice sharp.

"Yeah? Well, that's how you fucking act, and actions speak louder than words, Shanny."

I stepped closer, feeling the walls closing in. The hotel room felt like a cage, and every word exchanged was another blow. She opened her mouth to respond, but I could see the conflict on her face. Maybe she was torn between gratitude and resentment, caught in a whirlwind of expectations and reality.

"Look, I've given you everything," I continued, my voice dropping to a low growl. "I opened doors for you that your father couldn't even afford to knock on. I showed you a life that glittered beyond your wildest dreams. But if you can't respect that, then what the hell are we doing?"

Shanny crossed her arms tighter, her expression hardening. "You act like I don't appreciate it. I do, but I'm not just some trophy wife to be paraded around. I'm still me, and I need to honor my roots."

"Your roots? This ain't about roots, it's about respect!" I snapped, frustration seeping through every word. "You can honor your family without acting like you don't give a fuck about our marriage. It's like you want to keep one foot in your old life while you're living in mine. You can't have it both ways."

"Now it's an issue?" she yelled

"It's been an issue," I said back looking her in the face.?

The silence that hung in the air was heavy and thick with unspoken words and unresolved issues. It felt like we were dancing around the real problem, both too stubborn to take that final step toward understanding. The truth? I was never really in love with Shanny. But I had love for her.

When I was young, I got caught up in the street life, selling drugs with my brothers like most of the boys my age, just trying to come up and chase my dreams. But when I got pinched, it was behind some shit Ahmad, Armani and I were tied into together. The cops wanted me to snitch on everyone including our connect. I refused. I did my time like a man.

Walking away from my mom was one thing, but leaving Dior? That shit nearly broke me. I had made the grown man decision to sell drugs, so I made the grown man decision to sit that time out alone. Ahmad and Armani were the only ones that I allowed to see me and the only people that I called. They kept money on my books and our mom informed that I was good. I didn't want any of their lives to stop or be dragged down by the dumb mistakes I made. Especially not Dior. She had her whole future ahead of her, dreams that sparkled brighter than the hood we came from.

I couldn't let my choices taint her path. She deserved better. In some twisted way, I thought distancing myself would protect her, and keep her from the chaos I was tangled in. But now, looking at Shanny, I felt trapped in a life that wasn't mine.

Shanny's gaze flickered, and I could see the confusion mixed with hurt. "So, what? You think I'm holding you back? You think I don't care?"

"It's not about that," I replied, frustration spilling over. "It's about who I am and who I want to be. I don't want to be this dude who's stuck in a loveless marriage, pretending everything's fine when it's not. I want more than this, and I thought you did too."

Her eyes narrowed, but I could see the cracks in her facade. "Then maybe we need to figure out what that 'more' looks like for both of us."

"Yeah, maybe," I said, my voice softer now. "But I need you to understand—I can't keep living like this. I can't keep feeling like a failure every time I look at you."

She opened her mouth to respond, but the weight of everything hung between us. We were both lost, caught in a cycle of expectations and realities that threatened to drown us. The road ahead felt uncertain, but I knew one thing: I couldn't keep pretending. Not anymore.

Shanny's dad was my cellmate in jail, and I'll never forget that night when everything changed. I was attacked by some niggas from a gang that didn't fuck with my crew. If he hadn't been there, I'd be dead. But instead of minding his business like most would, he jumped in and saved my damn life.

After that, he took me under his wing like I was his own son. Even while behind prison walls he showed me how to be a better man. I felt indebted to him like I owed him everything. He came home before me and looked out for my mom, making sure she was okay while I was locked up. When I finally got out, my boss broke me off a heavy lump sum for keeping my mouth shut. Ahmad and Armani had some cash stacked up for me too. I tried to give Shanny's dad some cash as a thank-you, but he declined. All he wanted was for me to marry his oldest daughter, Shanny. She struggled to finish high school and as much as he loved her he considered her his problem child that he needed to know was good or he'd never be able to rest in peace when his time came. He wanted to make sure she was well taken care of.

At first, I turned him down. But then my mom had been murdered in a robbery, and I felt like I had failed her. I was pissed at my brothers and myself that she even went out that way and we weren't there to protect her. But also that I had lost time with her because I was in jail. She had put some much into raising us right and she would always have it in her mind that her baby boy went to jail. I threw myself into work, investing that payout and turning myself into the secret business mogul I am today. Owning a hotel, restaurant, a few investments, and a car rental company. The hustle consumed me, and it was the only way I could cope with the pain of losing her.

But then everything changed. Shanny's dad called me on his deathbed, battling stage four prostate cancer. His voice was weak, but the request was clear. He asked me again to marry Shanny. With the most important women I once considered family gone, I finally agreed.

In less than a year, I gave her the wedding of her dreams, put her in the house she always wanted, and opened her own salon so she could stop working for others. I had done everything she asked for and more, but deep down, I knew she didn't love me. She loved the money, the lifestyle, the image of what I could provide.

I could see it in her eyes every time she walked into a room, every time she flashed that smile that lit up her face when she talked about her salon or the latest designer bag. It made my blood boil and my heart ached at the same time. I wanted her to react like that about me. I wanted her to love me for me, not for what I could give her.

But here we were, stuck in a cycle of expectations, and I was starting to wonder if I'd made the biggest mistake of my life by saying yes.

Shanny walked over to me, her eyes softening as she wrapped her arms around my neck. She pressed her lips against mine, and for a moment, the tension between us faded into the background. If we got nothing else right in this messed-up marriage, our sex life was nothing short of amazing.

I could feel the heat radiating off her body as she moved closer, her hands sliding down to loosen the towel wrapped around my waist. My heart raced the familiar rush of desire coursing through me. I rubbed my hands over her curves, feeling the softness of her skin beneath my fingertips.

"Damn, you're beautiful," I murmured against her lips, lost in the moment.

She smiled, a teasing glint in her eyes. "You know how to sweet-talk a girl, don't you?"

"Only when it counts," I replied, my voice low and gravelly. I pulled her in tighter, feeling the warmth of her body against mine, and for a fleeting second, I wished we could just stay in this bubble, away from all the chaos.

But reality hung heavy in the air, a constant reminder of the cracks in our foundation. I pushed those thoughts aside for now, focusing on the way her body responded to my touch, the way she melted against me. It was a dangerous game we were playing, but at this moment, I didn't give a damn. I just wanted to lose myself in her.

As we made love this time, everything felt different. I hoisted her up onto the sink, her skin warm against the cool porcelain. Sliding into her, I lost myself in the rhythm, the chemistry sparking like a live wire between us. But when I kissed her, pulling back to look into her eyes, I was struck by a jarring realization. It wasn't Shanny I saw anymore; it was Dior.

Confusion coursed through me like a storm. What kind of twisted game was my heart and head playing? My body was here, lost in the moment, but my mind was racing, grappling with memories and feelings I thought I had buried. I could still hear Dior's laughter, and see her fierce gaze that could cut through the bullshit of our lives. It made my chest tighten, the weight of it almost suffocating.

"Fuck," I muttered, my voice barely breaking the charged silence. I wanted to shake it off, to focus on the warmth of Shanny beneath me, but the ghost of Dior lingered, haunting every caress. It was a mindfuck, and I didn't know how to untangle the mess of emotions swirling inside me.

We finished, and as Shanny and I cleaned ourselves up, I felt an odd mix of satisfaction and confusion swirling in my gut. "I'll walk you to your car," I said, trying to shake off the lingering thoughts of Dior as we headed toward the lobby. The air was thick with the scent of fresh coffee and the low hum of chatter, a stark contrast to the storm brewing in my mind.

Just as we stepped into the lobby, I was stopped in my tracks. "Mr. Riggins! Nice to see you this morning," my manager, Renee, greeted me with her usual bright smile. "How was the room? I hope it showed you I'm managing the hotel well."

"Everything was amazing," I replied, forcing a grin. "We're going to meet and talk later on today or this week."

She smiled and nodded; her approval evident in her eyes. But then Shanny cleared her throat, and I could feel the shift in the air.

"Sorry, Renee, this is Shanny, my…" Before I could finish the sentence, Shanny jumped in.

"His business partner."

I shot her a look, my eyebrows raised in disbelief. Did my wife just introduce herself as my damn business partner? The words hung in the air like a punchline, and I could feel the heat rising in my cheeks. What the hell was she playing at? My mind raced, torn between annoyance and the peculiar thrill of her boldness. I could see Renee's eyes flicker with curiosity, and I knew this wasn't going to end well.

"Well, Renee, I have some meetings and things to take care of, so I'll be in touch," I said, grabbing Shanny's arm to steer her toward the exit. My mind was still racing, and I needed distance to cool off.

Once we got to the parking lot, she unlocked her car, and I followed suit, my heart still pounding. I could feel the anger simmering beneath the surface, probably etched all over my face. As she slid into the driver's seat, her brow furrowed, and she shot me a concerned look.

"What's wrong with you?" she asked, her voice laced with confusion.

"Business partner?" I shot back, disbelief dripping from my tone.

"I just figured… Ummm…" she stammered, looking like she was searching for the right words.

"You are my fucking wife! But if you want to play it like we're just business partners, let me know. I can have the papers drawn up, and that can be that." The words tumbled out, sharper than I intended, but the frustration was boiling over.

"Relax, I didn't mean no harm," she said, her voice softening. "I'm going to do some shopping before heading into the shop. I'll see you later—back at our house. Have a good day." She said putting a lot of power behind our house then a smile when she said Have a nice day. She popped her lips out, expecting a kiss, but I just stared.

Ignoring her gesture, I closed the car door with a decisive thud, the sound echoing like my unresolved feelings. I watched her pull away, the taillights fading into the distance, and I was left standing there, torn between anger and a heavy heart. What the hell was going on with us?

Breanna J

THREE

Dior

Candlelight flickered softly, casting a warm glow that danced across the room. When Armand emerged from the bathroom, his skin glistened like it was kissed by the sun, and my heart raced at the sight. He walked toward the bed with an easy confidence that made my body ache with desire. Standing between my legs, he flashed that irresistible smile, his hand sliding under my chin, pulling my lips to his in a kiss that ignited a fire deep within me.

"Damn..." he breathed, his eyes roaming over me with a hunger that felt electric. I bit my bottom lip, savoring every moment, admiring him just as he was admiring me.

With a swift movement, he unclasped my bra, his hands cupping my breasts, fingers dancing over my skin with a gentle yet possessive touch. His lips found their way to my nipples, kissing and sucking each one, sending waves of pleasure coursing through my body. I arched my back, exhaling a soft moan, my fingers threading through his hair, urging him on.

He trailed kisses down my stomach, each one easing me back into the softness of the bed, a tantalizing path leading lower. As I laid back, he effortlessly slid my panties off, his gaze heated and insatiable. Grabbing my legs, he pulled me to the edge of the bed, a teasing smirk playing on his lips. "Now don't run," he warned, positioning my legs on his shoulders with a dominance that made my heart race.

The moment his tongue met my clit, it felt like a jolt of electricity. I gasped, the sensation taking the wind right out of me. Armand feasted on me, his every movement calculated to drive me wild, holding my legs tightly in place as I squirmed, overwhelmed by the pleasure.

I was lost in ecstasy, two orgasms washing over me like tidal waves, when he finally let go. Standing up, he dropped his towel, revealing his full glory. The sight made my breath hitch, and when he slid into me, a sultry moan escaped my lips, my body arching to welcome him.

And then, just like that, the sound of my own moan pulled me from the depths of my erotic dream. I woke up, breathing heavily, the remnants of that steamy encounter still buzzing in my mind. Glancing at the clock, I saw it flashing 8:05 AM, reality crashing in around me like a cold bucket of water.

Rolling over, I noticed Sergio wasn't in bed with me, and a small smile crept across my face knowing he didn't hear me say Armand 's name. Last night had been a whirlwind, and I couldn't help but replay the moments in my mind. I reached for my cell to see if he'd reached out, my heart racing a little.

> Just as I unlocked my phone, the bathroom door creaked open, and out walked Sergio, towel draped around his waist, water still beading on his skin.

"I see you made it home," he said, his tone casual but with an edge of something I couldn't quite place.

> Instead of engaging, I stayed quiet, scrolling through my messages and call log. Not one text or call from Armand. My heart sank a bit, but I brushed it off, not wanting to give Sergio any satisfaction.

"I hope you're getting up sometime soon. You really should wash that smell off of you," he said.

"What smell?" I replied, my eyebrows knitting together in confusion.

"The smell of cologne. If you're going to cheat, at least make sure not to bring the smell home."

> His words hit me like a slap to the face. "Cheat? Are you fucking serious? No one cheated on your ass, even though I probably had every right to." I shot back, sitting up in bed, my heart pounding with a mix of anger and indignation.

"What?" he said, now leaning on the bed, his face a mask of disbelief. I could see the tension building in his jaw, and for a moment, I wondered if this would blow up into something bigger. The air felt thick between us, charged with unspoken accusations and unresolved issues.

"I can't believe you're worried about me cheating when you still have another woman's name tattooed on you while we're married. What if the tables were turned?" I yelled.

"But they're not," he replied.

"But they could be. I've been holding my tongue, but the truth is, things could change fast. You're not doing anything in this marriage that's so amazing. And just so you remember, I was beautiful when you met me, and I'm a fierce woman now."

His chest rose and fell quickly as he stared at me.

"Dior, don't be stupid."

"Sergio, don't make me show you just how much you can hate me. I am your wife, and I called you in need last night," I shot back, my voice rising with anger. "You left me hanging to figure it out on my own. And now you have the nerve to accuse me of cheating? Your ass took off your ring because your finger itches, and I didn't say a damn thing about whether you were possibly cheating."

"How are you mad at me because you got yourself in a fucked-up position?" he countered, his tone defensive. "You knew that car was messed up when you took it out of here. I wasn't about to jump out of bed to save you from what you created."

"That's what husbands do." I was screaming in my head. Thinking of all the times I saw my dad save my mom even if it was from stuff she created.

"You're an asshole," I spat, swinging my legs over the side of the bed, the cool air hitting my skin like a slap.

"No, I'm real," he replied, shrugging it off as he turned back to get ready, his back to me.

I felt a storm brewing inside me, a mix of frustration and pain. It wasn't just about him not showing up last night or how Armand treated me like I mattered. It felt like I was at my breaking point, and all the little cracks were starting to show.

"You real? Nigga, you know nothing about being real. If you did, you'd do better. You're a fucking husband! You're supposed to protect, provide, comfort, and be there when I need you—and I'm feeling like I'm in this shit alone! I'm paying most of the bills. I'm the only one loving and caring!" My voice shook with emotion, each word a dagger aimed straight at him.

He turned to face me, his expression hardening like steel. I could see the tension in his jaw, the way his fists clenched at his sides, muscles coiling like a spring ready to snap. This argument wasn't just about last night; it felt like a boiling over of everything we'd been ignoring for too long. The silence between us was suffocating, and I knew we both needed to confront it before it consumed us whole.

"I'm doing my fucking best," Sergio said, though his words sounded more like a defense than the truth.

"No, the fuck you're not! You did more when we were just dating. We got married, and you dropped the ball and never picked that shit back up," I shot back, my voice rising with every syllable.

"So what are you saying, Dior?" His tone had a sharp edge, challenging me to dig deeper.

"I'm saying man the fuck up, Sergio! Do better!" I yelled, frustration spilling over like a boiling pot.

"How about if you don't like what I'm doing, you pack your shit and leave!" he shot back, his words hanging in the air like a challenge. I looked around the room, confusion washing over me. There was no way he was serious.

    I closed the distance between us, stepping right up to him, my heart racing. "This is my shit! I pay the bills! If you can't man the fuck up, you pack your shit and get the fuck out! And don't take the shit I paid for. Not a piece of clothing, that phone or that damn car outside. I ain't in the business of keeping no nigga that don't want to be kept. And I'm also not funding one that's out here doing whatever. So, if you want to leave, go." My voice was steady, but inside, I was a whirlwind of emotions—anger, hurt, and a desperate need for him to see how far we'd fallen.

He stared back at me, and for a brief moment, I caught a flicker of doubt in his eyes, a crack in that hardened exterior. But just like that, it vanished, replaced by the stubborn pride I'd come to loathe. The air between us crackled with tension, heavy with unspoken words and unresolved emotions. This was a turning point, a crossroads we couldn't ignore. We could either fight through this storm or let it rip us apart, leaving nothing but jagged pieces in its wake.

As I walked toward the bathroom, I could feel the weight of his gaze boring into my back. Sergio opened his mouth, probably to launch into another one of his relentless justifications. "I—"

"Shut up," I interrupted, my voice sharp. I slammed the door behind me, needing that moment of solitude. I was done talking.

I turned on the shower, letting the hot water cascade over me, drowning out the chaos that had become our life. Each droplet felt like a reminder of the comfort I'd once found in Armand's arms, that fleeting warmth that now felt like a distant dream. I closed my eyes, allowing the steam to envelop me. Guilt gnawed at my insides for thinking of him while standing here, wrapped in a life that felt more like a cage than a home.

I took my time, letting the water wash away not just the dirt, but the tangled mess of my thoughts. Memories of laughter, stolen kisses, and whispered dreams with Armand flooded my mind, and I hated myself for it. But I couldn't help it; he was a part of me, even if I was bound to someone else.

When I finally stepped out of the shower, the sound of Sergio leaving echoed through the house. Relief washed over me, a sweet reprieve from the tension. I didn't want to come out to a conversation about agreements or compromises. Not today. Today, I needed to breathe, to reclaim a sliver of my own identity, even if just for a moment.

My phone rang and it was Destiny calling.

"hello"

"girl, you ain't text or call to let me know you were home. Were you that drunk?" she asked.

"Nah, I got stranded and Sergio refused to come get me. Thankfully Armand just happened to be coming along and gave me a ride." I told her.

"What kind of ride did he give you," she said jokingly.

"Not that type nasty. I am married."

"And your husband can't fuck." she said.

"But I am still married." I told her.

"Bad dick calls for a divorce or at least some good outside dick to keep you sane."

"Girl, you play too much." I laughed.

"But I am so serious." she said back

"Whatever. I am okay though. Besides the little argument me and Sergio just had. He said I came home smelling like another man. Like he really accused me of cheating" I explained.

"Good, maybe the smell of another man on you will get him to tighten up." she said.

"I hope so but if it doesn't, I made it very clear that he can leave and not leave with anything I paid for."

"Yeah, ain't no way you going to tell me that fine ass man didn't slide his dick in you. Because normal Dior would not have told Sergio that." she said, sounding proud.

"I didn't sleep with Armand. I am just at my breaking point with Sergio. If he doesn't love me, I am not about to force him."

FOUR

Armand

  I left the hotel, the rich aroma of coffee still lingering in my nose, and headed over to check on Dior's car. As I pulled up, I spotted my boy Los leaning against a sleek ride, chatting up a dark-skinned woman who was definitely putting on the charm. The way she flashed that smile told me she was fishing for something more than just a conversation.
  As I got closer, I caught snippets of their exchange. "So, like I said, it's going to be $1200 for your repairs, hun," he said. "Can I pay you half and then we can go out to dinner and talk about the other half?"

"Yo, Los!" I called out, trying to break the tension. He flashed a quick grin and told the girl, "I'll be right back."

"What's up, my boy?" he said, his eyes lighting up at my arrival.

"Nothing much, just see you're still up to your usual," I replied, chuckling.

"Nah, that ain't me. It's these little bitches; they'd rather throw themselves at me than pay for anything. But that doesn't pay my bills or child support. It's sad, man. We really don't have any good women left in this world," he said, shaking his head.

"I wouldn't say that. There are still some good ones out there who don't just follow what the internet or society tells them is okay," I countered, my mind drifting to Dior.

"Yeah? Where are they at? 'Cause I need one," he shot back, a smirk on his face.

"Exactly," he said, as if he'd just won a debate.
"Hell, maybe you're right," I admitted, though I wasn't about to let him in on my thoughts about Dior. If I caught even a whiff that she was willing to give someone else a chance, I'd take it—no matter what it meant for Shanny. I'd do whatever it took, even if that meant leaving her behind.

"So, what's up with the car?" I asked, shifting the subject.

"Tell Shanny to start putting some coolant in her car. That's why it was overheating," he replied.

"That's it?" I raised an eyebrow, surprised.

"Yeah, these females don't know shit about cars besides how to drive them. They can barely figure out how to put gas in 'em," he laughed, shaking his head in disbelief.

"I'm surprised your ass hasn't kept up with it," he added, nudging me playfully.
    It blew my mind that Dior had a husband who couldn't even handle something as simple as checking the fluid levels in her car. I was seriously trying to figure out why she was even with that clown at this point. This was basic stuff to me. No matter how messed up things got between me and Shanny, I always kept the bills paid and the

Hall Pass

cars in good shape. I made it my business every Sunday to fill up the tank, ensuring she never had to step foot in a gas station if she didn't want to.

"It's not Shanny's car. It belongs to a friend; I was just helping her out because I saw her stuck on the side of the road," I explained, feeling a bit defensive as I spoke.

"A friend?" he asked, raising an eyebrow.

"Don't start your shit. It's just a childhood friend whose parents looked out for me just as much as my mom looked out for her," I shot back, trying to keep my cool.

"Okay, I understand and respect it. Like a sister," he replied, his tone softening.

I damn sure wouldn't say that—like a sister, I thought to myself. We lost our virginity to each other, and there's nothing I wouldn't give to feel her that way again. The thought sent a rush through me, a bittersweet memory lingering like an old song.

"Well, I put coolant in it," he said, giving me a knowing look that made me wonder just how much he really understood the tangled mess of my feelings for her.

I couldn't shake the feeling that Dior deserved someone who'd treat her right, someone who'd make sure her car was as taken care of as she was. That thought gnawed at me, a reminder of the kind of man I aspired to be, even if it felt like a distant dream.

"Thanks, man," I said, and for a moment, the weight of my troubles faded away, replaced by the camaraderie we always shared. But thoughts of Dior hung around like a melody I couldn't shake off—sweet yet haunting.

"You're welcome, don't worry about it. It's free," he said.

"Okay, cool. But can you take a look at everything else too? Oil, tires, make sure there aren't any lights blinking on her dash, and even wash the outside and detail the inside. I'll wait while you do it," I instructed, trying to keep my tone light, but the urgency behind my words was clear.

"Got you. But you know that shit costs, right?" he shot back, a smirk playing on his lips.

"Nigga, don't I always pay?" I replied, rolling my eyes, but I couldn't help but grin.

"You're right. You're the only one who comes up here and doesn't try to pull that friend discount crap." His smile widened, and I felt a sense of relief knowing I had his support.

I wanted to take the stress off Dior and ensure her car wouldn't be a headache anymore. She needed reliable wheels—something sturdy to keep her safe and mobile, especially after what happened last night. The thought of her stranded and vulnerable sent a chill down my spine. I wanted to be the one to protect her, to make sure she didn't have to face those kinds of things alone, just in case I wasn't there to save her.

As Los got to work, I leaned against a car, watching him in between checking emails and letting my mind wander.

My phone rang, and Simeon's name lit up the screen like a beacon.

Hall Pass

"Yo!" I answered.

"My bad, bro. I know we were supposed to meet up last night," he said, his voice a mix of regret and urgency.

"It's all good, don't worry about it," I shot back, brushing it off.

"I feel bad though. You my boy, and you needed to vent about Shanny, but Sabrina had me busy."

Sabrina was Shanny's younger sister, and unlike Shanny, their dad wasn't as concerned about her. He was more laid-back, treating her like an adult rather than a fragile flower. Simeon and Sabrina had hit it off at our wedding, and a few months later, they were already married. I couldn't help but feel a twinge of envy at the ease of their connection.

"That's cool, shit happens. I actually ran into an old friend, and we ended up catching up on things," I said, trying to sound casual.

"An old friend?" he questioned, his tone shifting to something more curious, maybe even a little protective.

"Yeah, my homegirl I went to school with."

"Man, you know Shanny's gonna flip," he said.

"Man, are you my friend or Shanny's? Plus, Shanny needs to focus on being a better wife, not worry about my female friends," I replied, frustration creeping into my voice. But the truth was, I didn't want to deal with her insecurities right now.

"Oh man, well let's reschedule. Let's go out for lunch," he suggested, eager to shift the vibe.

"I'm a little busy right now, but when I leave here and get some free time, I'll hit you up," I promised, feeling the weight of the day pressing down on me.

"Aight, bet. But before we go, we need to discuss a big charge that just popped on your account," he said, his tone shifting from casual friend to no-nonsense accountant in a heartbeat.

"What do you mean?" I asked, confusion clouding my mind.

"I thought you weren't buying any more cars," he said, skepticism thick in his voice.

"I didn't…" I started, but then it hit me. "Wait, someone did."

I fell silent, letting the realization sink in. "Man, I'ma hit you back," I said, my thoughts racing as I remembered I wasn't the only one with access to the accounts.

The sun beat down outside, casting long shadows that danced across the pavement, but my mind was elsewhere—lost in memories of Dior's laughter, the way her eyes sparkled when she talked about her dreams, their intensity almost blinding. I couldn't help but wonder if I could somehow be a part of those dreams, a constant in her chaotic world, or if I was just another fleeting moment in the whirlwind of her life.

"Yo, you good?" Los called out, snapping me back to reality.

"Yeah, man. Just thinking," I said, trying to shake off the weight of my thoughts.

"About your friend, huh?" he teased, knowing me all too well.

"If you only knew," I shot back, my heart racing at the thought of her.

"Just make sure you don't get too lost in your head, my dude. You gotta handle your business," he said, his tone turning serious.

"Trust me, I will. I just want to make sure she's okay." And as I watched him work, I felt a flicker of hope. Maybe, just maybe, I could be the one to bring some light into her life.

After Los checked everything on the car and slapped some fresh tires on it, I told him to follow me in my ride to drop off Dior's car. It was about that time, and I figured she was already at work. The address was right there on her business card, so I figured pulling up wouldn't be an issue.

When we arrived, I ordered an Uber for Los, leaving him to wait while I made my way inside to find Dior.

She worked at an upscale firm that had all the trappings of a white-owned business—sleek glass doors, polished floors, and a receptionist who looked like she'd stepped off a runway. As I approached the front desk, I could feel the receptionist's eyes on me, sizing me up. I asked for Dior, and while I waited, it was clear she was trying her best to flirt. You could tell she was one of those white girls who had sampled a taste of black dick and was now hooked, looking for any opportunity to reel me in.

"Can I help you with anything else?" she asked, her voice a little too sweet, her smile a little too wide.

"Just waiting for Dior Waye," I replied, keeping my tone casual, but her gaze lingered as if she was trying to figure out how to make her move.

A few minutes later, Dior appeared, her presence lighting up the room. She was radiant, wearing a fitted dress that hugged her curves just right, and her smile was like a breath of fresh air. "Hey! Follow me back to my office," she said, her eyes sparkling with excitement.

As I walked behind her, I caught the receptionist's glare, a mix of envy and frustration etched on her face. It made me smirk a little; clearly, she thought she had a shot, but Dior wasn't just an average girl.

Dior led me down a hallway adorned with modern art and sleek furniture, gliding with confidence, her heels clicking against the floor—a rhythm that matched the pounding of my heart. I could feel the tension in the air, a magnetic pull between us that had been building ever since our first encounter.

When we reached her office, she opened the door and gestured for me to step in. "Thank you again for helping me last night," she said.

"No problem," I replied, leaning against the doorframe, unable to take my eyes off her. "I just wanted to make sure you were taken care of."

And in that moment, with the city buzzing outside and the world feeling like it had faded away, I stood admiring her, knowing I'd do whatever it took to keep her safe and happy.

I stepped further into Dior's office and took a moment to soak it all in. The space was alive, filled with sketches and vibrant designs sprawled across a table in front of a large window. Sunlight streamed in, illuminating the creativity that buzzed in the air. I glanced at her designs, and damn, they were impressive.

"You like?" she asked, a hint of pride in her voice.

"Hell yeah, this shit is real dope," I replied, genuinely impressed.

"Thanks," she said, her smile lighting up the room. "With all this talent, why are you working for someone else?" I couldn't help but ask, curious about what held her back.

"Because having talent and no clients don't make money," she shot back, her expression momentarily serious.

"You're right. But I think I might have a client for you," I said, feeling a surge of excitement.

"It's the owner of a hotel. He's looking for a new look. Maybe that could help you on your journey to independence."

I could see her trying to hold back a blush, the corners of her mouth twitching upward. "Armand, why are you really here?" she asked, her tone softening, making me feel a little vulnerable.

"I came to bring you your car," I said, wanting to keep things straightforward.

"My car?" she replied, a frown creeping onto her face, clearly perplexed because I hadn't told her what was wrong with it.

"Yeah, I had my people look it over. You were overheating because you needed coolant. I had them take care of that, along with a car wash, an oil change, and some new tires," I told her, pride bubbling up in my chest.

"Oh my god, Armand! You didn't have to do all that. How much do I owe you? I can Cash App you right now," she said, reaching for her phone, brows knitting together in concern.

"Don't worry about it. I took care of it because I wanted to," I assured her, feeling warmth spread through me at her gratitude.

"Then how can I repay you?" she asked, her voice teasing yet sincere.

"When my friend calls you about working on his hotel, make sure you take that opportunity," I told her, already scheming in my mind. I had the hotel for a few years now, and it needed a new look. So I was going to have Renee reach out, keeping my role as the owner under wraps.
Dior's eyes sparkled with a mix of surprise and excitement. "Are you serious? That could change everything for me!"

"Hell yeah, I'm serious. You deserve this, Dior. Just promise me you'll seize the moment," I said, locking eyes with her, hoping she could see how much I believed in her.
She nodded, that blush creeping back onto her cheeks, and for a second, the world outside faded away. It was just us,

tangled in ambition and possibility, and I couldn't help but feel that this was just the beginning of something special.

I left Dior's office feeling like a king, a swagger in my step that couldn't be denied. Glancing at my watch, I realized it was time to meet up with my brothers, so I headed straight to the hood. There was a Jamaican restaurant we always hit up—our unspoken meet-up spot, where the food was as comforting as family.

I pulled up and jumped out of my car, the familiar scent of jerk chicken wafting through the air. My brothers were already there, plates piled high with their favorites. The owner caught my eye and gave me a nod, letting me know he'd bring my order out shortly.

"What's up, baby bro?" Ahmad greeted me, a wide grin lighting up his face. Every time I saw him, it felt like a celebration; he was the only one of us still grinding in the game.
"What's up, sir?" I shot back, grinning as we slapped hands. Then I turned to Amari and exchanged the same brotherly gesture.

I settled into my seat, the atmosphere buzzing with laughter and familiar banter. Ahmad wasted no time, diving right into business. "Y'all know Momma's birthday is coming up. I want to head up and clean off her gravesite and maybe do a BBQ at the house."

"I'm down for that," I replied, feeling warmth spread through me at the thought of honoring her memory.

"Now that that's out of the way, why the fuck are you sleeping at a hotel?" Armani jumped in, a knowing glint in his eye.

"Who's sleeping at a hotel?" Ahmad asked, suddenly alert.

"Shanny and I are going through some stuff right now, so I figured the best thing to do was to stay elsewhere," I responded, trying to keep my tone casual.

"I told you not to marry that bitch," Ahmad said, shaking his head.

"Don't start," I shot back, already feeling the familiar tension rise.

"Nigga, we taught you better than that. You don't let anyone put you out of the house you pay the bills at. Her ass could've left," Armani chimed in, concern lacing his voice.

"You know that's not how I move. Plus, I live in a white neighborhood. If shit gets out of control and the cops get called, guess who's black ass is going back to jail?" I countered, frustration bubbling beneath the surface.

"And we'll bail you out, and the twins' momma will beat Shanny's ass," Armani teased, trying to lighten the mood.

"All that shit ain't even worth it. Y'all know I own a hotel, right? So I just went there and took the platinum suite. It's not like I'm crashing in some motel. Shit is all good," I said, trying to downplay everything. I wasn't ready to dive deeper into what was really going on with Shanny, especially since my brothers were convinced she was nothing more than a gold digger.

As we waited for my food, the conversation shifted, but the weight of my situation hung in the air like a thick fog, a quiet storm brewing beneath the surface as I tried to savor this moment with my brothers. "Well, on a better note, I ran into Dior last night," I said, excitement creeping into my voice.

"Oh shit, how did that turn out?" Ahmad leaned in, his interest piqued.

"I swear, it was like no time had gone by. She's still so fine and has done so well for herself," I told them, a smile breaking across my face at the memory of her radiant energy.
"Man, make sure you tell her to pull up for Momma. She's always been like a little sis to us," Ahmad urged, nostalgia lighting up his eyes.

"I'm definitely gonna do that," I replied, feeling warmth at the thought of reconnecting.
"Nigga," Armani chimed in, his tone suddenly serious.

"What?" I shot back, defensive but curious.

"I know that look. You're the better one out of the three of us. Don't be a player; don't pull that girl into your world knowing you're married. You've already hurt her once when you left. The karma you'll feel if she gets hurt again will be crazy," Armani warned, his gaze piercing through my relaxed facade.

I nodded, taking in what he said. There was truth in his words, and it didn't sit well with me. The last thing I wanted was to drag Dior into my messy situation, especially with a past that was a tangled web of regret.

We finished off lunch, the conversation flowing easily between us, but my mind was elsewhere, caught in a whirlwind of thoughts about Shanny and the undeniable spark I felt for Dior. As laughter filled the air and the familiar warmth of brotherhood surrounded me, I couldn't shake the feeling that I was standing at a crossroads, and the choices I made next could change everything.

FIVE

Dior

Armand showing up at my job had me grinning from ear to ear for the rest of the day. I swear, I was practically glowing and walking on clouds. But the moment I slid into my car, the flood gates opened, and tears of joy streamed down my cheeks. The ride was like butter smooth as hell. Armand didn't have to go out of his way to clean my car, and make sure it was good, but he did and those were the little things that counted. And the fact that he was going to mention my name to a hotel owner for a design gig? That was monumental. It felt like a golden key unlocking doors that five years at my job hadn't even scratched the surface of.

As I pulled up to my house, the world outside felt muted, like nothing could touch my bliss. I walked in, tossed my purse onto the couch, and headed to the bedroom, ready to bask in the afterglow of my day with a nice bubble bath. But then I heard it—my name echoed through the air, pulling me back. I turned and made my way toward the kitchen, curiosity piquing.

There was Sergio, lounging at the kitchen island, a bottle of Rémy Martin in front of him and a cup in hand. He took a leisurely sip, savoring whatever was left in his glass before locking eyes with me. "So, I thought about what you said this morning," he said, his tone slightly teasing but with an undertone of seriousness.

I leaned against the doorframe, crossing my arms, my heart racing a little. "Oh yeah? And what's that supposed to mean?" I shot back, trying to play it cool, but I could feel the tension bubbling beneath the surface. "It means I really heard you and how you felt."

Hope surged in my chest, a flicker of belief that maybe my words had finally reached him, that he was ready to step up. "I'm glad, baby. I didn't want to come off as a bitch this morning," I said, my voice softening as I walked closer. "But I just needed you to understand how I felt. I don't need you to be perfect; I just need you to try a little harder." As I spoke, I gently cupped his face in my hands, feeling the warmth of his skin beneath my palms.

Sergio's expression shifted as he grabbed my wrists and pulled my hands away. "I heard you loud and clear, but what I heard is that you don't appreciate me," he said, his voice dripping with sarcasm. He gestured to a piece of paper lying beside him and slid it toward me. "So I came up with two ideas."

I glanced down at the paper, my curiosity piqued. "What's this?" I asked, confusion mingling with dread.

Hall Pass

He leaned back, a wicked grin spreading across his face. "We can get a divorce, and I'll take half of all this shit," he said, his tone cold and calculating.

"What?" I shot back, my heart racing. "You can't be serious."

"Or" he continued, leaning forward, his eyes narrowing, "we can do a separation for a while. You can go out there and see that the grass isn't greener on the other side."

I felt a whirlwind of emotions—speechless and furious all at once. "The decision is yours, Dior," he said, as if he were handing me a choice between life and death. "But one way or another, you're leaving here tonight. I already packed your stuff." He gestured nonchalantly to the corner.

I turned, my heart dropping as I saw my suitcases stacked neatly, as if he'd planned this all along. "Sergio, I know damn well you ain't packed up my shit," I screamed, my voice echoing off the walls, a mix of disbelief and anger coursing through me.

"So, what are you gonna do?" he asked, a smirk playing on his lips.

"I'm not leaving my damn house," I shot back, standing my ground.

"Yes, you are," he said, his tone unwavering.

"No, the fuck I'm not," I replied, my voice rising as adrenaline coursed through me.

He stepped closer, the scent of liquor heavy on his breath. "You can leave willingly like a lady, or I can make it a whole lot harder for you. Trust me, you're not gonna like that."

My heart raced, pounding against my chest like it was trying to escape. I turned away, fury and fear swirling inside me. I grabbed my purse and wheeled my suitcase toward the door, each movement feeling heavier than the last. As I stepped outside, the reality of what was happening hit me like a punch to the gut.

I slid into my car, and as I turned the key in the ignition, tears streamed down my cheeks. I fumbled for my phone and called Destiny, desperate for a friendly voice, but there was no answer. I dialed again and again, frustration building as the silence echoed back.

Finally, I drove to my parents' house, needing the comfort of home. I let myself in, the familiar scent of their living room wrapping around me like a warm blanket. They were curled up on the couch, engrossed in a show, but when they saw me, their expressions shifted from relaxation to concern.

"What's wrong, baby girl?" my dad asked, jumping up.

My mom was already ushering me toward the couch, her eyes scanning my face for answers. "What happened?"

Hall Pass

"Sergio put me out," I managed to choke out, my voice barely above a whisper.

"Out of what?" my mom shot back, her tone sharp, a hint of disbelief in her eyes.

"Out of my house."

"The house your name's on and you pay all the bills for?" she blurted out, her voice rising with indignation.

All I could do was look down, shame flooding my cheeks as I realized how ridiculous this was. I felt small and defeated, the weight of my situation crashing down around me.

"We had a heated argument this morning that turned into him throwing all my hard work in my face," I said, my voice trembling with the weight of it all. "He told me when I got home that we could either get a divorce and he'd take half of everything I've built, or we could separate for a while. But either way, I was leaving tonight because he packed my shit." My dad didn't say a word, but the anger etched on his face spoke volumes.

"I told you not to marry that boy; he was no good," she said, frustration simmering just beneath the surface. "But you swore you were in love. He got my baby at that house playing the man in the relationship, and he's gonna put you out? Who does he think he is? I told you…"

Breanna J

"Mom, I don't need to hear the 'I told you so' right now," I interrupted, my voice sharp.

"No, you need to hear it because this could've been avoided if you'd just listened," she shot back, her tone a mix of concern and exasperation.

I stood up, my heart racing. "I'm leaving," I declared, marching toward the door. I knew she was probably right, but I wasn't in the headspace to process that. This wasn't the time for "I told you so."

I rushed out to my car, adrenaline pumping, but my dad followed closely behind. Just as I reached for the door to slam it shut, he grabbed it, stopping me in my tracks. "Listen, baby girl," he said softly, his eyes filled with concern. "I know you're hurting right now, and we both know your mom can be a bit much, but she means well and says it all with love. What do you need right now?"

I looked up at him, trying to hold back the tears that threatened to spill over. "I don't know," I admitted, my voice barely a whisper.

"Take your time. We're here for you," he reassured me, his hand resting gently on my shoulder. In that moment, I felt the weight of my choices and the warmth of family, but I still felt so lost.

"Yes, sir," I replied, trying to keep my voice steady. "I'm just gonna go have a drink. But if it's okay with y'all, can I come back here tonight? I really don't have anywhere else to go. Destiny isn't answering."

"Of course. This is always your home, no matter your age, you don't have to ask." he said, his voice warm and reassuring. "Now give me a hug."

I climbed out of the car and wrapped my arms around my dad, the embrace grounding me in a way I desperately needed. His arms were strong and comforting, reminding me that no matter how chaotic my life felt, I still had my family.

"Remember, we love you, Dior," he said, pulling back and looking me in the eyes. His gaze was steady, filled with both concern and pride.

I climbed back into my car, feeling a mixture of relief and sadness wash over me. My dad shut the door gently, lingering for a moment as he watched me pull out of the driveway. I glanced in the rearview mirror, seeing him standing there, a pillar of strength amidst my storm. I needed this break, but the thought of facing the night alone gnawed at me. I drove away, the weight of uncertainty still heavy on my heart, but knowing I had a safe haven waiting for me when I needed it most.

I headed back to that same bar where Destiny and I had spent last night, the neon lights flickering like they were trying to tell me something. This time, instead of a table, I slid onto a stool at the bar, the wood cool beneath me. I waved the bartender over, her hair slicked back in a tight bun that screamed no-nonsense. "Give me the strongest thing you've got and keep it coming," I ordered, my voice low and heavy.

    As the first drink slid in front of me, I could feel the heat sizzling in my chest. Men started to hover, their eyes glinting with that predatory spark, thinking my dry tears were a sign of weakness. I rolled my eyes and ignored them, focusing on the burn of the whiskey. My phone buzzed in my pocket, and I fished it out, raising it to my ear. "Hello?" I slurred, the world around me beginning to blur.

"How's the car?" Armand's cheerful voice cut through the haze.

"Fine," I replied, trying to keep it casual but failing miserably.

"You good?" he asked, his tone laced with a hint of worry.

"As good as I'm gonna be," I shot back, throwing back another drink like it was water.

"You don't sound okay. Where are you?" he pressed.

"Same place as last night," I admitted, feeling the weight of my words settle in the pit of my stomach.

"The bar?"

"Yup. Hoping I can drink all my problems away." I laughed bitterly, but it felt empty.

"Dior, I'm on my way. Don't leave," he said, urgency pulsing through his words.

"Yup," I mumbled, dropping my phone back on the bar.

I wasn't sure how long it had been since I spoke to Armand. I lost track of time and drinks, each one numbing the reality that I was trying to escape. When Armand finally walked in, concern etched across his face, it felt like a punch to the gut.

"What happened? What's wrong?" He leaned closer, his eyes scanning me for signs of distress.

"He put me out," I mumbled, the bitterness rising in my throat.

"Who?"

"Sergio," I spat, the name bitter on my tongue.

"your husband?"

"That bitch-ass nigga put me out of my own house. Can you believe that? I pay most of the bills, the house is in my name, and he has the audacity to toss me out like yesterday's trash. But that was after he gave me this bullshit ultimatum—

divorce him and let him take half of everything I've worked for, or we separate." I signaled for another drink, needing the burn to drown out the chaos in my mind.

Armand's expression shifted, anger flashing across his features. "Dior, you deserve better than this. You know that, right?"

I took a deep breath, the weight of his words mixing with the alcohol swirling through my system. "Yeah, maybe. But right now, I just want to forget."

Armand settled onto the stool beside me, his warmth wrapping around me like a comforting blanket. I leaned into him, grateful for his presence. "Do you know how much I've changed to be in a relationship with him?" I started, my voice thick with emotion. "All those women who flirt with him, the way he looks at them with those wandering eyes? But God forbid I even think about admiring another man in his presence."

I took a deep breath, trying to keep my voice steady. "I don't take my insecurities out on him. I deal with them silently, like it's my own private battle. I give that man respect he doesn't even deserve. I don't sweat him about where he goes or what he does. When his mood is off, I give him space to process it like a man. But I always let him know I care, that I'm here as his safe space, ready to listen. Yet, I know he's not going to express himself like I do."

I glanced at Armand, then continued, "I keep myself up. I mean, look at me—I'm fine! He said I was controlling

Hall Pass

and always thought I'm right, so I took a step back, letting him lead knowing damn well he couldn't lead us to water if our lives depended on it. I listened. I let him paint a picture because I was an only child that everything I had was handed to me. But I worked hard to be here. My parents were broke. They didn't have any money. I had student loans just like everyone else. I'm still paying them off. When he told me school wasn't working for him and he'd rather work at his uncle's detailing shop than chase a degree, I stood by him. I didn't judge; I just wanted to support him and hold it down for our family. I gave him everything I had. I loved him the best I could, compromising to make sure I didn't push him away."

I paused, the weight of my words heavy in the air. "Do you know he doesn't even fuck me right? He's never given me an orgasm. But I don't throw that in his face."

"Dior, let me get you out of here," Armand said, concern etching his features.

"No, I'm not done drinking. I can have a few more and drive myself back to my parents'," I insisted, defiance rising.

"You're not driving anywhere like this," he replied firmly, crossing his arms.

"I got this," I shot back, but the confidence in my voice wavered.

"Your night is done. Bartender, please bring me the check," he said, his tone leaving no room for argument.

He settled my tab and helped me up from the bar, his grip steadying me. As I took a few steps, a wave of realization hit me—I was way drunker than I thought. The room swayed slightly, and I leaned into Armand, grateful for his strength. Maybe it was time to let someone else take the lead for a change.

As I sat in the car, the city lights flickering past like a blur, I glanced over at Armand. My eyelids feel heavy, weighed down by the mix of exhaustion and the alcohol still swirling in my system. The air was thick with unspoken words, and finally, I broke the silence.

"You know this is all your fault," I said, my voice low but steady. "Had you never left me, I wouldn't be here right now."

He turned to me, the concern in his eyes cutting through the haze. "Dior, don't say that. You know I didn't have a choice," he replied, his tone softening.

I shook my head, frustration bubbling to the surface. "No, really. If you hadn't gone to jail, maybe I wouldn't be fighting so damn hard to save a marriage with a man that doesn't value me. I wouldn't be drowning in this mess."

The weight of my words hung between us, and I could see the tension in his jaw. He wanted to argue, to defend himself, but I could tell he understood the truth in what I was saying. I leaned back in my seat, staring out at the passing lights, the reflections dancing in my mind like memories we both tried to forget.

"Sometimes I wonder what it would've been like if we never lost each other," I murmured, the vulnerability slipping through the cracks.

Armand sighed, his voice barely above a whisper. "Me too, Dior. But we can't change the past. We can only figure out what's next."

I turned to him, searching his eyes for something—maybe hope, maybe answers. "What's next for us, Armand?"

He met my gaze, the intensity of his stare igniting a flicker of something deep within me. "I don't know yet, but I want to find out. Together."

The atmosphere shifted, a fragile sense of possibility hanging in the air, even as my heart wrestled with the chaos.

SIX

Armand

I couldn't take Dior back to her parents' house—not like this. The last thing I wanted was for them to see her in such a vulnerable state, so I brought her to my hotel room instead. The moment we stepped inside, I scooped her up in my arms, her body feeling light against mine. I carried her to the bed, the soft sheets inviting us to sink into their comfort.

As I laid her down, she looked up at me, her eyes heavy with a mix of sleep and something more. "Armand, make love to me. Make me feel like you used to," she murmured, her words slurring together, but the desire behind them was unmistakable.

"Dior, you're drunk," I replied, trying to keep my voice steady despite the heat rising in my chest.

"A drunk mouth speaks of a sober heart," she shot back, an unexpected spark in her gaze before she grabbed me and pulled me down, planting a kiss on my lips. It was intoxicating, a reminder of everything we once had, and it made me feel like I was right where I needed to be. But I knew this wasn't the time.

Hall Pass

"Dior, you're drunk. Just rest. I'm gonna get you some stuff for the hangover. I'll be back," I told her, my heart aching at the thought of leaving her side.

"All I need is you," she whispered, her voice a soft plea that tugged at me.

I backed away reluctantly, forcing myself to leave the room. I headed to the nearest gas station, my mind racing with thoughts of her and the essentials I needed to grab. I picked up water, aspirin, and some snacks—anything to help her when she woke up.

When I returned to the room, I set everything up on the nightstand, the soft glow of the lamp illuminating the space. I took a seat in the chair across from the bed, watching her as she slept, her chest rising and falling gently.

My blood boiled as I thought about what she'd been through, knowing that someone had dared to treat her this way and had broken her down like this. The anger simmered just beneath the surface, but I couldn't let it overtake me. I had to be her rock right now, to protect her from the pain that had brought her to this moment—but there was going to be hell to pay.

I leaned back in the chair, my mind racing in a whirlwind of thoughts, determined to be there for her when she finally woke up. But her words from the car kept echoing in my head—a relentless loop of guilt and regret that felt like a punch to the gut. Was this all my fault? Where would we be if I had just chosen a different path—one that didn't lead me straight to jail? The weight of my thoughts pressed down on me, not allowing me a moment's peace.

I pulled out my phone and headed to the bathroom, the fluorescent light buzzing overhead. I called Ahmad, and he answered on the third ring, his voice a familiar lifeline.
"What's up, boy?"
"I need access to your tech guy," I said, urgency lacing my tone.

"Alright, what do you need him to do?" Ahmad asked, his curiosity piqued.

"I need intel on a guy named Sergio Waye," I replied, the name tasting bitter on my tongue.

"Okay, I'll get him on it. You good?" he asked, concern creeping into his voice.

"Yeah, just need that info, and ASAP," I told him, my heart racing.

"Okay, I'll hit you back," he said before hanging up.

As I paced the bathroom, I couldn't shake the feeling that I'd never felt this way about any woman—not even my momma. I wanted to protect Dior, to fight for her. The thought of her being hurt made my blood boil. I was a caged animal, restless and ready to break free.

By 6 AM, I was back in the chair, watching Dior sleep peacefully, her chest rising and falling like a calm tide amidst my storm. My phone buzzed, pulling me from my thoughts—it was Ahmad. I got up and headed back into the bathroom, closing the door behind me for a moment of privacy.

"Yeah?" I answered, my heart pounding.

Hall Pass

"Check your email," he instructed.

I quickly pulled up my email, adrenaline coursing through my veins as I opened the file. It was a comprehensive file on Sergio—complete with a picture of a sharp-dressed man sporting a confident smirk that twisted my gut. Details about his job, his hours, and even the exact time he clocked in flooded my screen.

"I got you what you wanted. Now tell me what's going on," Ahmad demanded.

"Don't worry about it. I just have something to handle," I replied, trying to keep my voice steady.

"Armand, before you bug out, talk to me. This isn't even like you," he pressed.

"What is there to talk about?" I shot back, frustration bubbling.

"What's going on? That dude Sergio is Dior's husband. I looked at the file—what's the deal?" he asked, disbelief creeping into his tone.

"He hurt her. He even kicked her out of their house," I said, my voice low, the anger simmering within me.

Ahmad was silent for a moment, processing the weight of my words. "Little bro, let me handle this," he finally said. "Nah, I got it," I retorted, my resolve hardening.

"Armand, let me handle it. I don't want you going back to jail. Don't let the lover boy in you make you stupid," he yelled, concern now tinged with desperation.

"I got it!" I shot back, frustration boiling over. He must have understood that he wasn't about to change my mind.

"You love her?" he asked, and I knew he could hear the truth in my silence.

"Never stopped," I told him, the admission hanging heavy in the air.

Ahmad sighed, the sound heavy with resignation. "Okay, listen. I'm going to give you an address. At this address, I keep a bag. Get the bag, use what's in there—nothing will trace back to you. When you're done, get rid of the bag and everything in it. Do you understand?"

"Yeah, I understand," I replied, the gravity of the situation weighing down on me.

"No, Armand, do you really understand what you're about to do?" Ahmad pressed, his voice a mix of concern and urgency.

I took a deep breath, the stakes higher than I'd ever imagined. "I understand. And I'm doing this for Dior."

"Because if you get caught, we're both going away," he said, urgency lacing his words.

"Yeah, I understand. Just send the address," I replied, my heart pounding in my chest as I hung up. A mix of relief and urgency coursed through me; I needed to act fast before the day slipped away.

Just then, my phone vibrated again, lighting up with Shonny's name. I hesitated, a knot forming in my stomach. I ignored it, the weight of the situation pressing down on me like a heavy fog. I splashed cold water on my face to shake off the fatigue that clung to me like a second skin. Each drop felt like a jolt to my system, but my mind was still racing, thoughts spiraling chaotically around what I needed to do next.

I stared at my reflection in the cracked mirror, the shadows under my eyes a testament to the sleepless night I'd endured. "Get it together, Armand," I muttered to myself. I could see the man I wanted to be—the protector, the fighter—everything Dior deserved. But right now, I felt like a soldier standing on the brink of a battlefield.

I ran my hand across my face, trying to quell the storm inside me. The thought of Dior, vulnerable and alone, spurred me on. I couldn't let her down. I had to be the one to save her from the mess Sergio had created.

As I paced the bathroom, the cold tiles biting into my feet, I recalled every moment we'd shared—the laughter, the stolen glances, the way she lit up a room just by being in it. I couldn't let that light fade away. Not on my watch.

I checked my phone again; there was a message from Ahmad with the address and a warning to be careful. The silence felt deafening. I needed to move. With one last look in the mirror, I steeled myself for what lay ahead. I had to keep my cool, even as the tension in my chest tightened like a vice grip.

With purpose, I stepped out of the bathroom, ready to face whatever came next. Time was ticking, and I wouldn't let it run out on Dior.

I called down to the main desk, my voice steady. I entrusted them to place the room in Dior's name, ensuring she was treated like a VIP guest. No cost for however long she stayed—she deserved that and more. Plus, if Shonny showed up looking for me, I wanted the system to reflect that the room was booked by an actual guest and not me. I hung up, the tension in my chest easing just slightly.

As I stared in the mirror, the reflection looking back at me was a mix of determination and despair. I couldn't change the past, but I could damn well fight for her future.

I checked on her one last time, her soft breaths filling the room, before grabbing my keys and heading out. Today was one of Sergio's early days, and I figured it was my best shot to handle him while she slept peacefully. I made a stop at the address Ahmad had given me and picked up a black duffle bag, my mind swirling with questions.

How the hell did Dior end up married to him? I couldn't wrap my head around it. His file had laid it all out—no college degree, just a guy who dropped out after a basketball injury. Now he was stuck working at a car detailing shop, his life seemingly on pause. What did she see in him?

As I pulled up to the shop, I parked in the back near the employee entrance, my heart pounding harder than usual. The smell of gasoline and fresh wax wafted through the air, mingling with the sounds of birds singing. I scanned the lot for Sergio, hoping he'd be easy to spot.

I opened the bag I'd grabbed on the way here, my heart racing as I pulled out the contents: a ski mask, some gloves, and, last but not least, a gun with a half-empty clip. Suddenly, everything Ahmad had said on the phone clicked into place, the gravity of my situation weighing down on me. I had to make sure I said nothing that would connect me to Dior.

Hall Pass

When I finally saw him walking up, my pulse quickened. "Sergio?" I called out, my voice steady despite the chaos swirling inside me.

"Yeah?" he answered, spinning around to face me, a cocky smirk plastered on his face that made my blood boil.
In an instant, I closed the distance between us and struck him with the butt of my gun, knocking him straight onto his ass. "Ya momma should've swallowed ya bitch ass," I spat, the words dripping with venom. I unleashed every ounce of pent-up anger as I pounded him, each blow fueled by the pain he'd caused Dior and the mess my life had spiraled into.

He crumpled beneath me, lying there motionless, and for a brief moment, I battled with the urge to pull the trigger. The thought of ending him right then and there flickered in my mind—a twisted sense of justice for what he'd done to her. I wanted him erased, to never be a problem for Dior again. But alongside that thought came a heavier one: did I really want to step into a world where I'd crossed that line? I had never taken a life; I never imagined I would even entertain such a thought. But damn, I loved Dior that much, and the desperation clawed at my insides.

Then, the sounds of the community waking up reached my ears—the distant rumble of cars, the chatter of early risers, the laughter of kids heading to school. That noise jolted me back to reality, and I realized I couldn't do it. I left him there, a broken man on the ground, and rushed back to my car, adrenaline coursing through my veins.

As I glanced over my shoulder, I checked my surroundings, every instinct on high alert. The sun was beginning to rise, casting a golden hue over the streets, but all I felt was the weight of what I'd just done. I could still hear his groans fading into the distance as I sped away, the knot in my stomach tightening with every heartbeat. I had made it clear I wasn't playing games anymore; I was going to have Dior.

SEVEN

Dior

I woke up in a hotel room, disoriented and unsure how I had ended up here or who I had come with. The alcohol from last night had turned everything into a hazy blur. As I sat up in the bed, stretching my limbs, I scanned the unfamiliar room for any clues—anything that might jog my memory. I was still fully dressed, a testament to the wild night I barely remembered.

On the nightstand, I spotted a Gatorade and some Advil along with a plate of eggs, toast, and bacon with a clear lid covering it, a small lifeline in this chaos. I swung my legs over the edge of the bed, my head pounding like a jackhammer, and reached for them. Just as I was about to pop the Advil and chase it with the neon-blue drink, the bathroom door creaked open. My heart raced, and I held my breath, bracing myself for the worst—an awkward encounter with a stranger or, God forbid, a regrettable choice I made while drunk.

But then he appeared: Armand, emerging from the bathroom wrapped in nothing but a towel, droplets of water glistening on his skin. Relief washed over me, quickly igniting an unexpected fire between my legs at the sight of him. "Damn, I'm sorry! I thought you were still sleeping. I was just grabbing some clothes," he said, his voice smooth yet slightly sheepish.

"No worries, do what you gotta do," I managed to reply, trying to play it cool despite the flutter in my stomach. I popped the Advil, downed some juice, and couldn't help but notice the suitcases lined against the wall as he rummaged through one, pulling out a pair of sweatpants. Was he living here? The thought flitted through my mind, mingling with the remnants of last night's debauchery. What the hell had happened? And, more importantly, what was going to happen next?

He slid the sweatpants beneath his towel, and then, with a casual flick, let the towel drop. My breath caught in my throat. His body was like a work of art—muscles defined, skin glowing, and those sweatpants hugging his waist just right, accentuating that perfect V shape leading down from his abs. The angel wings tattooed on his back seemed to unfurl with every movement, as if they were alive, calling to something deep within me.

"How are you feeling?" he asked, his voice playful, a hint of mischief dancing in his eyes.

"Like shit," I replied, rubbing my temples, trying to chase away the remnants of last night's debauchery.

He laughed, the sound rich and warm. "Dior 0, alcohol 1."

"Seriously, how much of a fool did I make of myself?" I asked, half-joking but genuinely curious.

"None at all," he assured me, his gaze steady.

"Did we do it?" I blurted out, my heart racing as I awaited his answer.

"Nah," he replied with a cocky smirk. "If we did it, it wouldn't be while you're weak and emotional, and damn sure not while you're drunk. I want you to enjoy it and remember it."

His words sent a heat rushing through me, igniting a knot in my throat. There was something about his confidence, the way he looked at me, that made me feel both vulnerable and alive. I could feel the tension crackling in the air between us. "

"So what happened?" I asked, a hint of shame creeping in as I braced myself for the answer.

"You vented, and I listened," he replied, a playful glint in his eyes. "Eventually, I felt like the alcohol was getting the best of you, so I closed your tab, and we left the bar. I knew you said you were staying at your parents', but I wasn't letting you go home like that. So, I brought you here and sat in that chair while you slept."

"Damn, that's the second time in a row you saved me. You're going to get tired of saving my ass soon," I said, half-joking but feeling a strange warmth at his words.

"Never," he said, his tone firm, locking eyes with me in a way that made my heart skip.

I couldn't hold back the burning question any longer. "Are you living here?"

"Yeah, for now," he said, glancing around the lavish hotel room, his expression unreadable.

"How are you affording this... Never mind, that's not my business," I said, the words tumbling out before I could stop them. I couldn't shake the nagging thought that this place looked expensive, and I'd never heard him mention a job. Maybe it was because of his criminal record—something beneath him that he didn't want to drag up. Or he was selling drugs like I knew his brothers used to.

"No biggie," he replied, shrugging casually. "When my mom passed, I got a little money, threw it in the bank, and I managed a bar."

As Armand spoke, my gaze was drawn to the imprint he had in his gray sweatpants. I tried to focus on his words, but the way the fabric clung to him made it hard to think straight. There was something intoxicating about him, a mix of charm and mystery that kept me hanging on every word. The air between us thickened, charged with unspoken possibilities, and I couldn't help but wonder what else lay beneath that confident exterior.

"So, are you going to take a few days off work?" he asked, his tone casual, but there was an edge of concern beneath it.

"For what? To sit at my parents' house and throw a pity party about how fucked up my life is? How did I marry a man who doesn't really love me, no matter how much I love him? He's not man enough to leave with exactly what he came in with," I replied, frustration bubbling to the surface.

"Not to mention he don't know how to fuck," he added with a laugh, and I choked on my drink at his bluntness.

"Did I tell you that?" I asked, surprised and somewhat embarrassed.

"Yeah, along with the fact that it's all my fault you're going through this because I went to jail." The room fell silent, the weight of unspoken words hanging in the air.

"Do you really feel that way?" he asked, breaking the tension.

"That he can't fuck?" I asked, trying to deflect.

"I don't give a fuck about that nigga's dick game. I care about whether you really think me leaving fucked you up in the long run."

I hesitated, grappling with the truth. Yes, that thought had always lingered in the back of my mind, but I'd never voiced it. "Dior?" he pressed gently.

"In a way, yes. We were young, but I loved you with everything in me. There was a safety I felt when I was around you—like the safety I felt with my dad. I could turn my brain off and still know I was going to be okay. There was a love I felt with you that, if I'm being honest, I never felt with Sergio. The way you looked at me, the way you made love to me... I unknowingly compare my husband to you. You have a hold on me, and in my head, I blamed you. Even before you came back into my life."

The words spilled out like an overflowing dam, raw and unfiltered. I realized how much I had kept bottled up, and the vulnerability of the moment made my heart race. Armand's gaze was intense, searching, and I could feel the air thickening between us, charged with the weight of our shared history and the complexities of our present.

Armand took a seat next to me. "Dior me leaving was never to hurt you." "I know" I said quickly then looking away. He turned my face to him. "No seriously. I'm not making excuses. I was doing shit that I knew the results of would be jail. When it happened I didn't want your life to end or you grow a hate for me while waiting on me or stopping your life because mine stopped." I always thought it was pride that made Armand push me away but finally hearing him explain gave me a scene of closure with that chapter of our lives. I kissed him on the cheek. "Thank you. I needed that."

"Dior, on some real shit, I love you. You are an amazing woman. Don't let this shit break you. I know it's hard—sometimes you bend, and you feel every damn emotion, but don't let this nigga or that situation take over you. Whether it's me or any other man, don't lose yourself trying to overplay your role for them. You are beautiful, and I mean that with all due respect—you are that bitch. Own it. Stand tall, walk confidently, and sit on your throne like the queen you are. Don't ever come off that pedestal.

As long as I'm around, I'm gonna keep reminding you of that. You deserve to hear it, to feel it, and to believe it. Life's messy, but you're tougher than any bullshit that comes your way. So let the world throw its punches; you've got the strength to take them and keep moving forward."

Armand words damn near had me ready to cry. But I needed to hear that.

"Are you ready to go home?" he said to me. "Yeah, you can take me to my parents. My clothes are there." I told him.

As we pulled up in front of my parents' house, it felt like we were transported back to our teenage years, when everything was simpler and love was just a heartbeat away. Armand had that old-school R&B playing softly, the kind that wrapped around us like a warm blanket. Even though I should have been tearing up with nostalgia, I couldn't help but smile from ear to ear. My gaze was glued to Armand, that familiar spark igniting something deep inside me.

"Why you looking at me like that?" he asked, his brow raised in playful curiosity

"I don't know, it's just something about you," I replied, feeling a mix of affection and admiration.

"What do you mean?" His voice was teasing, but I sensed the sincerity behind it.

"Nothing crazy. I'm just grateful," I confessed, my heart swelling.

"Grateful for what?" he probed, genuine interest lighting up his eyes.

"That God reconnected us when he did. With everything I have going on and all the shit you've done for me lately, it means more than you even know. You were like the missing piece I couldn't quite put my finger on. Someone real. Someone who won't lie or hide stuff from me," I told him, my voice soft but steady.

Armand smiled, that charming smile that always made my heart skip a beat. "I told you back when we were younger that I had you forever and always, and I meant just that."

I felt a blush creep into my cheeks, warmth flooding through me. "Ummm... you want to come in? I'm sure my parents would love to see you."

He glanced at the clock, then back at me, a grin spreading across his face. "Sure, why not? I haven't seen your parents in forever, and I always loved them."

Hall Pass

We climbed out of the car, and as we walked toward the house, a mix of excitement and nerves tangled in the air. When I stepped inside, the familiar scent of home enveloped me, and I headed straight to the kitchen, where Mom and Dad were bustling about.

"Look who I found!" I announced cheerfully, my voice echoing with delight as we entered the kitchen.

"Hello Mr. and Mrs. Matthews," Armand said.

"Armand, is that you?" My mom exclaimed, her face lighting up as she came around the island to greet him.

"Yes ma'am, it's me," he answered, his trademark smile lighting up the room as he embraced her. The warmth of that moment wrapped around me like the sweetest melody, and suddenly, everything felt right in the world again.

"Son, we missed you around here. It's good seeing you," my dad said, his voice deep and welcoming. Both of my parents knew about Armand's past, but I was relieved they didn't bring it up. It felt like a fresh start, a chance to rewrite our story.

"How is your momma? I've got to make my way over there to see her," my mom asked, her concern genuine and maternal.

Armand's smile faltered slightly. "She passed."

"Are you serious? My God," my mom gasped, her eyes wide with shock and sympathy. The air thickened with unspoken feelings, the weight of loss hanging between all us.

"Well, if your momma ain't here, who's been feeding you? I know you're probably still as picky as you were when you were younger," my mom said, trying to lighten the mood. "Have a seat! I cooked breakfast; I'll get you some."

"Don't worry about it, Momma, I got it," I chimed in, eager to help and fill the space with something comforting. I grabbed a plate and piled it high with crispy bacon, fluffy scrambled eggs, creamy grits, and a buttery biscuit, each item a little piece of home. With a smile on my face, I brought it over to Armand and set it down in front of him.

"Thank you," he said, his tone sincere, and I could see the appreciation in his eyes.

"Eat up, I'm about to run upstairs," I told him, feeling a rush of excitement mixed with nerves. I wanted to give him a moment to savor the food and soak in the warmth of the home we both cherished. As I turned to head up the stairs, I glanced back at him one last time, hoping this was just the beginning of something beautiful.

I walked into my old bedroom, a sanctuary filled with memories that made me smile. Just like I suspected, my bags were already waiting for me, a reminder of the chaos that had brought me back here. I pulled out some clothes for work and laid them on the bed, hoping to change quickly so Armand could take me to get my car afterward.

I jumped into the shower, letting the hot water wash away the lingering tension from the night before. But when I stepped out, I was shocked to see my mother sitting on the bed, arms crossed, a serious look etched on her face.

"Ma'am?" I said, still dripping wet. "What are you doing?"

"About to get dress." I told her "Now you know that's not what I'm talking about. I'm talking about that man you got sitting in my kitchen. I know me and your daddy raised you better than this. Just because your marriage is rocky doesn't mean you should jump into bed with the next guy."

"What, Momma?" I said, confusion washing over me.

"You left here hurt last night, but I know you're not dumb, you come back in her with a blast from the past this morning. That's a good man downstairs. But..." she continued, her voice firm but laced with concern.

"Momma," I started, feeling defensive.

"Dior, you're playing a dangerous game. Don't hurt that man because you're hurting, and don't put yourself in a situation that makes your marriage worse," she advised, her eyes searching mine for understanding.

"Momma, I didn't sleep with Armand," I finally blurted out, the words tumbling out in a rush. My heart raced as the truth hung heavily between us, a delicate balance of tension and relief.

She stared at me, her expression a mix of disbelief and concern. "The other night, I ran into Armand when Destiny and I were out. Later that night, I was stuck on the side of the road, and Sergio refused to come get me or help me."

"What?" she said, her brow furrowing.

"Armand just so happened to drive by and stopped to help me when he didn't have to. Last night, he called to check on me while I was at the bar. He realized how drunk I was and came to get me before I embarrassed myself once again when he didn't have to. Because he cares about me and you guys, he didn't want to bring me home for y'all to deal with my drunken mess. He took me to a hotel and put me in bed. I woke up this morning still in my clothes," I explained, my voice steady but my insides churning with vulnerability.

"I hope that's the truth," she said, her eyes narrowing slightly. Making me feel like a teenage girl.

"It is," I insisted, biting my tongue to hold back everything else I wanted to say about how much he meant to me.

Before the conversation could go any further, my phone started to ring, cutting through the tension like a knife. "I'ma let you get that. But we are going to talk later," she said, her tone softening a bit. "Hurry back down here before your daddy talks that boy's ears off."

"Yes ma'am," I replied, a hint of a smile breaking through my nerves.

"Hello?" I answered, trying to shake off the weight of our discussion.

"Hey bestie! I'm so sorry I missed your calls last night. What's up?" Destiny's voice was bright and familiar, instantly lifting my spirits.

"Girl!" I exclaimed, almost breathless.

"What? What happened?" she asked, concern creeping into her tone.

"A lot. Meet me at the diner on Lexington for breakfast so I can fill you in. I'm about to get dressed and have Armand take me to get my car, then I'll be there," I said, urgently coloring my voice.

"Armand?" she repeated, a teasing lilt in her tone. I could almost hear her eyebrows raising through the phone.

"Yeah, Armand," I replied, my cheeks warming at the thought of him. "It's complicated."

We hung up, and I quickly finished getting dressed, slipping into my favorite jeans and a snug top that hugged my curves just right. As I made my way back downstairs, the familiar aroma of my mom's cooking wafted through the air, making my stomach grumble. "How was your food?" I asked, stepping into the kitchen with a teasing smile.

"Man, you already know it was on point! I've never had anything your mom cooked that wasn't fire," Armand replied, grinning from ear to ear, his eyes sparkling with delight.

"Thank you, baby," my momma chimed in, her pride shining through her warm smile.

I turned to Armand, the thought of my car nagging at me. "Well, can you take me to get my car?" I asked, trying to keep my tone light.

"Of course," he said. But as I glanced back at my momma, I caught a glimpse of the look she shot me from across the kitchen—a mix of concern and encouragement that made my heart race.

I took Armand's empty plate and placed it in the sink, then leaned over to give my momma a quick kiss on the cheek. "You know what I said," she whispered, her voice low but firm. I nodded, feeling the weight of her words but also the thrill of what lay ahead.

I made my way to my dad, planting a kiss on his cheek too. "Armand, you be safe with my baby," he said, his tone protective as we walked toward the door.

"Yes sir, always," Armand called back, flashing my dad a confident grin that somehow reassured everyone in the room—even me.

As we stepped outside, the air wrapped around us like a warm embrace, buzzing with the vibrant energy of the city. I could feel the anticipation simmering just beneath the surface—a heady mix of excitement and nerves that made my heart race.

Once we settled into Armand's car, he burst into laughter, breaking the momentary tension. "That was definitely like old times. Your dad was grilling me, making sure I wasn't doing any unspeakable things to his daughter."

"Unspeakable?" I shot back, a smirk creeping onto my lips.

"Yeah, he wanted to make sure I wasn't fucking his daughter," he replied, his eyes dancing with amusement.

Hall Pass

I chuckled, rolling my eyes. "Well, the difference between back then and now is that you actually weren't lying when he asked."

"But don't feel bad," I said, his laughter infectious. "My momma came upstairs grilling me too."

We shared a laugh, reminiscing about those awkward teenage days as he navigated through the bustling streets. The familiarity of our banter felt comforting, like slipping into an old, well-loved hoodie.

When we finally reached my car, Armand was his usual self, a comforting presence in the chaos of my life. He helped me into my seat, making sure I was safely inside before leaning against the doorframe, his expression earnest. "The hotel room is open to you if you need it, or if you just don't want to stay at your parents'," he offered, a hint of concern in his eyes.

I smiled at him, warmth spreading through me. "Aww, I don't want to invade your space," I replied, trying to downplay how much I appreciated the offer.

"It's no biggie. I can always crash at Ahmad's or Armani's. I just want to make sure you're good," he said, his voice steady and reassuring.

"Thank you," I said, a genuine smile breaking across my face. It meant a lot to me that he cared so much.

"Are you about to head to work?" he asked, tilting his head slightly, a playful glint in his eyes.

"I'm meeting up with Destiny first, and then, yes, I am going to work," I informed him, shifting in my seat, the reality of my day looming ahead.

"Well, when you get a moment, hit me up. I want to take you out to do something," he said, his tone filled with anticipation.

I felt a rush of excitement at the thought. "Okay, I will," I promised, feeling a flutter in my chest.

He leaned in and planted a soft kiss on my forehead, and I nearly melted into my seat. That simple gesture felt like a shield against all the chaos in my life, grounding me in a moment of warmth.

Armand stepped back, walking over to his truck, but he didn't pull away until he saw me leave. I glanced in my rearview mirror, catching a glimpse of him standing there, and a smile tugged at my lips. It was a small moment, but it filled me with hope, reminding me that even amidst the storm, there were still lights to guide me home.

As I pulled out my cell to call Destiny and let her know I was on my way, the phone buzzed with an incoming call that stopped me in my tracks.

"Hello?" I answered, my voice steady but curious.

"Hi, is this the family of Sergio Waye?" the voice on the other end asked, its tone professional but laced with urgency.

"Yes, this is his wife," I replied, my heart beginning to race for an entirely different reason.

Hall Pass

"Hello, ma'am. I am calling from St. Mary's Hospital to let you know that your husband was brought here by ambulance and is currently in surgery."

The words hit me like a freight train, and the world around me blurred into a chaotic swirl of colors and sounds. I gripped the steering wheel tighter, my knuckles turning white as I struggled to process the shock. The vibrant city lights outside faded into a hazy backdrop, and panic surged through me, each heartbeat echoing louder than the last.

"My heart dropped. What do you mean surgery? Surgery for what?" I demanded, my voice trembling.

"It's best if you get here as soon as possible. A doctor can tell you face to face," the voice replied, its calmness only heightening my anxiety.

"I'm on my way," I said, urgency flooding my words. I hung up and slammed the wheel to the right, making a swift U-turn that sent my heart racing even faster.

As I pulled into the hospital parking lot, déjà vu washed over me like a cold wave. This place felt hauntingly familiar. Back in college, Sergio had been one of the star players on the basketball team while I was just the nerdy girl, buried in books. I remembered how he'd been struggling in English, and they assigned me as his tutor. One thing led to another, and one night, when we were supposed to be studying, I found myself in Sergio's bed, the soft sheets tangled around us as we explored something new and thrilling.

After that night, he'd claimed me as his girl, and I felt like I had stepped into a dream. But then came the night of the big game. I had overslept, completely missing the first half, and when I finally rushed into the gym, breathless and wide-eyed, my heart dropped at the sight before me. Sergio was being placed on a stretcher and wheeled out to the back of an ambulance, the crowd around him a blur of concern and chaos.

I followed the ambulance to the hospital, my heart pounding in my chest, and I remembered pacing the sterile floors, anxiety twisting in my stomach as I waited to hear how he was. Taking a deep breath, I pushed through the hospital doors, the sterile smell of antiseptic hitting me like a punch to the gut. The fluorescent lights buzzed overhead, casting a harsh glare on the linoleum floors, and I felt a familiar knot of dread tighten in my stomach. This time, I was determined to be there for him, no matter what it took.

That night changed everything. I still remembered how everyone said Sergio had been overly aggressive in the game, fueled by adrenaline and the need to prove himself. In a moment of sheer determination, he dunked over the opposing team, a move that sent the crowd into a frenzy. But when he came down, he landed wrong. The sickening thud of his body hitting the floor echoed in my mind, his leg twisting in a way that made my heart drop. The injury took him out of college basketball and shattered his dreams of going pro. I still remember telling his mother what happened. And the look on Sergio's face when they told him he'd never be at the same capacity to play again.

After that, Sergio was never really the same—his spark dimmed, replaced by frustration and anger that seeped into every part of his life.

Now, standing in the same spot, the memories flooded back like a tidal wave, and I couldn't shake the fear clawing at my insides. Would history repeat itself? Would I have to face that pain again?

Hall Pass

I walked up to the front desk, my heart racing and breaths coming in quick bursts. "Hi, I got a call that my husband, Sergio Waye is here," I said, my voice steady despite the chaos swirling inside me.

"Please have a seat, ma'am. Someone will be out to talk to you," the receptionist replied, her tone professional but distant.

I turned away from the desk, but anxiety clawed at me, making it impossible to sit still. I paced the waiting area, glancing at the flickering TV in the corner, but the images blurred together. Minutes felt like hours.

Finally, a doctor emerged, his expression serious. "Ma'am, I'm Dr. Terry. Your husband came in fighting for his life after being badly beaten."

The weight of his words crashed over me like a tidal wave. I stumbled back, my breath hitching. "What do you mean 'badly beaten'?" My voice was barely a whisper, fear creeping into every syllable.

Dr. Terry's eyes softened with concern. "He was involved in an altercation, and we're doing everything we can. I need you to come with me; we have to discuss his condition."

My heart raced as I followed Dr. Terry down the stark, white hallway, each step echoing with the weight of my fear. Memories of our past—the laughter, the late-night talks, the moments of pure love interwoven with the jagged edges of pain—flashed through my mind like a slideshow. I realized, with fierce determination, that this time, I wouldn't let him go without a fight.

"Beaten?" I asked, my voice trembling when we got to a private area.

"Yes, and whoever did this wanted your husband dead. We've stopped the internal bleeding, but right now it's touch and go until he wakes up," the doctor explained, his expression grave.

"Can I see him?" I asked, tears pooling in my eyes, blurring my vision.

"Yes, follow me," he said, leading me to a dimly lit room that felt worlds away from the chaos outside.

As I stepped inside, my breath hitched in my throat. The person lying on the bed, wrapped in bandages and surrounded by machines, was someone I barely recognized. His face was bruised and swollen, a harsh reminder of the violence he had endured. All I could do was hold his hand, feeling the warmth of his skin against my trembling fingers, and let the tears flow freely.

Just then, my phone buzzed in my purse, slicing through the silence. I fumbled to pull it out, answering as my heart raced. "Hello?"

"Where are you at, girl? You've had me waiting for an hour!" Destiny's voice came through, laced with irritation.

"I'm so sorry, D. I'm at the hospital," I replied, my voice cracking.

"What happened? Are you okay?" she asked, her tone shifting to frantic concern.

"Yeah, I'm okay, but Sergio's here and in bad shape. Someone attacked him," I cried out, the reality of the situation crashing over me like a wave.

Destiny fell silent for a moment, processing the news. "He's not even recognizable," I added, my voice barely above a whisper.

"You really crying over that nigga?" she asked, a note of disbelief in her voice.

"What do you mean? This is my husband," I shot back, my emotions flaring.

"That's treated you like shit for a while now. I would've paid my respects and been on my way.

He didn't run to save you when your car broke down," she said, her words sharp and unyielding.

"Two different situations, Destiny," I retorted, frustration bubbling up.

"Shit, either way, I'm matching energy all the way around," she replied, her tone firm.

I took a deep breath, feeling the weight of her words, but my heart remained tethered to Sergio. No matter the past, he was still the man I loved, and I couldn't just walk away. "I get it, but right now, I need to be here for him," I said softly, looking down at his battered face, willing to be there with him as he fought through this darkness.

EIGHT

Armand

I woke up in a hotel room, disoriented and unsure how I had ended up here or who I had come with. The alcohol from last night had turned everything into a hazy blur. As I sat up in the bed, stretching my limbs, I scanned the unfamiliar room for any clues—anything that might jog my memory. I was still fully dressed, a testament to the wild night I barely remembered.

On the nightstand, I spotted a Gatorade and some Advil along with a plate of eggs, toast, and bacon with a clear lid covering it, a small lifeline in this chaos. I swung my legs over the edge of the bed, my head pounding like a jackhammer, and reached for them. Just as I was about to pop the Advil and chase it with the neon-blue drink, the bathroom door creaked open. My heart raced, and I held my breath, bracing myself for the worst—an awkward encounter with a stranger or, God forbid, a regrettable choice I made while drunk.

But then he appeared: Armand, emerging from the bathroom wrapped in nothing but a towel, droplets of water glistening on his skin. Relief washed over me, quickly

Hall Pass

igniting an unexpected fire between my legs at the sight of him. "Damn, I'm sorry! I thought you were still sleeping. I was just grabbing some clothes," he said, his voice smooth yet slightly sheepish.

"No worries, do what you gotta do," I managed to reply, trying to play it cool despite the flutter in my stomach. I popped the Advil, downed some juice, and couldn't help but notice the suitcases lined against the wall as he rummaged through one, pulling out a pair of sweatpants. Was he living here? The thought flitted through my mind, mingling with the remnants of last night's debauchery. What the hell had happened? And, more importantly, what was going to happen next?

He slid the sweatpants beneath his towel, and then, with a casual flick, let the towel drop. My breath caught in my throat. His body was like a work of art—muscles defined, skin glowing, and those sweatpants hugging his waist just right, accentuating that perfect V shape leading down from his abs. The angel wings tattooed on his back seemed to unfurl with every movement, as if they were alive, calling to something deep within me.

"How are you feeling?" he asked, his voice playful, a hint of mischief dancing in his eyes.

"Like shit," I replied, rubbing my temples, trying to chase away the remnants of last night's debauchery.

He laughed, the sound rich and warm. "Dior 0, alcohol 1."

"Seriously, how much of a fool did I make of myself?" I asked, half-joking but genuinely curious.

"None at all," he assured me, his gaze steady.

"Did we do it?" I blurted out, my heart racing as I awaited his answer.

"Nah," he replied with a cocky smirk. "If we did it, it wouldn't be while you're weak and emotional, and damn sure not while you're drunk. I want you to enjoy it and remember it."

His words sent a heat rushing through me, igniting a knot in my throat. There was something about his confidence, the way he looked at me, that made me feel both vulnerable and alive. I could feel the tension crackling in the air between us. "

"So what happened?" I asked, a hint of shame creeping in as I braced myself for the answer.

"You vented, and I listened," he replied, a playful glint in his eyes. "Eventually, I felt like the alcohol was getting the best of you, so I closed your tab, and we left the bar. I knew you said you were staying at your parents', but I wasn't letting you go home like that. So, I brought you here and sat in that chair while you slept."

"Damn, that's the second time in a row you saved me. You're going to get tired of saving my ass soon," I said, half-joking but feeling a strange warmth at his words.

"Never," he said, his tone firm, locking eyes with me in a way that made my heart skip.

I couldn't hold back the burning question any longer. "Are you living here?"

"Yeah, for now," he said, glancing around the lavish hotel room, his expression unreadable.

"How are you affording this… Never mind, that's not my business," I said, the words tumbling out before I could stop them. I couldn't shake the nagging thought that this place looked expensive, and I'd never heard him mention a job. Maybe it was because of his criminal record—something beneath him that he didn't want to drag up. Or he was selling drugs like I knew his brothers used to.

"No biggie," he replied, shrugging casually. "When my mom passed, I got a little money, threw it in the bank, and I managed a bar."

As Armand spoke, my gaze was drawn to the imprint he had in his gray sweatpants. I tried to focus on his words, but the way the fabric clung to him made it hard to think straight. There was something intoxicating about him, a mix of charm and mystery that kept me hanging on every word. The air between us thickened, charged with unspoken possibilities, and I couldn't help but wonder what else lay beneath that confident exterior.

"So, are you going to take a few days off work?" he asked, his tone casual, but there was an edge of concern beneath it.

"For what? To sit at my parents' house and throw a pity party about how fucked up my life is? How did I marry a man who doesn't really love me, no matter how much I love him? He's not man enough to leave with exactly what he came in with," I replied, frustration bubbling to the surface.

"Not to mention he don't know how to fuck," he added with a laugh, and I choked on my drink at his bluntness.

"Did I tell you that?" I asked, surprised and somewhat embarrassed.

"Yeah, along with the fact that it's all my fault you're going through this because I went to jail." The room fell silent, the weight of unspoken words hanging in the air.

"Do you really feel that way?" he asked, breaking the tension.

"That he can't fuck?" I asked, trying to deflect.

Hall Pass

"I don't give a fuck about that nigga's dick game. I care about whether you really think me leaving fucked you up in the long run."

I hesitated, grappling with the truth. Yes, that thought had always lingered in the back of my mind, but I'd never voiced it. "Dior?" he pressed gently.

"In a way, yes. We were young, but I loved you with everything in me. There was a safety I felt when I was around you—like the safety I felt with my dad. I could turn my brain off and still know I was going to be okay. There was a love I felt with you that, if I'm being honest, I never felt with Sergio. The way you looked at me, the way you made love to me... I unknowingly compare my husband to you. You have a hold on me, and in my head, I blamed you. Even before you came back into my life."

The words spilled out like an overflowing dam, raw and unfiltered. I realized how much I had kept bottled up, and the vulnerability of the moment made my heart race. Armand's gaze was intense, searching, and I could feel the air thickening between us, charged with the weight of our shared history and the complexities of our present.

Armand took a seat next to me. "Dior me leaving was never to hurt you." "I know" I said quickly then looking away. He turned my face to him. "No seriously. I'm not making excuses. I was doing shit that I knew the results of would be jail. When it happened I didn't want your life to end or you grow a hate for me while waiting on me or stopping your life because mine stopped." I always thought it was pride that made Armand push me away but finally hearing him explain gave me a scene of closure with that chapter of our lives. I kissed him on the cheek. "Thank you. I needed that."

"Dior, on some real shit, I love you. You are an amazing woman. Don't let this shit break you. I know it's hard—sometimes you bend, and you feel every damn emotion, but don't let this nigga or that situation take over you. Whether it's me or any other man, don't lose yourself trying to overplay your role for them. You are beautiful, and I mean that with all due respect—you are that bitch. Own it. Stand tall, walk confidently, and sit on your throne like the queen you are. Don't ever come off that pedestal.

As long as I'm around, I'm gonna keep reminding you of that. You deserve to hear it, to feel it, and to believe it. Life's messy, but you're tougher than any bullshit that comes your way. So let the world throw its punches; you've got the strength to take them and keep moving forward."

Armand words damn near had me ready to cry. But I needed to hear that.

"Are you ready to go home?" he said to me. "Yeah, you can take me to my parents. My clothes are there." I told him.

As we pulled up in front of my parents' house, it felt like we were transported back to our teenage years, when everything was simpler and love was just a heartbeat away. Armand had that old-school R&B playing softly, the kind that wrapped around us like a warm blanket. Even though I should have been tearing up with nostalgia, I couldn't help but smile from ear to ear. My gaze was glued to Armand, that familiar spark igniting something deep inside me.

"Why you looking at me like that?" he asked, his brow raised in playful curiosity

"I don't know, it's just something about you," I replied, feeling a mix of affection and admiration.

"What do you mean?" His voice was teasing, but I sensed the sincerity behind it.

"Nothing crazy. I'm just grateful," I confessed, my heart swelling.

"Grateful for what?" he probed, genuine interest lighting up his eyes.

"That God reconnected us when he did. With everything I have going on and all the shit you've done for me lately, it means more than you even know. You were like the missing piece I couldn't quite put my finger on. Someone real. Someone who won't lie or hide stuff from me," I told him, my voice soft but steady.

Armand smiled, that charming smile that always made my heart skip a beat. "I told you back when we were younger that I had you forever and always, and I meant just that."

I felt a blush creep into my cheeks, warmth flooding through me. "Ummm... you want to come in? I'm sure my parents would love to see you."

He glanced at the clock, then back at me, a grin spreading across his face. "Sure, why not? I haven't seen your parents in forever, and I always loved them."

We climbed out of the car, and as we walked toward the house, a mix of excitement and nerves tangled in the air. When I stepped inside, the familiar scent of home enveloped me, and I headed straight to the kitchen, where Mom and Dad were bustling about.

"Look who I found!" I announced cheerfully, my voice echoing with delight as we entered the kitchen.

"Hello Mr. and Mrs. Matthews," Armand said.

"Armand, is that you?" My mom exclaimed, her face lighting up as she came around the island to greet him.
"Yes ma'am, it's me," he answered, his trademark smile lighting up the room as he embraced her. The warmth of that moment wrapped around me like the sweetest melody, and suddenly, everything felt right in the world again.

"Son, we missed you around here. It's good seeing you," my dad said, his voice deep and welcoming. Both of my parents knew about Armand's past, but I was relieved they didn't bring it up. It felt like a fresh start, a chance to rewrite our story.

"How is your momma? I've got to make my way over there to see her," my mom asked, her concern genuine and maternal.

Armand's smile faltered slightly. "She passed."

"Are you serious? My God," my mom gasped, her eyes wide with shock and sympathy. The air thickened with unspoken feelings, the weight of loss hanging between all us.

"Well, if your momma ain't here, who's been feeding you? I know you're probably still as picky as you were when you were younger," my mom said, trying to lighten the mood. "Have a seat! I cooked breakfast; I'll get you some."

"Don't worry about it, Momma, I got it," I chimed in, eager to help and fill the space with something comforting. I grabbed a plate and piled it high with crispy bacon, fluffy scrambled eggs, creamy grits, and a buttery biscuit, each item a little piece of home. With a smile on my face, I brought it over to Armand and set it down in front of him.

"Thank you," he said, his tone sincere, and I could see the appreciation in his eyes.

"Eat up, I'm about to run upstairs," I told him, feeling a rush of excitement mixed with nerves. I wanted to give him a moment to savor the food and soak in the warmth of the home we both cherished. As I turned to head up the stairs, I glanced back at him one last time, hoping this was just the beginning of something beautiful.

I walked into my old bedroom, a sanctuary filled with memories that made me smile. Just like I suspected, my bags were already waiting for me, a reminder of the chaos that had brought me back here. I pulled out some clothes for work and laid them on the bed, hoping to change quickly so Armand could take me to get my car afterward.

I jumped into the shower, letting the hot water wash away the lingering tension from the night before. But when I stepped out, I was shocked to see my mother sitting on the bed, arms crossed, a serious look etched on her face.

"Ma'am?" I said, still dripping wet. "What are you doing?"

"About to get dress." I told her "Now you know that's not what I'm talking about. I'm talking about that man you got sitting in my kitchen. I know me and your daddy raised you better than this. Just because your marriage is rocky doesn't mean you should jump into bed with the next guy."

"What, Momma?" I said, confusion washing over me.

"You left here hurt last night, but I know you're not dumb, you come back in her with a blast from the past this morning. That's a good man downstairs. But…" she continued, her voice firm but laced with concern.

"Momma," I started, feeling defensive.

"Dior, you're playing a dangerous game. Don't hurt that man because you're hurting, and don't put yourself in a situation that makes your marriage worse," she advised, her eyes searching mine for understanding.

"Momma, I didn't sleep with Armand," I finally blurted out, the words tumbling out in a rush. My heart raced as the truth hung heavily between us, a delicate balance of tension and relief.

She stared at me, her expression a mix of disbelief and concern. "The other night, I ran into Armand when Destiny and I were out. Later that night, I was stuck on the side of the road, and Sergio refused to come get me or help me."

"What?" she said, her brow furrowing.

"Armand just so happened to drive by and stopped to help me when he didn't have to. Last night, he called to check on me while I was at the bar. He realized how drunk I was and came to get me before I embarrassed myself once again when he didn't have to. Because he cares about me and you guys, he didn't want to bring me home for y'all to deal with my drunken mess. He took me to a hotel and put me in bed. I woke up this morning still in my clothes," I explained, my voice steady but my insides churning with vulnerability.

"I hope that's the truth," she said, her eyes narrowing slightly. Making me feel like a teenage girl.

"It is," I insisted, biting my tongue to hold back everything else I wanted to say about how much he meant to me.

Before the conversation could go any further, my phone started to ring, cutting through the tension like a knife. "I'ma let you get that. But we are going to talk later," she said, her tone softening a bit. "Hurry back down here before your daddy talks that boy's ears off."

"Yes ma'am," I replied, a hint of a smile breaking through my nerves.

"Hello?" I answered, trying to shake off the weight of our discussion.

"Hey bestie! I'm so sorry I missed your calls last night. What's up?" Destiny's voice was bright and familiar, instantly lifting my spirits.

"Girl!" I exclaimed, almost breathless.

"What? What happened?" she asked, concern creeping into her tone.

"A lot. Meet me at the diner on Lexington for breakfast so I can fill you in. I'm about to get dressed and have Armand take me to get my car, then I'll be there," I said, urgently coloring my voice.

"Armand?" she repeated, a teasing lilt in her tone. I could almost hear her eyebrows raising through the phone.

"Yeah, Armand," I replied, my cheeks warming at the thought of him. "It's complicated."

We hung up, and I quickly finished getting dressed, slipping into my favorite jeans and a snug top that hugged my curves just right. As I made my way back downstairs, the familiar aroma of my mom's cooking wafted through the air, making my stomach grumble. "How was your food?" I asked, stepping into the kitchen with a teasing smile.

"Man, you already know it was on point! I've never had anything your mom cooked that wasn't fire," Armand replied, grinning from ear to ear, his eyes sparkling with delight.

"Thank you, baby," my momma chimed in, her pride shining through her warm smile.

I turned to Armand, the thought of my car nagging at me. "Well, can you take me to get my car?" I asked, trying to keep my tone light.

"Of course," he said. But as I glanced back at my momma, I caught a glimpse of the look she shot me from across the kitchen—a mix of concern and encouragement that made my heart race.

I took Armand's empty plate and placed it in the sink, then leaned over to give my momma a quick kiss on the cheek. "You know what I said," she whispered, her voice low but firm. I nodded, feeling the weight of her words but also the thrill of what lay ahead.

I made my way to my dad, planting a kiss on his cheek too. "Armand, you be safe with my baby," he said, his tone protective as we walked toward the door.

"Yes sir, always," Armand called back, flashing my dad a confident grin that somehow reassured everyone in the room—even me.

As we stepped outside, the air wrapped around us like a warm embrace, buzzing with the vibrant energy of the city. I could feel the anticipation simmering just beneath the surface—a heady mix of excitement and nerves that made my heart race.

Once we settled into Armand's car, he burst into laughter, breaking the momentary tension. "That was definitely like old times. Your dad was grilling me, making sure I wasn't doing any unspeakable things to his daughter."

"Unspeakable?" I shot back, a smirk creeping onto my lips.

"Yeah, he wanted to make sure I wasn't fucking his daughter," he replied, his eyes dancing with amusement.

I chuckled, rolling my eyes. "Well, the difference between back then and now is that you actually weren't lying when he asked."

"But don't feel bad," I said, his laughter infectious. "My momma came upstairs grilling me too."

We shared a laugh, reminiscing about those awkward teenage days as he navigated through the bustling streets. The familiarity of our banter felt comforting, like slipping into an old, well-loved hoodie.

When we finally reached my car, Armand was his usual self, a comforting presence in the chaos of my life. He helped me into my seat, making sure I was safely inside before leaning against the doorframe, his expression earnest. "The hotel room is open to you if you need it, or if you just don't want to stay at your parents'," he offered, a hint of concern in his eyes.

I smiled at him, warmth spreading through me. "Aww, I don't want to invade your space," I replied, trying to downplay how much I appreciated the offer.

"It's no biggie. I can always crash at Ahmad's or Armani's. I just want to make sure you're good," he said, his voice steady and reassuring.

"Thank you," I said, a genuine smile breaking across my face. It meant a lot to me that he cared so much.

"Are you about to head to work?" he asked, tilting his head slightly, a playful glint in his eyes.

"I'm meeting up with Destiny first, and then, yes, I am going to work," I informed him, shifting in my seat, the reality of my day looming ahead.

"Well, when you get a moment, hit me up. I want to take you out to do something," he said, his tone filled with anticipation.

I felt a rush of excitement at the thought. "Okay, I will," I promised, feeling a flutter in my chest.

He leaned in and planted a soft kiss on my forehead, and I nearly melted into my seat. That simple gesture felt like a shield against all the chaos in my life, grounding me in a moment of warmth.

Armand stepped back, walking over to his truck, but he didn't pull away until he saw me leave. I glanced in my rearview mirror, catching a glimpse of him standing there, and a smile tugged at my lips. It was a small moment, but it filled me with hope, reminding me that even amidst the storm, there were still lights to guide me home.

As I pulled out my cell to call Destiny and let her know I was on my way, the phone buzzed with an incoming call that stopped me in my tracks.

"Hello?" I answered, my voice steady but curious.

"Hi, is this the family of Sergio Waye?" the voice on the other end asked, its tone professional but laced with urgency.

"Yes, this is his wife," I replied, my heart beginning to race for an entirely different reason.

"Hello, ma'am. I am calling from St. Mary's Hospital to let you know that your husband was brought here by ambulance and is currently in surgery."

The words hit me like a freight train, and the world around me blurred into a chaotic swirl of colors and sounds. I gripped the steering wheel tighter, my knuckles turning white as I struggled to process the shock. The vibrant city lights outside faded into a hazy backdrop, and panic surged through me, each heartbeat echoing louder than the last.

"My heart dropped. What do you mean surgery? Surgery for what?" I demanded, my voice trembling.

"It's best if you get here as soon as possible. A doctor can tell you face to face," the voice replied, its calmness only heightening my anxiety.

"I'm on my way," I said, urgency flooding my words. I hung up and slammed the wheel to the right, making a swift U-turn that sent my heart racing even faster.

As I pulled into the hospital parking lot, déjà vu washed over me like a cold wave. This place felt hauntingly familiar. Back in college, Sergio had been one of the star players on the basketball team while I was just the nerdy girl, buried in books. I remembered how he'd been struggling in English, and they assigned me as his tutor. One thing led to another, and one night, when we were supposed to be studying, I found myself in Sergio's bed, the soft sheets tangled around us as we explored something new and thrilling.
After that night, he'd claimed me as his girl, and I felt like I had stepped into a dream. But then came the night of the big game. I had overslept, completely missing the first half, and when I finally rushed into the gym, breathless and

wide-eyed, my heart dropped at the sight before me. Sergio was being placed on a stretcher and wheeled out to the back of an ambulance, the crowd around him a blur of concern and chaos.

    I followed the ambulance to the hospital, my heart pounding in my chest, and I remembered pacing the sterile floors, anxiety twisting in my stomach as I waited to hear how he was. Taking a deep breath, I pushed through the hospital doors, the sterile smell of antiseptic hitting me like a punch to the gut. The fluorescent lights buzzed overhead, casting a harsh glare on the linoleum floors, and I felt a familiar knot of dread tighten in my stomach. This time, I was determined to be there for him, no matter what it took.

    That night changed everything. I still remembered how everyone said Sergio had been overly aggressive in the game, fueled by adrenaline and the need to prove himself. In a moment of sheer determination, he dunked over the opposing team, a move that sent the crowd into a frenzy. But when he came down, he landed wrong. The sickening thud of his body hitting the floor echoed in my mind, his leg twisting in a way that made my heart drop. The injury took him out of college basketball and shattered his dreams of going pro. I still remember telling his mother what happened. And the look on Sergio's face when they told him he'd never be at the same capacity to play again.

After that, Sergio was never really the same—his spark dimmed, replaced by frustration and anger that seeped into every part of his life.

    Now, standing in the same spot, the memories flooded back like a tidal wave, and I couldn't shake the fear clawing at my insides. Would history repeat itself? Would I have to face that pain again?

Breanna J

I walked up to the front desk, my heart racing and breaths coming in quick bursts. "Hi, I got a call that my husband, Sergio Waye is here," I said, my voice steady despite the chaos swirling inside me.

"Please have a seat, ma'am. Someone will be out to talk to you," the receptionist replied, her tone professional but distant.

I turned away from the desk, but anxiety clawed at me, making it impossible to sit still. I paced the waiting area, glancing at the flickering TV in the corner, but the images blurred together. Minutes felt like hours.

Finally, a doctor emerged, his expression serious. "Ma'am, I'm Dr. Terry. Your husband came in fighting for his life after being badly beaten."

The weight of his words crashed over me like a tidal wave. I stumbled back, my breath hitching. "What do you mean 'badly beaten'?" My voice was barely a whisper, fear creeping into every syllable.

Dr. Terry's eyes softened with concern. "He was involved in an altercation, and we're doing everything we can. I need you to come with me; we have to discuss his condition."

My heart raced as I followed Dr. Terry down the stark, white hallway, each step echoing with the weight of my fear. Memories of our past—the laughter, the late-night talks, the moments of pure love interwoven with the jagged edges of pain—flashed through my mind like a slideshow. I realized, with fierce determination, that this time, I wouldn't let him go without a fight.

"Beaten?" I asked, my voice trembling when we got to a private area.

"Yes, and whoever did this wanted your husband dead. We've stopped the internal bleeding, but right now it's touch and go until he wakes up," the doctor explained, his expression grave.

"Can I see him?" I asked, tears pooling in my eyes, blurring my vision.

"Yes, follow me," he said, leading me to a dimly lit room that felt worlds away from the chaos outside.

As I stepped inside, my breath hitched in my throat. The person lying on the bed, wrapped in bandages and surrounded by machines, was someone I barely recognized. His face was bruised and swollen, a harsh reminder of the violence he had endured. All I could do was hold his hand, feeling the warmth of his skin against my trembling fingers, and let the tears flow freely.

Just then, my phone buzzed in my purse, slicing through the silence. I fumbled to pull it out, answering as my heart raced. "Hello?"

"Where are you at, girl? You've had me waiting for an hour!" Destiny's voice came through, laced with irritation.

"I'm so sorry, D. I'm at the hospital," I replied, my voice cracking.

"What happened? Are you okay?" she asked, her tone shifting to frantic concern.

"Yeah, I'm okay, but Sergio's here and in bad shape. Someone attacked him," I cried out, the reality of the situation crashing over me like a wave.

Destiny fell silent for a moment, processing the news. "He's not even recognizable," I added, my voice barely above a whisper.

"You really crying over that nigga?" she asked, a note of disbelief in her voice.

"What do you mean? This is my husband," I shot back, my emotions flaring.

"That's treated you like shit for a while now. I would've paid my respects and been on my way.

He didn't run to save you when your car broke down," she said, her words sharp and unyielding.

"Two different situations, Destiny," I retorted, frustration bubbling up.

"Shit, either way, I'm matching energy all the way around," she replied, her tone firm.

I took a deep breath, feeling the weight of her words, but my heart remained tethered to Sergio. No matter the past, he was still the man I loved, and I couldn't just walk away. "I get it, but right now, I need to be here for him," I said softly, looking down at his battered face, willing to be there with him as he fought through this darkness.

NINE

Dior

I had spent so much damn time at the hospital waiting for Sergio to wake up that I wasn't even sure what day it was anymore. The sterile smell of antiseptic and the constant beeping of machines had become my unwelcome companions. Armand had called and texted, but I ignored every single one. I didn't need his well-meaning distractions; my focus was completely consumed by Sergio.

The only thing I managed to do amidst the chaos was reach out to the hotel where he connected me with a design project. I didn't want them to think I didn't want the opportunity and I sure didn't want to make Armand look bad. I explained my situation to the manager, who was surprisingly understanding. She assured me that whenever I was ready to come in for a walkthrough to discuss designs, just let her know. But for now, my priority was here, in this sterile room, tending to the man I made a vow to.

"Fuck," Sergio moaned, breaking the heavy silence and causing me to jump out of my chair to rush to his side. It was only his second day awake. The day before, he hadn't said much—just lay there, drifting in and out of consciousness. The doctors had assured me that just him waking up after everything he'd been through was progress, but hearing his voice now sent a ripple of hope through me.

"Baby, you okay?" I said with my heart racing. But the look of disgust he shot my way when he realized it was me stung like a slap.

"What are you doing here?" Sergio rasped, struggling to sit up, his voice rough and laced with confusion. I could see the pain etched on his face, a mix of frustration and vulnerability that made my heart ache. Before I could respond, the door swung open, and a couple of doctors filed in, their presence a stark reminder of the reality we were facing.

"Mr. Waye, nice to see you awake," one of them said, clipboard in hand, ready to assess his condition. Sergio nodded, still processing everything, and I felt a flutter of anxiety in my stomach. This was just the beginning, and I was determined to be by his side every step of the way.

"You still have some recovering to do," the doctor continued, his tone professional yet gentle. "But with time and therapy, we hope to get you as close to normal as we can." Anger flashed across Sergio's face as the doctor spoke, his jaw tightening with each word. When the doctors finally exited, he turned to me, his expression hardening.

"Why are you still here? You can leave too," he said, his voice gaining strength with each syllable.
"Sergio, I'm not leaving you like this. You need someone here with you," I insisted, trying to keep my voice steady.

"Not you," he shot back, the venom in his words stinging more than I expected.

Hall Pass

"Sergio! " I cried out, desperation creeping into my voice.

"Leave!" he yelled, and I felt my heart drop.

"No! I am your wife, it is my job to be here." I yelled back, my frustration boiling over.

We continued going back and forth until A nurse peeked her head in, eyebrows raised. "I'm gonna need y'all to keep it down," she said, before walking away. The silence that followed was heavy. I looked back at Sergio, my chest tight with emotion. "I don't know why you treat me like this. I've been good to you. I've stood beside you. I've loved you even when you made it hard."

Tears rolled down my cheeks, each drop a testament to the love I felt for him, despite the hurt.

Just then, Destiny walked in, her presence like a whirlwind. "Girl, I heard you all the way down the hall." She must have instantly read the tension in the room. "Them tears don't mean shit. Ever since you came into my life, it's been one thing after another, and I'm sure me being in this hospital bed has something to do with you too."

My blood boiled, but I was trying to keep the peace. "Oh hell no," Destiny said, her voice rising. "Destiny, just leave it alone," I pleaded, desperate to avoid a bigger fight.

"Hell no! This weak-ass niggas got you fucked up, and I'm not letting that slide."

"Bitch, you can leave just like I told this bitch!" Sergio spat, his words cutting deep. Hearing my husband disrespect me like that was the final straw.

"You know what? Fuck this and fuck you!" I shot back, my voice trembling with anger. "You ungrateful son of a bitch! You will not lay in this hospital bed and disrespect me when you should be praising me for making sure you're still breathing!"

The words hung in the air, heavy with truth and hurt, an electric tension crackling between us. For a moment, everything felt unbearably raw. "I make sure you're good, I keep our home together, I go above and beyond to be a good wife, and you're going to blame me for everything that's gone wrong in your life? You are a sick son of a bitch. The last time you were laid up in that hospital bed, I was there morning, noon, and night. And despite what you just pulled on me, I've been right here this time. The truth is, this might just be your karma for how you treated me," I spat, my voice trembling with anger and hurt.

"Fuck you," he shot back, spitting in my direction.

"Nigga, I will—" Destiny started to say, but I cut her off.

"See, Sergio? I was trying to be nice, but now? Fuck it and fuck you you no-good sorry ass excuse for a man, lover and a husband you are the biggest mistake I ever made and regret. I regret loving you. I regret marrying you. I regret meeting you. I regret ever letting you think them ten strokes you give were ever good enough. But I got something for your ass. I'm moving back into my house. And I'm changing the locks, so when they finally let you out of here, don't even think about coming to my place. As a matter of fact don't call my phone when they tell you you can't be released unless someone's there to help you. You clearly didn't value the wife I was to you, so now you get the bitch you created in me. I'm going to do what you said and see if the grass is greener on the other side. And trust me, I already know the first patch I'm trying out. I'm sure he can last longer than ten strokes, and maybe when I'm done with this little hall pass, I'll think about being your wife again."

Destiny burst out laughing, her joy a sharp contrast to the storm brewing inside me. "Dior, don't you dare disrespect me," he interjected, his voice rising.

"Disrespect you? Shut up! Now it's an issue because you're on the other end, but it was fine when you were doing it to me. Ain't that some shit? Shit ain't fun when the rabbit's got the gun. But just wait—you ain't seen shit yet." I grabbed my stuff, each movement fueled by a mixture of rage and liberation.

"Damn, nigga, you done woke up the beast," Destiny said, laughing as we walked out together. I stepped into the elevator, and as soon as the doors slid shut, all the strength I had summoned in that room crumbled. Tears poured down my cheeks, soaking into Destiny's shoulder as she held me tightly. For those few moments, I let it all out, determined that none of these feelings would leave this hospital with me.

"We're almost to the ground floor," Destiny whispered softly, her voice a gentle anchor in the chaos. I stood up, wiped my face, and readjusted myself, putting on a brave smile as the elevator doors opened.

As we stepped into the parking garage, the air felt different—fresher, like a new beginning. I slid into the driver's seat, and Destiny turned to me, concern etched on her face. "You, okay?"

"Hell yeah, I feel free. I'm about to get some new locks and find someone to put them on," I replied, my voice steadying with each word.

"Okay, well, call me if you need me. I'll swing by later with wine," she said, her support a comforting balm.

"Okay," I told her, and as I revved the engine, I felt the weight of the world lift just a little bit more. This was just the beginning.

TEN

Armand

Days had dragged on, each one blurring into the next, and still, there was no word from Dior. I called and texted until my fingers ached from the relentless tapping, but all I got in return was a deafening silence. That shit gnawed at me—worrying about her, wondering what the hell was going on. And on top of that, I was knee-deep in this mess with Shanny, which felt like a goddamn circus. To keep my head above water, I threw myself into my work, hoping the grind would drown out the chaos swirling around me. I was still held up in that hotel, the sterile walls closing in around me, a stark contrast to the whirlwind of emotions churning inside. Avoiding Shanny had become my new full-time job, each day feeling like a marathon of denial. The weight of our crumbling marriage pressed down on me, suffocating and relentless, like a heavy fog I couldn't escape. In my mind, it was over and done. I just needed to find a way to break free from her grasp. Shanny was hell-bent on turning my life into a nightmare, her toxicity wrapping around me like a snake. Honestly, even if Dior weren't back in my life, I didn't want Shanny anywhere near me. I'd rather embrace the solitude than deal with that mess. Better off alone, I told myself, but deep down, I couldn't shake the gnawing feeling that I was missing out on something real.

Breanna J

As I sat in my makeshift office at the hotel, staring at the bland walls and listening to the distant hum of city life, there was a knock at my door. "Come in," I called out, my voice flat. Renee walked in, her brow slightly furrowed, holding an iPad like it was a lifeline.

"Hey, boss, you got a few minutes to talk?" she asked, her tone light but professional.

"Yeah," I replied, leaning back in my chair, trying to shake off the weight of my thoughts.

"So, I've been thinking—if we want to promote your restaurant, maybe we should offer 10% off or $10 for all our guests who come over to eat," she suggested, her eyes sparkling with enthusiasm.

"Okay, I like that," I said, feeling a flicker of interest in my otherwise clouded mind.

"Yeah, and what if we think about offering some type of late night free delivery from the restaurant to the hotel? I mean, it's only two or three streets away," she continued, jotting down notes with purpose. "I think it will make those customers who are checking in late or just up late more tempted to order." She added

"Alright, start putting it in motion," I instructed, a hint of excitement creeping into my voice.

Hall Pass

"Okay!" she said, tapping away on her iPad, her focus unwavering. "Oh, and Mrs. Waye got back to us. She's willing to decorate the hotel, but she needs some time before she can start because her husband is in the hospital."

That hit me like a punch to the gut. The thought of Dior—my Dior—catering to her bitch-ass husband in the hospital sparked a storm of emotions in me, a chaotic blend of jealousy and longing that I couldn't shake. It was absurd, really, how this woman could still twist my insides even through the haze of my current hell. I shook my head, trying to push the thoughts away, but deep down, I couldn't help but wonder if she was still the one who could light up my darkened world, like a neon sign in a foggy alley.

I flashed back to the last time I actually got to talk to her. I'd been calling, over and over, each ring echoing my frustration and worry. I'd almost convinced myself this was it—my final attempt. So when she finally picked up, relief washed over me like a cool breeze on a stifling summer day.

But as soon as I heard her voice, I knew something was off. "How was your day after we separated?" I asked, trying to keep it light, but the tension crackled between us.

"It was a lot," she replied, her tone heavy with unspoken words.

"Really? I'd love to hear about it. Did you eat? Want to grab some food and talk?" I offered, hoping to coax her out of whatever funk she was in.

But then, she blurted it out, and it hit me like a punch to the gut. "Armand, Sergio is in the hospital, and I'm here with him." My heart dropped. I felt a rush of regret, a dark wave crashing over me for not finishing what I'd started with that bastard.

"Is he okay?" I asked, trying to sound calm, but my voice trembled with concern.

"It's still touch and go. He needs me here with him. I hope you understand," she said, her words slicing through the air like a knife.

I took a deep breath, trying to play it cool, but all I could think about was how much I wanted to be there for her—not just as a friend, but as something more.

"Look, when Dior finally comes in to start work on the hotel, by no means does she to know I own this place," I said, my voice steady but my heart racing. Renee shot me a side-eye, her brow furrowing. "As long as it stays a secret to her about my role in this hotel, you'll get a raise," I added, trying to keep my tone businesslike.

"Say no more. For all she'll know, I own this mutha fucker… My bad." She slapped a hand over her mouth, eyes wide with faux innocence. I couldn't help but laugh. I was very aware of who I hired. Renee had the white girl voice, and she was smart. But her tattoos she kept covered and her address let you know she was from the hood "No worries. We're behind closed doors; it's cool to be yourself," I told her. I could tell she was grateful for the levity, even if just for a moment.

"So how am I supposed to handle her payments when she asks?" Renee probed, her tone shifting to practicality.

"All her payments will be wired directly from the business account," I replied, trying to keep the logistics clear in my mind.

"Okay, and who's going to be doing the meetings with her? Your business partner?" I sensed the sarcasm dripping from her words, but I decided to let it slide this time.

"You will be doing all the meetings. You know the vision we discussed for the hotel," I instructed firmly, my tone leaving no room for negotiation. "If you have any questions, just reach out and ask me. But I need you to understand—by no means should my name be mentioned to her. This is our little secret, and I'm counting on you to keep it under wraps."

As I watched Renee nod in understanding, a strange mix of hope and dread twisted in my stomach. The thought of Dior walking through those doors, her laughter echoing through the halls, sent shivers down my spine. Knowing that I was supporting her dream was big to me. Would she still remember the way we used to dream together, those late-night talks filled with wild ambitions and soft smiles? Or had those moments faded into the background noise of her life, drowned out by the chaos of her current situation? I had to keep my distance, but it was hard to ignore the magnetic pull she had on me, like a moth drawn to a flame.

"Understood," Renee said, her voice steady.

Just as we delved deeper into the hotel business, my office door swung open with a bang, and in charged Shanny, a whirlwind of energy and attitude. Renee and I exchanged a glance, both taken aback by the sudden disruption. "Can I help you?" I asked, eyebrow raised, trying to regain control of the situation.

"Get out so I can speak to my—" Shanny halted mid-sentence, catching herself. I wasn't about to let her disrespect my space or my team.

"That's not how you talk to any of my staff," I said, my voice firm, asserting dominance over the room. Shanny took a deep breath, the tension thick between us.

"Can we please have the room so I may talk to my business partner?" she asked, her tone softening but still laced with urgency.

I shot a quick glance at Renee, who looked as if she was caught in a storm of confusion, and nodded my head, giving her the silent signal to step out. She gathered her papers, casting one last wary look at Shanny before leaving the room.

As the door clicked shut behind Renee, I turned my full attention to Shanny, the air thick with unspoken words and unresolved tension. What did she want now? In this game of high stakes and hidden agendas, I knew I had to tread carefully. The last thing I needed was to be pulled into a drama that could unravel everything I was trying to build.

Shanny launched into her rant, her voice slicing through the silence like a knife. "So this shit is going too damn far, Armand! First, you're not coming home, and then the shit that happened at the house, now you've taken my name off the bank accounts. I was out shopping, and all my damn cards declined!" The desperation in her voice echoed in the room.

I leaned back in my chair, a smirk creeping across my face. "I didn't take your name off all the accounts. The ones you actually contribute to? Your name is still on those. See, somewhere along the line, I let you think you ran shit. You thought you had the upper hand, that you controlled everything. But the truth is, I made this version of you. This spoiled, self-centered mutha fucker. I created this lifestyle you live. So just like you figured out how to keep me in this marriage and miserable, I'll do the same."

Her demeanor shifted, a flicker of vulnerability creeping into her eyes. "But I don't want you to be miserable, Armand."

I couldn't help but laugh. Now that she didn't have access to my money, she suddenly wanted to play nice. It was almost comical. Her love for cash was stronger than any affection she'd ever shown me. "Listen, I want you to be happy. I want to be happy. I want us to be happy. I just need you to compromise a little. I mean, how many men can say their wife has a girlfriend and she's willing to share her with him?" I rolled my eyes, the absurdity of it all washing over me.

Shanny crossed her arms, her expression a mix of indignation and reluctant curiosity. "Compromise? You think I'm just going to sit back and watch you chase after whoever the hell you want while treating me like the sticky shit on the bottom of your shoe. I want a divorce?"

"Why?" she asked "If you want to keep living like the queen you think you are, it might be time to expand your horizons a bit. I'm not asking for much—just a little understanding that this isn't the same game we were playing before." I told her.

The tension hung thick between us, a tightrope stretched taut, and I could see the wheels turning in her mind. She was calculating her next move, weighing her pride against the comfort of her lavish lifestyle. In this twisted dance of love and power, the stakes were high, and I was more than ready to play.

"You do realize sex doesn't solve everything," I said, leaning back in my chair, crossing my arms. "I can have any bitch I want. I'm not worried about fucking Angel."

"When has sex not helped us hash out our issues, Armand? You beat this pussy up to take out your frustration, and I leave relieved and happy. Plus, we've never done it here, on your desk," she purred, inching closer and rubbing her hand against my chest.

"Not this time," I said, gently moving her hand away. She stepped back, confusion flickering across her face. "What's up with you?" she asked, a hint of frustration creeping into her voice.

Hall Pass

"Just matching your energy," I replied coolly.

"Wrong energy, babe. What is wrong? If you want to try new pussy go ahead and get it out of your system and let's stop talking about divorce," she shot back, trying to close the distance again. But I held my hand up, stopping her in her tracks. For once, it seemed she was finally catching the hint.

"Armand, I need money," she said, her tone shifting to something more serious.

I raised my eyebrows. "So go to the salon I bought you and do some hair to put some money into those accounts you have access to."

"I will…" she started to say with aggression, but I cut her off.

"You will what? State your threat?" I said, rising from my chair without raising my voice, but with an intensity that filled the room. "What are you going to do, go tell the police what you saw? That's fine. Do it! Because I'll sit in jail happy. But you? You will suffer. If I go to jail, I'm away from you. And not only that—if I'm in there and not out here working, where is the money coming from to fund your lifestyle? That means the salon will close, and when you don't have my money to spend on her, how long do you think Angel will stay?" I let a smirk play on my lips, knowing I had her on the ropes.

Her eyes narrowed, the realization crashing over her like a wave. For all her bravado, she knew I was right. The weight of the situation settled between us like a heavy fog, and suddenly, the game didn't feel as fun anymore. She was smart enough to understand that this dance was a dangerous one, and the music could stop at any moment.

"I—" she began, but I cut her off.

"When you thought blackmailing me was a good idea, that's when you changed everything between us," I said, my voice steady.

"So what am I supposed to do now?" she asked, her tone shifting from defiance to desperation.

"Just what I said. And maybe if you act right, I'll give you an allowance," I replied, watching her expression flicker between shock and indignation.

Shanny opened her mouth, but no words came out. I could see the gears turning in her mind, the realization that her usual tactics weren't going to work this time. "Have a nice day," I told her, the finality in my tone leaving no room for negotiation.

"Armand…" she started, but I cut her off again.

"Have a nice day, Ms. Griffin. And please close my door behind you." I picked up my phone, my focus shifting away from her.

As I watched Shanny exit the office, I was certain this wasn't over just because she was leaving. We had just entered a tense game of chess, and I was going to have to stay one step ahead of her. I could feel the stakes rising—she wouldn't just let this go without a fight.

I sank back down into my chair and dialed Simeon's number.

"What's up, man?" he answered, his voice relaxed.

"How much money can I move from my account without flagging the government? And is there any way you can transfer it to an offshore account that Shanny has no access to and no way to find?" I asked, my mind racing as I plotted my next moves.

"Yeah, I can help with that," he replied, the casualness in his voice reassuring. "Just give me a second to run the numbers. We can keep this low-key, but you need to keep your head on straight. You know how these things can unravel."

"Trust me, I'm well aware," I said, glancing at the closed door. "Just make sure it's done discreetly. I can't afford any slip-ups."

"Got it. I'll get back to you in a few," he said before hanging up.

I leaned back in my chair, contemplating the layers of this mess. Shanny and I were caught in a tangled web of emotions and power plays, a high-stakes game where every move mattered. I needed to be ready for whatever she threw my way next. The game was just beginning, and I was determined to come out on top.

"Bro, can I ask you something?" Simeon's voice pulled me from my thoughts.

"What," I replied, my tone clipped.

"Bro, what are you doing? First, you have me remove Shanny from all the accounts, and now this?" His confusion was palpable, and I could almost hear the gears turning in his head.

"I'm just preparing. All I need is you to move enough money into an account that can't be tracked," I told him, my voice steady but laced with urgency.

"Prepare for what?" he pressed, skepticism creeping into his tone.

"A fresh start," I said, letting the weight of my words hang in the air.

The silence on the line stretched, and I could sense him processing my intention. A fresh start—it sounded simple, but it was anything but. I needed to untangle myself from Shanny's grasp, and that meant cutting ties in a way that left no trace.

"Look, I get it," he finally said, his tone shifting to something more serious. "But you realize this isn't just about money, right? You're talking about a complete overhaul of your life. It's risky."

"Risky is my middle name," I shot back, a wry smile tugging at my lips despite the gravity of the situation. "But I've been playing it safe for too long and look where that's gotten me. It's time to shake things up."

"Alright, man, I'll see what I can do," Simeon said, the resolve returning to his voice. "But you need to be careful. Shanny isn't going to take this lying down."

"Trust me, I know. But I'm ready for whatever she brings. I won't give her the satisfaction of watching me crumble," I replied, my determination solidifying with every word.

As we wrapped up the call, I felt a surge of adrenaline coursing through me. This was it—the moment I'd been waiting for. The chance to reclaim my life and step into a future that didn't include Shanny's drama. It was time to play my cards right and make my move.

Breanna J

ELEVEN

Dior

Although most would have thought I'd be devastated by everything going down between Sergio and me, I drove home smiling, feeling an unexpected rush of freedom. The bustling streets of the city whizzed by, each honking horn and revving engine mirroring the chaos in my mind. Thoughts crashed into one another like waves in a storm, each one more turbulent than the last, threatening to pull me under. Just as I felt myself slipping into that emotional whirlpool, my phone buzzed, yanking me back to reality.

"Hello?" I answered, my voice exhausted but cheerful.

"Hey, baby," my momma's familiar voice greeted me, warm yet commanding, like she could wrap me up in a hug through the phone.

"Hey, momma," I replied.

"How are you?" she asked, her concern wrapping around me like a heavy blanket.

"I'm good. How are you and daddy?"

"We're fine. We're getting ready to come up to the hospital to sit with you and Sergio for a while," she said, her tone shifting to one of seriousness, the kind that always made me sit up a little straighter.

"Don't bother," I shot back, my tone sharper than I intended, the words tumbling out before I could catch them.

"Why not? What's wrong? Did things take a turn for the worse?" Her voice tightened, concern flooding through the line like a dam about to burst.

I could almost see her frowning, the worry etched across her face like a storm cloud. But the truth was, I felt oddly liberated. Sure, things were messy between Sergio and me—hell, they were a goddamn wreck. But in that moment, I could finally breathe, the air tasting sweeter than it had in ages.

"I'm not there," I admitted, the truth hanging between us like thick smoke, heavy and suffocating.

"Now, Dior, why aren't you at the hospital with your husband? I know I raised you to stand by that man in times like this."

I rolled my eyes, irritation flaring like a match striking against a rough surface. "I can't stick beside someone who doesn't want me there."

"Dior!" she exclaimed, disbelief and disappointment lacing her tone, a combination I knew too well.

"Momma, the man spit at me and put me out of his damn hospital room! How much more disrespect am I supposed to take? What else do you want from me?"

"Who are you talking to?" she yelled, her voice sharp enough to cut through the chaos of the city outside my window.

"Respectfully, this is my marriage. I have to handle it the best way I know how."

"First off, you're going to show me some respect when you speak to me. Secondly, I'm sure a lot of what you're feeling has to do with Armand being back in the picture. Now, I'm not saying Sergio is perfect, but you stood before God and everyone else and said 'for better or for worse.'"

"And I've been here through better and worse," I shot back, my voice rising with every word. "I rushed to the hospital after he kicked me out of my own house, Momma. I've chosen to be a good wife over my own feelings. Now I'm choosing to love myself because he doesn't."

"Dior, I'm just saying—"

"Just saying what?" I interrupted, my heart racing like a subway train speeding through the city. "That I should ignore my own goddamn needs for a man who can't even appreciate my presence? I get it; you want me to play the loving wife, but sometimes love isn't enough. I need to put myself first, even if it feels like I'm breaking every rule you taught me."

The silence on the other end felt heavy, like the weight of a thousand unsaid words hung in the air, thick enough to choke on.

"Momma, I'm driving. I'll have to call you back," I said, desperation creeping into my voice as I hung up, craving a moment of silence to gather my frayed thoughts.

Pulling up to my house, I managed a forced smile, but it faded the instant I stepped inside. In just a few days, Sergio had transformed our once-cozy home into a disaster zone. Dishes piled high in the sink like a monument to neglect, clothes strewn across the floor as if a fashion show had gone horribly wrong and beer and liquor bottles all over—it looked like a tornado had hit. I stood frozen in shock, the chaos around me a stark reminder of why I was choosing myself.

"This is just another reason why I'm picking me," I muttered under my breath, pulling my phone from my purse with newfound resolve. I opened Google, searching for locksmiths to change the locks, feeling a surge of determination coursing through my veins. But before I could find a number, the doorbell rang, slicing through my thoughts like a knife.

When I opened the door, a knot formed in my throat, and my phone slipped from my grasp, clattering to the floor. "Momma!" I exclaimed, a tidal wave of shock and fear washing over me.

"Yeah, momma! If you ever think you can hang up on me and I won't show up, you're sadly mistaken. I'm your momma, and you're going to respect me, despite whatever you've got going on," she declared, her eyes blazing with maternal authority that could have put a drill sergeant to shame.

"Yes, ma," I mumbled, chastened, feeling the weight of her presence fill the doorway. She stepped inside, taking in the chaos with a frown that could curdle milk. "What the hell happened here?"

I felt a mix of embarrassment and defiance bubble up. "It's not like I'm the one who turned this place upside down," I shot back, trying to mask my vulnerability.

"Dior, this isn't about blame," she said, her tone softening just a fraction. "This is about taking care of yourself, and this—" she gestured to the mess "—this isn't it."

I sighed, the tension in the room thick enough to cut with a knife, a palpable heaviness that seemed to cling to the air like smoke. Maybe she was right, but the thought of putting myself back together felt like an impossible task, like trying to piece together a shattered mirror—every shard reflecting a different version of myself I wasn't sure I wanted to see.

"Now, here. Get your stuff," she said, shoving my suitcase into my arms with surprising force, the weight of it feeling like a reminder of all the baggage I was trying to escape.

"Momma, I'm sorry," I said, my voice breaking a little, the words slipping out before I could stop them.

"Don't be sorry. Be aware that no matter how old you are, I am not your little friend. And don't let it happen again," she replied curtly, her tone leaving no room for debate. With that, she turned on her heel, her presence a whirlwind of authority that left me standing there, suitcase in hand, knowing I had to figure out my next move.

I spent the day calling locksmith after locksmith, my hope dwindling with every unanswered call. The minutes turned into hours, and with each ring that met silence, my frustration mounted. I scrubbed my house clean, scrubbing away the remnants of Sergio's neglect, but instead of feeling accomplished, I felt more defeated, like I was just polishing a rusted surface that would never shine again.

Finally, with my patience wearing thin and desperation creeping in, I decided to reach out to the one person I knew would always come through for me. She was a wild card—my best friend Tasha, with her vibrant energy and no-nonsense attitude. If anyone could help me navigate this chaos, it was her. I scrolled through my contacts and hit the dial button, the anticipation bubbling in my chest like a pot about to boil over.

"Hey, girl, what's up?" Tasha answered, her voice a burst of sunshine that cut through the dark clouds hanging over me.

"I need you," I admitted, the weight of my day spilling out in a rush. "Can you come over?"

"Damn right, I'm on my way. You sound like you need a drink and a plan," she replied, her tone shifting to one of determination.

"More like a miracle," I muttered, feeling a flicker of hope igniting in my chest. Maybe, just maybe, with Tasha by my side, I could start to reclaim the pieces of myself I thought I'd lost.
"Well what do you need?" She asked "help cleaning and changing the locks." I said. "Cleaning?" She asked. "Yeah this man left this house so nasty" I proclaimed. "Well I'll

come help you clean but friend I don't know anything about changing locks." "Okay I said feelings a little defeated.
We hung up

There was only one other person I could think to call and I was nervous as the phone rang.

"What's up, stranger?" Armand answered, his voice smooth and familiar, pulling me from the chaos of my thoughts like a comforting balm.

"Nothing much. I need a favor, though," I said, trying to keep the desperation from creeping into my tone.

"What's that?" His genuine curiosity laced his words, sparking a flicker of warmth in my chest.

"Do you know anyone who can change my locks right now? I've got cash on hand," I replied, my heart racing at the thought of finally feeling secure in my own space again.

"I got you," he said without hesitation, the confidence in his voice igniting a small flame of relief.

"OMG, seriously? Who is it?" I asked. "me" "you? Yes I got tools and you know where we used to live, I had to change the locks there anytime my mom kicked out one of my brothers." He said, "Are you sure I don't want to bother you?" "I got you" he said " "at this point I'll take anyone. I've called every locksmith on Google, and they're all booked solid. You'll be saving my ass," I told him, gratitude washing over me like a wave.

"Yeah, just send me the address and I'll be there," he said, his tone reassuring and steady.

Hall Pass

We hung up, and I quickly texted him my address, my fingers flying over the screen. He told me to give him 30 to 45 minutes, which I figured was just enough time to wash off the sterile scent of the hospital and the grit of cleaning up the mess Sergio had left behind.

When Armand finally arrived, he wasted no time getting to work. As I watched him move around, changing the locks, I couldn't help but admire the way his muscles shifted beneath his shirt. The way he concentrated, his brow furrowed, sent a thrill through me. I noticed the beads of sweat forming on his forehead and trailing down his temples, glistening in the dim light of my living room. But as I watched, that initial thrill was tinged with confusion; the vibe between us felt off.

Each time I tried to spark a conversation, he responded in clipped sentences, almost as if he were keeping his distance. "How's your family?" I ventured, trying to bridge the gap, but he merely shrugged, his focus still on the lock in his hands.

"Good," he replied shortly, not meeting my gaze.

"Still in town?" I pressed, desperate to coax him out of whatever shell he was hiding in.

"Yeah," was all he offered, his tone flat, as if he were guarding some secret he wasn't ready to share.

The air between us crackled with unspoken tension, a strange mix of nostalgia and something else I couldn't quite place. I wanted to lean in, to reclaim the easy camaraderie we once shared, but it felt like there was an invisible wall between us, one that I didn't know how to break down.

I shook off the feeling, focusing instead on the simple act of watching him work, marveling at how someone who once felt so close could now feel so distant.

After what felt like an eternity, Armand finally finished up and began packing his tools. I offered him something to drink, grateful for the excuse to prolong our time together, to bridge the distance that had formed between us. We stood in my kitchen, sipping sweet iced tea, the silence growing heavier with each passing moment, saturated with unspoken words and lingering glances.

"Here you go." I slid two hundred dollar bills across the table, the crispness of the cash a stark contrast to the warmth of our shared space.

Armand looked at it, then pushed it back toward me. "I'm all set," he said, his tone firm yet gentle.

"Armand, can I take you out to dinner? My treat, just to thank you," I asked, my heart racing with a mix of hope and nerves, the words spilling out before I could second-guess myself.

"Sure," he replied, his expression softening for just a moment, a flicker of something familiar sparking in his dark eyes.

"Okay, I'll drive," I said, a smile breaking across my face, relief flooding through me. He grabbed his tools and tossed them into his car, while I texted Destiny I was heading out, and we were off, the city lights flickering like stars as we navigated the streets, a familiar blend of excitement and apprehension swirling in my stomach.

I had the perfect spot in mind—a little hole-in-the-wall place that served up live music and soul food that could make your taste buds dance. When we arrived, the air was thick with laughter and the mouthwatering aroma of fried fish, instantly putting me at ease, the vibrant atmosphere wrapping around us like a warm embrace.

We settled at a cozy table tucked into a corner, the sound of a live band playing a smooth blend of jazz and blues filling the air. I could feel the rhythm of the music pulsing around us, wrapping us in its embrace. I nudged him gently, excitement bubbling up. "You've got to try the catfish here; it's amazing!"

He raised an eyebrow, intrigued. "Alright, I'll give it a shot." His lips curled into a smile that felt like a spark igniting something deep within me.

He ordered the catfish with rice and gravy and mac and cheese, while I went for the greens and, of course, the mac and cheese—my guilty pleasure. As we waited for our food, the conversation flowed more easily, the tension from earlier beginning to dissipate like smoke in the wind.

"Tell me, how's life treating you?" I asked, genuinely curious, wanting to peel back the layers and find out what lay beneath his guarded exterior.

"Can't complain," he replied, leaning back in his chair, a hint of a smile playing on his lips. "Just trying to keep busy, you know?"

I nodded, sensing there was more he wasn't saying. "Busy is good. Keeps the mind off things."

"Yeah, it does." He paused, his gaze drifting for a moment. "But I've been thinking about making some changes. Maybe it's time for a new direction."

"Like what?" I pressed, intrigued by the idea of him shaking things up, the thought stirring something hopeful within me.

"Just... exploring new opportunities, you know? Life's too short to stay in one place," he said, a thoughtful look crossing his face as the music swelled around us.

As our dishes arrived, the rich scents mingled with the melodies in the air, and I couldn't help but feel that maybe tonight was a step toward something new for both of us.

As the food arrived, the conversation flowed more easily, but I still felt that lingering tension. "Armand, can I ask you something?" I finally ventured, my curiosity getting the better of me.

"What's up?" he asked, taking a sip of his drink and swaying slightly to the live band's rhythm, a hint of a smile playing on his lips.

I took a deep breath, feeling the weight of the question on my tongue. "Why do you seem so distant today? I mean, I know things have been weird between us, but I thought we were cool."

He looked at me, the playfulness vanishing from his eyes, replaced by something deeper. "It's complicated, Dior. You know how it is."

Hall Pass

"Yeah, but I'm here. You can talk to me," I pressed, wanting to break through whatever wall he had built around himself.

He took a moment, his gaze drifting to the lively band before returning to me. "I just don't want to complicate things more than they already are."

He paused for a moment, his eyes scanning the vibrant band that filled the corner of the dimly lit bar, before locking onto mine with an intensity that sent shivers down my spine. "I just don't want to complicate things more than they already are," he said, his voice low, almost swallowed by the upbeat rhythm surrounding us.

As the music swirled around us like a warm embrace, I felt a stirring deep within me. There was a whole world of emotions and desires waiting to be explored, and I was more than ready to dig deeper.

We shared small talk over our meals, laughter punctuating the air as we navigated the delicate balance between friendship and something more. When our plates were empty, there was no urgency to leave; the live band had us spellbound. The moment the soulful intro of Luther Vandross's "Take You Out" filled the room, excitement bubbled between Armand and me.

"Can I have this dance?" he asked, his hand outstretched, an invitation I couldn't refuse. I smiled, rising to my feet, my heart racing as he led me to the dance floor. The world around us faded away as we swayed to the music, lost in our own rhythm. His arms wrapped around me felt like home, and as he leaned in to sing softly in my ear, I melted. Heat pooled low in my belly, and my desire for him was a growing list of wants and needs.

Then it happened. With his arms enveloping me, our lips collided in a kiss that ignited a fire within. It was passionate, consuming, and my body screamed for more. Just as I felt myself getting lost in him, he pulled back, his expression a mix of shock and something else—something dangerous.

"We need to go," he said, urgency lacing his tone.

"But..." I started, searching for the words to keep him close.

"I've got an early day tomorrow. I need to get back to the hotel and get ready," he replied, his voice firm.

We left the restaurant, and I drove in silence, the weight of unspoken words hanging heavily between us. I couldn't hold it in any longer. "Armand, seriously, what's the problem?"

He remained quiet, a serious look etched on his face, and I could feel the tension radiating from him. Frustrated, I pulled the car over to the side of the road. "Armand, talk to me."

"What the fuck do you want me to say, Dior? You're a married woman, and I want you. I want you bad," he shot back, his voice raw with emotion.

"You want me sexually?"

"I want you sexually, emotionally—I want you in every way. I want you as mine. That's why I always come when you call, but you're married and committed to him,

Hall Pass

despite what I think and how I've seen him treat you. There's nothing I can do about that."

"But…" I started to say, desperate to bridge the gap between us. "Can we just hurry and get to your house?" He said.

I turned back in the driver's seat, putting the car back in drive as I felt a mix of determination and longing swelling inside me. I wanted to tell Armand that I felt the same way he did—that I craved him, too.

When we finally arrived at my house, Armand jumped into his car with a speed that caught me off guard. I couldn't even thank him, my heart was heavy with all that had been left unsaid.

I paced back and forth. In my living room thinking. I wanted Armand and I wanted him bad. My phone rang and I looked at it. Hello I answered Destiny's call. Girl I am so sorry I dozed off. She said, It's okay but I'm a call you back I said , rushing off the phone giving no time for questions. I got an idea and knew I needed work on it before my nerves got the best of me. I went upstairs to my bedroom and opened a draw I hadn't used in a while. I pulled out lingerie that still had tags on it. I held it up to myself in the mirror. "yeah this the one." I said to myself, smiling. I went to the closet and pulled out some gold heels. Then I showered and got myself together.

Once I was pleased with what I saw I headed out my door and got into my car. With my plan in mind. I got to the hotel and parked in the garage. I walked through the hotel lobby in my trench coat and heels feeling sexy. I got on the elevator and headed to Armand's room. When I got to the front of his door I let out an exhale before knocking.

"I want you," I blurted out, the words spilling from my lips when the door opened and Armand stood before me with no shirt and his glasses on. "And I think you want me too. And before you mention my husband, let me be clear—fuck him." The air between us crackled with tension, the challenge and invitation hanging like a promise.

"Want me?" he asked, his voice low and rough, sending shivers down my spine. I opened my jacket, letting it fall to reveal the lingerie that clung to my body. My hands rested on my hips, a bold display that made Armand's eyes darken with desire. He licked his lips, taking in every curve as if I were a feast laid out just for him.

In a heartbeat, he scooped me up into his arms and carried me into his room, placing me gently on the bed. The moment his lips found mine, it ignited something primal within me. Our kisses deepened, moving from my lips to my neck as I ran my hands over his chest, feeling the hard planes of his body. "Damn, I want you," Armand murmured, a low growl escaping him that sent a rush of heat through me.

"Dior, what do you want from me?" he asked, his eyes searching mine, filled with a mix of urgency and need.

"Make love to me," I breathed, my heart racing. "Tell me how you want me to do it. I want to hear it from you." The air was thick with our shared longing.

"I want you to make my body yours. Choke me. Pull my hair. Slap my ass. Do it all—just make me cum over and over again," I confessed, my voice steady but dripping with desire.

"Your wish is my command. Dior, if I put my dick in you, you're mine!" he declared, his words sending a thrill through me just before he ripped the lingerie from my body. He planted kisses all over me, trailing down my skin before his lips found my nipples, sucking and teasing until I moaned out in pure enjoyment.

When Armand settled between my legs, lifting them onto his shoulders, my body ignited. "Relax," he said, looking up at me with that smirk that always made my heart race. His kisses were gentle at first, teasing me until I felt like I was melting. Then, when his tongue finally made its appearance, my eyes rolled back in bliss. He didn't stop until I drenched his beard with my pleasure. "That's what I like. One down. Let's see how many more I can get out of you," he said, grinning wickedly.

He stood up, dropping his pants to the floor, his gaze locked on me. "Are you sure you want to do this?" he asked, his voice low and filled with a mix of concern and hunger.

Instead of answering, I slid off the bed, circling around him, feeling powerful. I pushed him back until his body hit the bed, and then I climbed on top of him, guiding his dick inside me myself. "Fuck," we both moaned in unison, the sound blending into the heat of the moment.

I rode Armand, using his chest for leverage when I needed to bounce harder. I lost myself in the rhythm, riding him until I reached another release, my body trembling with pleasure. But in one swift movement, he flipped me over, reclaiming control.

That man had me moaning and screaming and calling him daddy as he fucked me so good, twisting me into every position imaginable. "Right there daddy" was like words of encouragement. He turned my body into a playground, pushing me to the edge again and again. I begged for orgasm after orgasm, and he delivered, each wave of pleasure crashing over me like a tidal wave, leaving me breathless and craving more.

TWELVE

Armand

As Dior lay in my arms, the warmth of our bare skin against each other felt electric, a connection deeper than just the physical. The sun began its slow ascent, casting a golden glow that danced across the room, illuminating the chaos of our passion from the night before. In that moment, everything felt perfect—like this was exactly where I was meant to be, and this was how life was supposed to unfold.

Dior stirred, stretching like a cat awakening from a deep slumber. She looked up at me, her eyes sparkling with that morning light, and a smile broke across her face. "Good morning," she said, her voice a soft melody that wrapped around me.

"Good morning, beautiful," I replied, unable to keep the grin off my face.

"Last night was amazing," she said, biting down on her lip,

a playful glint in her eye that made my heart race.

"It really was," I agreed, reliving the intensity of every moment we'd shared. But her gaze turned serious, and I sensed the weight behind her words. "And I meant what I said," she continued, her voice steady.

"And what was that?" I asked, wanting to ensure that the passion of the night has not merely been some fleeting fantasy that evaporated with the dawn.

"That once you stuck your dick in me, I'm all yours and you're all mine." She said it with such conviction that it sent a thrill through me.

"I don't recall that last part," I said playfully, a smirk creeping onto my lips.

"It was implied," she shot back, her eyes narrowing in mock indignation.

"Dior, I'm—" I started, feeling the need to address the elephant in the room, the weight of my marriage hanging heavy over us.

She cut me off, her voice firm. "Tell your old hoes you're off the market. You're all mine now." If only it were that simple, I thought, the complexities of life swirling around us like the city traffic below.

"Dior, are you sure this is what you want? You're fresh out of a situation, and I'm not trying to get hurt," I said, my concern spilling over into my words.

Hall Pass

She sat up, locking her gaze onto mine, and the intensity of her stare made my heart skip. "I want you. I'll get the divorce papers today if that will prove it. I don't want to hurt you; I want to give you the same love you give me—if not more," she declared, her voice unwavering.

In that moment, I could see the truth in her eyes—a fierce determination that ignited something deep within me, like a fire rekindling after a long winter. It was as if I were standing at the edge of a new beginning, the promise of something real and beautiful ready to unfold before us. The city outside buzzed with life, cars honking and the distant sounds of street vendors calling out, but here, in our little world, everything felt suspended in time, as if we were the only two souls that mattered.

Dior got up, her silhouette framed by the morning light streaming through the window as she headed to the bathroom. I slid on some boxers and turned on the music, letting the soft tunes fill the space. Funny enough, Charlie Wilson's "Charlie, Last Name Wilson" came on, and I couldn't help but smile. I walked over to the bathroom door, leaning against the frame as I belted out the lyrics:

"Hey D, how you doin'

My name is Armand, last name Riggins

I was wonderin' if I could take you out

Show you a good time, invite you to my house…"

I danced a little, shaking my hips in a way that made her laugh. She looked up from washing her face, water glistening on her skin. "You play too much," she said, amusement dancing in her eyes.

"Yeah, but I'm serious. I do want to take you out. I'm not trying to have you as some fuck buddy sneaking you around," I told her, my tone shifting to something more earnest.

"When?" she asked, her curiosity piqued.

"Shit, today if you're with it," I said, and a smile broke across her face, lighting up the room.

"I definitely am. Just say when and where," she replied, her excitement palpable. The fact that she was all in without needing to know the details was exactly what I craved—something I never got from my own wife.

"Okay, so go handle your day. I have to meet up with my brothers, and then I'll text you what to wear and where to meet," I said, trying to keep my voice casual.

"Okay," she replied, her smile still lingering.

Dior walked back into the room, picking up her lingerie from the floor, and I couldn't help but tease her. "Where are you going with that?" I asked, raising an eyebrow.

"Home," she said, a hint of confusion in her voice.

"Nah, that's mine. Here, put on these sweats and this shirt." I handed her some comfortable clothes, taking the lingerie from her hands. She looked at me, a smirk on her lips, and I took a moment to inhale the lingering scent of her lingerie—intoxicating and all too familiar.

Dior got dressed, and I threw on some sweats, feeling the weight of the day ahead. I walked her out of the hotel, the air thick with anticipation. As we reached her car, I opened the door for her, and she slid in gracefully. Leaning down, I planted a soft kiss on her lips, feeling the warmth and promise in that brief moment.

"I'll see you later," I said, savoring the moment as her lips finally pulled away, her eyes sparkling with mischief.

"Yes sir," she replied, the glint in her eye making my heart race like I'd just downed a shot of espresso. I backed up, watching as she pulled away, the city lights catching the shimmer of her car, making it look almost magical as it disappeared into the hustle and bustle of the streets. The day was just beginning, but I already knew it was going to be one for the books.

I hopped into my own car, the engine rumbling to life beneath me, and dialed a number I hadn't called in what felt like ages. "Hello?" Phil's voice came through, smooth and steady.

"Hey Phil, it's Armand," I said, trying to keep my tone light.

"Hey, you're not in trouble, are you?" My lawyer inquired, his tone shifting to that of a concerned friend.

"Not precisely, but I do need your services," I replied, feeling the weight of what I was about to ask settle in my chest.

"What can I do for you?" he asked, his curiosity piqued.

"I need divorce papers drafted," I stated, the words hanging heavy in the air.

"Huh?" He questioned, clearly caught off guard.

"I'm divorcing Shanny. Draw up the papers. Offer her whatever you think is fair to keep her on her feet and let me know when I can pick them up," I told him, my resolve strengthening with each word.

"Ummm, okay, will do," he said, his voice steadying.

"Thank you," I replied, feeling a sense of relief wash over me as I hung up.

After last night, I didn't want to play games with Shanny anymore. If Dior was willing to end her marriage for me, then so was I. I didn't want to hurt her; she brought me a peace I'd been searching for, and I'd do anything to be with her.

I pulled up to the gym, the atmosphere buzzing with energy, and my mood was soaring. I was the first of my brothers to arrive, and with my adrenaline rushing, I decided to dive right into my workout. Ahmad rolled in next, his presence filling the space with camaraderie, followed closely by Armani, who was always the last to arrive but somehow still managed to catch up with us.

We pushed through our sets, the weights clanging and the smell of sweat mixing with the faint scent of rubber mats. As the workout dragged on, I could see Ahmad and Armani starting to tire, their breaths coming in deep gasps. They stepped to the side to catch their breath, and Ahmad broke the silence.

Hall Pass

"Okay, so Momma's birthday BBQ is this weekend at her house. I'm covering all the food and I'll do the grilling. Can you niggas cover the drinks and liquor?" he asked, a grin spreading across his face.

"Yeah, that's cool with me," Armani replied, wiping the sweat from his brow.

"Armand?" Ahmad called out, snapping me back to reality.

"Yeah," I answered, putting down the weights I'd been hoisting.

I could feel the warmth of brotherhood wrapping around us, the kind of bond that made everything else fade into the background. The gym was alive with energy—weights clanking, sneakers squeaking on the polished floor—while we mapped out the BBQ plans. But beneath the banter, I couldn't shake the feeling that everything was shifting, that new beginnings were on the horizon. It was time to embrace the chaos of the heart and see where this wild ride with Dior would take me.

"Damn, nigga, what done got into you? You over there going hard, looking extra focused today," Ahmad said, breaking through my thoughts.

"Nothing," I replied, trying to keep my cool. We weren't kids anymore, so discussing where my dick had been last night felt unnecessary.

"Nothing? You know we know you, right? You're lying. What's up with you, little nigga?" he pressed, his voice teasing but laced with genuine curiosity.

"Nothing," I insisted again, a little too defensively.

"Okay then, you'll tell us when you're ready. But what happened with that little situation with Dior?" Ahmad's question hung in the air, and the mere mention of her name sent warmth coursing through me, a familiar rush that felt both exhilarating and terrifying.

"Damn, nigga, you cheesing hard over there. You still fucking with her?" Ahmad said, catching me off guard. I tried to fix my face, not realizing I was grinning like a fool.

"We're cool, and everything is handled. Just so y'all know, I'm divorcing Shanny. My lawyer is drawing up the papers, so she won't be at Momma's party," I told them, my voice steady despite the turmoil inside.

"You a dumb ass nigga," Armani chimed in, shaking his head.

"Nigga, how?" I shot back, a flash of irritation sparking in my chest.

"You're getting a divorce? That bitch is married! She belongs to someone else. Get the fuck out your feelings about her before you fuck up your life again," he said, his tone blunt and unyielding.

"Watch your fucking mouth," I warned, rising from the bench, adrenaline surging through me.

"See? She's got you all sensitive, and your nose wide open over her ass. But remember, I'm the big brother, and I will fuck you up," he said, stepping toward me, his nostrils

Hall Pass

flaring with defiance. Both of our chests puffed out, a silent challenge hanging in the air.

I wasn't sure what the hell his issue was with Dior. Growing up, she had always been sweet to him, the kind of girl who'd share her snacks and laugh at his corny jokes, while he was my right hand, my ride-or-die. The tension simmered between us, thick enough to cut with a knife, and for a moment, I wondered if he could see the depth of my feelings for her. But did it even matter? This was my life, and I was ready to take the plunge, no matter the risks involved. As I stared him down, the weight of my choices pressed on my shoulders, but I was determined to carve my own path, even if it meant going against the grain.

"Ain't nobody got me shit. And let me be clear: you may be the big brother, but we're not kids anymore. You can try and find out how this shit will end," I shot back, my voice rising. "I don't understand why you're so emotional over my fucking life."

"I'm your fucking brother! I'm supposed to care! Fuck, nigga! I thought going to jail made you smarter and tougher!" he yelled, his frustration spilling over.

"Caring and being a fucking hater for no fucking reason are two different things. And as for what jail did to me, I already told you—you can try me and find out how tough it made me," I retorted, my anger flaring.

"Nigga, hate on you for what? When all this shit blows up in your face, it's going to be us you run to for help," he shot back, his eyes locked onto mine.

"I don't need y'all to fix shit for me. Never have. We both know I handle all my shit—along with shit that's not mine—like a real man," I snapped, feeling the adrenaline pumping through my veins.

"Nigga, was that supposed to be a shot?" Armani chimed in, eyes narrowed.

"Both y'all need to chill and shut the fuck up; you're making a scene in here," Ahmad interrupted, trying to diffuse the tension.

"Fuck that, nigga," Armani muttered under his breath.

"Shut the fuck up! Both you niggas are taking it too damn far. Armani, that's your brother. You can care, but it's his fucking life. Let him live it his way. He already gave up part of it for some shit that wasn't his fault," Ahmad said, fixing his gaze on Armani, trying to bring him back to reason.

It was our brotherly secret that I went to jail for Armani. He had always been the flashy one, the kid with the freshest sneakers and the latest gear. I was out there selling drugs for a better life, while he was doing it just to keep up appearances. He didn't have a car because I had one and was always there to drive him around.

One night, he went to see a girl with a bag full of work and two guns. Her dad came home unexpectedly, and Armani had to jump out the window, leaving everything behind. He called me in a panic, and I rushed out, leaving Dior to come get him. I was so busy talking shit to him, my nerves rattling, that I was driving reckless and got pulled over.

Hall Pass

The police pulled us over and searched the car. When they found the bag, neither of us said a word. Because it was my car, they placed the bag on me. I didn't snitch and say it was Armani's out of loyalty, knowing he was already on probation. He had been caught with some work before, but the amount was small enough that they figured he was using it, not selling it. They gave him probation, hoping he'd turn his life around.

I thought they'd hit me with the same deal as Armani. Instead, the judge looked at me like I was a lost cause, his eyes cold and unyielding. "This isn't baseball," he said, his voice slicing through the tension in the courtroom. "You should have learned from your brother's mistakes. Since you didn't, I'm going to teach you." He sentenced me to six years, and in that moment, everything changed. The very foundation of our brotherhood felt shaken, and I knew I'd have to navigate this new reality alone, carrying the weight of our choices like a badge of honor—and a curse.

"You always take his side," Armani spat, frustration radiating from him like heat from asphalt on a summer day.

"How old are you, my nigga? This ain't about sides," Ahmad shot back, raising his voice before glancing around the gym, aware of the eyes on us.

Armani, unable to contain his anger, grabbed his stuff and stormed off, leaving a heavy silence in his wake. "You niggas," Ahmad muttered as he took a seat, the weight of the moment settling on his shoulders.

"Man, I didn't want this to happen," I said, my voice laced with regret.

"Y'all better fix this shit before Momma's party," he fussed, his tone a mixture of disappointment and brotherly concern.

I said nothing, the words stuck in my throat. Instead, I grabbed my things and headed out, feeling the gym's energy shift as I walked away. I got into my car and exhaled deeply, trying to push the frustration away. I wanted to be mad, but just then, a text came through, shifting my mood like a sudden breeze on a hot day.

"Hey, just thinking of you," Dior had texted, and a smile crept onto my face.

I responded quickly, "You're always on my mind. I want you to meet me at Stanley Farm at 6 PM."

"What to wear?" she replied, and I could almost hear the playful tone in her voice.

"Nothing. Lol," I texted back, chuckling at the thought of her reaction.

She shot back with a "Lol," and I could picture her rolling her eyes, a smile tugging at her lips.

"Nah, all jokes aside, wear what you'd like," I added, wanting her to feel comfortable.

"Okay, I'll see you at 6 PM," she texted back.

With that simple exchange, the weight of the gym drama faded, leaving only the electric anticipation of our date. I left the gym behind, the bullshit between me and Armani confined to that space, and shifted my focus to the evening ahead. I had plans to put together, and I wasn't about to let anything ruin the thrill of what might unfold with Dior. Just the thought of her sent a rush of adrenaline through me, igniting a flicker of hope amidst the chaos of my life.

Time flew by as I waited, buzzing with excitement for Dior to arrive. I rode out on one of the horses, feeling the rhythm of the earth beneath me. "What kind of black cowboy shit is this?" I heard Joely call out from behind me, her voice dripping with playful sarcasm. "It's our date," I replied, pulling my horse to a stop.

She stood there, dressed in a flowing black sundress, leaning over the fence, her laughter lighting up the evening. "This is not what I was thinking when you said date," she said, a teasing smile playing on her lips. "I figured that out, so I came prepared. Follow me," I told her, taking her hand and leading her toward the house connected to the barn.

Inside, I rummaged through some clothes, thinking about the size I'd seen in her lingerie and grabbed a pair of fitted jeans, a fringed jacket, and some foldover cowboy boots. When she stepped out of the bathroom, everything fit her like it was made just for her—like she was born to wear it.

"You ready?" I asked, my heart thumping in anticipation. "To what?" she replied, her smile brightening the dim light around us. "To ride a horse," I said, guiding her toward the door.

"I've never done that before," she confessed, a hint of nervousness in her voice. "Don't worry," I reassured her, trying to keep my own excitement in check.

We made our way to the barn, where two horses stood waiting, their coats glistening in the fading sunlight. "This is Rose and Ray," I said, introducing her to the animals. "Hi," she said softly, reaching out to pet Rose. I couldn't help but smile, watching her gentle interaction.

"Who would've thought you'd be a horseback-riding cowboy from the hood?" she joked, her eyes sparkling with mischief.

"My momma always loved horses and used to talk about how she'd ride one if she ever got the chance. When she died, I made it my mission to learn how to ride," I shared, the weight of the memory hanging in the air.

"Wow, you did a lot when she died," she said softly, her expression shifting to one of genuine admiration. " Losing her gave me a different outlook on life." I said. "Understand. But I don't want to fuck up our date, so I have to tell you, as cute as they are, you're not putting me on one of these horses by myself." She wore the most serious face, and I couldn't help but chuckle.

"Okay, well will you get on one with me?" I asked, raising an eyebrow.

"Yeah, as long as you don't go fast and you don't let me fall off," she said firmly, her tone half-joking but laced with sincerity.

"I got you," I assured her, the promise hanging between us like an unspoken bond.

I showed her how to mount the horse, and as I settled in behind her, I could feel the tension in her body. She held on tight, her hands gripping my thighs, a little apprehensive but trusting. I placed one hand over hers, feeling her warmth seep into me, and soon she rested her head against my back, her body relaxing as the rhythm of the ride took over.

As we rode, the world around us faded, and I stopped under a sprawling tree where I had set up a little picnic—wine, a blanket, and fresh fruit waiting for us. We sprawled out beneath the branches, exchanging small talk, but mostly just savoring the moment, the connection between us deepening with every shared laugh.
"Armand can I ask you something and you won't be offended?" She asked me "yes what's up?" I asked "can you afford this? I can help pay if you need me to." She said, I fought with the urge of wanting to tell her money was not a problem for me but at the same time wanting to see if unlike Shanny she would love me even if she thought I was broke.

"Don't worry about it. I got it. I normally save to take one ride per month

"Okay" she says before letting silence find us

"I love this," she said, her voice soft as she nestled against me. "What?" I asked, genuinely curious.

"Moments like this. I've never experienced anything like it before. It makes me..." She paused, her cheeks flushing slightly.

"Makes you what?" I prodded, intrigued.

"Horny," she said boldly, her eyes sparkling with mischief.

"Oh really?" I replied, leaning in to kiss her forehead gently, my heart racing.

"Yeah," she said, sitting up, her gaze locking onto mine with an intensity that made my pulse quicken. Without breaking eye contact, she leaned in, kissing me softly at first, then with a hunger that sent a jolt of electricity through me. Her control in the moment had my body responding, every nerve ending alive with desire.

"Looks like you're feeling it too," she smirked, her fingers trailing over the outline of my excitement. I didn't say a word; the look I gave her was more than enough to confirm what we both already knew.

She began to unbuckle my jeans and I didn't stop her. She stuck her hands in my pants massaging my manhood. "fuck" "do we have to worry about anyone coming out here?" she asked me. "nah it's just us" I told her. With no hestation she pulled my dick from my pants and sent it to the back of her throat. "oh damn" I moaned out. Her head game was something crazy. I had spent some much time pleasing her last night that I didn't know what I was missing. The sound of her pleasing me filled the air. I pulled her hair up out the way and watch her with my mouth open in amazement. She looked up at me making eye contact as she took in every inch of my dick she could. She went on and on until I released. She let the cum slid down her throat as she stood up took off her pants and climbed back on top of me.

She eased my dick inside of her and rode me like I was a horse. I unzipped the jacket she had on and took her breast out and sucked on each one. When I felt her walls tighten she was getting to her peak. I grabbed her hips and helped her grind just a bit more forcefully. We both came together and neither of us rushed to separate when we were done. We actually sat for a while entangled and attached to each other.

THIRTEEN

Dior

The time Armand and I had been spending together felt nothing short of magical, a whirlwind of laughter, stolen glances, and late-night conversations that stretched until dawn. So when he casually asked me to join him for his mother's birthday BBQ, I didn't hesitate for a single second.

"Girl, you sure I can't come to the BBQ with you?" Tasha asked, her tone playful yet laced with genuine curiosity.

"Girl, I'm a guest! How the hell am I supposed to bring a guest?" I laughed, rolling my eyes at her, the affection radiating between us like the summer sun.

"I'm just saying, you said he has brothers, I'm trying to get the hook up. I want to brag about my own Armand too," she replied, her voice teasing with a hint of envy.

"Honey, there's only one Armand, and he's all mine," I said cheerfully, my heart fluttering at the thought of him. Just then, my phone dinged, and I felt a rush of excitement. It was Armand letting me know he'd be pulling up shortly.

"Girl, I gotta go! I need to finish getting dressed; Armand just said he's almost here," I told her, my pulse quickening as I thought about seeing him again.

"Okay, have fun!" she said, her voice brightening my mood even more.

"I will!"

"And Dior…"

"Yes?" I answered, sensing the serious note creeping into her voice, which always made me pause.

"I'm really happy to see this new you. I love you, girl. Talk to you later!" She hung up, and I smiled at my reflection in the mirror, feeling a rush of warmth.

My skin was glowing, the kind of glow that felt like it came straight from within, my smile brighter than ever. "Happy" felt like an understatement for how I was feeling. I slipped into my favorite sundress—a flowy, floral number that danced around my knees and clung to my curves just right—and added a pair of strappy sandals that made my legs look endless. I brushed my hair until it shimmered and adorned myself with just a hint of lipstick that whispered confidence.

As I glanced back at my phone, anticipation bubbled in my chest like soda fizzing over. Armand was more than just a guy; he was the spark that ignited something deep within me—something I hadn't realized I'd been missing until he came along. The thought of him waiting outside made my heart race, and I couldn't help but grin at the idea of him introducing me to his favorite people. Today was going to be special, a day filled with laughter and memories,

Hall Pass

and I was ready to dive headfirst into whatever magic awaited us at that BBQ.

When Armand pulled up, I rushed outside, the excitement propelling me forward. "You look amazing," he said as I slid into the car, his eyes lighting up with genuine admiration, making my stomach flutter.

"Thank you," I replied, warmth creeping into my cheeks. He always had a way of making me feel special, like I was the only person in the room.

As we headed to his mom's house, waves of nostalgia washed over me. Pulling up in front of the familiar, cozy home brought back a flood of memories—sun-soaked summers and endless laughter. The block was alive with people walking toward the house, their voices mingling in the air like a sweet symphony. The rich, smoky aroma of BBQ wafted through the open windows, making my stomach growl in anticipation.

We walked to the backyard, and I clung to Armand's arm as he expertly navigated through the crowd. The atmosphere was vibrant, families mingling, kids darting around, their laughter echoing like music. We approached a small circle where I spotted his brother, Ahmad. Despite the years that had passed, he still looked the same—just older, with that rugged charm that came with facial hair.

"Bro!" Ahmad exclaimed, slapping Armand's shoulder before pulling him into a brotherly hug. He peeked around Armand and grinned at me. "Hello there, beautiful," he greeted, his voice warm and familiar, just like it was when we were younger.

"Hey!" I smiled back, feeling a flutter of nostalgia wash over me.

"Give me a hug, girl!" He opened his arms wide, and I embraced him tightly, soaking in the warmth of family.

"Time has treated you well; you look amazing," he said, his eyes sparkling with genuine admiration.

As I stood there, enveloped in warmth and laughter, I couldn't shake the feeling that this day was just the beginning of so many beautiful moments to come. But just as I was settling into the joy, I noticed a shift in the air when Armani stepped into the circle. "Bro," he said, tension crackling between the two of them.

"Bro," Armand replied back, a smile breaking over his face, but I could feel the unspoken words hanging in the air. I wasn't sure what was going on, but I caught the look of approval Ahmad gave them as they slapped hands and embraced.

When they finally pulled apart, Armani turned to me, his eyes sparkling with that familiar mischief. "Dior," he said, enveloping me in a warm hug that felt like home. The guys introduced their women: Kelly, Armani's baby mama, flashed a friendly smile, while Tasha leaned in, her laughter infectious as Ahmed playfully referred to her as his "friend."

The atmosphere buzzed with camaraderie, a perfect blend of joy and togetherness. Kids were darting around playing tag, their laughter ringing out like music, while the mouthwatering aroma of grilled meats wafted through the air, tickling our senses. Us ladies busied themselves making plates for our men, then settled down beside them, cards in hand and drinks flowing freely. It was the kind of effortless vibe that filled my heart with warmth.

"So, Dior, how's it going with Armand?" Tasha asked, her tone teasing but genuine.

I couldn't help but blush as I replied, "Honestly, it's refreshing. After all the bullshit, it feels good to be with a real man. He makes it easy for me to just be myself, to lean into my role. It's comforting to surrender and just be a woman." I grabbed Armand's arm, feeling that electric connection between us.

"You need to take some lessons from your brother," Kelly shot back at Armani with a playful smirk, and we all laughed.

As I nestled next to Armand, warmth radiating between us, my phone buzzed insistently in my pocket. It was my mom. I tapped Armand's shoulder and held up my phone, and he nodded, his expression shifting to one of concern mixed with encouragement. "Take it inside," he said softly. I nodded, already feeling the pull of the conversation I needed to have.

I slipped into the house, seeking the sanctuary of the bathroom for a little privacy. By the time I settled against the cool tiles, my phone had stopped ringing. I quickly dialed her back, hoping to catch her before the moment slipped away.

"Hey, Momma," I said when she answered, trying to keep my voice light.

"Where are you?" she asked, her tone laced with urgency.

"I'm out. Why? What's wrong? Are you okay?" I shot back, my heart racing.

"I'm at your house with your husband, fresh out of the hospital, and this man can't get into the house. Did you change the locks?" she said, frustration evident in her voice.

"He can't get in because he no longer lives there, and he was made aware that the locks were changed," I explained, trying to keep my cool.

"Dior…"

"Momma, I'm not trying to be disrespectful, but you've got to take yourself out of this. You don't know everything that's going on or what's gone on. We had a conversation, and Sergio is very aware I told him not to come to my house."

"Dior, I raised you better than this. What would Jesus do?" she pressed, her voice rising.

"Momma, if you're worried about what Jesus would do, then you take him into your house. But I'm done, and I will be divorcing him. I was just giving him enough respect to wait until he got out of the hospital before serving him the papers."

The weight of my words hung in the air, a stark contrast to the warmth I'd just left behind. I took a deep breath, reminding myself that I was no longer bound by the past. Today was about new beginnings, and I was determined to embrace them.

Hall Pass

Momma fell silent on the other end of the line, and I could practically feel her anger radiating through the phone. "Momma, I love you. May I hang up?" I asked gently.

"Yes, bye Dior," she snapped, her tone sharp with attitude before she hung up. I set my phone down on the counter and exhaled, staring at my reflection in the mirror. The vibrant colors of my dress contrasted with the gravity of the conversation I'd just had. I was stronger than the weight of family expectations; I had to be.

Pulling myself together, I stepped out of the bathroom, only to nearly collide with Armani. The smell of liquor wafted off him like a heavy cloud, and I wrinkled my nose, trying to sidestep the awkwardness. "Excuse me," I mumbled, intent on moving past him.

"So you gonna keep acting like this?" he asked, a challenge simmering in his voice.

"Acting like what?" I shot back, confusion etching my brow.

"Like you care about my brother," he slurred, his words dripping with disdain.

"I don't just care about your brother; I love him," I stated boldly, my heart racing as I stood my ground.

"You love him, but you kissed me," he retorted, his eyes narrowing.

I looked around, incredulous. "I know damn well you're not bringing that shit up. Don't say I kissed you. That was years ago. Armand was in jail, and you kissed me. I told you in that very moment that the kiss was wrong, that it should've never happened and was never going to happen again." My voice rose, fueled by a mix of frustration and disbelief.

I was appalled he even dared to bring this up, especially now that Armand was finally home. His absence had been suffocating, but his family had been my lifeline—checking in, offering support. Armani had taken me out for dinner and drinks to celebrate my birthday while Armand was locked up, and though I wasn't sure what his intentions were, I never expected this confrontation to rear its ugly head.

"Your husband is a nigga that ain't shit; your new nigga shouldn't be soft like my little brother. You need a real man," Armani sneered, his bravado grating on my last nerve.

"I hope you don't think that real man is you?" I shot back, my voice steady despite the chaos swirling inside me.

Armani raised an eyebrow, a smirk forming on his lips. "I don't want you. I never have, never will. Even when Armand was in jail, I wasn't lowering my standards to want you. You're not a real man; you're a hater and fucking disloyal. If this shit wouldn't break Armand, I'd tell him. But I'm gonna do you a favor and act like none of this ever happened. Now get out of my way."

I pushed past him, my heart racing as I navigated through the crowd, determined not to let Armani's toxicity ruin my day. The vibrant energy of the BBQ wrapped around me like a warm embrace, laughter and chatter filling the air like sweet music. Armand was out there, and I wasn't about to let anyone dim the light of this moment. Today was mine, and I was ready to claim it.

Hall Pass

I slid back into my seat next to Armand, forcing a smile as I tried to mask the anger and discomfort that Armani had stirred up, not to mention the tension from my earlier phone call with Momma. I focused on Armand's radiant grin, hoping it would wash away the negativity.

After a while, I noticed Armani rejoining the table, his presence loomed like a dark cloud. I did everything in my power to avoid making eye contact or engaging with him, the last thing I wanted was to reignite that tension.

As Mary J. Blige's "Real Love" played softly in the background, I playfully sang along to Armand, letting the rhythm lift my spirits. But the joyful atmosphere shattered in an instant when gunshots rang out, slicing through the laughter and sending everyone into a panic. It was like a scene from a movie—chaos erupted as Ahmad flipped over the card table, and all three brothers instinctively pushed us women behind it, pulling out their guns, looking battle-ready.

We crouched low, hearts racing, adrenaline coursing through our veins while the world outside spiraled into confusion. The sounds of screeching tires filled the air, and I held my breath, praying for everyone's safety.

When the panic finally subsided and the echo of speeding cars faded into the distance, we cautiously emerged from behind the table. "Fuck," Ahmad muttered, shaking his head in disbelief. "Can't believe someone fucked up Momma's party like that."

"This is the hood; why is someone shooting up a damn BBQ a surprise to y'all?" Armani said dismissively as he walked off, his bravado still intact even in the face of danger.

The once lively backyard was now eerily empty. We all pitched in to pick up the remnants of the party, collecting trash and trying to restore some sense of normalcy before we decided to head home.

Our drive home was enveloped in silence, the weight of what had just happened hanging heavily in the air. I finally broke the quiet. "Baby, I'm really sorry they fucked up your mom's party," I said softly, glancing at him.

"It's cool. This was my brothers' idea anyway. Now I can do what I really wanted, which is go to her gravesite, put some flowers out there, and clean it up," he replied, his voice steady but tinged with sadness.

"Do you want me to come with you?" I asked, genuinely wanting to be there for him.

"No. Thank you, but I want to spend this time with just her." I nodded, understanding the need for solitude in moments like this. I didn't know how it felt to celebrate a parent who was no longer here, so I didn't want to be pushy.

As we pulled up in front of my house, I turned to Armand, my heart aching at the look on his face. It was a mix of grief and determination, and all I wanted to do was comfort him. "Am I going to hear from you later?" I asked, hoping for a glimmer of connection.

"Probably in the morning, not tonight," he said, his voice soft but resolute.

"Maybe I'll just stop by to check on you in the morning. I'll be there to start working on the contract," I suggested, wanting to keep that thread of connection alive.

"Okay, baby," he replied, a flicker of appreciation crossing his features.

We shared a lingering kiss, one filled with unspoken promises before I stepped out of the car and walked into the house. As I closed the door behind me, I leaned against it, taking a deep breath. This was not how I thought today was going to go. But in the midst of chaos, I realized that it was moments like these that truly mattered.

FOURTEEN

Armand

Spending time with my mom at her gravesite was exactly what I needed. The weight of everything on my mind felt lighter as I knelt by her headstone, the cool breeze whispering through the trees around me. Yesterday was a shit show. I'd gone inside the house to check on Dior and ended up overhearing her and Armani deep in conversation. I wasn't mad at her—not really—but I couldn't shake the feeling that I was stuck in some twisted game of chess, and I had no idea how to make my next move.

The urge to leap across that card table and strangle Armani when I saw him again was almost overwhelming. The only thing that saved him was the fact that he was still breathing after that drive-by. How could my own big brother betray me like that, especially while I was doing a bid for him? I could practically hear Momma's voice echoing in my head. If she were here, she would've kicked his ass for sure. She didn't play when it came to loyalty. We were raised with the mantra that family was all we had, so why the hell would he do this to me?

I tossed and turned in bed, the sheets twisted around my legs, my thoughts spiraling like the smoke from a burnt-out cigarette. I was so lost in my head that when my alarm blared, I nearly jumped out of my skin. Sitting up, I rubbed my eyes and tried to shake off the lingering anger. Dior was coming to the hotel today, and I wanted to be long gone before she arrived. I couldn't risk any slip-ups, especially with anyone referring to me as "boss."

I'd already sent an email with my orders; I was going to leave a check on my office desk that needed to be filled in for her, and now I was headed to the restaurant. The last thing I needed was someone screwing that up. I took a deep breath, steeling myself for the day ahead. Time to put on my game face.

As I finished dressing, my phone rang, breaking the morning silence. I picked it up from the nightstand and saw Ahmed's name flashing on the screen. "Yo," I answered, bracing myself for whatever chaos was about to unfold.

"Hey, we're having a bro breakfast. Be there," he said, hanging up before I could even get a word in. Classic Ahmed—always the one to dictate the agenda like he was some kind of patriarch. I rolled my eyes, irritated. He'd played the role of our dad for so long that even as grown men, he still felt like he ran the show. Well, both he and Armani were about to find out I didn't answer to either of them. I had my own businesses and shit to handle, and I was tired of feeling like a kid looking for approval.

Plus, I had no desire to sit across from Armani and break bread like everything was all good between us. The tension between us was thick enough to cut with a knife. I could already picture him smirking, trying to act like we were still boys when the truth was far more complicated. No, I was going to do what I did best: throw myself into my work and keep my head down. It was better that way—safer, too.

If I focused on the grind, I could avoid the urge to confront Armani and potentially screw things up even more.

With a final glance in the mirror, I adjusted my tie, feeling the fabric hug my neck just right, and stepped out into the bustling city. The sounds of the urban jungle enveloped me—honking cars, distant sirens, and the murmur of pedestrians filled the air. It was time to face the day, but that didn't mean I had to play nice.

I headed to the restaurant, and a surge of satisfaction washed over me when I saw it was damn near packed. Business-wise, the hotel was one thing, but the restaurant was like my baby. I had created it from scratch, every detail, from the layout to the meals on the menu. The savory aromas wafting in the air were a testament to my hard work, and seeing it thrive made my chest swell with pride.

As I walked into my office, a sense of purpose propelled me forward. My phone buzzed, breaking my focus. "Phil, what can I do for you?" I said, sinking into the familiar warmth of my leather chair.

"I got the divorce papers back today," he replied, and I felt a flicker of hope.

"I'm divorced!" I said, bubbling up. I figured that would be the best news to kick start my day.

"No," he said, his tone flat. "Where she was supposed to sign, she actually wrote 'fuck no.'"

"What? This girl…" I groaned, burying my head in my hands. "It was a really good offer— $100,000! She keeps the salon and still gets half of yall joint investments."

Hall Pass

"Ugh, just throw in the house and all the cars for all I care. I just want out, and I want it ASAP," I snapped, frustration boiling over.

"I'll redraft and send it again. Does she have a lawyer I can reach out to? Maybe see what she wants to make this smoother?" Phil asked, his voice steady.

"She has what I give her access to," I replied, my tone resigned.

"Okay… well, I'll be in touch," he said before hanging up.

Before I could drop my phone on my desk, it buzzed again. This time, Shanny's name lit up the screen. "Hello," I answered, bracing myself.

"Hello, husband. That is what you wanted me to call you, right?" she said, her voice dripping with sarcasm.

"What do you want, Shanny? I'm not playing games with you today," I shot back, irritation creeping into my voice.

"Games? I thought you liked games, 'cause sending divorce, papers to the house was clearly a game," she retorted, her tone sharp.

"Shanny, why didn't you just sign the damn papers so we can end this?" I pressed, my patience wearing thin.

"Because we promised 'until death do us part.' I mean, you were almost dead, but I decided to send warning shots," she said, her laughter chilling.

"That was you that shot up my momma's damn party!" I yelled, the memories flooding back like a bad dream.

"Well, I figured since I wasn't invited, no one should be there," she shot back, unapologetic.

"You're fucking crazy! I really should fuck you up," I said, my heart racing.

We both knew this was more than just a war of words; it was a battle of wills, and neither of us was backing down. The city outside buzzed on, oblivious to the chaos simmering between us, a stark contrast to the storm raging in my heart.

"Crazy in love," she said, laughter ringing through the phone like a taunt.

"Love my ass. You don't love me; you love the lifestyle," I shot back, irritation creeping in.

"It's still love, right?" she replied, her voice playful, as if we were discussing the weather instead of the wreckage of our lives.

"Shanny, you're going to get new divorce papers. I'll give you $100,000, the house, and the cars. Just sign it, and we'll be done," I said, hoping to end this circus.

"That plus whatever I sign on that check sounds pretty good," she quipped, and I felt my stomach drop.

"What check?" I asked, dread pooling in my gut.

Hall Pass

"The one you left on your desk. I mean, I came to see you in person so we could talk, and to my surprise, you're not here," she said, her tone dripping with mock innocence.

"Get out of my office and leave the check," I said, trying to keep my cool, but the anger was bubbling just beneath the surface.

She laughed, the sound sharp and irritating. "Shanny, please don't make me be a person I don't want to be," I pleaded, knowing all too well how far she could push me.

I heard her laughter again before the call ended, leaving me staring at my phone in disbelief. "Fuck," I muttered, frustration spilling over.

I got up and started pacing my office, the walls closing in around me, the weight of the situation pressing down like a vice. I needed to act fast. I grabbed my phone and dialed a number I knew by heart.

"Yo," a familiar voice answered, smooth and confident.

"Did you move that money for me?" I asked, urgency in my voice.

"Yeah, I moved about $100,000 into an offshore account that will collect in trust," he replied, and a wave of relief washed over me.

"Good. Now lock down all my accounts," I said, my tone shifting to one of command.

"What?" he asked, confusion lacing his voice.

"Lock them down now. Shanny has a blank check she got from my office, and I don't want her pulling all my money," I explained, the panic rising.

"Okay, I got you," he said, understanding dawning.

"Thanks," I said, hanging up and running a hand through my hair. The last thing I needed was her draining my accounts while I was trying to fight my way out of this mess.

With the city still buzzing outside, I felt the weight of the world pressing down on me. I was in it deep, and there was no turning back now. I hung up and made my way over to the small bar in the corner of my office, pouring myself a shot. The smooth burn of the whiskey was just what I needed to momentarily drown out the storm brewing inside me.

Before I could even regroup, my office door swung open. "Yo, bro," Ahmed said, stepping in with a grin that faded as soon as Amani followed.

"We missed you at breakfast," he continued, his tone casual, but I wasn't in the mood for pleasantries.

"Yeah, I didn't have time, and I don't have it now either," I shot back, my irritation flaring.

"Fuck wrong with you?" Armani chimed in, a hint of concern mixed with annoyance in his voice.

"I'm busy," I replied, giving him a look that could slice through steel.

Hall Pass

"You've never been too busy for your family before, so what's really going on?" Ahmed pressed, his brow furrowing as he sensed the tension.

I could feel my blood boiling, a dangerous mix of frustration and anger bubbling just beneath the surface. "I'm just busy, so can y'all leave? I'll hit you up when I have free time," I said, my voice cold.

"Armand," Armani called out, and I shot him a glare that could melt ice.

"Nigga, don't say my fucking name," I spat, the words laced with venom.

"That bitch must've done something," he said, rolling his eyes as if he already knew the answer.

"No, she ain't do shit; you did," I said, finally losing it.

"Me? What the fuck I do?" he shot back, his tone defensive.

"I've been trying to figure out why you were so against Dior. My heart wanted to believe you were just being a concerned big brother because you knew she had a husband and I had a wife, but something in my gut wouldn't let me believe that."

"That's exactly what it is," he insisted, but I could see the cracks in his facade.

"Nigga, stop fucking lying. You pressed up on Dior while I was locked up, and you didn't want it to get back to me how my own brother was trying to backdoor me," I accused, my voice rising with each word.

"Armani, you didn't," Ahmed interjected, sadness washing over his features.

"He did. I overheard him talking to Dior yesterday when I went to check on her," I said, my heart racing.

A smirk crept across Armani's face, a look that made my stomach turn. "She should've been mine anyway," he said, as if he were claiming a trophy.

"Bro, what the fuck is wrong with you?" Ahmed asked, disbelief etched across his face.

"Armand has always been Mr. Perfect. I saw and wanted Dior first, but yet he got with her," Armani sneered.

"That's your fucking brother! Are you really sitting here telling me you've been walking around jealous for years?" Ahmed challenged.

"Never jealous. That nigga ain't me," Armani spat, his pride blinding him.

"You're right; I'm not you. I'm a real man and a real brother. I'd never press up on any of your girls. I believe in loyalty. You kissed her, and she turned you down even when I wasn't there. You pressed her yesterday, and she turned you down again because she loves me, not you. And your ass called me weak. You even said you'd lie on her and claim y'all fucked if she ever told me. Yeah, nigga, I heard it all. So tell me to my face how weak I am. Go ahead, tell me so I can show you what type of weak nigga I am," I spat, my voice low and dangerous.

"Nigga, you're weak, and in the right moment, that little bitch is gonna crumble. And when she does, I'm gonna have my dick down her throat," he retorted, arrogance dripping from his words.

The air in the room crackled with tension, each second stretching out like a drawn bowstring, ready to snap. I could feel the heat of our confrontation simmering just beneath the surface. This wasn't just a fight between brothers; it was a battle for respect, loyalty, and the love of a woman who had become the epicenter of our war.

In a flash, I charged at him, pinning Armani against the wall, my fists flying as I landed punch after punch. The adrenaline surged through me, drowning out the chaos around us, even as I heard Ahmed yelling, desperately trying to separate us. The world narrowed down to just me and Armani, our history colliding in a whirlwind of anger and betrayal.

When Ahmed finally managed to pull us apart, we were both breathing heavily, adrenaline still coursing through our veins. Armani wiped blood from his lip, a grimace twisting his features. "Little nigga, I'm gonna fuck you up," he spat, fury etched in every line of his face.

"Fuck you, bitch-ass nigga! I can't believe I did a bid for your snake ass," I shot back, the words laced with venom. The betrayal cut deeper than any physical blow ever could.

"Both you niggas chill the fuck out!" Ahmed intervened, trying to mediate the chaos.

"Get the fuck out my business!" I yelled, my voice echoing in the small room, frustration boiling over.

"Nigga, fuck this place!" Armani retorted, his rage palpable as he swiped his arm across my bar, knocking all the bottles to the floor in a cascade of glass and liquor.

"And fuck you, nigga. Just so we're clear: don't speak to me, don't come around me or my girl. If you do, I'm gonna beat your ass again," I warned, my voice low and dangerous, dripping with menace.

"Fuck you," he shot back, spitting towards me, but Ahmed's quick reflexes caught him, causing the spit to miss me by inches.

In a moment of pure instinct, I reached out and landed one last punch square in his mouth, feeling the satisfying impact resonate through my knuckles. But before I could follow up, Ahmed hoisted him away, his grip firm and unyielding.

"Enough!" Ahmed shouted, his voice booming like thunder in the storm of our anger.

The tension hung in the air, thick and suffocating. I stood there, breathing heavily, the reality of our shattered brotherhood weighing down on me like a lead cloak. This wasn't over—not by a long shot.

Hall Pass

FIFTEEN

Dior

My heart ached for Armand. I knew his mother was everything to him, and the way her birthday party had spiraled into chaos cut deep. Ms. Riggins was the glue that held her family together, the peacekeeper among her sons and a calming presence for everyone else. I could feel the weight of his grief, especially after last night when he needed his space. I respected that, but today was a different story. Today, he was going to see or hear from me, no matter what.

But first, I needed to focus on the task at hand: showcasing my skills at this hotel. Sure, Armand had opened the door for me, but I was determined to prove that I was that bitch when it came to getting the job done.

I stood in front of the mirror, taking in my reflection. The tailored black pantsuit hugged my curves just right, giving me an air of power and confidence. "Dior, you got this," I murmured, pumping myself up. "This is another new beginning for the life you want and deserve. Own this opportunity." I grabbed my portfolio and purse, feeling the thrill of a fresh start, and headed to the hotel.

As I walked in, I held my head high, exuding confidence. "Are you Dior Waye?" a well-dressed young lady asked as I approached the front desk.

"Yes, I am," I replied, forcing a smile even though my heart was still heavy for Armand.

"Nice! I'm Renee," she said, her friendly demeanor instantly putting me at ease.

"Cool. Nice to finally put a face to the name and voice on the phone," I said, recalling our conversations.

"Right?" she laughed, a warm sound that echoed through the lobby.

"Follow me; let's go talk," she instructed after we shook hands.

As we walked through the hotel's bustling corridors, Renee shared the rich history of this place, her voice tinged with pride. "This hotel has been black owned for a few years," she said, her eyes sparkling with determination. "But it's time for an upgrade." Her tone shifted, becoming serious. "Everything about the look and design has been stuck in the 80s. It's like time forgot about us, you know?"

I nodded, a surge of excitement coursing through me. I could already envision the transformation—bold colors, modern touches, and a vibe that screamed sophistication. This wasn't just about showcasing my skills; setting the tone for me as a business I was ready to dive in, no matter how messy things got.

Hall Pass

We stepped into the office, and both of us halted at the sight of a woman lounging at the desk, her feet propped up nonchalantly. "Ms. Griffin, what are you doing here?" Renee asked, an edge of surprise in her voice.

"I was looking for my business partner," she replied coolly, not even bothering to remove her feet from the desk.

"He's not here; he's out of the office for the day. Is there anything I can help you with?" Renee offered, trying to keep things professional.

"No, you're not him," Ms. Griffin shot back, her tone dripping with condescension.

"Fine. I have a meeting to handle here," Renee said, her voice firm.

Ms. Griffin's gaze swept over me, her eyes narrowing as she sized me up. I felt a chill run down my spine, but I forced myself to stand tall. I was in business mode, and I wouldn't let the hood in me slip out to confront her. She stood up, grabbing something off the desk and tossing it into her purse. "Okay, I'll reach out to him later," she said, her tone dismissive as she strutted towards the door, she got near me and stopped making eye contact "I like your perfume" she stated. "Thank you" I replied and she continued walking, leaving a lingering discomfort in the air.

Once she left, Renee and I took our seats, the tension from Ms. Griffin dissipating as we focused on the task at hand. "So, the vision we want for the hotel is class, elegance, and luxury," Renee explained, her enthusiasm contagious.

Ideas started flooding my mind like a rush of adrenaline. I could see it all—the grand lobby adorned with sleek, modern furnishings, a color palette that radiated warmth and sophistication. I quickly passed her my portfolio to browse through while I pulled out my iPad to draft some initial concepts.

"This is just the beginning," I said, my fingers flying over the screen. "We can create a space that not only reflects our heritage but also attracts a new clientele. Imagine rooftop events, art displays from local artists, and a bar that serves signature cocktails inspired by our culture."

Renee's eyes lit up as she leaned closer, captivated by the possibilities. "Yes! That's exactly the energy we need and we have a restaurant a few streets over," she exclaimed, her enthusiasm infectious.

With each idea we tossed around, I could feel the weight of the day lifting just a little. When I finished outlining my concepts, I handed my iPad to her, watching as her eyes sparkled with excitement.

"This is it! This is the exact look we're aiming for!" she declared, her voice brimming with energy.

"Perfect! So I can start ordering the materials right away, and we can stage an area for your boss to see," I replied, my heart racing at the thought of taking action.

"That would be perfect! How much do we need to pay you today?" she asked, her brows furrowing in concentration.

"$5,000 should be good. That'll serve as the deposit for my services and cover some initial supplies," I said, feeling a surge of confidence.

"Cool, let me grab the check," she said, turning toward the desk. As she rifled through the drawers, I noticed a flicker of confusion cross her face.

"Um, this is embarrassing, but can we wire you the payment? I can't seem to find the checkbook at the moment," she admitted, her cheeks flushing slightly.

"Sure, no problem," I said, flashing her a reassuring smile. I handed over my banking information, feeling a rush of excitement as I gathered my things. I could already envision the look on Armand's face when I shared the news.

Once I left the office, a wave of exhilaration washed over me. I had to share this moment with Armand. I hurried up to his room, knocking on the door with anticipation, but there was no answer. A twinge of disappointment hit me, but I pushed it aside.

Feeling buoyant, I headed to my car, the sun shining down and warming my skin. As I drove home, a smile spread across my face. I replayed the day's events in my mind—the ideas, the energy, and the promise of what was to come.

This was just the beginning, and I couldn't wait to bring Armand into the fold, to show him that even amid the chaos of our lives, we could carve out something beautiful together. The future felt bright, and I was ready to embrace every challenge that lay ahead, no matter how daunting.

I arrived home, the excitement of the day still clinging to my shoulders. I dropped my things by the door and made a beeline for the kitchen, craving a glass of wine to help me unwind. Balancing my regular job, Armand's emotional rollercoaster, and this new project felt like juggling knives, but I was in a good place—a place buzzing with excitement and possibility. I knew I could handle it.

Just as I was pouring my wine, the doorbell rang, interrupting my moment of bliss. I set my glass down and walked over to answer it, still feeling that thrill of the day coursing through me.

"Momma!" I exclaimed, surprised to see her standing there, her serious expression striking a stark contrast to my mood.

She slid past me without a word, her demeanor more intense than I'd ever seen. "What's going on with you?" she asked, her tone sharp and probing, cutting through the air like a knife.

I followed her into the living room, confusion swirling in my chest. "Oh my God, Momma, I have my first private project that's not through my job! I'm so excited. This could be the spark for me to finally work for myself, like I've always wanted!" I said, trying to infuse some joy into the atmosphere, hoping to lighten her mood.

"That's nice, baby, but that's not what I'm talking about," she shot back, her words slicing through my enthusiasm like a hot knife through butter.

"Then what are you talking about, Momma?" I pressed, my brow furrowing as I tried to bridge the gap between us.

Hall Pass

"You're divorcing your husband and out in public with another man—at a cookout where drive-bys are happening," she said, her voice steady but filled with concern that sent a chill down my spine.

"How do you know about that?" I asked, a mix of disbelief and frustration creeping into my voice. The heat of the day's excitement faded, replaced by a knot of anxiety in my stomach.

"I hear things, sweetheart. You think your life is a secret? Your decisions affect more than just you," she replied, her eyes narrowing slightly as she studied me.

I took a deep breath, the weight of her words settling heavily on my shoulders. "It's not like that, Momma. I'm trying to figure things out. It's complicated."

"Complicated?" she echoed, her tone laced with disbelief. "You're risking everything for what? A fling? You need to think about your future, are you thinking about what this could mean for you."

I felt a surge of defensiveness rise within me. "This isn't just a fling! Armand is different. He sees me, the real me."

"Is he worth the trouble?" she asked, her voice softening but still probing.

I hesitated, staring into her eyes. "I don't know yet, but I need to find out. I can't keep living a life that doesn't feel like mine. I have to take risks, Momma."

Her expression softened, and for a moment, I saw the worry ease in her features. "Just be careful, baby. I want you to be happy, but I also want you safe."

I nodded, feeling the weight of her concern wrap around me. "I promise. I'll be careful. But with Armand is the safest I felt in a long time."

But as I said it, I couldn't shake the feeling that my choices were pulling me into uncharted territory—exciting and terrifying all at once.

"I'm your momma I know you and I know what best for you listen to me so you don't make a mistake ," she replied, her eyes locking onto mine like a spotlight, fierce and unyielding.

"Well, you don't know everything especially when it comes to my personal life I am grown enough to make decision based off what I feel is best for me and if it goes wrong I'm grown enough to deal with it , and I asked you yesterday: stay out of it," I snapped back, the heat rising in my chest as anger flared.

"I am your mother, and I will not let my daughter be a hoe. I didn't raise you like that. You fight for your marriage!" she yelled, her voice echoing off the walls, filling the room with tension.

"A hoe, Momma?" I scoffed, incredulous. The word hung in the air like a weight, twisting my stomach.

"Yes, with a man who's just going to break your heart again when he goes back to jail," she spat, her words cutting deeper than I wanted to admit.

"Momma, you don't know what you're talking about! You can't judge Armand by his past," I argued, trying to stay firm, even as doubt began to creep in.

Hall Pass

"You're being fucking stupid," she shot back, her frustration palpable, her voice rising like a wave ready to crash.

"Momma, I think it's time for you to go," I said, my patience wearing thin, the edges of my resolve fraying.

"No, we are going to talk about this. And you're going to talk to me now because your husband is at my house sleeping in my guest room," she declared, her eyes fierce, a storm brewing just beneath the surface.

I took a seat, stunned into silence, just staring at her. "Talk, girl," she demanded, her voice rising, leaving no room for escape.

"You want me to talk, Momma? Here it is: fuck that marriage, fuck Sergio. I'm happy, and I won't change that to go back to hell. If you can't understand that, fuck it, and fuck—"

Before I could finish, Momma slapped the taste out of my mouth, the sharp crack echoing in the room. "If you dare think you were about to say 'fuck me,' you had another thing coming," she said, her voice low and dangerous, a warning laced with authority.

I touched my cheek, the sting igniting both shock and anger within me. "Momma, this isn't fair!" I exclaimed, my voice trembling between defiance and hurt.

"Fair? Life isn't fair, darling," she replied, her tone softening just a fraction, but her eyes remained steely. "But I'm trying to protect you from making a mistake that could cost you everything."

"Everything? You think I'm throwing everything away? I'm trying to live, Momma! I'm trying to find my own happiness!"

She sighed, rubbing her temples as if trying to process the whirlwind of emotions swirling between us. "You think happiness comes from running away? You need to face your problems, not run into the arms of another man."

"Maybe I need to run away from my problems!" I shot back, frustration bubbling over. "Maybe I need to find out who I am without all the baggage!"

"You're not just running from your problems; you're running from your family, from your responsibilities," she countered, her voice rising again, but I could see the worry etching deeper lines on her face.

"I refuse to go back to a life that feels like a prison!" I yelled, the words spilling out before I could hold them back.

Momma's expression softened for a moment, the fierce mother bear giving way to a glimpse of the worried mother beneath. "I just want what's best for you, baby. I don't want to see you hurt."

"I know, Momma," I said, my voice dropping to a whisper. "But I need to live my life for me now, not for anyone else."

The tension hung thick in the air, a palpable energy crackling between us as we stood locked in our emotional storm. I could see the fight in her eyes flicker, wavering just a bit. "Just promise me you'll think before you leap," she said, her voice barely above a whisper, a hint of desperation lacing her words.

"I promise, but I have to leap first." My voice was steady, but inside I was a whirlwind of confusion and anger.

"I'm trying to stop you from making the same mistakes I did," she yelled, her eyes wild, fierce with emotion. "Because when life humbles you, you don't want to come back to your marriage with a baby that's not your husband's."

"What?" The shock washed over me like ice water, freezing my thoughts. The look on her face told me she'd just revealed more than she intended.

"Are you telling me Daddy is not my dad?" I blurted out, the words tumbling from my mouth before I could catch them. I felt ridiculous asking, but the weight of the revelation surged within me.

"I...," she stammered, her voice faltering.

"You what?" I pressed, my heart pounding in my chest, anxiety twisting my insides.

"I never wanted you to find out like this," she said, tears streaming down her face, leaving trails through her carefully applied makeup. Her vulnerability was almost painful to witness.

"You didn't want me to find out like this, or at all? Does he even know?" I demanded, feeling the ground shift beneath me.

"Yes, he knows. And he was there to agree to sign the birth certificate and be your dad despite what I did. He loves you as if you were his blood," she said, her voice trembling, each word a fragile thread connecting us amid the chaos.

"You need to leave," I said, my anger boiling over, hot and fierce.

"Dior," she cried, desperation coloring her tone, as if the weight of her own choices bore down on her.

"Leave!" I yelled, the sound reverberating in the room, shaking the very foundation of our relationship.

Momma stepped closer, reaching for my hand. "Baby, I just don't want you to make the same mistakes I made," she pleaded, her voice thick with emotion.

"I'm not you! Whatever bed I make for myself, I'll deal with it. Now get the fuck out of my house. I have nothing else to say to a person who lied to me all my life. No wonder you and Sergio get along so well—neither of you really loved me." Momma swung this time I caught her arm. We stared at each other.

Each word felt like a dagger, slicing through the silence. I watched her face fall, the realization of the chasm between us widening. This wasn't just a fight; it was a reckoning. The truth hung heavy in the air, and I felt more alone than ever, grappling with a reality that was crumbling around me.

As she turned to leave, I could see the heartbreak etched in her features, but I stood firm. I needed to reclaim my life, my choices—not just for me, but for the future I was desperate to forge, even if it meant stepping into the unknown.

The finality of my words hung in the air, heavy and unyielding. As she stood there, tears pooling in her eyes, I felt a tempest of rage and sorrow churning inside me. This was it. The lines were drawn, and there was no going back.

    Once Momma left, I stormed into the kitchen needing something stronger then wine, I grabbed a bottle of liquor that Sergio had left behind. I poured myself a generous drink, feeling the liquid warmth wash over me as I threw it back in one go. The glass shattered against the wall, sending shards flying as I muttered, "Fuck." My heart raced—how the hell did I end up here? I began to pace, frustration fueling my steps, each one echoing the chaos in my mind.

I wanted to let my emotions take over, to scream and shout, but I had too much at stake now to lose control. Still, I needed to release this pressure building inside me or I was going to crack.

I picked up my phone, dialing Armand's number. "Hey," he answered, his voice a lifeline in my storm.

"I need you to come to my house," I said, urgency threading through my tone.

"You good?" he asked, concern lacing his words.

"Just come over," I insisted, the raw need for his presence spilling out.

"Iight," he replied, and we hung up.

It felt like no time at all before I was opening the door to him. "Fuck me! Don't ask me any questions. I don't want to talk. Just fuck me," I blurted out before he could step fully inside.

When the light from the house hit his face, I noticed the marks and bruises marrying his skin. "What happened to you?" I asked, an alarm creeping into my voice.

"No talking," he said, his voice low and commanding as he scooped me up, carrying me effortlessly to the couch. The air felt electric between us.

He wasted no time, ripping my clothes off with an urgency that matched my own. He slid into me with ease, but every stroke that followed was filled with a forceful, passionate pleasure that made my breath hitch. "Oh my God," I moaned, feeling every inch of him as he claimed me.

I took his hand, placing it on my neck, my heart racing with both desire and defiance. "Choke me," I instructed, my voice a sultry whisper. As he bit down gently on my neck, the thrill of it sent shivers down my spine, drowning out the chaos of my earlier conversation with my mother.

In that moment, I lost myself completely, surrendering to the wild, intoxicating blend of pleasure and pain. "Harder Daddy." Every thrust, every touch pushed me further into a realm where nothing else mattered—just the two of us, lost in the heat of the moment, free from the burdens of the world outside.

SIXTEEN

Armand

That session I had with Dior was exactly what I needed to take the edge off, but let's be real—it was just a temporary fix and now I laid here wide awoke with my mind racing. The way she melted into my embrace, her body relaxing as I carried her gently to her bed, was intoxicating. I couldn't help but lean down and place a soft kiss on her forehead. She didn't even stir. Watching her peaceful face, framed by a cascade of dark curls, I felt an unfamiliar warmth spread through me, a flicker of something I hadn't allowed myself to feel in a long time. But the moment was fleeting. The reality of our chaotic lives crashed over me like a wave, pulling me back from the blissful escape.

As I pulled away from her house, the streets blurring past me, it felt like the last few days had ignited something deep within—something raw and powerful, like a beast clawing to break free. I drove back to the hotel, my mind racing, thoughts spiraling, pacing mentally like I was stuck in a relentless loop. It felt like I was being taken for a joke, and I didn't like it one bit. I needed to regain control, so I headed straight for my suitcase, fumbling through the chaos until I found the cold, hard steel of the gun that I was supposed to get rid of but couldn't. I slipped it into my jacket, the weight pressing against my chest a stark reminder of the darkness that had been creeping in, like shadows swallowing the last light of day.

With fierce determination burning in my eyes, I drove with purpose, anger coursing through my veins like wildfire. The city lights blurred past me, neon reflections dancing in the rearview mirror as I parked around the back of my house. I pulled the hood of my jacket up, shielding my face from the world—anyone who might see the storm brewing inside me wouldn't stand a chance. As I stepped into the familiar surroundings, they felt suffocating—like a cage of memories and regrets pressing down on my chest.

Climbing the stairs, each step creaked in protest, echoing in the stillness around me, my heart pounding so loud I could barely hear anything else. The walls seemed to close in, a claustrophobic reminder of everything that had gone wrong. I knew I had to confront whatever awaited me at the top. This wasn't just about me anymore; it was about protecting what little I had left—a fragile connection with Dior that flickered like a candle in a storm, and the promise of something more if I could navigate the chaos threatening to consume us both.

When I finally opened the door, I was met with a sight that twisted my gut into knots—Shanny and Angel sleeping peacefully in our bed, their faces serene, blissfully unaware of the turmoil brewing just outside their dreams. Anger surged through me like a tidal wave as I approached her. I pulled out the gun, the cold metal pressing against my palm, a chilling reminder of everything that had led me to this moment. Memories flooded back—her lack of love, the constant disrespect, that chaotic outburst at my mother's birthday party that had turned a celebration into a battlefield, the blackmail that had left me feeling trapped and powerless.

My hand tightened around the grip of the gun, the weight of it heavy with dark possibilities. But just as quickly, I released it. The thought of killing Shanny flickered through my mind like a twisted fantasy, something straight out of a noir film, but the reality was far grimmer.

I could killed her and leave the gun right here in Angel's hands as if she did it. But would I be able to live with myself knowing she had driven me that far. Angel rolled over opening her eyes and looking at me. I quickly put a finger over my mouth signally for her to be quiet. The risk of getting caught, the thought of making Dior relive the trauma of my absence—this time, possibly for good—wasn't worth it. I tucked the gun back into my jacket, stepping away from the bed, my heart heavy with the weight of what I was leaving behind.

Once outside, tears streamed down my face, a raw mix of pain, frustration, and anger spilling over like a broken dam, flooding my senses. I was furious about everything swirling around me—about how I had clawed my way back to Dior, only to feel like I was losing ground in every other aspect of my life. It felt like I was running a marathon just to find myself back at the starting line. The victory of getting her back felt bittersweet, overshadowed by the chaos that loomed like dark clouds on the horizon, threatening to unleash a storm I couldn't control.

In that moment, I realized I was standing on the edge of something monumental, teetering between hope and despair. If only I could find a way to balance the shards of my life before they cut me too deep, before the jagged pieces of my reality became unbearable.

Sitting in the car, the engine humming softly, I could hear my momma's voice echoing in my head: "What's more important to you? The good or the bad?" It was a question she'd always posed when we complained about life's burdens. She'd remind us that misery loved company, and if we let the bad overshadow the good, we'd miss out on so much worth holding onto. Those words were like a lifeline, pulling me back from the edge of my spiraling thoughts.

I pulled out my phone, hesitation creeping in as I dialed Ahmad's number, the late hour gnawing at my nerves. I wasn't sure if he'd pick up. "Yo," he answered, his tone instantly alert, cutting through the darkness like a knife.

"Bro, I need you," I said, urgency lacing my voice, each word a plea for support.

"Say less, give me your location," he replied, ready to spring into action, his unwavering loyalty a comfort in the chaos.

Hall Pass

We hung up, and I immediately shared my location with him, knowing that at this moment, I needed my brother by my side. The night felt suffocating, heavy with unresolved tension, but with Ahmad coming, a flicker of hope ignited within me—a small flame in the vast darkness.

He pulled up without hesitation, the headlights cutting through the night as he jumped into the car beside me. "What's going on?" he asked, his brow furrowed with concern, the weight of my turmoil evident on his face. I could see him assessing me, his eyes sharp and searching, as if he could read the storm brewing beneath my skin.

"Everything's a damn mess, man. You know Shanny's still in the picture, and it's just... it's complicated," I admitted, my voice trembling slightly. I could feel the walls closing in again, but having Ahmad there felt like a shield against the chaos.

He nodded, understanding etched in his gaze. "Let's figure it out together. You're not alone in this." His words wrapped around me like a warm blanket, a comforting reminder that even when everything felt like it was crumbling, I had someone solid in my corner, ready to face the storm with me.

"I almost fucked up," I admitted, my voice low and shaky, the weight of my confession hanging heavy between us.

"What'd you do?" he pressed, a hint of alarm creeping into his tone, his concern palpable.

"I was ready to kill Shanny," I confessed, the words spilling out before I could stop them, each syllable tasting bitter on my tongue. "I went in there loaded and ready."

"But you didn't," he replied, the question hanging in the air like a fragile thread, a moment of tense silence wrapping around us.

"No, but I wanted to. She won't let me out of this marriage. And then she shot up Momma's party, and I had all that shit with Armand on my mind." The memories flooded back, each one sharp and jagged, slicing through the fragile calm I'd been trying to maintain.

Ahmad's jaw tightened, the muscle flexing as he processed my words. "So she did that drive-by," he said, anger flickering in his eyes like a spark in dry grass.

"Yeah, because I served her with divorce papers," I replied, the bitterness in my voice palpable, a jagged edge I couldn't quite smooth over.

Hall Pass

He fell silent for a moment, weighing the situation carefully, his brow furrowing deeper with each thought. "Listen, I'm glad you didn't do that shit. It's not you. I don't want to see you behind bars again, especially not over some bitch," he said, his voice firm but laced with brotherly concern. "I know your mind is all over the place right now, but you gotta find some peace and center yourself. If Dior does that for you, so be it. Fuck Armand."

I nodded, feeling the weight of his words sink in, wrapping around my frayed nerves like a lifeline. "I told him that shit he did was fucked up," I added, frustration bubbling back to the surface, the anger simmering just beneath my skin.

"Good," Ahmad said, his tone sharpening with a fierce intensity. "You can't let him think he can walk all over you. You've been through enough, and you deserve better than this mess." His words were like a rallying cry, igniting a spark of defiance within me.

I leaned back against the headrest, letting out a slow breath as the tension in my shoulders began to ease just a bit. With Ahmad beside me, I felt a flicker of hope igniting in the darkness, a small flame that pushed back against the shadows closing in. The road ahead was still murky, filled with uncertainty and potential pitfalls, but at least I wasn't navigating it alone. Together, we'd find a way through this chaos, and maybe—just maybe—I could reclaim the parts of my life that still mattered.

"Yeah, it was. But you can't let that consume you," Ahmad continued, his voice steady and urgent. "You got too much going on to lose your head over this. You got dreams, man. You've got Dior back in your life, and you can't let this chaos drown out the good." His intensity grounded me, like an anchor in a storm.

I took a deep breath, feeling the weight of my worries start to lift. "I know you're right. I just feel so lost sometimes. Like I'm fighting a war on all fronts." The admission hung heavy in the air, a vulnerable crack in my tough exterior.

"Then let's fight it together," he said, his voice steady and reassuring, a balm for my frayed nerves. "You ain't alone in this. I got your back, no matter what." His sincerity wrapped around me, creating a shield against my doubts.

With those words, a wave of relief washed over me. I wasn't in this battle alone, and maybe—just maybe—I could navigate the chaos without losing myself in it.

"Bro, listen, on some real shit: if Dior makes you happy and brings you peace, then so be it. Follow your heart. I can't stop you or make you feel bad for doing that, and no one else can either. I love you." He told me, his voice thick with emotion before pulling me into a brotherly hug that felt like home. It was a reminder that no matter how tangled life got,

I had someone who believed in me, who saw the light flickering within the storm.

As we broke apart, a renewed sense of purpose surged through me. With Ahmad by my side, I felt ready to face whatever chaos lay ahead, armed with the knowledge that I could fight for the life I wanted—one step at a time.

We sat there, sharing thoughts and laughter, the weight of our conversation hanging in the air like an unbreakable bond. Eventually, Ahmad glanced at the time and decided it was time to head home. As he stepped out of the car, I felt a twinge of gratitude for his unwavering support.

I drove around aimlessly for a while, the night wrapping around me like a heavy blanket. I wasn't ready to go back to the hotel, not yet. The thought of being alone with my thoughts felt suffocating. I picked up my phone and dialed a familiar number.

"Hello?" Dior's sleepy voice came through, wrapped in warmth and a hint of confusion.

"Hey, I had to step out while you were sleeping. Can I come back?" I asked, my heart racing at the thought of seeing her again.

"Of course," she replied, her voice soft, and I could almost hear the smile behind it.

With no hesitation, I headed back to Dior's house. When I arrived, she met me at the door, wearing nothing but a loose-fitting T-shirt that barely did justice to her figure. I couldn't help but let a grin break across my face as I stepped inside. Leaning in, I gave her a gentle kiss, feeling the warmth radiate between us. "I love you," I whispered, knowing it was early and fully prepared for the possibility that she might not say it back.

"I love you too," she replied, her gaze locking onto mine with an intensity that sent shivers down my spine. I kissed her again, deeper this time, and as I lifted her effortlessly into my arms, she wrapped her legs around me, holding on tight.

I was grateful that Dior had welcomed me back into her space. Being wrapped up in her presence, I felt a sense of peace I hadn't known in ages. I drifted off to sleep, the rhythm of her breathing beside me a soothing lullaby.

When I woke up, the delicious smell of bacon filled my nose, pulling me from my dreams. I rolled over, but the bed was empty. A hint of disappointment washed over me, but my curiosity quickly took over. Following the mouthwatering aroma, I padded barefoot toward the kitchen.

Hall Pass

As I entered, there was Dior, standing at the stove. I'd seen her in lingerie before, and damn, she was sexy as hell. But this morning, even in her oversized T-shirt and fluffy slippers, there was something breathtakingly beautiful about her. The way the fabric hugged her curves, combined with the casualness of her hair pulled up in a messy bun, had my heart racing and my dick rock hard. She turned, catching me staring, and I could see the hint of a smile playing on her lips, as if she knew exactly what kind of effect she had on me.

"Morning, sleepyhead," she teased, her eyes sparkling with mischief.

"Morning," I replied, unable to hide my grin. "What's for breakfast?"

"Just the best damn bacon you'll ever taste," she shot back playfully, and I couldn't help but chuckle. In that moment, everything felt right—like the chaos of the past was finally melting away, leaving only this delicious morning together.

"Hey, bae," she said, her smile brightening the room as she turned around and caught me admiring her. "Hey," I replied, my voice low, feeling the heat rise in my cheeks. As she moved closer, I could tell she wasn't wearing anything underneath that T-shirt, and her hard nipples were a tempting distraction. I felt my dick rising to attention, the air thick with unspoken desire.

"Ready to eat?" she asked, her eyes sparkling with mischief before she leaned in to give me a soft kiss.

"Yeah, but first let me..." I murmured, my hands instinctively lifting her onto the kitchen counter. With a playful tug, I lifted her T-shirt, rubbing my fingers across her pussy. The instant contact sent a shiver through her, and a smile spread across my face at the sound of her soft moans—music to my ears.

In one fluid motion, I snatched the T-shirt off her, laying her back on the counter. I tasted her sweet juices, savoring every moment as I massaged her nipples, my fingers working their magic. I didn't stop until her legs were shaking, and my craving for her was finally fulfilled.

Once she regrouped, I helped her down from the counter with a smirk plastered on my face. She slipped into her clothes, but the playful tension still hung in the air. I went to wash my face, splash some water on it to clear my head, and when I returned, I found her busy fixing plates for both of us. I had to admit, Dior cooked just as well as her momma—maybe even better.

As we sat down at the table, I couldn't shake the feeling that something was different about her. Even last night when I arrived, there had been an underlying tension, but I couldn't quite pinpoint what it was. Finally, she broke the silence that hung thick between us. "So, I was thinking, instead of wasting money staying at a hotel, you can stay here with me."

"Is that so?" I asked, raising an eyebrow.

"Yeah, I mean, I like having you around. I know we're not technically in a relationship, but…" She trailed off, her gaze flickering with uncertainty.

"Do you want to be in a relationship with me?" I asked, cutting straight to the heart of it.

"Well, I figured because of my situation…"

"That wasn't what I asked you," I replied, my tone firm but gentle.

"Yeah," she answered, a playful smile breaking across her face.

"Okay, then that's what we are," I said, returning my focus to my plate, feeling a sense of relief wash over me.

"But what about—" she started, but I stopped her mid-sentence.

"I told you I love you, and I meant that. I love you, Dior. I'm in love with you. I don't give two fucks about that nigga who had you. I'm here now to reclaim what was mine from the jump. That's why he didn't know what to do with you. So like you told me yourself, fuck that nigga. Plus, I told you once I put my dick in you, you were mine. And I've been fucking you raw," I said, my voice low and serious.

"Yeah, we gotta stop that too before there's a little us running around here," she shot back, a hint of laughter dancing in her tone, her eyes sparkling with mischief.

"That's the point, I mean you was calling me daddy so I figured you were ready to be a mom" I replied with a wink, watching a smile bloom on her face like a flower in the sun. The playful banter felt like a promise of what was to come, a shared moment that pulled us closer together. I couldn't help but feel that maybe, just maybe, we were on the right path, carving out our own little world amidst the chaos.

But as the laughter died down, silence settled in, and I seized the opportunity to dig deeper. "So why didn't you tell me about Armani?" I asked, my tone shifting to something more serious.

"Huh? What about Armani?" she asked, confusion clouding her features.

"Why didn't you tell me that Armani pressed up on you while I was locked up? And then again at my momma's party, when he tried you?" My voice was steady, but beneath the surface, I felt a mix of anger and concern brewing.

Dior put her fork down, her expression turning serious as she met my gaze. "I didn't want to cause any issues. I handled it and figured it was over."

"You're never causing an issue by telling me what's going on or when someone's trying you. I will burn this damn city down to the ground for you and over you. Know and believe that," I told her, my voice firm, conviction pouring from my heart.

"But he's your brother. I didn't want you to think I'm lying on him," she replied, her brow furrowed in concern.

"Have you ever lied to me before?" I asked, searching her eyes for sincerity.

"No."

"Exactly. I'm not going to think you're lying because it's my fucking brother. Blood doesn't make you loyal, and he showed that. He learned how unloyal motherfuckers get handled." The heat in my voice was palpable.

"How do you know what happened?" she asked, her curiosity piqued.

"I heard y'all at mom's house, and then me and him had a conversation," I said, the memories flooding back.

"Is that where the marks and bruises came from?" she inquired, her voice laced with concern.

"Yeah, but I'm fine," I reassured her, even though the memory still stung.

We finished breakfast, the tension lingering in the air as we headed back upstairs. I sat on the edge of the bed while she got dressed, my eyes glued to her. I couldn't help but admire her, the way she moved with a grace that made my heart race. She was officially all mine, and that thought filled me with a sense of pride.

"So, are you going to bring your stuff over?" she asked, glancing back at me with a hopeful smile.

Hall Pass

"Yeah, baby, I'll bring it before I head to the restaurant," I replied, feeling a warmth spread through me at the thought of making her place my own.

"Okay, well, I'll leave the spare key for you. I'm not sure if I'll be in the office or hotel today?" she said, a bright smile lighting up her face, making the morning light dance around her.

"How's the hotel going?" I asked, genuinely curious.

"Good, just waiting for that first payment to be wired to me," she said, her excitement palpable.

"You haven't been paid?" I asked, a sinking feeling hitting me as I realized Shanny had probably pocketed that check.

"No, not yet, but they said it will be wired to me." She shrugged it off, but I could see the worry hidden behind her smile. I took a mental note, trying not to show any expression, though my gut churned.

"Dior, baby. I need to tell—"

"Baby, can we talk about it a little later? That session we had got me running late. I gotta go. I love you," she interrupted, her voice soft but firm.

"Yeah, that's fine," I said, wanting to get it off my chest about Shanny but knowing I needed to respect her time. As she rushed out, I felt the weight of my unspoken words heavy on my shoulders, but for now, I'd let it go. There would be time later to unravel this mess. For now, I just wanted to hold onto the promise of us.

SEVENTEEN

Dior

I drove to work feeling joyful, the morning sun spilling golden light across the city streets. But that bliss was quickly snatched away when my phone started to ring, and I saw my momma's name flashing on the screen. "Not today," I muttered, attempting to ignore the call, but somehow I accidentally answered it.

"Dior," she called out, her voice a mix of urgency and not being sure if I was there .

"Mother," I replied, cursing myself inwardly for picking up. "I really don't have time for this."

"Baby, I just want to talk to you and explain," she said, her tone softening.

"Momma, respectfully, I don't want my day ruined. I'm heading into work, and I can't carry this with me." I felt the knot in my stomach tighten as I spoke.

"The sooner we talk about this, the better," she insisted, her voice steady.

"In order for the conversation to work, we both have to be ready, and right now, I'm not. I can't be sure of what I might say to you based on what you tell me." The silence that followed was deafening, stretching into uncomfortable territory.

"Dior, I love you. How I made you was a mistake, but you were never a mistake," she finally said.

I felt tears prick at the corners of my eyes, but I refused to let my day spiral down that path. "Momma, I've got to go. I'm pulling up for work," I said, my voice firm as I maneuvered into a parking spot.

I hung up and exhaled deeply, trying to shake off the weight of the conversation. Regrouping was essential; I had too much riding on me being at my best to let her drag me off track. I took a moment, reminding myself of the progress I'd made, the new chapter I was writing.

Hall Pass

As I stepped out of the car, the click of my heels echoed against the pavement, a steady rhythm that grounded me. Just as I started to walk toward the entrance, I heard a voice behind me.

"Dior!"

I spun around to see Sergio standing there, his hands shoved deep into his pockets, a mix of hope and desperation etched on his face. "What are you doing here?" I asked, annoyance creeping into my tone.

"I just want to talk to you," he said, his gaze searching mine.

"But I don't want to talk to you. That's why I didn't answer your texts and calls," I shot back, irritation bubbling at the surface.

"You're looking amazing. You're glowing," he said, clearly ignoring my words, his eyes roaming over me like I was a mirage.

"That's what change will do for you," I replied sharply, crossing my arms as I stared him down.

"I've really been missing you, and I love you," he declared, his voice earnest.

I couldn't help but laugh, a harsh sound that sliced through the air. "Now you love me? Where was that love when I needed a husband? Where was that love when I needed someone who protected and provided for me? Where was that love when I needed a husband who supported and pushed my dreams?" My heart raced as I let it all out, each word laced with the pain of my past.

"I fucked up," he admitted, his expression turning serious. "I was fucked up, and I see that now. But I'm ready to be better. I'm ready to be everything you need and more."

"Is that so?" I replied, raising an eyebrow. "You think it's that simple? You think you can just waltz back into my life and rewrite the script?"

He stepped closer, his eyes pleading. "I know I can't change the past, but I can change the future. Just give me a chance. I've changed, Dior."

I took a deep breath, my emotions swirling. It was easy to get lost in the memories of what once was, the man I had fallen in love with. But I couldn't ignore the years of hurt that lay between us like a chasm.

Hall Pass

"I don't know if I can trust you again, Sergio," I said finally, my voice softer but resolute. "You broke my heart once. What's to stop you from doing it again?"

He opened his mouth to respond, but I raised a hand. "I need time. I need to figure things out for myself first. Right now, I'm focused on my life, my goals, and my happiness." turning to walk away. "I want to be apart of that. He called out.

"The only issue is that doesn't work for me," I called over my shoulder, my voice steady and clear, echoing off the walls. "I told you I was going to see what else is out there for me, and if I decide to come back, it'll be on my terms. But right now, it's looking like I'm not coming back because I've messed around and found out that what you made seem like a big deal or a bother, another man will do times two." I locked eyes with him, standing my ground like a warrior ready for battle.

"Are you talking about the nigga your momma told me about?" Sergio shot back, his tone dripping with disdain. I rolled my eyes, a mix of irritation and amusement bubbling inside me. "Maybe," I replied, crossing my arms defiantly.

He stepped closer, his expression hardening. "I just feel like your mother is right. You don't want to keep playing with fire because I'm not taking you back if you get pregnant. I heard about this nigga. He's been to jail. What are you going to do when he goes back?" His voice was laced with a condescending edge, like he was trying to play the concerned husband.

"I don't give a damn what you heard, Sergio. Jail or not, you're not even half the man that he is. So fuck you and whatever my momma told you. I'm good. We're good. You can expect the divorce papers soon," I spat, my words sharp and unyielding.

"Dior, I'm giving you this hall pass, but you are still my wife and will remain my wife. No matter what I have to do," he said, his voice dropping to a husky whisper as he rubbed his hand across my cheek, sending a chill down my spine.

I jerked away from his touch, my skin prickling with discomfort. "Don't you dare touch me," I hissed, my heart racing from the mix of anger and betrayal. I waited until he had turned away, his figure receding into the distance, before I walked into work, my mind a whirlpool of emotions.

With that, I turned away, my heart pounding in my chest like a drum in a parade. I had to keep moving forward, even if the past was clawing at my heels, trying to drag me back into its shadows. The entrance to the building loomed ahead, a glass door that felt like a gateway to my future. I was determined to leave Sergio behind—at least for today. As the door swung shut behind me, sealing off the memories and the chaos, a flicker of resolve ignited within me. I was ready to embrace whatever lay ahead, shedding the weight of yesterday like an old skin.

The fluorescent lights buzzed overhead in my office, casting a sterile glow that felt at odds with the storm brewing within me. I closed the door behind me, the click echoing like a gunshot in the silence. Sinking into the plush chair, I pressed my phone to my ear, needing to reach out to someone who understood the turmoil I was feeling. Destiny's familiar voice was a lifeline amidst the chaos.

"Hey, girl," she said, her tone bright but instantly shifting when she sensed my mood.

"Hey, Destiny," I replied, my voice wavering. "You won't believe the morning I've had."

"Tell me everything," she urged, the concern in her voice wrapping around me like a warm blanket. I took a deep breath, ready to spill it all—the confrontation, the truth, and the emotional rollercoaster that had pulled me in every direction. I needed to lay it all out, to find some clarity in the mess that was my life.

As I began to recount the morning's events, the weight on my shoulders slowly started to lift, piece by piece. I could feel the storm inside me begin to calm, and with every word, I was inching closer to reclaiming my narrative—the life I was determined to build without the shadows of my past looming overhead.

"You got a minute?" I asked, letting out a shaky exhale. All the tears I had been fighting, the ones I had been holding in, came rolling down my face like a sudden downpour.

"Of course," she replied, her voice laced with genuine concern.

I took a deep breath, trying to steady myself, and began to tell her about last night—the bombshell my mother had dropped on me. "So, my mom told me something that turned my whole world upside down."

"Are you serious right now?" she exclaimed, disbelief crackling through the phone line. "So, your entire life has been a lie? How the hell could your mom not tell you this? And your dad—damn, how could he hold that secret? He's a strong man, raising another man's child and loving you like his own. It's wild to think you could grow up not knowing you're not his."

I ran a hand through my hair, the weight of the revelation pressing down on me like a heavy fog that wouldn't lift. "It's not just that. My mother—she always told me my dad was my dad. And now, with Armand back in the picture and everything falling apart, she finally comes clean. My dad raised me, loved me unconditionally, but I'm not even his biological daughter." I felt tears prick at the corners of my eyes, but I blinked them away. "I don't know who I am anymore. It feels like I'm stuck in a world where I'm constantly rediscovering myself."

"Dior, that's... that's a lot to process." Her voice softened, understanding washing over her words. "How could she keep that from you for so long?"

"Because she's terrified of the truth," I sighed, my voice trembling with the weight of it all. "She didn't want to shatter the life we had built together. She would have probably taken this secret to her grave, pretending to be the perfect mother and wife. But now, how do I look at that man the same way? It's like I'm staring at a stranger in the mirror, and I don't recognize the reflection anymore."

A silence stretched between us, thick with unspoken fears and uncertainties that hung in the air like a storm cloud. My heart pounded in my chest, each beat a reminder of the jagged edges of my reality, the pieces of my life that felt so hopelessly out of place.

"Your dad is still your dad—he raised you, he loved you. That counts for something, doesn't it? The one that donated sperm to make you doesn't even fucking matter," Destiny said, her voice cutting through the heaviness.

I took a deep breath, trying to anchor myself in the reality of the love I'd received my whole life from a man who didn't have to give it to me. "I guess. But it's just so overwhelming. And on top of that..." I hesitated, glancing at the office door, making sure no one was eavesdropping. "I'm with Armand now."

Destiny gasped. "Wait, wait a damn minute. The Armand? Your first love? The one from that restaurant? Mr. Smooth Himself?"

"Yeah," I admitted, feeling my cheeks flush with a mix of nostalgia and guilt. "We're moving in together. He's moving out of the hotel and into my house."

"Wow. That's huge! You don't think you're moving a little quick?" she asked, her brow furrowing with concern.

"No, I love him and he loves me. What's understood doesn't need explaining to anyone else," I told her, trying to sound more certain than I felt.

"Yeah, but what do you really know about this man now? I don't want you falling in love with the person he used to be while ignoring who he is now. You're moving him into your house straight from a hotel. Why doesn't he have his own place? Does he have bitches hiding out in the cuts? Because if I find out you're getting played, I swear I'll slap a hoe over my best friend. And what's his money situation like? You don't need to be taking care of another grown man. If that's the case, you might as well stay with Sergio," she said, her voice a mix of concern and protective instinct.

"I know he's not the little boy he was when he got locked up. I know that when I'm with him, I feel protected. He provides for me in a way that money can't. He makes it okay for me to be a woman, to not have to be strong all the time or the 'I got this' type. He listens to me, sees me in ways that Sergio never did."

Destiny paused, her expression softening. "I just want you to be careful, Dior. Love can be beautiful, but it can also blind you to the truth. Armand might be different now, but it's a big leap from hotel life to sharing a space. Just promise me you'll keep your eyes wide open."

"I promise," I said, feeling a flicker of warmth in my chest. "But I really believe in him. He's showing up for me in the way I asked For and I can't ignore that."

Destiny sighed, half-exasperated, half-supportive. "Okay, okay. Just be smart about it. If he messes up, I'll be right here, ready to knock some sense into you both."

We both chuckled, the tension easing just a bit, but deep down, I knew this was only the beginning of a complicated journey—one that would test not just my heart but my sense of self as well.

"Okay, friend. I get it, and I love that for you. If you feel this is right, I'm riding it out with you. But… what about Sergio?"

My stomach knotted at the mention of his name, the memory of our last conversation replaying in my mind like a bad mixtape. "He showed up at my office today, in the garage of all places. Can you believe that? He's trying to win me back. Well, shit, I don't even know if I can say 'win me back' because the things he said felt more like a threat than a plea."

"Ugh, that's so typical Sergio. Did you tell Armand?" Destiny replied, disgust coloring her tone like a splash of paint on a white canvas. "He thinks he can just waltz back into your life after everything he's done? You deserve way better than that. If Armand is giving you what you need, then fuck Sergio. You deserve someone who respects you. This is the happiest I've seen you in ages, and girl, you're glowing."

"I know, I know. But it's complicated. I'm still married, even if it's falling apart at the seams. I never thought I'd be in this position, juggling my past and my present like some twisted circus act. But somehow, I fell in love. I tried to fight it, but I can't— I love Armand. I want to divorce Sergio, and Armand is willing to stand by me through it all." My voice cracked, the turmoil spilling over like a shaken soda can.

"Okay, you need to breathe," Destiny said, her tone shifting to a more soothing rhythm, like a gentle tide coming in. "What you really need is a break. Seriously, maybe you should take a vacation. Get away from this mess and clear your head. Just you, somewhere beautiful."

I considered it, the thought of sun-soaked beaches or tranquil mountain retreats a tempting escape from the chaos swirling around me. "I don't know. It sounds good, but I can't just run away from everything."

"Sometimes running away is the best way to find yourself again and figure out how to handle it all," Destiny insisted, her eyes sparkling with conviction. "You can't keep navigating this storm the way you are. Get some perspective. And hey, you could invite Armand, right?"

"Yeah, because nothing screams 'let's figure out our complicated lives' like a romantic getaway," I said, half-joking, half-serious, a wry smile creeping onto my lips.

"Exactly! You need that space, that clarity. And if Armand's willing to step up now, why not see where it goes? You could explore your feelings without the weight of everything else pressing down on you. Plus, you deserve some joy amidst all this mess."

I felt a flicker of hope at Destiny's words, like a small flame igniting in the darkness of my uncertainty. Maybe a break was exactly what I needed—time to breathe, reflect, and finally see what my heart truly wanted without the relentless noise of my past drowning it out. As I considered the possibilities, a surge of determination rose within me. It was time to take control of my life, one way or another.

I leaned back in my chair, letting my mind race through the options. The idea of going somewhere alone with Armand was tempting—maybe a secluded beach or a cozy cabin where we could really connect. "I'll think about it. I just… I need to figure out what I want first," I replied, my voice steady despite the whirlwind inside.

"Good," Destiny said, her tone warm and encouraging. "And remember, no matter what, you're not alone. I'm here for you."

As the conversation wrapped up, I hung up and stared out the window, my gaze drawn to the sprawling city skyline beneath me. The weight of my decisions felt heavier than ever, but Destiny's words lingered in my mind like a soothing balm. Maybe a break was exactly what I needed—a chance to breathe, to think, to reclaim myself amidst the chaos of my life.

With newfound resolve, I opened my laptop and started searching for ideas for a potential getaway. My heart raced at the thought of rediscovery. I didn't just want to escape; I wanted to carve a path forward, to navigate the tangled web of my heart and mind, and emerge whole on the other side.

Scrolling through my feed, I stumbled upon a Facebook post about a huge festival coming to ATL. My pulse quickened as I read the lineup—Nas, Ne-Yo, Chingy, Mary J. Blige, Usher, Lyfe Jennings, and so many more artists I loved. The thought of immersing myself in music, surrounded by vibrant energy and the rhythm of life, felt like exactly what I needed.

As I determined if I could swing the trip on such short notice, my phone chimed, breaking my concentration. I picked it up and saw it was a notification from PayPal. The hotel had finally processed my payment and, to my surprise, had given me twice what I had originally asked for. A rush of excitement shot through me—I took that as a sign.

"Okay, universe," I whispered to myself, a smile creeping onto my face. "You want me to take this leap, huh?"

I quickly started securing the trip, my fingers flying across the keyboard as I booked the hotel and snagged tickets for the festival. Each click felt like a step toward reclaiming my freedom, an affirmation that I was ready to embrace the unknown.

Breanna J

With every detail falling into place, I could almost hear the distant sound of music calling my name. This wasn't just about a getaway; it was about opening a door to new possibilities, rediscovering who I was, and maybe—just maybe—finding a deeper connection with Armand along the way. I was ready to dive into this adventure, to face whatever came next head-on.

My excitement bubbled over, and I quickly dialed Armand's number. "Hey, boo," he answered, his voice wrapping around me like a warm embrace.

"Hey, baby! So, I know it's last minute, but there's a big music festival going on in ATL this weekend. I was thinking we should go as a getaway for both of us. I really could use it. Plus, I know you love Nas, and he's performing. I already paid for everything—you just have to show up," I said, trying to keep my tone light, avoiding any hint of pressure.

"Well, if you paid already, let's do it! But what's going on that you're trying to run from?" he asked, his voice shifting to a more serious tone. I sighed, the weight of my thoughts pressing down on me.

"Dior, talk to me," he urged, concern threading through his words.

"There's some stuff going on with my mom that I'm not

Hall Pass

really ready to discuss yet. But then Sergio showed up at my job today—he cornered me in the parking garage, and it made me really uncomfortable."

"Are you okay?" he asked, his protective instinct flaring.

"Yeah, it's just some of the stuff he said," I explained, my heart racing as I recalled the encounter.

"What did he say?" Armand's voice was laced with tension, and I could hear the anger simmering beneath the surface.

"Nothing for you to worry about," I tried to brush it off.

"Tell me, Dior," he insisted, and I could feel the heat radiating from him.

"Just that he was giving me a hall pass, but I am still his wife and will remain his wife. No matter what he has to do," I said, my voice barely above a whisper.

"Oh, that's what he said? Okay, bet," Armand replied, the intensity in his voice unmistakable.

"Armand, don't worry about it. Sergio's just talking, and it doesn't matter. It's just me and you now. Let's go on this trip and enjoy ourselves without worrying about anything else," I said, trying to soothe the storm brewing in his chest.

"Okay. What time are we leaving?" he asked, his curiosity piqued.

"There's an 8 AM flight on Friday. We'll make it in time to see Monica and Jasmine Sullivan perform that night," I said, excitement bubbling up again.

"Alright, babe. Once I get all my stuff to the house tonight, I'll start packing," he said, and I could feel the anticipation radiating through the phone.

"Alright, baby! I'm so excited. I love you," I said, my heart swelling.

"I love you too, and I'll see you later," he replied before we hung up, leaving me with a warm glow of anticipation.

As I set my phone down, the reality of our trip began to sink in. This wasn't just a break; it was a chance to create new memories, to dance freely beneath the stars, and to explore the depths of my connection with Armand. The festival wasn't just a backdrop; it was a promise of adventure and the potential for something beautiful.

EIGHTEEN

Armand

I hung up, and although I had told Dior I'd drop the issue with Sergio pulling up on her at work, it didn't sit well with me. Now that I was officially in the picture and wasn't going anywhere, it was time for him to know and respect that. After what I'd done to him last time, I wasn't sure how he was moving or if he was even protecting himself. So, I called Ahmad.

"Yo," he answered, his voice casual but alert.

"Ay, you want to make a move with me?" I asked, my tone serious.

"I got you," he said, sounding ready for whatever was coming. We hung up, and I sent him my location.

Hall Pass

When he pulled up, I instantly regretted calling him. Armani stepped out of the car with him, looking more sheepish than I'd ever seen him. "Listen, before you get mad, the nigga knows he fucked up and wants to apologize," Ahmad said as they approached.

"Nah, I'm good. He can go," I replied, my irritation flaring.

"He's your fucking brother," Ahmad shot back, frustration creeping into his voice.

"And that didn't matter to him when he crossed me," I snapped, my anger boiling over.

"Armand, what I did was fucked up. I'm sorry. I never wanted to hurt you," Armani said, his voice low and heavy with regret. I just looked at him, my expression hard as stone.

"Armand," Ahmad called out, trying to mediate the tension.

"Iight, heard you. You can leave now," I said, my voice cold.

"Nigga," Armani muttered, running a hand through his hair. "Just because you said a wack-ass sorry doesn't fix shit. You dogged me and crossed me. That's not brother shit. I love you, but I'ma love you from a distance."

"But I—"

Ahmad stepped in, trying to keep the peace. "Armani, he heard you. But you can't force anything. You have to respect how he feels based on what you did." Armani nodded, slowly absorbing the truth in Ahmad's words.

"Man, I'ma make this shit up to you," Armani said, his voice cracking slightly.

"Yeah, well for now, leave," I said, my tone final.

"Armani, just go," Ahmad added, handing him his keys as if to emphasize the point.

As we watched Armani leave, Ahmad turned to look at me, concern etched on his face. "What's going on?"

"That nigga Sergio pulled up on Dior at her job, had her uncomfortable and everything. I want to go see him. I

Hall Pass

already made some calls, and I know he's back at work," I explained, my jaw clenched.

Ahmad gave me a skeptical look but followed me to my car, the tension thick in the air between us.

The sun hung low in the sky, casting long shadows on the pavement as I gripped the steering wheel, anger simmering just beneath the surface. Next to me, Ahmad leaned back in his seat, arms crossed, a storm of anticipation brewing in his eyes.

"Man, you sure about this?" he asked, his voice low and cautious.

"Yeah, I need to handle this," I replied, my voice steady. "I can't let him think he can just run up on her like that. Not now. Not ever."

"Just remember, this isn't just about you. It's about her too," Ahmad reminded me, his tone sharp but caring.

"I know. That's why I have to do this," I said, determination coursing through me like electricity. I started the engine, the rumble echoing in the tightening silence of the car. Whatever happened next, I was ready to face it head-on.

"Are you sure about this?" Ahmad asked, his voice steady but laced with concern. "Confronting Sergio could escalate things, and you don't want that."

My jaw tightened as I imagined the image of Dior's husband, Sergio, waiting in the garage, a smug look plastered on his face as if he owned the damn place. "I'm not going to let him think he can just pop up on her like that. She deserves better than that bullshit."

"Yeah, but you also don't want to put Dior in the middle of this," Ahmad warned, his eyes serious. "She's already dealing with a lot right now."

"I know," I replied, my determination etching deeper lines into my features. "But that's exactly why I need to step up. I'm not letting some guy who's been half playing the husband act think he can still mess with her head. Not anymore."

Ahmad sighed, knowing his brother's heart was in the right place, even if his approach was reckless. "Okay, but let's keep it civil. We're not here to start a fight."

As they pulled into the parking lot of Sergio's workplace, I spotted Sergio leaning against his car, arms crossed, the casual arrogance radiating from him as he scrolled through his phone. The sight ignited a fierce protectiveness within me, the kind that made my blood boil. I parked and turned the car off. I reached over and pulled the gun from the glove box. Then turned to Ahmad. "Let's go." "Nigga why you still got that shit."

I said nothing but tucked it in my pants.

We stepped out into the late afternoon sun, the breeze ruffling our shirts as we made our way toward Sergio. The tension in the air thickened with each step, anticipation crackling like static electricity. When Sergio finally glanced up, his expression shifted from indifference to irritation, recognizing the two brothers approaching.

"What do you want?" His tone was curt, his posture defensive, as if he could dismiss us with a mere wave of his hand.

I took a step forward, my eyes narrowing, the fire in my gut burning hotter. "We need to talk."

"Do I know you?" Sergio shot back.

"I'm sure you know of me, so hear me clearly: don't show up at Dior's job or anywhere else."

Sergio straightened, his casual arrogance faltering. "I don't have anything to say to you, man. This is between me and Dior."

"Not anymore," I replied, my voice low and steady, each word laced with authority.

"You can't just roll up on her and act like she doesn't have a choice in this. You don't get to break her heart, mess with her head, and then pretend you're still in control."

Ahmad stepped in, trying to keep the peace. "Look, Sergio, we're not here to fight. We just want to ensure you understand the boundaries. Dior's not some pawn in your game."

Sergio scoffed, his bravado returning. "You think you can come here and dictate how I handle my marriage? You don't know what the hell you're talking about."

"I know enough," I replied, my voice steady as a rock. "I know you don't get to scare her or corner her at her job. You think this is some kind of power play? You're wrong. It ends now. I'm here, and she's mine. I will do whatever it takes to protect her."

Hall Pass

The tension hung thick in the air, narrowing the world down to just the three of us, each man standing firm in his conviction. I could feel Ahmad's presence beside me, a steadying force, but right now, it was all about making sure Sergio understood the stakes.

"Back off, Sergio. Let her breathe," Ahmad added, his voice calm but firm, like a steady anchor in a storm.

Sergio's eyes flickered with anger, but beneath it lay a hint of uncertainty. "You don't know what you're getting into," he warned, his bravado wavering. But I wasn't backing down. Not now. Not ever.

Sergio smirked, clearly unfazed by the confrontation. "And who are you to tell me what to do? You think you have any claim on Dior?" His voice dripped with condescension, as if dismissing me were as easy as swatting a fly.

"Dior is my girl now," I shot back, my voice steady but charged with intensity. "You may think you can just pop in and out of her life, but you're not going to disrespect our relationship."

Sergio laughed, a harsh sound that sliced through the tension. "You think this is some kind of game? You're just a rebound, man. She'll come back to me."

"No, she won't," Ahmad interjected, stepping closer, shoulder to shoulder with me. "Dior deserves someone who respects her, not someone who thinks he can manipulate her emotions like a puppet."

Sergio's demeanor shifted, laughter fading as he stepped closer, eyes narrowing. "You really think you can swoop in and play the knight in shining armor? She's still my wife, no matter what's going on between you two." His voice dripped with contempt, as if the very idea of my involvement with Dior was laughable.

I clenched my fists, feeling the fire rise within me, the heat of protectiveness igniting my resolve. "She's not your possession, Sergio. You've treated her like a stranger while you've been busy living your own life. You're lucky she hasn't cut you out completely."

Sergio's expression hardened, but for a moment, a flicker of uncertainty crossed his features. "You think you know her better than I do? You don't know the half of what we've been through." His voice dropped, bravado cracking just a bit.

"Maybe not," I replied, my voice low and deliberate. "But I know she deserves better than this. You need to back off. For good."

Hall Pass

"And if I don't?" Sergio challenged.

I eased my hand to my shirt, revealing my gun.

Sergio's eyes darted from the gun to me, and a tense silence hung between us, thick with unspoken words and unresolved emotions.

Ahmad glanced at me, gauging the situation, while Sergio weighed his options, his mind racing.

"Fine," he finally said, begrudgingly. The fight was draining from him. "But don't think this changes anything. She'll realize she made a mistake." Desperation laced his voice, revealing cracks in his facade.

"I'm betting on the opposite," I shot back, holding Sergio's gaze with fierce intensity. "She's finally free to choose what's best for her, and that's me. So you better stay out of her way." The words hung in the air, heavy with the promise of unwavering commitment.

As Sergio turned to leave, I felt a weight lift slightly from my shoulders. He knew this wasn't over, but I had made my point. I wasn't just some guy in the background anymore; I was ready to stand up for Dior, ready to fight for her happiness.

Ahmad clapped a hand on my shoulder, grounding me. "You did good, bro. But let's keep our heads cool moving forward. We don't want to give him any more fuel."

I nodded, my heart still pounding, but a sense of clarity settling in. "I just want to make sure she's safe. She deserves so much more than he's given her."

As we walked back to the car, the sun dipped lower in the sky, casting a warm glow around us—a golden reminder that even in the darkest moments, there was still light ahead. And for me, that light was Dior.

As I turned to leave, a surge of adrenaline mixed with relief flooded through me. I had stood my ground, made it clear that I wouldn't let Sergio disrupt the fragile peace we were trying to build. Ahmad followed closely, our footsteps echoing sharply in the parking lot, like a drumbeat marking our moment of victory.

"You alright?" Ahmad asked, concern etched on his face, his brow furrowed as he surveyed me.

"Yeah, thanks for having my back and defending Dior," I replied, exhaling slowly as the weight of the confrontation began to lift.

Hall Pass

"If you're this serious about her, then that's it. I'll defend her to the grave," he said. "Thanks, bro. I just needed him to know I'm not backing down." The conviction in his voice was palpable, a testament to the resolve swelling within him.

"Good. But let's keep an eye on him. He's not the type to take this lightly," Ahmad warned, glancing over his shoulder as if expecting Sergio to rush back at us.

As we climbed into the car, the leather seats cool against our skin, I couldn't shake the feeling that this was just the beginning. I focused on the road ahead, determination settling in my chest like armor. I was ready to fight for Dior, ready to show her that this time, things would be different. No more shadows from the past—only a future I was determined to build with her.

The engine roared to life, and as we pulled out of the parking lot, I felt the weight of the world lifting, if only a little. I turned to Ahmad, who was still watching me closely. "You think I did the right thing?"

"Hell yeah," Ahmad replied, a grin spreading across his face. "You showed him you're not afraid. That's exactly what she needs right now."

I nodded, a flicker of hope igniting within me. "I just want her to feel safe, to know that I've got her back. She deserves better than what Sergio gave her."

"Just remember, man, this battle isn't over. You'll have to stay vigilant. But you're not in this alone." Ahmad's voice held reassuring weight, a reminder that we were a team.

As we drove through the city, the skyline illuminated by the setting sun, gratitude swelled within me for my brother. I wasn't just fighting for Dior; I was also fighting for myself—a chance to redefine my future.

With every mile that passed, my resolve grew stronger. I would be the one to show Dior what true love looked like— no games, no manipulation, just raw, honest connection. As the evening sky painted the horizon in hues of orange and pink, fierce determination surged within me. I would do whatever it took to protect the light that was Dior.

Just as we pulled out of the parking lot, Ahmad began to talk, his voice lively with plans for the upcoming festival. Suddenly, our conversation shattered as another car barreled into us at high speed. The impact slammed my head against the steering wheel, a shock of pain reverberating through my skull. For a moment, everything blurred, the world fading into a ringing silence.

Hall Pass

When I finally managed to pull myself together, adrenaline kicked in. I quickly turned to check on Ahmad. "You good?" I rasped, my voice strained.

"Yeah, I think so," Ahmad groaned, rubbing his head as we both climbed out of the car, still dazed. The scene around us was chaotic, bystanders gathering with expressions of concern and curiosity.

Then, a woman emerged from the other car, fury etched on her face. "You really going to keep playing with me, Armand?" she screamed, her voice sharp and accusatory.

I recognized her instantly. Shanny, my estranged wife, stormed toward me like a whirlwind. "Did you really do what I think you did last night? You came into my house and were going to try to kill me?"

"Next time, make sure I'm fully asleep and wipe the scent of that other woman off you!" she shouted, her eyes blazing with anger.

I tried to feign confusion. "What other woman are you talking about?"

"The same one you have working at the hotel! I caught a whiff of her perfume when I saw her in your office that day, and then when you came home last night, it was all over you!" The venom in her voice was palpable, each word a dagger aimed at my heart.

"Shanny, this isn't the time or place! People are watching us," I snapped, frustration boiling over. "This is childish and stupid. Why would you do this, especially in broad daylight? Get in your car and leave now!"

Ahmad growled, trying to diffuse the tension crackling in the air.

I looked at Shanny, and she shot me a look filled with hatred, hurt, and a tangle of other emotions. "This isn't over, dear husband," she spat, her tone dripping with sarcasm.

"Sign the damn divorce papers," I shot back, my voice steady despite the chaos.

As she walked toward her car, she called back one last time, "I'm not signing anything. I vowed 'til death do us part. I might be the one to send you to your death."

Her words hung in the air, heavy and foreboding. A chill ran down my spine, a sense of impending doom mixing with the adrenaline still coursing through me. As Shanny climbed into her car, I knew this confrontation was far from over. She had made it clear she wasn't just going to walk away quietly, and I was left grappling with the reality of what lay ahead.

With Ahmad by my side, I took a deep breath, trying to shake off the tension. "Let's get the hell out of here," I said, urgency in my voice palpable. Today had turned into a nightmare, but I was determined not to let Shanny or Sergio control my life any longer. I would fight for Dior, for our future, and for the peace I so desperately craved.

Breanna J

NINETEEN

Armand

When I came home that day, Armand's stuff was finally there. My house, once a shell of what it could be, felt like a real home—filled with warmth, laughter, and the unmistakable energy of a man. With Armand in my bed, everything clicked into place. We spent hours moving Sergio's things to the garage, each box we shoved aside symbolizing a step away from my past and closer to the future I envisioned with Armand.

As the sun dipped below the skyline, I whipped up dinner, the aroma of spices wafting through the air, mixing with the excitement buzzing between us. Armand took the cars to fill them up with gas and get them washed—his strong hands working diligently, a contrast to the clutter we'd just cleared. After we devoured the meal, he gave me that playful grin of his and told me to take a shower while he handled the kitchen cleanup. I couldn't help but smile; he made even the mundane feel special.

Once I was fresh and cozy, we snuggled in bed, the flicker of the TV casting soft shadows around us as we lost ourselves in a movie. The world outside faded away, and

Hall Pass

for those moments, it was just us, wrapped up in each other's warmth.

Now, here we were, days later, gearing up for our trip. We were taking an Uber to the airport since Armand's car was still in the shop after a hit-and-run accident. I wasn't about to shell out a fortune for my car to sit idle at the airport all weekend.

I had to admit, I secretly hated planes. Something about putting my life in the hands of a stranger behind the cockpit made my stomach churn. So, I turned my thoughts elsewhere. "So, bae, your birthday's coming up. Are you excited?" I asked, trying to keep the mood light.

He chuckled, his eyes sparkling with mischief. "I think every black man that makes it to any birthday after 18 is excited," he shot back, his grin infectious.

"What do you want to do?" I pressed, eager to hear his thoughts.

"Baby, as long as I'm with you, that's a good birthday to me," he replied, his voice smooth like honey.

While Armand's answer was sweet, I had bigger plans swirling in my mind. Turning 30 was a milestone—a celebration worthy of everything he'd overcome. He deserved to go big, to feel cherished and celebrated. I had an idea brewing, but I needed his brothers on board to pull it off. Hopefully, the tension between him and Armani had simmered down enough for everything to go smoothly. I was determined to make this birthday unforgettable for the man who had already made my life so much richer.

As Armand leaned back, visibly relaxing, I pulled out my iPad and began scribbling down my ideas. Just as I got into a groove, the plane hit some turbulence, rattling us like a roller coaster. My instinct kicked in, and I grabbed Armand's hand without a second thought. He chuckled softly before letting go, wrapping his arm around me and pulling me as close as he could. "We good, little momma, relax. I got you," he said, his calm voice washing over me like a soothing balm.

When we finally landed in Florida, I practically bolted off the plane. As soon as I powered on my phone, notifications flooded in—texts from Sergio, asking where I was, how he missed me, and all that bullshit. Armand appeared behind me, his presence a solid wall of protectiveness. "What does that nigga want?" he asked, a mix of irritation and concern flickering in his eyes.

"He's just talking," I replied, trying to brush it off.

"I told that nigga to leave you alone," he shot back, anger painting his face.

"You talked to Sergio?" I asked, my heart racing. Shock crossed Armand's features as he realized he'd let it slip.

Hall Pass

"Yeah, after he pulled up on you, Ahmad and I rolled up on him," he explained defensively. "But I asked you to leave it alone."

"I was doing my fucking job defending you," he replied, frustration lacing his voice.

"No, you lied to me," I said, my anger boiling over as I started to walk away.

But he grabbed my arm, his grip firm yet gentle. "Our trip just started. Don't ruin it over that shit," he said, his voice low but intense. I looked at him, feeling the weight of his gaze, but I remained silent, pulling my phone back out to order an Uber to the hotel.

In the car, the air was thick with tension. I stared out the window, my thoughts racing, fingers tapping away at my phone to text Destiny, letting her know we made it safe. Once we arrived at the hotel, I checked us in and led us up to our room.

Finally, Armand broke the silence. "Can you stop with the silent treatment, please? I only went to see that nigga so he knew he had someone who wasn't going to allow any games when it came to you. I needed him to understand that you have someone who's ready to step up for you. And however he wants to take that, we can handle it. I don't care," he said, his voice a mix of frustration and sincerity.

I looked at him, a whirlwind of emotions swirling inside me. "I'm about to get ready for the concert," I said, turning away and locking myself in the bathroom.

Inside, I texted Destiny, pouring out my frustration. She responded almost instantly: "Friend, I get it. You're mad because he didn't tell you, and you asked him to let it go. But as a man, he did what he was supposed to do—make it clear that no one's going to play with his bae. Not even your soon-to-be-ex-husband. Let it go, you're overdoing it. Be flattered that you have a man who cares enough to step up for you. This trip is for you to relax and enjoy each other. So just do that."

Destiny was spot on. I took a deep breath, washing away the anger that had knotted itself in my chest, and stepped out of the bathroom. Armand was perched on the edge of the bed, his eyes glued to a basketball game flickering on the screen. The tension in the room was still thick, but it softened under the hypnotic pull of the game. I realized that despite the bumps we'd hit, I wanted to make this trip special. I needed to let go of the past and focus on the man waiting there for me, his presence both grounding and intoxicating.

"I'm sorry for giving you the silent treatment," I said, my voice barely above a whisper. He turned, his gaze shifting from the screen to me.

"It's cool. I'm sorry I didn't tell you I pulled up on that

Hall Pass

nigga after you specifically said not to. But just know, I did it out of love." His voice held a mix of regret and stubborn pride, and I could see the tension in his jaw relax just a bit.

"I know, baby. I get it now, and I understand. I just don't want any issues between us." I walked over, wrapping my arms around him and pressing a kiss to his lips. It felt like the world faded away for a moment, just us and the warmth of our connection.

He tugged at my towel playfully, a mischievous glint in his eyes. "Let's do some making up," he said, his voice low and teasing.

"No, we gotta get ready," I replied, half-laughing, half-serious.

"Ugh, I'ma let you slide this time because I know how bad you wanna see Jaszmine Sullivan," he said, chuckling as he turned back to the game.

After we got dressed, I couldn't help but admire how good Armand looked—his fitted shirt accentuating those broad shoulders, making my heart race. We snapped a few pictures, capturing our smiles, his arm wrapped possessively around my waist, before heading out to the outdoor concert. We both opted for comfortable sneakers, ready to dance the night away.

When we arrived, the atmosphere was electric, even

under the dark sky. The crowd was thick, and our last-minute decision to come left us navigating through a sea of people, straining to see anything through the dim lighting.

"What's wrong?" Armand asked, his brow furrowed as he noticed my frown.

"I can't see," I admitted, frustration creeping into my voice.

Without missing a beat, he scooped me up and tossed me onto his shoulders. Suddenly, I had a perfect view of the stage, the crowd swaying to the rhythm of anticipation. But my attention was quickly pulled away as Armand leaned down, kissing my inner thighs, sending shivers through me.

"Bae," I laughed, half-amused and half-flustered.

"What? You're watching your show, and I'm making one of my own," he shot back, that cheeky grin lighting up his face.

He resumed kissing my legs, and I squirmed, trying to suppress the playful giggles bubbling up inside me. "Bae!" I called out again, a teasing lilt in my voice.

He paused, looking up at me with that devilish smirk I couldn't resist. "Let's play a game," he proposed, his eyes twinkling with mischief.

Hall Pass

"What game?" I asked, intrigued.

"If you make it obvious what I'm doing to you up here, you gotta buy the drinks and dinner tonight. If you don't, I will." He winked, a challenge hanging between us like electricity.

"May the best win," I replied, a confident smile spreading across my face as he buried his head back between my legs.

I felt his tongue part my lips, a rush of heat surging through me as I struggled against the urge to move. This was unexpected, thrilling—so sexy that it left me breathless. The darkness around us provided a perfect cover, allowing me to focus on controlling the sounds that threatened to escape my lips. It was a challenge I was determined to win.

I was so caught up in the moment that the concert faded into the background, the pulse of the crowd becoming a distant thrum. I clutched Armand's head, biting my bottom lip as he shamelessly devoured me, his lips and tongue igniting sensations that sent shivers down my spine. He didn't stop until I came, the world around us dissolving into bliss. When he finally slid me down onto my feet, he licked his lips, that playful smirk spreading across his face. My legs felt like jello, shaky yet craving more.

"I guess I owe you drinks and dinner," he said, teasingly.

"Fuck that. We'll order room service. Let's go back to the room," I shot back, grabbing his hand. With the other, I quickly ordered an Uber while we made our way to the exit, the excitement of the night still buzzing between us.

When we got back to the room, we were filled up, but it wasn't with food or drinks. The atmosphere crackled with unspoken desire, and we dove into each other, the night carrying us away into a realm of pleasure.

The next morning, we woke up eager for what the day had in store. Today was the day of the big concert featuring Nas, Ne-Yo, and a lineup of major names. The early morning sun spilled across the Florida coast, painting the horizon in vibrant shades of orange and pink. As we stepped out of the hotel, the salty breeze tousled my hair, carrying the scent of the ocean. It felt like a fresh restart, a clean slate for both of us.

We were in a good mood after last night, and Florida was providing a welcome distraction from the troubles that had weighed us down back home. The energy in the air was palpable as we arrived at the concert. The vibe was electric, each beat resonating with our hearts. We danced and sang as if we had no cares, lost in the rhythm of the moment. For a brief time, it felt like we had forgotten about the trauma that clung to us like shadows, replaced instead by the promise of music and escape.

Hall Pass

"I can't believe we're actually here," I exclaimed, a smile stretching from ear to ear, a perfect blend of excitement and relief. I adjusted my oversized sunglasses and took a sip of my drink, feeling the cool liquid refresh me.

"Me either. I'm enjoying it," he replied, his eyes sparkling with enthusiasm.

"Do you want to walk the beach until the next set?" I asked, already envisioning the scene.

"Sure," he said, grinning.

The beach was relatively empty, with only a few joggers and people lounging in the sun. As we walked along the shoreline, I took in the breathtaking scenery, waves crashing softly against the sand. "This place feels magical," I told him, my voice almost a whisper as I gazed out at the horizon.

Armand nodded, his expression serious yet warm, and I felt a wave of comfort wash over me. "Just us and the music for the next few days. No past, no worries." He took my hand, his grip anchoring me in the moment, the warmth radiating from his skin grounding me amid the chaos of life.

We sat on the beach for a while, the sound of the waves lapping against the shore creating a soothing rhythm. The sun hung low in the sky, casting a golden hue that danced on the water, and I felt a sense of peace enveloping us. Just as I started to lose myself in the serenity, a striking couple approached us, exuding confidence and charm.

"Hey! I'm Kayla, and this is my man, Derrick," the woman said, her light skin glowing in the fading sunlight. She had an infectious smile that drew you in instantly.

"Hey!" Armand and I both greeted in unison, intrigued by their energy.

"I don't mean to be strange, but I was telling my man how perfect you two are together," Kayla continued, her eyes sparkling with excitement. "I'm a photographer, and I'd love to take some photos of you guys!"

Armand and I posed for Kayla, our smiles genuine and carefree, the chemistry between us palpable. I was filled with anticipation, eager to see how her photos would turn out. Once she had snapped a good number of shots, Kayla turned to me, her eyes bright. "Could I get a few shots of just you?"

I hesitated, surprised by the request. But Armand, ever the supporter, encouraged me with a nod. "Go for it," he said, his confidence in me bolstering my own.

Kayla and I moved closer to the water, the waves kissing our feet as she began to snap photos. The men stood back,

Hall Pass

watching with a mix of curiosity and amusement. We engaged in small talk between her clicks of the camera.

"So, are you from around here?" she asked, her voice casual yet inviting.

"No, we're just here for the concert," I replied, my heart racing with a mix of excitement and nerves.

"Oh, cool! So what are you guys interested in?" she asked, her tone shifting slightly, a glimmer of something playful in her eyes.

"Huh?" I said, feeling the conversation take an unexpected turn.

"Well, Derrick and I both think you two are very attractive, and maybe later, you'd want to come by and we could… you know…" She trailed off, leaving the implication hanging in the air.

A wave of realization washed over me. "Oh!" I exclaimed, the pieces clicking into place. "We are flattered, but girl, I'm an only child, and I don't know how to share—especially not my man." I shot her a teasing smile, hoping to lighten the mood.

Her expression shifted to disappointment, but she quickly masked it with a nod. "Okay, no worries!"

We returned to the guys, and I took Armand's hand, grateful for his steady presence. I thanked Kayla for the experience and shared my email address, eager to see the photos she promised to send.

As we turned back toward the festival grounds, the remaining lineup of artists promised a weekend filled with rhythm and connection. My heart felt full, and my spirit soared; it was as if we were on the brink of something extraordinary, ready to embrace whatever life threw our way. The air buzzed with anticipation, and I knew that this was just the beginning of our adventure together.

As we strolled, the sounds of guitars strumming and drums beating floated toward us like a siren's call, pulling us deeper into the vibrant festival atmosphere. The crowd buzzed with energy, a mix of laughter and anticipation swirling around us. Colorful festival flags danced in the breeze, and the scent of street food wafted through the air, making my stomach rumble.

But as the day continued, dark clouds began to gather ominously on the horizon. I pointed at the sky, my brow furrowing. "Is it just me, or does it look like rain?"

"Just a little cloud cover," Armand reassured me, his voice steady, but I could see the flicker of concern in his eyes. We pushed through the throngs of festival-goers, soaking in the melodies, the art, and the fleeting moments of joy. When Mary J. Blige took the stage, we lost ourselves in the music, our bodies swaying together like we were the only two souls in the universe. Every beat

Hall Pass

resonated within us, and I felt the weight of the world lift, if only for a moment.

Hours slipped by like grains of sand, the sun beginning its descent as the evening approached. But then, the wind picked up, swirling around us with an unsettling ferocity. The festival organizers announced that due to an unexpected weather warning, the festivities would be paused. Armand and I exchanged glances, the thrill of escape slowly being replaced by an ominous sense of foreboding.

"Let's get back to the hotel," Armand suggested, gripping my hand a little tighter, as if grounding me against the uncertainty. I quickly ordered an Uber, but just as we settled into the wait, the first drops of rain began to fall, light at first but quickly intensifying.

"We should find somewhere to wait it out," I said, glancing at the gathering clouds. We hurried toward a nearby café that had lights glowing warmly in the windows, a beacon of comfort amid the brewing storm. But as we reached the entrance, the rain transformed into a torrential downpour, drenching us in seconds.

"Shit!" I laughed, pulling my hair back as if that would shield us from the deluge. Armand pulled me close, shielding me with his body as we dashed into the café, laughter bubbling between us despite the chaos outside. The cozy interior was filled with the comforting aroma of coffee and baked goods, an inviting escape from the storm.

As we shook off the rain, I could see the flicker of excitement still dancing in Armand's eyes, even as the world outside raged. "Guess we're stuck here for a bit," he said, a playful grin spreading across his face.

"Looks like it," I replied, feeling a warmth spread through me that had nothing to do with the coffee brewing behind the counter. We settled at a small table by the window, the rain tapping rhythmically against the glass like nature's own metronome. Despite the weather, I felt this was just another thread in the tapestry of our adventure together.

The café quickly filled with people trying to ride out the sudden storm, the atmosphere buzzing with anxious energy and nervous chatter. I glanced at my phone, realizing the Uber request had canceled. A knot tightened in my stomach as I pressed against Armand, feeling scared and unsure how things had spiraled so quickly. I watched the rain lash against the windows, each drop a reminder of the chaos outside. "What if it gets worse?" I asked, my voice barely audible over the din of worried conversations and clattering dishes.

"It's just a storm," Armand promised, his tone steady and reassuring. "We'll be okay."

But as the minutes dragged on, the rain transformed into a furious hurricane, the wind howling like a beast unleashed from the depths of hell. The café's lights flickered, casting eerie shadows on the walls before plunging us into darkness. Panic rippled through the crowd, and I began to tremble as I watched a worker frantically board up windows and doors, trying to keep everyone safe.

"Stay close," Armand instructed, his voice unwavering despite the chaos surrounding us. We huddled together, surrounded by strangers who shared in our fear. The storm raged outside, and the walls shuddered under the relentless assault of wind and rain.

"Armand, I'm scared," I whispered, my eyes wide with terror, searching for comfort in his gaze.

He cupped my face, forcing me to meet his eyes, which held a fierce determination. "No matter what happens, I won't let anything happen to you. We'll get through this together." But even as he spoke, I could feel the truth lurking beneath his words—we were at the mercy of the storm.

Suddenly, the café's roof creaked ominously, and a loud crash echoed outside. A wave of water surged against the windows, and instinctively, Armand pushed me behind him, his body a protective barrier. "We have to get out of here," he said, urgency flooding his voice.

We pushed through the panicking crowd, Armand leading me toward the back exit. The alley outside was a whirlwind of debris and rain, and for a split second, the world felt surreal, like we were caught in a nightmare, unable to catch a break.

"Where do we go?" I shouted over the storm's deafening roar.

"There's an old warehouse down the street I saw. Fewer windows, safer. We can take shelter there!" Armand yelled, determination etched on his face.

"Armand, I don't know! Maybe we should just go back inside. We're not from here; we don't know anything about this weather or any of the places!" I protested, panic creeping into my voice.

"Do you trust me?" He asked, locking his gaze onto mine, his intensity grounding me.

"Yes," I replied, my heart racing as I looked into his eyes, seeing the unwavering resolve that made me believe in him.

"Then follow me. I promise I got you. I will die for you. You're going to make it home," he said fiercely, grabbing my hand as we sprinted into the storm, the wind battering against us like a relentless wall.

As we reached the warehouse, we stumbled inside, gasping for breath. The interior was dark and damp, but it offered sanctuary from the chaos outside. Armand quickly scanned the area, his instincts kicking in as he found a corner that seemed relatively stable. "Over here!" he urged, pulling me toward the wall, where we could catch our breath.

The sound of the storm raged outside, but in that moment, huddled together in the shadows of the warehouse, I felt a flicker of hope. Against the backdrop of fear, I found solace in Armand's presence, knowing that together, we could weather any storm.

We clung to each other, the howling winds and crashing rain making the world outside feel both distant and immediate. I could sense the concern etched on Armand's face as he held me close. "I'd do anything for you," he said, his voice steady, though I could hear the underlying tension. "Even if it means—"

"Don't say that," I interrupted, my voice cracking under the weight of raw emotion. "You don't know what you're talking about."

"I do," he insisted, his heart pounding in his chest. "If it comes down to it… I would sacrifice everything to make sure you're safe."

My eyes glistened with unshed tears, the fear of losing him crashing over me like a tidal wave. "I can't lose you, Armand. Not after everything we've been through."

"You won't," he vowed, pulling me even closer, his warmth enveloping me like a protective shield. "We're going to get through this. Together."

The storm howled outside, the walls rattling around us as if the universe itself was testing our resolve. In that moment, as the wind roared and the world outside crumbled, we held onto each other tighter, two souls intertwined in the eye of the storm, vowing to face whatever came next.

As we listened to the chaos, I knew that no matter what trauma awaited us after the storm, we would face it together. And that knowledge was enough to keep me grounded.

Finally, dawn broke, the storm subsiding and leaving behind a landscape of rain-soaked ruins and an eerie gloom. But amidst the wreckage, I felt a surge of relief that we were alive and safe. When the warehouse owner arrived to check on the building, he was shocked to find us there. He explained that he had released his workers and rushed home to his family, never thinking to check if anyone was locked inside. "I'm just glad I could help," he said, shaking his head in disbelief.

With trees down and debris scattered everywhere, Uber rides were nowhere to be found. So, we decided to walk back to the hotel, witnessing the resilient spirit of Florida as people began piecing their lives back together. Each step felt heavy, but also liberating, as if we were shedding the weight of the storm with every footfall.

When we finally reached the hotel, we threw our phones on the charger, grateful that the place had power thanks to a generator. I rushed to pack my things while Armand sat on the edge of the bed, a look of contemplation on his face. "What are you doing?" I asked, glancing up from my hurried movements.

"Taking a breather," he responded, his tone casual but his eyes betraying the storm of emotions swirling within him.

"Breather? We gotta get the hell out of Florida now," I fussed, urgency creeping into my voice.

Tears rolled down my cheeks as I stuffed my belongings into a bag, the weight of the night's events crashing down on me. I had never experienced anything like this before, and the magnitude of it was overwhelming.

Armand came over and wrapped me in his arms, his warmth enveloping me like a balm. "Relax!" he said softly, his voice soothing as I cried into his shirt. "I told you I had you. I wasn't going to let anything happen to you, and I meant that."

I pulled back slightly, looking into his eyes as gratitude flooded through me. I leaned in and kissed his lips, a silent prayer of thanks to the universe for bringing a man like him into my life. In that moment, beneath the weight of the world, I found my strength in him, and together, we would continue to rise.

TWENTY

Armand

Florida was a wild ride, and somehow we made it back home safe. But damn, everything felt different. The storm had grounded flights, and Dior was itching to escape. We ended up snagging a rental from Enterprise, who, bless their hearts, let us return it to a location in our city.

Once back, we tried to settle into our routine. Dior was killing it at her job, diving headfirst into the hotel renovations. Whatever amount Renee told me she was requesting, I doubled it when I sent it over. The restaurant? Thriving like never before. Life was good, and for the first time in a while, it felt like we were on the right track.

But, of course, there were still those pesky shadows lurking in the background. Shanny hadn't signed the divorce papers yet, but she was keeping her distance, so I was counting that as a win, however small.

Every morning, we had this little ritual of eating breakfast together. Dior would get ready, and I'd grab her things and walk her to the car like I was her damn chauffeur. Just a typical Tuesday morning, we flung the door open to head out, and there he was—Sergio. My jaw clenched, and I felt that familiar surge of rage boiling up. "The fuck you doing here?" I shot at him.

"The fuck are you doing here?" he shot back, his tone dripping with defiance.

"I live here," I replied, my voice steady but laced with irritation.

"Dior, you got this nigga living in my house," he sneered.

I could see Dior's annoyance flaring. "Sergio, what do you want? Damn, you're like an STD—you just won't go away," she snapped.

"I came to take you to breakfast," he said, but I couldn't help but laugh, a harsh, mocking sound.

Dior turned to me, her expression firm. "Baby, go back inside and get ready. I got this," she said, her voice leaving no room for argument.

"Yeah, go in the house. Let me talk to my wife," Sergio chimed in, a smirk plastered across his face.

"Nigga, shut up. She don't want shit from you. I make sure she's fed every morning before she leaves this house, and I fuck her good so she don't need your ten strokes," I shot back, my chest tightening with every word.

"Nigga, I—"

"You what, my boy?" I challenged him, the tension crackling in the air.

"You always want to be tough while people are around," he taunted.

I stepped forward, the space between us narrowing. "Dior can step inside, and it'll just be me and you out here. We can handle this like men."

"Bae," Dior called out, her voice slicing through the hostility. I glanced over at her, and she held my gaze. "Go in the house. I got this," she insisted, her tone leaving no room for debate.

Hall Pass

I knew she could handle herself, but the urge to protect her surged within me like a tidal wave. This wasn't over—not by a long shot.

I grabbed her face, pulling her close for a deep kiss that tasted of passion and defiance. I squeezed her ass, feeling the heat radiate between us before reluctantly letting her go. I locked eyes with her, my voice firm. "You yell if you need me." I could see the anger flickering in Sergio's eyes, but honestly? I didn't give a damn.

I stepped back from the door, leaving it ajar so I could still hear the tension thickening in the air. "Sergio, I know you've got the divorce papers. Why the hell haven't you signed them?" Dior's voice was steady, but I could sense the volcano simmering beneath the surface.

"Because I'm not giving up on us," he shot back, his tone defiant.

"Us is over," she retorted, her resolve unshakeable.

"We aren't until I say so," he barked, his voice rising as I eased my way back toward the door, ready to intervene if things escalated.

"No, we are. See that man in there?" She pointed back at me, her fierce gaze never leaving Sergio's. "If I call him, he'll come take your head off. He doesn't play about me, and I'm sure you know that already. This house actually feels like a home with a real man in it."

"But this is our house," he insisted, desperation creeping into his voice.

Dior smirked, a sharp edge to her smile. "The deed to this house has just my name on it, remember? Your credit isn't good enough for anything but a secured credit card, Sergio."

"Dior," he called out, frustration lacing his tone.

"Boy, stop saying my name. Just stop popping up on me. I'm all set on you signing the divorce papers. Let me be. Plus, the way he's been fucking me all up and through here—on the tables, the couches, in the shower, and in the bed—I'm sure you don't want to think about that." She crossed her arms, her attitude radiating strength. "Now leave, Sergio, because what you're not going to do is make my man feel any type of way in his own home."

"Dior." He barked again, and I stepped back into view behind her, ready for whatever came next.

Hall Pass

"Nigga, you think you can scare me?" I challenged, my voice low and steady. "I can show you better than I can tell you." I tried to step around Dior, but she planted herself firmly in front of me, using all her strength to block me. I wasn't about to hurt her trying to get past.

"We aren't even doing all that. Just leave, Sergio," she demanded, her voice unwavering.

He opened his mouth to say something, but she cut him off. "Leave, or I'll let him whoop your ass, then I'm gonna call the police and tell them you were trespassing. I'm sure you have no money for bail."

"And a pretty nigga like you? They'll have fun with you in there," I chimed in, a smirk creeping onto my face.

Sergio's eyes burned with rage, but slowly he backed away, the fire in him dimming. "You're going to come back," he muttered, climbing into his car, a defeated look shadowing his face.

As Sergio's car disappeared down the street, Dior turned to me, her expression unreadable—a storm of emotions swirling in her eyes. Without a word, she leaned in and kissed me—soft yet electric, a brief moment that ignited something deep within me. Then she walked to her car, leaving me standing there, a whirlwind of emotions battling inside. This battle wasn't over, but at least we were in it together.

Once I got dressed, I headed over to Los's shop to check on my car. The familiar scent of grease and the sound of tools clinking greeted me as I walked into the garage. To my surprise, Los was actually working on my ride, his hands deftly maneuvering around the engine.

"So, what's my damage looking like?" I asked, trying to keep it light.

"Nigga, who you pissed off?" he shot back, a knowing smirk creeping across his face.

"Man, I don't even wanna talk about it," I replied, shaking my head, the weight of the morning still pressing on my chest.

"Got caught up in your shit, didn't you?" he teased, but I could see the concern behind his playful tone.

"Not even like that. It's just Shanny won't let me go. I mean, she isn't in love with me, we aren't in love with each other. So I don't understand why she's making this divorce hell," I confessed, running a hand through my hair in frustration.

Los paused for a moment, his expression shifting as he absorbed my words. "I need you to think about what you just said. Think about the life you've given her. You're walking away to be happy with someone else, possibly providing them the same life you once provided her. You want her to just be okay with that? At the end of the day, you're threatening her survival. Of course she's gonna fight this divorce."

"But I've offered her money," I countered, feeling defensive.

"Sometimes it's more than just the money. When you're a real man, you provide, you protect, you encourage. You create a safe space, you give comfort—even when they don't tell us. There's a chance the next guy who comes along won't provide that. Why would she want to let that go?" He paused, letting his words sink in. "When was the last time that woman had to pump gas or take her car in for a checkup? When's the last time she actually saw a bill? Let alone had to pay for one? When was the last time she ever had to feel fear, knowing you wouldn't be there to at least try to save the day? When's the last time she had a worry that you didn't take off her hands, leaving it just her issue?"

I hadn't thought about it that way. His words hit hard, unraveling my perspective.

"So I sit and suffer?" I asked, my voice barely above a whisper.

"I would never tell you to just sit and suffer," he replied, his tone softening. "But what I am saying is that sometimes it's not as easy and simple for the other person as we think. Remember the last time you were here? I saw that look in your eye. You needed to get your shit in order to avoid crap like this. Now look at your car—it's fucked."

I glanced over at my ride, and the reality hit me hard.

"Can I fix it? Sure, but technically it's totaled out," he continued. "I can contact your insurance company and let them know it's totaled, and you can get that check, or I can fix this and we go from there. It's up to you."

I thought for a moment, weighing my options like I was balancing a scale. The thought of being tied to Shanny and her endless drama felt heavier than the burden of car repairs. "Go ahead and total it out," I finally said, a sense of resolve settling in my gut. "I'd rather get something else."

After that, Los and I exchanged a few more thoughts about the situation before I let him walk away to handle the insurance company. I headed into work, but a nagging

Hall Pass

feeling tugged at me—Dior hadn't reached out.

For the rest of the day, I found myself waiting anxiously for her text while scrolling through listings for new cars. But the silence stretched on, heavy and uneasy. Finally, I couldn't take it anymore. I pulled out my phone and typed, "Hey baby girl, you good? It's not like you to not hit me throughout the day."

I saw the bubbles pop up, a flicker of hope igniting in my chest, but then they disappeared. A moment later, they reappeared again, and my heart raced. "Honestly, I just feel mixed emotions about this morning. I never wanted to drag you into this shit with Sergio and me," her message finally came through.

I couldn't help but respond. "I kinda figured that was on your mind. Do you still love him?"

"No," she shot back instantly, and I felt a weight lift ever so slightly.

"Do you feel like we're moving too fast? Because I will step back, let you fully handle that, and be here waiting when you're ready. I told you I was rocking with you through it as long as you wanted me to. But it's up to you. You have to tell me what you want."

"I want you. I'm so happy with you," she replied, her words pouring out like a confession. "I just don't want the drama to cause you to leave me or not love me anymore. I'm just in my head and I can't help but think I'm fucking up your life."

Her words hit me like a ton of bricks, each one landing hard. "Babe, I'm glad you expressed that to me. I never want you to hold stuff in or overthink when it comes to us. That will only lead you to come up with thousands of possibilities in that beautiful head of yours. I'm not going anywhere as long as you want me here. I love you, girl. I'm in love with you. I will fight for us. Plus, I'm hooked on that good thang you're putting on me."

Dior responded with a string of laughing emojis, and I couldn't help but smile. I wanted her to know I meant every word. After that, I made sure everything was good at the restaurant and called to check on the hotel as I headed home.

When Dior finally got home from work, I heard her enter the house, her presence immediately filling the space with warmth. She headed straight to the bedroom, slipping into her usual routine of undressing before starting dinner. I followed her into the room, a glass of her favorite wine in hand, eager to surprise her.

As I entered, I found her admiring the flowers and treats

Hall Pass

I had laid out on the bed, a smile breaking across her face. I handed her the glass of wine and guided her over to the bed, gently sitting her down.

"Got a little something to help you unwind," I said, watching her take a sip, the tension in her shoulders beginning to ease.

I knelt down and took off her shoes, my fingers brushing against her skin as I worked. As she sipped the wine, I unbuttoned her shirt, the fabric parting to reveal her skin beneath. I helped her slide out of her bra, my heart racing as I took in the sight of her, the atmosphere between us charged with unspoken desire.

In that moment, everything felt right. We were a team, and I was ready to protect what we had at all costs.

Dior looked at me, her eyes shining with a mix of love and vulnerability. I helped her out of the rest of her clothes, and as I stood her up, she pressed her bare body against me, wrapping her arms around my neck. The warmth of her skin sent a jolt of electricity through me.

"How was the rest of your day after we talked?" I asked, guiding her toward the bathroom. I had run her a bath, filling it with warm water, rose petals floating lazily, and candles flickering softly in the dim light.

"Aww, what is this for?" she asked, glancing around the bathroom, her surprise evident.

"I just wanted you to have a relaxing night. I've been seeing your grind, and I know you've been working hard to make this good for us. Tonight, I want you to let me do all the worrying while you unwind," I said, my heart swelling as a tear rolled down her cheek. I gently wiped it away and helped her step into the tub.

"I've never had anyone do anything like this for me," she said, her voice trembling with emotion before she leaned in to give me a soft kiss.

"What one won't do, another damn sure will," I replied, a playful grin spreading across my face.

She settled into the tub, and then looked up at me with a playful glint in her eyes. "What's wrong?"

"Get in with me," she demanded, her voice leaving no room for argument. I stripped off my clothes and jumped in, positioning myself against the back of the tub so she could lay back against me, her body relaxing into mine.

Hall Pass

As the warm water enveloped us, she began to share about her day at the hotel. Her eyes sparkled with pride as she recounted the projects she was working on, and I couldn't help but smile from ear to ear, feeling just as proud of her achievements.

"So, bae, we're going to do a small dinner for your birthday next week at your mom's. I talked to your brothers, and they were down," she said excitedly.

"You talked to Armani and Ahmad?" I asked, raising an eyebrow.

"No, I reached out to Ahmad on Facebook, and he said he'll handle Armani," she replied with a grin. "It's a '90s/early 2000s themed dinner. And I already ordered our outfits!"

"Okay, baby," I chuckled at her take-charge attitude. "I wanted to see if you're okay with my best friend Destiny coming to the dinner too," she said, a note of uncertainty creeping into her voice.

"The one that was with you that night?" I asked, trying to recall.

"Yeah," she responded, her eyes searching mine for

reassurance.

"Yeah, of course. She seems cool, and plus she's your people. We haven't had her over with everything going on, so it'd be good for us to get to know each other," I said, giving her a reassuring nod.

"Cool," she replied, her smile returning.

"Will your parents be there too?" I asked, noticing the shift in her demeanor when she quickly said no.

"They still not okay with us being together?" I joked, trying to lighten the mood.

"I don't know, and I don't care," she shot back, but I could feel the tension radiating from her.

"Bae, what's going on with you and your parents?" I asked gently, sensing the weight behind her words. I felt her exhale, a long, heavy breath that spoke volumes.

"So you remember that night I called you over and told you to fuck me and not say anything?" she began, her voice dropping to a whisper.

Hall Pass

"Yeah," I said, the memory flooding back vividly.

"My mom came over to talk to me about Sergio, and she ended up telling me that the man I always knew as my dad wasn't my real dad," she admitted, her voice trembling.

"What the fuck?" I was completely shocked, processing the gravity of her revelation.

"She went into details about how they split for a while. She was dealing with someone else, and when shit went left, she came back to my dad pregnant with me. He still loved her, took her back, and accepted me as his own."

Her words hung in the air, heavy with the weight of the past. I pulled her closer, wanting to shield her from the pain of it all. "Damn, that's a lot to unpack," I said softly, my mind racing as I tried to process her story. "I'm here for you, no matter what."

"Damn," was all I could manage after Dior revealed that bombshell.

"Yeah, I haven't talked to her since then," she admitted, her voice tinged with frustration.

"Dior, you gotta talk to your momma," I urged, feeling the seriousness of the situation.

"I will eventually," she replied stubbornly, crossing her arms as if to shield herself from the conversation.

"Make it soon. It's been long enough. Right or wrong, they love you, and it's not your dad's fault. They did what they thought was best. People like me wish they could still talk to their parents, and you're holding onto this grudge and not speaking to them."

"Okay, bae, I will," she finally conceded, her tone softening just a bit.

We climbed out of the tub, and I laid her gently across the bed, pouring scented oil into my hands. As I worked the oil into her skin, I could feel her muscles relaxing more and more under my touch. When Dior rolled over, she leaned in and gave me a soft kiss, but her hands wandered down to my towel. I stopped her gently.

"Not tonight," I said, and she looked at me like I had two heads.

Hall Pass

"What? We haven't done anything since we came back from Florida because of my period. Now it's off, and you're saying no?" she fussed, her brows furrowing in confusion.

"Yeah, I know, but tonight is all about intimacy, not lust. I want you to feel good without me fucking you. I want to engage those other senses and let you know I see you, I hear you, I connect with you emotionally, and that I care."

Her expression softened at my words. She smiled and laid back on the bed, letting me get back to work. Telling her no was hard because I was always ready to dive into Dior's ocean, but tonight I wanted to be different. I went to the foot of the bed, gently placing her feet in my lap and massaging them, feeling the tension melt away under my fingers.

"Listen, I want you to take tomorrow off and make no plans," I told her as I worked on her arches.

"Huh?" she responded, raising an eyebrow.

"I want you to take tomorrow off," I repeated, my tone firm yet playful.

"Okay, but what are we going to do?" she asked, curiosity dancing in her eyes.

"You'll see," I teased, a grin spreading across my face. The rest of the night melted away with laughter and easy conversation. I ordered food, and we enjoyed a cozy movie marathon, wrapped in each other's warmth.

The next morning, I woke Dior up with breakfast in bed. She was cuddled up in my arms, and as I gently shook her awake, I said, "Baby, get up and throw on a sundress or something. We're going for a ride."

With no hesitation, she jumped up and did what I asked, her excitement contagious. We hopped into the rental car, and as we drove, we made small talk about how I was picking up my new car as a birthday gift for myself.

Pulling into a gas station, I turned to her with a smile. "Bae, grab whatever you want," I told her, feeling generous.

"Okay, big spender," she laughed, her eyes sparkling with mischief.

"Girl, you can have whatever you like," I replied, quoting T.I., and we both burst into laughter as we headed inside to grab our snacks.

Hall Pass

The day felt full of promise, and I couldn't wait to see what adventures awaited us. With Dior by my side, everything seemed brighter, like the sun had decided to shine just for us. I was ready to embrace whatever came next.

We met back at the register, giggling as we cashed out with our snacks. Once back in the car, I turned the key and pulled away, heading toward a park I knew was usually quiet and secluded. But as we drove, I couldn't shake the feeling that we were being followed. I tried to keep my cool, not wanting to alarm Dior, but when I glanced in the rearview mirror, my stomach dropped. It was Shanny, her car tailing us too closely for comfort.

I pressed the gas a little harder, weaving through the streets and trying to make it through any yellow lights that flickered in front of me. "You okay, baby?" Dior asked, her voice laced with concern as she reached for my hand resting on the armrest.

"Yeah, just trying to remember where this park is," I replied, forcing a smile that didn't quite reach my eyes.

As luck would have it, I hit a yellow light that instantly turned red just as I passed through it, leaving Shanny stuck behind us. I quickly took the first corner I saw, eager to lose her in the maze of city streets.

Finally, we arrived at the park, and my heart eased. It was a weekday, so I figured it would be one of those peaceful days with little to no traffic. "What are we doing here?" Dior asked, her curiosity piqued as I parked the car.

"We're going to have ourselves a picnic," I told her, and her face lit up with excitement. She jumped out of the car, and I popped the trunk, grabbing a blanket from the back.

We laid out on the grass, the sun warming our skin, music playing softly from my phone. I had given Dior one rule: neither of us could look at our phones. We were there to give each other our undivided attention. As we settled into the moment, laughter and stories flowed easily between us, and the world around us faded away.

With nothing but each other to focus on, one thing led to another. Before I knew it, Dior had pulled up her dress, straddling me while I guided her hips up and down, one of her breasts in my mouth.

"Serigo, baby, we gotta stop—someone might see us," she said, her eyes fluttering closed as pleasure washed over her.

"So…" I teased, my breath hot against her skin.

"We need to…" she moaned, her voice trailing off mid-sentence as the sensations took over.

"Are you asking me or telling me?" I whispered in her ear, a playful lick sending shivers down her spine.

"I… I… I… damn, daddy," she gasped, completely lost in the moment as she bounced on my lap.

"I'll stop when you come," I promised, my hands still guiding her movements.

Dior didn't respond. The fear of being caught seemed to dissipate, and my shy lover transformed into a confident goddess, spinning around on me as if we were the only two people in the world. She gripped my ankles tightly, the reverse cowgirl position giving me an intoxicating view of her ass bouncing up and down.

She rode me harder, her rhythm building as my legs began to tense up. With one final thrust, we both reached the edge, and she held on tight as we both came, a wave of pleasure crashing over us. In that moment, nothing else mattered—just Dior and me, lost in our own world, free from the chaos outside.

TWENTY-ONE

Dior

Life has been good. There was such a difference with Armand here; I wasn't asking for things anymore—he was handling everything like a real man should. I woke up excited, bubbling with anticipation. It was the day before Armand's birthday party, and after all the love he'd poured into me lately, I couldn't wait to celebrate him.

I rolled over, ready to give him a good morning kiss and maybe some head, but then I realized he wasn't there. Confused, I sat up and scanned the room, finally noticing a note lying on the pillow where he should've been.

Good Morning,

Sorry I couldn't be there to see your beautiful face when you woke up. Just know I love you and I'm so grateful to be walking into my 30s with you by my side. I'll never stop telling you that. There will be days when I piss you off. There will be days when you piss me off. But there will always be a solution because of our love and communication. I am so happy to have you back and to be spending the rest of my days basking in your beauty and making sure I never lose you again. Because I can't live without you or that good ass pussy.*

Love you,

Armand

Reading Armand's note made me laugh and smile hard. I had said it time and time again, but it was the little things he did that melted my heart. I got dressed for work, grinning like a fool. But as I walked outside to my car, I felt a little off; something was different, and I couldn't quite put my finger on it.

When I opened the door, my breath caught. Inside were three dozen of the most beautiful roses and a teddy bear that smelled just like him. Along with that, he'd left my morning iced coffee, perfectly made. I stood there, blushing, overwhelmed by his thoughtfulness before finally climbing into the driver's seat.

I drove to work with the windows down, blasting "Best Part" featuring H.E.R., feeling every word resonate deep within me. When I arrived at the office, I walked in feeling like I owned the place, confidence radiating from me.

A few hours into my day, I sat at my desk chatting with Destiny. "Girl, sometimes I question why I even gave Sergio the time of day. If I'd known life was going to be this good, I would've just waited for Armand to get out of jail peacefully. In such a short time, he's given me everything Sergio wouldn't. I don't feel any confusion about how he feels about me. I know he loves me. He protects me and my heart."

"Friend, I am so happy for you. For real, this is what you deserve," Destiny said, her smile infectious even through the phone

"Thanks," I replied, beaming. I was smiling from ear to ear, feeling like I was floating, all while working on bathroom designs for the hotel since my project for work was already wrapped up.

As we talked, my phone chimed, and I felt a thrill run through me when I saw it was a text from Armand. *I'm downstairs with lunch for you. I rushed to the window and spotted him sitting on the hood of a parked car outside. My heart raced at the sight of him sitting there, looking fine as hell. I quickly ended the call with Destiny and dashed out of my office.

Hall Pass

When I reached the car, Armand greeted me with that radiant smile I loved. He looked so good with his fresh haircut and smelled even better, a mix of cologne and something uniquely him. "Get in," he said, his tone playful.

"I got work to do," I replied, half-heartedly, but I couldn't help the smile creeping onto my face.

"And I'm gonna let you do it. But I brought you lunch because I wanted to see your face and kiss those lips since I missed them this morning," he said, his gaze intense.

"Then give me a kiss," I said, leaning inand planting a soft kiss on his lips.

"That was nice, but not the lips I was talking about," he said, giving me a seductive grin before licking his lips, his eyes dancing with mischief.

The air around us crackled with tension, and I felt a rush of excitement. Today was going to be special, not just because of the birthday party tomorrow, but because of every little moment we were creating together. I was ready to dive headfirst into whatever adventures awaited us.

A tingle went down my body and My pussy got wet. I instantly decided to match his energy. Then come on we can go to my office. I said.

We went up to my office and i closed my door and locked it and pulled down the shades. I walked over to the table and knocking everything off on it. I pulled my dress up and bent over the table. "Oh so that's the type of time we on." Armand asked. "Yup" I said looking back at him with a smile on my face. Armand walked over to me and bent down. "You know I got to lick it before I stick it." he said to me before pulling my panties to the side and licking my pussy. When he was done he so gently slid into me taking my breath away. "Damn daddy" I said as I looked back at him and he began giving stroke after stroke.

When we finished, we pieced my office back together, the air still thick with the remnants of our intimate moment. Armand flashed that seductive grin and headed out, mentioning something about picking up his new car. "See you at home," he said, and just like that, I was left alone in the quiet of my workspace. I sank back into my chair, daydreaming about everything we had just done—the way he had ignited a fire within me, sending shivers of excitement coursing through my veins all over again.

Lost in thought, I was jolted back to reality by a sharp knock on my door. "Come in!" I called out, my voice a mix of curiosity and apprehension. The door creaked open, and there he stood—my father. "Daddy," I breathed, the word tumbling out before I could catch it. "Baby girl," he responded, his voice warm yet laced with an undercurrent of tension. The room fell silent, thick with unspoken words. It had been ages since we'd seen each other, not since Momma dropped the bombshell that he wasn't my real father.

Hall Pass

"Can we talk?" he asked, stepping inside with a hesitant air. I nodded, rising from my desk, my heart racing. "Sure."

"How have you been?" he inquired, his eyes searching mine. "Good," I replied, trying to sound casual, but the weight of everything hung heavily between us.

"I don't even know where to start," he admitted, running a hand through his hair in that familiar way I remembered. "About what?" I asked, my brow furrowing.

"Why you and your momma aren't talking," he said, giving me a look that spoke volumes. "Daddy, you don't have to—"

"Yes, I do," he interrupted, his tone firm yet gentle. "You're walking around mad at the world, and you don't know the whole story."

"She told me she stepped out on you. What else is there to know?" I shot back, a mix of hurt and defiance bubbling to the surface.

"That I forced her to. We all make mistakes, Dior. The man I am today isn't the man I always was. I had my growing up to do. I didn't treat your momma the best because I was too damn busy thinking about myself. I didn't even realize what I had until it was gone. I fell apart without her. And I told God if He brought her back to me, I'd love and cherish her right. So when she did come back, I didn't care that she was pregnant with you. I was ecstatic, thinking God had given me double the reason to keep my word."

His voice trembled with emotion, and I felt my defenses waver. "That man didn't want you, and when your momma wouldn't get rid of you, he didn't want her anymore either. But I wanted both of you! The day that doctor placed you in my arms, there wasn't a DNA test in the world that could tell me you weren't my daughter. My heart already said you were. And when your mother and I couldn't have any more children, I knew this was how it was supposed to be. I am your father, Dior. Until the day I take my last breath. I love you with every bit of my being, and I'd give my last breath for you and your momma. Don't let the secrets and mistakes of our past make you forget that."

Tears streamed down my cheeks, a river of emotion I couldn't contain. For a moment, I was utterly speechless, enveloped in my father's embrace. His arms wrapped around me like a fortress, strong and unwavering. He was right; no DNA test in the world could alter the truth of what I felt. This was my dad—the man who had shaped my understanding of love and loyalty. I would never disrespect him by denying that bond.

I cried, and he held me tight, a shared sorrow binding us

together. It wasn't until I felt warm droplets hit the top of my head that I realized he was crying too. In all my life, I could count on one hand the number of times I had seen him like this. I gently wiped a tear from his cheek. "Daddy, don't cry," I murmured, my voice shaky but steady. He smiled, a bittersweet curve of his lips. "I will always be your little girl. Your Dior. No matter what. I don't care what DNA says."

He pulled me back in, this time hugging me tighter, as if he feared I might slip away. "You don't know how much I needed to hear that," he said, his voice thick with emotion.

We stood there for a while longer, the world outside fading into the background. Eventually, he got ready to leave, and just as he reached the door, he turned to look at me, his expression serious. "Make sure you call your momma," he said.

"I will," I promised, though I wasn't sure how that conversation would go.

"Yeah, 'cause her emotions are all over the place. She's going crazy with that boy in my house. I can't believe we housing a little boy that didn't even know how to treat my baby when he had her."

I burst out laughing, the tension easing from my shoulders. "Daddy I know he's my husband, and I should be with him, but I'm happy with Armand," I admitted.

"Then, baby, be with Armand. I support whatever makes you happy. But that boy needs to get out of my house," my dad said, a playful glint in his eye.

"Okay, Dad," I chuckled as he left.

Once he was gone, I sank into my chair, feeling a wave of relief wash over me. This was great, especially with

Armand's party tomorrow.

The day finally arrived, and I was buzzing with excitement—maybe even more than Armand. I had planned a 90s/early 2000s theme for his birthday bash, and I was dressed to impress, channeling Kelly Rowland from the Destiny's Child "Soldier" music video. As I stood in front of the mirror, carefully putting in my earrings, Armand stepped out of the bathroom, embodying the era. He had a fresh low cut with deep waves, a crisp white T-shirt, baggy jeans, and those iconic all-white Nike Air Force Ones. When he smiled, his gold teeth glinted, adding to his charm.

"Damn," was all I could manage, my heart racing.

"What? I look bad?" he asked, checking himself out in the reflection.

"Nah, you look good—good enough that I think we could be an hour late to this party," I teased, a smirk playing on my lips.

"Is that so?" he replied, raising an eyebrow, the corner of his mouth quirking up.

"Hell yeah," I shot back, stepping closer and starting to unbutton my pants.

Before I knew it, Armand had yanked off his T-shirt, scooped me up, and tossed me onto the bed. What was supposed to be a quickie turned into a two-hour delay, our moans and passion echoing off the walls.

When we finally arrived at Armand's momma's house, the street was packed with cars and people. "I thought you said this was just a little get-together?" he asked, opening the

Hall Pass

car door for me and helping me out.

"You knew damn well we weren't going small to celebrate my man's dirty 30," I replied, planting a teasing kiss on his lips.

He smiled, grabbing my hand as we made our way into the backyard. The atmosphere was electric; friends were slapping Armand on the back, shouting birthday wishes. Ahmad was there too, strutting over with a new girl on his arm, both of them dressed like Nelly and Ashanti.

"Welcome to your 30s, little bro!" Ahmad exclaimed, giving Armand a hearty slap on the back before pulling him in for a hug and slipping an envelope into his hand.

"You didn't have to do this," Armand said, looking genuinely touched.

"Man, shut up! It's your day. Use it to take your lady on a vacation. After all the planning she did, it's both of y'all birthdays," Ahmad said, and laughter erupted around us.

As we celebrated, I could feel the electric buzz of the night, knowing it was just the beginning of an unforgettable evening. The DJ was spinning all the 90s and early 2000s hits, setting the perfect vibe. I had arranged for a mobile bartender to mix up cocktails, and two photographers roamed the party—one capturing candid moments and the other snapping posed shots at our stylish backdrop, reminiscent of the clubs we used to hit up. To top it all off, I'd even hired a cook so everyone could indulge in delicious food throughout the night.

Armand stood there, taking it all in, his eyes lighting up with each detail. "Thank you, baby," he said, leaning in to give me a kiss that sent butterflies dancing in my stomach.

Just then, Armani approached with Kelly trailing behind him. They looked like they had stepped right out of a 90s music video, but something felt off. The tension between Armani and Armand crackled in the air, and I silently prayed that the night wouldn't take a turn for the worse.

"Happy birthday, bro," Armani said, exchanging a slap up with Armand. But the camaraderie felt forced, and I could see the uncertainty etched on Armand's face. After a moment, he pulled Armani into a brief embrace, and I felt a sense of relief wash over me. The last person to join our little circle was Destiny. I introduced her, and we all moved to join the festivities.

The party was in full swing, laughter and joy filling the air. We brought out the cake, and I couldn't resist the temptation to playfully smear frosting on Armand's face. He laughed, his smile infectious, and we lost ourselves in the rhythm of the music, swaying to slow jams that made it feel like time had stopped. It was just us, wrapped in our own world—until a voice shattered the moment.

"Really, Armand? This is what we're doing?" The woman's voice rang out like a siren, and I turned, my heart sinking as I recognized her from the hotel.

"Shanny, why are you here?" Armand said, instinctively pushing me behind him, a protective gesture that sent chills down my spine.

"Armand, who is that? I've seen her before," I asked, my voice trembling as confusion and dread washed over me.

"I'm his wife!" she yelled, the words slicing through the air like a knife. Ahmad stepped in, trying to defuse the situation. "This isn't the time or place for this," he said, gently attempting to guide her toward the exit.

"Why isn't it? Y'all are here celebrating my husband's birthday like one big happy family, and I'm not invited?" she shot back, her tone bitter.

"Shanny, you know why you weren't invited here," Armand replied, frustration lacing his voice.

"Wait, you're married?" I asked him, my heart racing, tears threatening to spill over.

"It's not like that," Armand said, his eyes pleading.

"Very married, baby girl. We have a house together, cars, and we own that hotel you saw me at," Shanny interjected, her voice dripping with disdain.

"Shanny, leave!" Armand yelled, desperation in his tone.

"Are you married?" I pressed, tears forming in my eyes as my heart shattered.

He looked at me with such sadness, his expression almost breaking me. "Legally, yes. But—"

I slapped him, the sting of betrayal coursing through me. "I trusted you… you lied to me," I managed to choke out before turning to walk away, my heart heavy with disbelief.

Armand grabbed my arm, desperation etched on his face. "Don't do this! Let me explain first," he pleaded.

"You should've explained when I told you about my husband! You should've explained when we sat at that table and made this a thing. You should've explained before moving into my house! I'm out here doing all this for us!" I shouted, my voice rising with anger as everyone watched in silence.

"That's because he's mine!" Shanny spat, her expression triumphantly smug.

"Bitch, shut up!" Destiny yelled

"Bitch, I will dog walk you," she shot back, her bravado only fueling my rage.

"You ain't gonna do shit while we're here," Armani's baby mama chimed in, trying to add fuel to the fire.

"Everyone chill! We're not about to take it there. Shanny, you need to leave," Ahmad said, trying to restore order.

"No, she doesn't, because I am," I declared, striding toward the exit, my heart racing with adrenaline.

The moment I turned my back, I could hear Kelly's voice rising behind me, laced with venom. And then, just like that, chaos erupted. A loud crash echoed through the yard, and I spun around to see Shanny sprawled on the ground, while Armani had Kelly in a grip that looked like it could snap her in half.

"Nah, because I hate a messy, bitch! Tell the truth—he's been trying to divorce you. We all know!" Kelly yelled, her voice a cocktail of anger and desperation, cutting through the tension like a knife.

I stepped outside, the cool night air hitting me like a splash of cold water. I called an Uber, trying to escape the madness, when I heard Armani's voice behind me. "Dior, let me take you home."

I didn't reply, just kept walking, but he wasn't letting up. "Dior, please let me talk to you." He turned me to face him, the desperation in his eyes almost softening my resolve. "No need," I replied, not even bothering to meet his gaze. "Go back and check on your wife and enjoy your party."

"Fuck her," he shot back, his anger spilling over.

"It's fuck her, but you did me and her wrong," I countered, crossing my arms defiantly.

"I didn't do shit to Shanny," he insisted, his voice rising.

"So cheating on her is nothing? How does that work? When you were laid up with me, playing house, where was she?" I pressed.

"She was living her best life with her bitch," he spat, bitterness dripping from each word.

I couldn't help but laugh, a harsh sound that echoed in the stillness. "I should've listened to my momma and stayed with Sergio. At least he didn't sign the papers, and I could go home and pretend none of this shit ever happened."

"So you're going to go back to a nigga who didn't do for you what I do? One who makes you feel like shit?" Armand shot back, frustration etched across his face.

"What's the difference between you and him at this point? We're in here playing house, and you're fucking married," I retorted, my voice steady.

"Dior, want me to take you home?" Destiny appeared, her presence a welcome distraction.

"Yes, please," I told her, relief flooding my veins. As I turned, I caught sight of Shanny stepping out front, a devilish smirk spreading across her face with a busted lip.

"I don't want her!" Armand yelled, causing the smirk to vanish from Shanny's face.

"You belong to her, and I have someone I belong to," I said, my voice firm as I began to walk away with Destiny.

The night had spiraled into chaos, and I felt like I was trapped in a whirlwind, the reality of the situation crashing down around me. The city lights blurred in the distance, mirroring the tumult inside me. All I wanted was to escape, to breathe, but I was tangled in a mess I couldn't easily walk away from.

TWENTY-TWO

Armand

It had been days since my birthday, and the weight of it all felt heavier than the last bottle I'd drained. Back at the hotel, I didn't even give a damn about the upscale top room. Instead, I locked myself away in one of the smallest, dingy rooms we had—my own little sanctuary of misery. The walls were closing in, and all I did was drink, drowning my thoughts in cheap whiskey. I'd bombarded Dior with calls and texts, but silence was all I got in return.

When I finally found the strength to head to her place, I was met with a fortress. Every door was chained up tight, like she was guarding against a hurricane. I was just a stray dog on the outside, scratching at the door, but she wouldn't let me in.

As I lay sprawled on the bed, a knock echoed through the silence. At first, I ignored it, hoping it would go away, but the knocking grew more insistent. Reluctantly, I pulled myself up, dragging the nearly empty bottle with me, my head spinning from the booze. I swung the door open, standing there in nothing but my boxers, the reality of my state hitting me like a truck. "What?" I barked, irritation spilling over.

It was Renee, the assistant I'd always considered a bit too professional for her own good. "Sir, I'm sorry to bother you, but I need your signature on some documents that can't wait any longer," she said, a clipboard in hand. She stepped into the room, her heels clicking on the floor, and I couldn't help but feel her gaze on me.

I glanced at the papers—payroll and other boring shit that felt like a million miles away from my current reality. But as I scribbled my signature, I couldn't shake the feeling of being scrutinized. When I looked up, I caught Renee staring—not at my face, but way lower. "You like what you see?" I slurred, a smirk creeping onto my lips.

"Huh?" she replied, caught off guard.

"Do you like what you see? Do you want some of this?" I asked, my hand casually grabbing my dick, the whiskey emboldening my words.

"Ummm…" she hesitated, her cheeks flushing as I took her hand, pulling her into the dimly lit room. The air was thick with tension, a heady mix of desperation and reckless desire swirling around us like the city's vibrant nightlife just outside the window. I could feel the pulse of the streets, the distant sounds of laughter and sirens, a stark contrast to the storm brewing between us.

"Sir?" she said softly, not fighting against my pull.

"Suck it," I shot back, my voice low and teasing.

"But sir, you are my boss," she replied, her eyes wide, a mix of shock and intrigue.

"You want me to pay you to suck it? So be it. Suck it, and I'll throw an extra grand in your check," I told her, the whiskey giving me a confidence I didn't know I had.

She hesitated for a moment, weighing her options, then dropped to her knees, tugging down my boxers to reveal my dick. I took a sip from my bottle, watching her intently, the warmth of the liquor coursing through me. Just then, the room door swung open, and in walked my brothers.

"Nigga, what you doing?" Ahmad exclaimed, eyes wide with disbelief.

"Ayo, shorty, get out," Armani said, his tone sharp.

"Nah, she stays. You get out," I countered defiantly.

"Excuse me, miss, please do yourself a favor and leave," Ahmad said, stepping forward to help Renee up from the floor. She looked a little confused as she wiped her mouth, like a deer caught in headlights.

"But I need that $1,000," she protested, glancing between us.

Ahmad pulled out some cash, slipping a few bills into her hand. "Now please leave," he repeated, his voice more insistent.

Renee grabbed her clipboard, her expression a mix of embarrassment and confusion, and headed for the door. Ahmad followed her out, throwing a glance back at me.

"Nigga, so now you paying for bitches to give you head?" Armani asked, shaking his head in disbelief.

"Man, miss me with that shit," I muttered, walking over to the bed and taking a seat, my head spinning with a mix of anger and frustration.

I heard the door click shut, and then Armani reappeared, his brow furrowed. "What the fuck are you doing? That bitch works for you! Do you know how you could've just fucked everything up for yourself?"

"Everything is already fucked up! Shanny fucked up my life!" I yelled, the words spilling out, raw and unfiltered.

"She might have helped, but she ain't fuck everything up by herself. You played a part in that, too. You were so in love but didn't tell Dior the truth," Armani said, his voice steady but firm.

"Nigga, fuck you. You just wanted to fuck my bitch," I shot back, anger flaring.

"And as fucked up as that is, I was real with her. You hid stuff from her, pretending to be Prince Charming instead of keeping it real. You should've laid all your shit on the table and let her decide if she still wanted to fuck with you."

"Nigga, you want me to beat your ass again?" I asked, rising from the bed, fists clenched, adrenaline rushing through me. Armani pulled up his pants, a challenge glinting in his eyes.

"Do what you gotta do, but you need to wake the fuck up, man," Armani shot back, the tension in the room thick enough to cut with a knife.

"Sit down. Your ass is drunk," Ahmad said, pushing me back onto the bed with a forceful hand. "Truth is, Armani's right, whether you want to hear it or not. You helped fuck up your own shit. Now you're in here all depressed like it's the end of the world. You need to pull your shit together."

The liquor had my emotions all out of whack, and before I knew it, tears were spilling down my cheeks. "Bro, she won't even talk to me. I love that girl. I can't see my life without her," I poured out, my voice cracking, the weight of my feelings crashing over me like a tidal wave.

"But you fucked up. You have to accept that and give her the time and space to think and deal with her own emotions," Ahmad said, his tone softer now, almost sympathetic. "That girl changed her life for you."

"I'ma kill Shanny," I muttered, the rage bubbling up inside me like a volcano ready to erupt.

"No, you ain't," Ahmad countered, shaking his head.

Hall Pass

"Yes, I am! We'd be fine right now! I'd still have Dior if it wasn't for that crazy ass, and y'all know that!" I snapped, the bitterness spilling over.

"And that may be a little true," Armani admitted, crossing his arms. "But had you told Dior when Shanny showed up at that party, you could have avoided her feeling used, lied to, hurt, embarrassed—any of those feelings. She would've already known, and Shanny would've just seemed like the bitter bitch she is, trying to stop you from getting a divorce."

It was hard to hear, but deep down, I knew he was right. I had given Shanny the leverage she needed to set my relationship with Dior ablaze, and now I was left picking up the ashes. The memory of Dior's laughter, her smile—it felt like a ghost haunting me, a reminder of everything I had lost.

"Damn it," I muttered, running a hand through my hair, frustration boiling inside me. "I didn't want it to end like this."

"Then do something about it," Ahmad urged, his eyes locked onto mine. "Stop wallowing in self-pity and fight for her. Show her you're serious this time. You've still got a chance, but you need to man up and own your shit."

I looked at them, the weight of my situation crashing down like a tidal wave. They were right; I had to find a way to fix this, to confront my mistakes head-on. But how could I do that when I felt so damn broken? Outside, the city pulsed with life—the sirens, the laughter, the neon lights flickering in the night—but all I felt was a hollow ache inside. I knew I had to step back into that chaos and reclaim what was mine.

"All I want is my girl back," I cried out, the desperation in my voice raw and unfiltered.

"Well, you may have fucked that up," Armani shot back, his words cutting like glass.

"Nigga, fuck you," I snapped, the anger bubbling over.

"Armani, just leave," Ahmad interjected, his voice cutting through the thickening tension like a knife.

"Why the hell I gotta go? This nigga needs tough love," Armani shot back, his defiance echoing in the cramped room.

"Nigga, you don't know shit about love or what I need! I don't fuck with you right now, so why the fuck are you even here? Your ass is foul, and I'm pretty sure you told Shanny to crash the party just because you can't stand seeing me happy," I snapped, the anger spilling over like a boiling pot.

"Bitch, I'm your brother! All I want is to see you happy!" Armani yelled, his frustration palpable, the tension crackling between us like electricity.

"Call me a bitch again, and we're gonna have a problem," I warned, my heart racing, every beat a reminder of how close we were to crossing a line.

"Armani, just leave," Ahmad said, his voice steady but strained with the weight of our mounting conflict. The room fell silent, the air thick with unresolved emotions, a storm brewing just beneath the surface.

"Fuck it, I'm out." Armani spat out his words like venom, turning on his heel and storming toward the door. It slammed shut behind him, leaving a heavy silence that felt almost suffocating. The aftermath of our argument hung in the air, like smoke from a fire that refused to die down.

Ahmad turned to me, concern etched on his face. "You can't let this shit consume you, man. You need to fight for Dior, but you gotta do it the right way. Pull your shit together."

I nodded, knowing he was right. The anger had ebbed,

replaced by a gnawing urgency in my gut. I couldn't let this be the end—not when there was still a flicker of hope. Outside, the city pulsed with life, its chaos a stark contrast to the turmoil swirling in my chest. Somewhere in that vibrant mess, Dior was waiting for me to make my move.

Ahmad's voice cut through my thoughts again. "Look, I'm not talking to you as a brother right now, because clearly that's not what you need. You need some real talk. You've been laying in your own shit for days. Get the fuck up. Get back on your grind, and do it now. You're not a bitch, so stop acting like one."

"Ahmad, I love her," I said, feeling the weight of my words.

"Yeah, but right now she ain't here. So get your shit together. If she comes back, I'm sure this isn't what she wants to see."

With that, Ahmad left, the door clicking softly behind him but the conversation still echoing in my mind. I lay back on the bed, my body numb, my thoughts racing. I replayed all the times I wanted to tell Dior about Shanny but held back. I missed her like crazy, and I had promised I wouldn't hurt her again—but here I was, having done just that. I told her she deserved better, but I hadn't done better myself, and now she was drifting away, maybe for good.

Hall Pass

As I lay there, the sun began to rise, casting a golden hue across my room. It felt like a new day, but I was still trapped in my own darkness. I picked up my phone, hesitating before sending a text.

"I'm not sure if you've blocked me or if I'll ever hear from you again, or if you'll even open this message, but Dior, please know I meant it when I said I never wanted to hurt you. I fucked up. I hid things because I didn't want to lose you again, but I was scared and wrong. If you give me just one chance to talk face to face, I promise I'll do more than just apologize. I'll explain everything. Just... please let me in."

I hit send, my heart pounding like a bass drum, hoping against hope that she would see it—that maybe this was the first step toward making things right. The weight of uncertainty pressed down on me like a heavy fog.

I pulled myself from the bed, forcing my body into motion, and headed downstairs. I needed to drown my feelings in work, just like I had done so many times before. I walked into my office and sank into my chair, exhaling slowly as I tried to shake off the remnants of the argument. I pulled out my phone, staring at the screen, hoping for a response from Dior—even if it was just a "leave me alone." But deep down, I wasn't surprised when silence greeted me.

Just as I was about to lose myself in my thoughts, a knock echoed at my office door.

"Come in," I called out, my voice barely masking my frustration.

The door swung open, and Renee stepped inside, her expression serious. "Renee, close the door so we can talk," I instructed, my tone firm. She complied, shutting the door behind her, and I motioned for her to take a seat.

"Listen, what happened yesterday was fucked up on my part," I started, the words tumbling out before I could second-guess myself.

"Don't worry about it," she replied, brushing it off with a wave of her hand.

"No, I owe you an apology. I don't know if you realize it, but I was in a bad headspace and had been drinking. That's no excuse." I paused, taking a breath. "But I'm still going to give you the money as promised."

"You don't have to," she said, crossing her arms. "Your brother gave me enough. Honestly, I knew you were weak at that moment and used it to my advantage. I've wanted to do this for a while; I just didn't want to risk my job. The money was just a nice incentive, but I would've done it either way."

"Still, I want to apologize. As a man who respects women and as your boss, I was wrong. I don't need any lawsuits on my hands," I said, trying to keep my voice steady.

"Relax, you don't have to worry about that. I love my job here and appreciate the opportunities you've given me. But just know, if the chance ever arises for us to do that while you're sober, let me know. I promise it'll stay between us." She winked, a playful glint in her eye.

We cleared the air, laughter slowly replacing the tension. I quickly shifted the subject, wrapping up any business matters that needed discussing. As Renee exited my office, Shanny came sliding in, her smile bright but laced with mischief.

"Nice to see you're finally out of hiding like a little bitch," she teased, her voice dripping with sarcasm.

My jaw tightened as I looked at her, irritation flaring. "I know damn well, after all the shit you've caused, that you shouldn't be standing in my office right now."

"Damn, you that hurt over that basic bitch?" she shot back, her attitude unrepentant.

"Watch your fucking mouth," I demanded, feeling the anger boiling just below the surface.

"I'm just saying," she shrugged, her nonchalance only fueling my frustration.

"Shanny, get the fuck out," I told her firmly, my patience wearing thin. I could feel the tension in the air, thick and heavy, like a storm ready to break.

As Shanny rolled her eyes and strutted out, I couldn't shake the feeling that everything was spiraling out of control. My mind was still reeling from the confrontation with Armani and the unresolved feelings for Dior. I needed to get my head straight, but the chaos around me made it damn near impossible.

"Nah, we need to talk now that your little bitch ain't in your head making you act funny toward me," Shanny said, her voice sharp and demanding. I frowned, refusing to give her the reaction she craved.

"Now that this divorce shit is over…" she trailed off. I cut her off.

"I still want a divorce. Whether I'm with Dior or not, I'm not going to be with you. Now you need to sign those damn papers or else," I stated, my tone firm.

"What did that bitch do to you?" she shot back, venom lacing her words and anger painting her face. "You keep talking about Dior, and you're gonna see a side of me you didn't know was there. You don't even know her. You could take some lessons from her about being a real woman because she's more of a woman than you are or could ever be."

"Fuck her. She came in trying to take you from me and making you act different," Shanny spat, her frustration boiling over.

"No, stupid. I went after her. She was my first real love. If I hadn't gotten locked up, I would have been married to her instead of you. She didn't make me move differently; she didn't even know you fucking existed. I don't love you and never have. I don't know why that's so hard for you to understand, Shanny, and I never will. I'm not going to stop trying to get Dior back, so just divorce me. You will always be the bitter non-factor."

"But you married me," she retorted, crossing her arms defiantly.

"I married you because your dad asked me to. We went on three dates before I proposed. It wasn't because you were that damn cute or special. Or that the pussy you gave me the first night was that great. I put a ring on your finger out of a promise to your dad because I owed him. He needed to know you'd be taken care of, or your ass was gonna end up broke and homeless. Now that's some honesty for your ass."

"Oh, now you're feeling bold?" she shot back, her eyes narrowing.

"No, now I feel whole. Outside of Dior, I don't owe nobody shit. When I married you, I didn't give a fuck about love. I didn't think it was in the cards for me, and I was okay with it. But Dior came along and showed me I deserved to be loved. She gave me a reason to love, and she made it easy to do. She had every reason not to love me, not to give me another chance. But she still did, with an open heart, wanting nothing but my love in return. If she takes me back, the man I'll be to her is one you could never get out of me."

The look on Shanny's face twisted into something dark. "Well, since we're giving out honesty, here's some for your ass," she said, suddenly pulling something from her bag and hurling it at me. When I picked up the object from my desk, my heart sank. It was a pregnancy test.

"What the fuck is this?" I demanded, my stomach dropping.

"What does it look like?" she responded, a smirk playing on her lips.

"Who's is it?" I pressed, my pulse racing.

"Mine. You're going to be a daddy."

"Bullshit!" I yelled, my anger flaring. "I figured since we were handing out honesty, here you go. Checkmate, bitch," she shot back, heading toward the door.

"Fuck!" I screamed, flipping my desk over in a fit of rage. Papers scattered everywhere, and I pulled out my phone, dialing Ahmad's number in a panic.

"What's good, bro? How you feeling today?" he answered, his voice calm.

"The bitch is pregnant! This can't be my fucking life!" I screamed, my frustration spilling over.

"Slow down. Who's pregnant? Dior?" he asked, confusion creeping into his tone.

"No, fucking Shanny!" I told him, pacing the room.

"How the fuck did that happen? You was fucking both of them?" he asked incredulously.

"No! The last time I touched Shanny was the morning after seeing Dior for the first time, and I haven't been with her since," I explained, gripping the phone tightly.

"So then how do you know she's pregnant?" he probed.

"She just came in my office talking shit and threw a pregnancy test at me," I said, the reality sinking in.

"And you believe her?" he asked, skepticism dripping from his words.

"Why would she lie about being pregnant?" I shot back.

"That bitch is crazy. Did you forget she ran her car into yours in broad daylight? She could have had someone else take that test just to keep stringing you along, thinking that it would stop you from leaving her," he warned.

"Well, if she's pregnant, I can't leave her. I know how it was for us growing up without a father. I'm not about to do that to mine," I replied, my resolve hardening.

"And I respect that, bro. I would expect nothing less from you. But don't be no damn fool. If you don't see her pee on that test yourself, don't believe she's pregnant. And even after that, a DNA test is needed," he said, his voice steady.

When I sat back and thought about what he was saying, he was right. "You know what? You're right. I'm gonna call you back," I told him, hanging up and grabbing my keys. I headed out, driving to the nearest CVS and grabbing three different types of pregnancy tests before making my way back home.

When I arrived, Shanny was lounging on the couch, watching TV. I dropped the bag of tests on the coffee table with a thud. "Go take them," I ordered, my heart racing.

"It's too late for a Plan B," she said, a hint of defiance in her voice.

"That's not a Plan B," I shot back.

"Then what is it?" she asked, sitting up, her curiosity piqued as she opened the bag.

The tension in the room was thick, wrapping around us like a heavy fog, and I couldn't shake the dread settling in my stomach. Whatever came next could change everything.

When Shanny realized it was a pregnancy test, her defensiveness kicked in like a switch. "I gave you a pregnancy test. Why do I have to take three more?"

"Because I need to be sure," I responded, my voice steady but laced with urgency.

"Sure of what?" she shot back, crossing her arms defiantly.

"Sure that you're actually pregnant," I said, meeting her gaze with a hard stare.

"I told you I was, and I gave you that test. How much more do you want from me?" she challenged, her voice rising.

"For you to take the damn test and stop playing games," I insisted, trying to keep my frustration in check.

"No, I don't have to pee," she replied, a smirk creeping onto her face.

"Fine. I'll wait," I said, taking a seat on the edge of the couch, my patience wearing thin.

"I don't get why you're acting like this. You know you fucked me and what could happen," she said, her tone a mix of indignation and entitlement.

I didn't respond; I just looked at her, the silence thickening the air between us.

I sat there for what felt like hours, the clock ticking loudly, each second amplifying my anxiety. "Shanny, take the test!" I yelled, my voice echoing off the walls.

"No! You're not going to treat me like some hoe just lying to you. Then call the doctor now and make an appointment, and I'll go with you," she snapped.

"No," she answered, her defiance infuriating me further.

"Do you see why it's hard for me to believe you? If you're really pregnant, why won't you just take the test?" I pressed, trying to keep my voice calm.

"Because my fucking husband should believe me!" she shot back, her anger flaring.

I could feel my temper rising, a fire igniting within me. Something told me my best bet was to leave before I said something I couldn't take back. I grabbed my keys and walked toward the door.

"You leaving?" Shanny asked, her voice dripping with sarcasm.

"I am," I replied, keeping my tone even.

"Fine, don't come back!" she said, but I could hear the crack in her bravado.

With the most calm voice I could muster, I turned to her. "If you are actually pregnant, I want a DNA test. If it's mine, I'm going to be the best father I can be and take care of my child—but me and you will still be done."

She interrupted me, her eyes blazing. "And if you divorce me, you'll never see our child. I'll be damned if you

Hall Pass

have my baby around another bitch!"

I held my ground, refusing to let her words shake me. "I will do what I want with my child. Don't let your mouth write a check that you know you can't uphold. I will pull every dollar from you and make you look like you're unfit to take care of a child, and I'll get full custody. I just hope that you are pregnant because if this is another one of your games, you're going to hate what happens next."

With that, I turned and walked out the door, the weight of the conversation hanging heavy in the air behind me. The cool breeze hit my face as I stepped outside, and I took a deep breath, trying to clear my head. Whatever storm was brewing inside me, I knew I had to face it head-on.

TWENTY-THREE

Dior

I lay in the soft cocoon of my blankets, the early morning light filtering through the curtains, casting a warm glow across my room. I closed my eyes, surrendering to the pull of sleep once more, my mind drifting into a realm where the boundaries of reality blurred with desire.

In this dreamscape, Armand appeared, his presence as magnetic as it had always been. The dimly lit room was filled with the heady scent of sandalwood and his signature cologne—an intoxicating blend that sent my heart racing and wrapped me in memories. I could see the way the light danced upon his skin, highlighting the strong contours of his jaw and the slight curve of his lips, which formed that familiar, mischievous smile that had once made me forget the world around me.

We were wrapped up in each other, the warmth of his body igniting a fire within me that I thought had long since cooled. The tension that had built up over the past few days—the painful revelation of his marriage—melted away, leaving only the raw, unfiltered connection we had once shared. My fingers brushed over his hair as he leaned closer, the heat of his breath warming my skin. "Dior," he murmured, his voice a low, sultry whisper that sent shivers down my spine, awakening every nerve in my body.

I could feel the weight of his gaze, burning with an intensity that was both comforting and agonizing. The memory of his birthday party flooded my mind, vibrant laughter and celebration abruptly overshadowed by the sting of betrayal when I learned the truth. Yet here, in this dream, the world outside faded to nothing, and all that mattered was the space between us, charged with a longing that felt both familiar and forbidden.

"Why haven't you talked to me?" he asked, his voice laced with an urgency that made my heart ache. In the dream, I wanted to reach out, to bridge the chasm that had opened between us, but the words caught in my throat, tangled in the web of hurt and confusion I had woven since that night.

I leaned in, my lips brushing against his, a gentle inquiry that demanded an answer. The kiss ignited a fire within me, a desperate need to reclaim the connection we had shared before the truth shattered my trust. I could feel the warmth of his body pressing against mine, the way he held me as if I was the only thing that mattered in his world.

The kiss deepened, and time seemed to stretch, the outside world fading into nothingness. My hands wound around his neck, pulling him closer as if I could fuse our bodies together, erasing the distance that felt like an insurmountable chasm. The taste of him was intoxicating, a blend of sweetness and spice that left me yearning for more, a flavor I had missed more than I cared to admit.

Just as I surrendered to the moment, embracing the dream's intoxicating pull, a flicker of doubt wormed its way into my mind. Could I really trust him again? Was this bliss just an illusion, a fleeting escape from the harsh reality that awaited me? But in this dream, those questions faded away, leaving only the heady thrill of his presence, the promise of what could be if we could navigate the storm that had torn us apart.

"Dior," he whispered again, his voice laced with both longing and regret, pulling me deeper into the depths of our tangled emotions. It was a question and a plea all at once, and as I melted into him, I felt a surge of hope. Whatever lay beyond this moment, I was ready to face it—together or apart.

But just as the dream began to spiral into something deeper, a distant sound pulled me from the warmth of his embrace. The reality of my waking life rushed back, cold and stark against the heat of my dream. With a start, I opened my eyes, the echoes of Armand's absence lingering like a haunting whisper in the air.

I sat up, my heart pounding, the remnants of the dream clinging to me like a gossamer thread. Guilt washed over me, mingling with the vestiges of desire still flickering in my chest. I hadn't spoken to him since that night, and the thought of facing him, of confronting the truth we had both been avoiding, felt like standing at the edge of a steep hill, the drop into uncertainty looming beneath me.

But deep down, I knew I couldn't run forever. The dream had stirred something within me, a visceral reminder of what was at stake. I glanced at my phone, its screen dark and silent, and felt a pang of longing. It was time to decide: to confront the shadows of our past or to let the silence stretch on, a chasm that might never be crossed again.

As I swung my legs over the side of the bed, the chill of the wooden floor sent a shiver up my spine. I took a deep breath, steadying myself for what lay ahead. The air was thick with unspoken words, and I could feel the weight of my choices pressing down on me like a storm cloud ready to burst. I knew I had to make a move. I couldn't let fear dictate my next steps any longer. With resolve, I reached for my phone, ready to bridge the distance that had grown between us.

But as I picked it up, doubt crept in. I placed the phone back down, not yet ready to check it. Instead, I let my legs dangle over the edge of the bed, the cool floor grounding me in reality. I could no longer hide from the truth or from the man who had stolen my heart even as he shattered my trust. Today, I would reach out. Today, I would face him. Just not right now.

Breanna J

Life had to go on. I was hurting, angry, embarrassed, and a whirlwind of other emotions since Armand's party. But even with all of that, I wouldn't dare hide away and miss out on money. My bills wouldn't grant me that luxury. Plus, the same day as the party, I'd come home and gone left eye with a hint of Bernadine, waiting to exhale on Armand's stuff he had left at my place. It didn't erase what had happened, but damn if it didn't ease some of the pain, if only for a moment.

Armand had come by my house a few times, and he'd called and texted, but I wasn't ready to talk. In my mind, there was nothing he could say that would change what had happened. I expected more from him—more honesty, more courage.

Now knowing that he owned the hotel, I hadn't been going there to work. I didn't want to run into him or his wife. I wasn't sure what I would do if I saw either one of them. Still, I kept putting together looks and ideas, trying to keep my mind occupied and off the drama.

When I finally headed into work, my morning routine felt so different. As I sat in my office, my phone rang. "Hello?" I answered.

"Mrs. Waye, you have a visitor down here," the front desk girl said.

"Is it Armand Riggins?" I asked, my heart sinking.

"No, ma'am," she replied.

"Okay, give me a few. I'll be right down," I told her, trying to shake off the anxiety coiling in my stomach.

When I stepped off the elevator, I was surprised to see Armani in the lobby. "Clearly, I need a new place to work because why does everyone keep thinking it's okay to pop up here on me?" I said, rolling my eyes.

"Man, chill," Armani replied, holding up his hands in a gesture of peace.

"I don't care how mad I am at your brother; I'm not fucking with you," I shot back, my voice colder than I intended.

"Look, I'm not here for that," he said, clearly exasperated.

"Then why are you here?" I asked, crossing my arms with an attitude.

"Man, my brother loves you. He's in love with you—something he's never been with anyone else, not even that waterhead wife of his," he said, his tone serious.

"I don't care about that. Your brother is a liar and a cheater," I shot back, my heart racing with anger.

"Shut up and just listen," he insisted, his voice firm.

I rolled my eyes defiantly but stayed silent, curiosity edging out my irritation. "Armand loves you, and for good reasons. Women like you don't come around often. That might be why my ass wanted you. You're a dope-ass woman. You're loyal, you're loving, and you've got your shit together, Dior. Anyone can see that you and Armand are meant for each other. Yes, he's married, and I'm not trying to downplay that. But he doesn't love her. He doesn't even care about her or treat her the way he treats you."

"Life has taught me that two men can share the same name and still not be the same man," he continued.

"That shit don't make sense," I said, shaking my head.

"It does. The Armand you got was the real one—the

loving one, the whole man. The one she got was based on a debt he felt he owed her father," Armani explained.

"What debt?" I asked, my curiosity piqued despite myself.

"That's for Armand to tell you. But I will tell you this: he's been trying to divorce her. She won't sign the papers because that would change her whole lifestyle. She's a hood bitch who got lucky marrying a dude who provides her with shit she can't even spell or pronounce. She's a fucking gold digger. So, of course, she won't leave easily," he answered.

"I don't care. And tell your brother not to send anyone else to my job to plead his case," I said, my voice firm.

"You're so fucking stubborn," Armani shot back. "Armand didn't send me here. I looked you up and came on my own because this shit has really got my brother fucked up. And as much as you're trying to stand here and act tough, I know it's got you fucked up too. He's not himself."

I exhaled in irritation. I was hearing Armani, and a piece of me was happy to hear that Armand was suffering, but Armani's words couldn't change how I felt.

"What will it take to make this better?" Armani asked,

his tone softening.

"Nothing can make it better. As long as he has a wife, there ain't shit that can make it better. Now you have a good day; I have a job to do," I said, turning to walk away from him.

Back in my office, I picked up my phone, ready to cuss Armand out for sending Armani to my job, but I couldn't. My hand began to shake, and tears rolled down my face. For the rest of the day, I sat in my office, working with the door closed, avoiding all calls.

Even with what had happened at work today, I couldn't muster the strength to reach out to Armand. I drove straight home, craving nothing more than to crawl into my damn bed and hide from the world. But when I pulled into my driveway, the sight of my mother and Destiny waiting for me made my stomach churn. "Why the fuck won't everyone just leave me the hell alone?" was all I could think as I parked, frustration boiling beneath the surface.

"Why are y'all here?" I asked as I stepped out of the car and walked toward the front door.

"We're here to check on you," Destiny replied, her tone gentle but firm.

"Why?" I shot back.

"Because, just like I knew he would, that damn boy hurt you," my mom said, crossing her arms as she eyed me with concern.

I shot her a glare. "You told her," I accused, looking back at Destiny.

"I was worried about you. You weren't answering anyone's calls or texts," Destiny said, her voice softening.

"Because I needed my time and space. I'm fine, see? I'm fine. I'm fine!" I insisted, trying to push them away.

"I knew…" My mom started, but I cut her off.

"If you're here to say 'I told you so,' save it. I don't want to hear it!" I yelled, the words spilling out in a rush of anger.

"Listen, Dior, no one is here to say anything. We just want to make sure you're okay. Can we come in and sit with you for a little?" Destiny asked, her eyes pleading.

Breanna J

I knew that unless I let them in, they wouldn't leave. With a heavy sigh, I opened the door and stepped inside, leaving it ajar for them to follow. The house was dark, the curtains drawn tight, and I hadn't bothered to clean. I was sure both of them were surprised by the state of the place, but I didn't care. I was just functioning through my emotions.

I walked upstairs to my room, stripped off my clothes, and crawled into bed. Moments later, Destiny and my mom kicked off their shoes and climbed in beside me, sandwiching me with their warmth and love. I lay there, fighting back tears, feeling like I had already done enough crying. Eventually, exhaustion took over, and I drifted off to sleep.

When I woke, the house smelled of bleach and Pine-Sol. I blinked against the brightness, confused for a moment, and then glanced around my room. It was clean, spotless even. I got up to pour myself a drink and realized my mom and Destiny must have tag-teamed the cleaning, transforming my chaotic space into something almost serene. There was food simmering on the stove, the rich aroma wafting through the air, a comforting reminder that life still went on outside my emotional turmoil.

I grabbed a glass of wine and headed back to my room. As I settled into bed, I figured there was no better time than now to acknowledge all the texts and calls I had been ignoring for days. The most recent message was from my dad. I was sure my mom had gone home and spilled everything. But being the man he was, he didn't want to push me; he simply let me know he was always there if I needed him and that he loved me.

Then I read the next message, and it felt like the air had been knocked out of my lungs.

"Dior, I know I've sent plenty of messages and calls, and I know you're not talking to me, but I don't want to hurt you any more than I already have. I want you to hear it from me—Shanny might be pregnant."

My eyes filled with tears, and in a fit of rage, I hurled my phone at the wall, the screen shattering on impact. Just then, the doorbell rang. I pulled myself from bed, thinking it was Destiny and my mom returning. But when I opened the door, I found Sergio standing there.

I fell into his arms, crying. "How in the hell could Armand be doing this to me?" I thought. He was married and had a baby on the way. My heart shattered all over again, and I couldn't hold back the tears.

That night, for the first time ever, Sergio brought me comfort. He didn't say anything; he just held me, his presence a quiet reassurance. I wasn't even sure if he realized

I was crying over another man the whole time.

The next morning, I woke up to find Sergio still there, asleep on the couch. Tiptoeing to the bathroom, I caught a glimpse of myself in the mirror. I looked like a mess—hair wild, eyes puffy. Just as I was about to step out, the bathroom door opened, and Sergio walked in. I instinctively grabbed my towel tightly, even though he had seen me naked plenty of times before.

He planted a soft kiss on my shoulder that sent a shiver down my spine. "How are you feeling this morning?" he asked, his voice low and soothing.

"I'm okay," I replied, sliding past him and heading back to my room to get dressed. I heard him turn on the water and then come back out. He walked over to me, taking my hand gently. "Let me talk to you," he said, leading me to the bed.

He sat on the edge and pulled me between his legs. "Tonight, I want to take you out to dinner somewhere nice, just to help you relax."

"Umm…" I hesitated.

"I'm not trying to pressure you. All you have to do is get dressed. I'll pick you up, I'll pay, I'll do everything," he said, his tone earnest.

I just looked at him. Although I had told Armand I was going back to Sergio, it was mostly to hurt him; I hadn't really planned on it. Last night, Sergio had just happened to catch me at a weak moment.

"Please, just give me this one chance. If I fuck it up, you don't have to hear from me or speak to me again," he pleaded, his eyes sincere.

I looked around the room, the memories of last night flooding back, and finally nodded. "Okay."

TWENTY-FOUR

Armand

I hadn't heard from Shanny about her taking the pregnancy test or making a doctor's appointment, and the uncertainty gnawed at me like a bad hangover. So, I threw myself into work to keep my mind straight and busy. The restaurant was my sanctuary, and tonight, I was down a bartender and a waiter. Thank God, I was the kind of owner who had no issue jumping in and getting my hands dirty. I slid behind the bar, ready to pour my heart into the drinks and the chaos.

I even called Renee, begging her to come in for some overtime. She agreed, and I breathed a little easier knowing she'd be waiting tables while I juggled cocktails and orders.

In the midst of crafting a complicated drink, I looked up and froze. There she was, standing at my hostess desk—Dior. Had the moment finally arrived for us to talk? She looked so damn beautiful, it was like she had stepped out of

Hall Pass

a dream, and I couldn't tear my eyes away from her. I passed off the drink and wiped my hands, preparing to walk over to her when, out of nowhere, Sergio strolled in and grabbed her hand.

Anger surged through me like a lightning bolt. No fucking way had she brought this dude to my restaurant. I watched as my hostess led them to a table in the corner. Sergio seemed excited, practically beaming, but I hadn't seen a single smile from Dior. I stood there, fists clenched, watching them for what felt like an eternity before I decided to confront the situation.

"Welcome. What can I get for you tonight?" I forced a smile, but I could feel the tension radiating off me. Sergio looked up, a smirk creeping across his face. But when I glanced at Dior, shock and disbelief were etched on her features.

"Bring us your most expensive bottle of wine," Sergio ordered, his tone dripping with arrogance. "She must be paying, because we both know you can't afford that."

A fire ignited in my chest. "What did you say?" I shot back, my voice low and dangerous.

"I don't repeat myself, and I know damn well you heard me," I said, sizing him up, letting the heat of the moment fuel my defiance. Dior's head dropped, the weight of the situation visibly crushing her.

But you know what? I was still the owner, and I wasn't about to let this asshole ruin my night. "I'll bring you what you asked for," I said, nodding coolly as I turned away from the table. I could hear Sergio muttering some smart comment about me working as a waiter, but his words only fueled my resolve. Tonight was mine, and I wasn't going to let anyone take it away from me.

I grabbed the expensive wine and an ice bucket, feeling the weight of the moment settle on my shoulders. My staff asked if they could handle it, but I declined. I wasn't about to let anyone else serve them. I headed back to the table, my heart pounding. "So, what can I get for you two? I know you love salmon, and we have some really good salmon over rice tonight," I said, directing my gaze at Dior, who was doing everything in her power to avoid eye contact with me.

"We would like—"

"Nigga, I'm not talking to you. I'm talking to my girl. I don't really care what you want," I cut in sharply, my voice low but firm.

"So again, baby, what can I get you?" I asked her, trying to keep the tension from spilling over.

Hall Pass

"Armand, don't do this," she said in a whisper, a plea wrapped in concern.

"Do what?" I shot back, my gaze still locked on her.

"Nigga!" Sergio barked, his voice loud and brimming with bravado.

"Nigga, what?" I replied, turning to him with a look that dared him to step out of line.

Sergio shot me a death stare. "Nigga, you're going to lose your job today," he threatened.

"I doubt it," I said, my confidence unwavering. "Send us over a new waiter or your boss," Sergio demanded, trying to assert his power.

"What for? You think if you complain, you'll get free food? Man, listen, don't worry about it—I got this for you. Let me feed my girl, because you don't know shit about taking care of her. That's how she ended up back with me in the first place," I said, my voice dripping with defiance.

"Both of you, stop," Dior interjected, tension rising between us.

"You don't know shit about me. Don't worry about me and my wife. Save your little waiter money," Sergio said, standing up, puffing out his chest.

I laughed, a sharp sound that cut through the atmosphere. "Sit your little silly ass down. Nigga, nothing about my money is little. I own this place. We aren't the same. Everything about me is grown man and big dog energy," I said, my voice steady. Dior looked at me, shock written all over her face when she realized I owned the place.

"Stop," she demanded, but the look on Sergio's face let me know I had just hit a nerve, and I could see the anger simmering beneath his skin.

"Damn, baby, so you really went back to this clown-ass nigga who still ain't got a clue on how to handle you," I said, as if Sergio wasn't even at the table.

"Armand, you really need to stop. I am not your concern. Where is your wife?" she shot back, trying to deflect the tension.

"Whatever. I bet he still can't fuck you right. Remember

Hall Pass

how I used to place your legs on my shoulders, kissing and licking your inner thigh while your body would tense up, craving more?" I said, watching her adjust in her seat, a flush creeping up her neck.

"Stop," she said in a low tone, but I could see the fire in her eyes, the way the past hung between us like thick smoke, thickening the air around us.

"It's okay, baby. I know you're sitting over there right now with your legs crossed as tight as you can, trying to control your pussy from getting wet. Even when you're mad at me, your body still calls for me."

"I will fuck you up in here," Sergio yelled, his voice laced with bravado.

"Is that what you think?" I shot back, my tone dripping with disdain.

"Armand, please stop," Dior said, her voice strained.

"Tell me I'm wrong. Tell me that even sitting here with this clown, your body doesn't still want me," I challenged, leaning in closer, letting the tension simmer.

"Can we go?" Dior asked, her eyes flicking to Sergio, a plea wrapped in frustration.

"You know I'll let y'all be great. I'll send a different waiter over," I said, but before I left, I planted the smoothest kiss on Dior's hand as we made eye contact, holding her gaze just a moment longer.

The tension at Dior's table was thick enough to slice through with a knife. I pulled out my phone, heart racing, and sent a text: "I want to taste that sweet pussy right now and make you squirt a little. Meet me in the back." I watched her look at her phone, anticipation curling in my gut.

My phone buzzed, and I glanced down at her response: "You really think I'm going to do that when I'm here with my husband?"

"Why not? He was the dumb one to bring you right to me. You know, like I know, he can't make you feel like I do."

"No, thank you. I'm all set," she shot back, putting her phone down, the finality of her words cutting through me like a cold breeze.

I was beyond pissed. The air was electric, buzzing with

unspoken words and simmering emotions. "You okay?" Renee asked, her voice low and soothing as she gently rubbed her hand across my back, sending a jolt of warmth through me.

"Yeah, I'll be alright," I replied, trying to shake off the storm brewing inside me.

She narrowed her eyes, a hint of concern mixed with something else—something playful. "You sure? You look pissed. I can help you with that," she said, her tongue flicking out to wet her lips, drawing my attention like a moth to a flame.

"Renee, we are at work," I shot back, trying to keep my tone serious despite the heat rising in my cheeks.

"And? Shit, there's no point in me acting scared or shy anymore," she countered, her confidence radiating off her in waves. "I told you, given the chance, I would satisfy you."

I glanced at her, then shot a look over to Dior's table, where the tension was palpable, a stark contrast to the heat sparking between us. Back to Renee, whose sultry gaze was challenging me, daring me to take a step further.

"Meet me in my office," I said, my voice dropping to a

low growl, the weight of the moment pressing down as I felt the pull between us grow stronger.

She took a moment to appraise me, her gaze flickering with a playful spark that sent a thrill through my veins. "With pleasure," she purred, her smile a tantalizing promise as she sauntered away, her curves swaying with a hypnotic rhythm that made it impossible to look away. The noise of the bar faded into a dull roar as I watched her go, anticipation coiling tighter in my chest like a spring ready to snap. This night was about to get a whole lot more interesting.

I cast another glance at Dior's table, the tension there palpable. A wicked idea sparked in my mind, and I called my waiter over. "Yes, sir?" he said, a hint of curiosity in his tone.

"You see that table right there?" I gestured casually. "Everything they order is on me." The waiter raised an eyebrow, but I continued, "If Sergio is anything like me, knowing that the guy who's been fucking his wife paid for their meal will drive him nuts." I shot off a quick text to Dior: "Meet me in the back now or I'm coming back to the table." I smirked at the chaos I was about to unleash, then made my way to my office.

As I pushed open the door, my breath caught in my throat. There she was—Renee—perched on my desk, clad in nothing but her lacy panties and a matching bra. The sight of her made my pulse quicken, desire flooding my senses. I closed the door behind me, the soft click echoing like a starting gun.

I strode over to her, the air thick with tension. Without hesitation, I gripped her neck gently, my thumb brushing her jawline. She bit down on her lip, her eyes sparkling with a mix of defiance and desire—a sexy little gesture that sent a rush of heat coursing through me. The world outside faded away; it was just us, caught in this electric moment, where every unspoken word hung heavily in the air.

I pulled a condom from my pocket, but she looked down and said, "We don't need that. Just pull out; I want to feel all of you." I ignored her, focusing on the hunger building inside me as I unbuckled my pants, ripped open the condom, and slid it on.

I moved Renee's panties to the side and slid right in, releasing every bit of frustration I was feeling with each aggressive thrust.

Renee gripped the edge of my desk, her nails digging in as I pounded into her, the rhythm building with each thrust. The world outside faded away, consumed by the heat of the moment—until the office door swung open.

"Are you fucking serious, Armand?" Dior's voice cut through the air like a knife, and I turned, a smirk creeping across my face.

"This is what the fuck you do to me!" Renee screamed, her voice a mix of pleasure and frustration.

"Can you close the door and get the hell out?" Renee shot back, her eyes flashing with irritation.

"Bitch, I'm gonna beat your ass! I ain't like you anyway!" Dior charged at her, fury radiating off her as the tension in the room skyrocketed.

In that moment, the atmosphere crackled with a dangerous energy, a wild cocktail of lust and rage that threatened to spill over. I felt like I was caught in the eye of a storm, the kind that whips up chaos and leaves everything in disarray. Should I push forward into this tempest or retreat into the safety of silence? One thing was crystal clear: this night was spiraling out of control, and I was standing right in the middle of it.

"Chill," I said, stepping in to grip Dior by the shoulders, trying to steady her.

"Get the fuck off me!" she spat, slapping my arm away like it was a mosquito buzzing too close.

Hall Pass

My heart raced, pounding against my ribcage as I struggled to keep my cool. "You're in here fucking this little bitch from the hotel, and you sent me a text to come back here just so I could walk in on that? You fucking sick, Armand. Have you not caused me enough pain?"

"Hold up. You brought your husband to my restaurant, right?" I shot back, desperate to deflect the blame, even though I knew it was flimsy at best.

"I didn't bring him here! He brought me! I didn't drive! I didn't even know you worked here!" Dior blurted out, her voice trembling with hurt and anger.

"Cause he doesn't. He owns it," Renee chimed in, that smug smirk playing on her lips like she was savoring the drama unfolding before her.

"Bitch!" Dior yelled, her frustration radiating off her like heat from pavement in the summer.

In that moment, I felt the weight of my actions crashing down on me, a tidal wave of regret. I had acted out of anger and jealousy, not realizing that Dior was caught in the crossfire of this messy situation. "Every time I expect more from you, you prove me wrong and just hurt me more," she said, tears streaming down her face as she turned to leave, each step a dagger to my heart.

"Dior, wait! I'm sorry, I fucked up," I called, gently grabbing her arm, desperate to hold on.

"You keep fucking up, and I've run out of space and emotions," she replied, her voice breaking like glass as she pulled away from my grip.

"Dior, please wait. Let me explain," I pleaded, desperation creeping into my tone, the air thick with unresolved tension.

"Don't worry about her. Let's finish," Renee said, stepping closer and rubbing my back, her touch trying to pull me back into the moment, a distraction I didn't want.

"Get off me. I don't want you," I said, the words tasting bitter on my tongue, each syllable laced with regret.

"But—"

"But nothing. Get dressed and get out," I told her firmly, my mind racing as I watched the two women I cared about caught in this tangled mess. The night had spiraled into chaos, and the last thing I needed was to lose Dior for good.

Hall Pass

Later, I sat at my desk, furious with myself, replaying the night's events like a broken record. Then my phone began to ring, jolting me from my thoughts. When I pulled it out, I saw it was Armani. I ignored the call and placed the phone back on my desk, but he called again, urgency dripping from his voice. "What?" I answered, irritation bubbling beneath the surface.

"I need you," he said, the urgency palpable, slicing through my anger like a knife.

Despite our rocky relationship, my heart wouldn't allow me to leave him in a fucked-up situation. "Send me the address; I'm on the way," I said, rushing to grab my things, my mind racing with the chaos of the night.

I slipped out the back, my heart pounding, unsure if Dior and Sergio were still tangled up in that chaotic mess. The weight of my decisions pressed heavily on my shoulders like a lead blanket. The night wasn't over yet, and deep down, I sensed it was about to get even messier.

I drove for twenty minutes, the city lights blurring past me, before I finally pulled up to the address Armani had given me. The house loomed in front of me—old, rundown, and definitely a place I had never seen before. Anxiety twisted in my gut, and I regretted not calling Ahmad before rushing out here. If Armani had gotten himself into some shit, I had no protection whatsoever.

I stepped out of the car, my nerves buzzing as I approached the door. I rang the doorbell, and to my relief, Armani swung it open. "What's going on?" I asked, trying to keep my voice steady despite the unease crawling up my spine.

"Follow me," he said, leading me through the dimly lit house. The inside felt like a ghost of its former self—cracked walls, peeling paint, and a lingering scent of mildew. It hit me like a ton of bricks: this place had once been a trap house, a hub for trouble and desperation.

He opened the basement door, and I hesitated, staring down into the darkness. "Come on, nigga," he urged, his tone sharp. With a deep breath, I followed him, my mind racing with dread about what lay below.

When I reached the bottom of the stairs, my breath caught in my throat. "What the fuck are you doing?" I demanded, taking in the sight before me. Shanny was tied up to a pole in the middle of the basement, fear in her eyes.

"Nigga, what you mean, what am I doing? This bitch has been an issue after issue," Armani replied, his voice tense.

Hall Pass

"So you thought the solution to my problems was to kidnap my wife and tie her up in a basement?" I shot back, disbelief washing over me.

He pulled out divorce papers from his back pocket and handed them to me. "She signed these."

"Nigga, it was never this deep to go to this extreme," I said, my heart racing as I crossed the basement toward Shanny. I gently removed the tape from her mouth. "Are you okay?" I asked, my voice laced with concern.

"So this is what you do to me? You have your crazy-ass brother kidnap me," she spat, anger mixing with relief.

"I had nothing to do with this," I told her, my heart aching at the betrayal.

"Don't explain shit to her," Armani snapped, his frustration palpable. I turned to face him, anger boiling inside me.

"Nigga, do you understand that I'm a nigga with a strike already against me? They'll put me under the jail and throw away the key if she goes to the cops about this!" I said, my voice rising, desperate to make him see reason.

"She's not going nowhere," Armani said, pulling out a gun, the metal glinting ominously in the low light.

"Armani, you're fucking tripping," I said, my heart racing as panic surged through me.

"Listen, I'm trying to make things right between us. You want Dior back? Well, the only way for that to happen is if this bitch is gone." He pointed the gun at Shanny, and my world tilted dangerously on its axis.

Shanny's eyes got big. "Aramni you can't do that dumb shit." I said to him. "why not? what else do you owe this bitch? because the only way you going to get Dior back is if this bitch is gone and out the picture." he said. "because she may be pregnant with my baby." I said walking back to Shanny and untieing her.

I helped Shanny off the ground. "hell nah this bitch not sending me to jail for trying to help you." he said. "i never told you to do this shit." i said back steping in front of Shanny. "bro just let me do it. You cant miss a baby you never meet." he said. "are you fucking crazy." I said to him. Armani click the gun and I kew that he was not at a point of reasoning. I punched him and we began to fight. the last thing I remember was the sound of a gun going off and a burning feeling.

TWENTY-FIVE

Dior

After seeing Armand in that office with another woman, there was no ifs, ands, or buts about it—I didn't give a fuck about whatever point Sergio was trying to make. It was time for us to go. The silence in the car was thick as we drove home, each of us lost in our thoughts, the tension crackling like static in the air.

When we finally pulled up to my house, I stepped out and headed inside, slamming my purse down on the table with a force that echoed through the empty space. "So can you cook since we left before eating?" Sergio said, his voice dripping with sarcasm.

"What?" I shot back, my eyes narrowing at him.

"I mean, it's only fair you let your little nigga fuck up our night," he replied, a cocky grin on his lips.

"No, both of you fucked up the night and had me all kinds of messed up. Next time you want to play this bullshit game of whose dick is bigger, keep me out of it. Now you can go," I snapped, turning on my heel and heading for the stairs.

"Nah, I think I'll stay," he said, following me closely.

"I think you won't. Ain't shit changed; you still don't live here," I shot back, my voice steady but my heart racing.

"Dior, you are my fucking wife!" he yelled, frustration boiling over.

"And your what? The consolation prize? No your what I fucking settled with. The love of my life is the man I just left at the restaurant. Had he not fucked up, I wouldn't have married you. And if he hadn't fucked up again, I wouldn't be standing here looking at you now."

"Dior, who the fuck you talking to?" he said, grabbing my arm as I turned to walk away.

I looked at his hand gripping me, then back at his face, anger igniting a fire in my chest. "You may be crazy, but you're not stupid. Get your fucking hands off me," I told him, my voice low and dangerous.

We stared each other down, the tension electric, until the shrill ring of my phone shattered the moment. I pulled it from my purse, still giving Sergio the death stare. "Hello," I answered, my voice tight.

"Armand has been shot. Get to the hospital now."

My heart dropped, panic flooding my veins. Without hesitation, I grabbed my keys and bolted for the door.

"Where are you going?" Sergio called after me, but I didn't answer. I jumped into my car and sped off, my mind racing with dread.

I drove at breakneck speed, praying with every ounce of my being. "Lord, you can't take him from me. Not like this."

When I pulled into the hospital parking lot, I spotted Ahmad jumping out of his car, his expression grim. We rushed inside together, my heart pounding in my ears, dread coiling tighter in my stomach. There, in the waiting room, was Armani—his clothes soaked in blood, his face pale and stricken with fear.

"What the fuck happened?" Ahmad asked, his voice

rising in disbelief.

"I fucked up," Armani kept saying, his voice shaky and filled with despair.

"Armani, what did you do? Is he okay?" I pressed, my heart racing as I reached for him, desperate for answers.

"I don't know. He hit me and we started fighting, and I dropped the gun. She picked it up and she shot him," he finally admitted, tears streaming down his cheeks.

"What?" Ahmad said, his eyes wide with shock. "Who is she?" I demanded, my heart sinking further.

"Shanny. I fucked up and—" Before Armani could say anything else, Ahmad cut him off.

"Shut up. Not here. When they ask, you found him like that. Did you drive him here?" Ahmad questioned, his tone sharp and commanding.

"Yes. Ahmad, I'm sorry, I didn't want him to get hurt," Armani said, his voice breaking.

Hall Pass

"Shut up," Ahmad snapped, his eyes hard with a mix of anger and concern. The weight of the situation crashed down around us, suffocating in its intensity. I could only think about the chaos that had led us here, how one reckless moment had irrevocably altered our lives.

I paced the floor, my stomach twisted in knots, anxiety clawing at my insides. It felt like we sat there for hours, waiting for news, the sterile smell of the hospital mingling with the heavy silence. Finally, a doctor emerged, his expression serious. "Riggin family?" he called out, and we all stood up, hearts racing.

"Yes, we are his brothers, and that's his girl," Ahmad said, stepping forward.

"Well, Mr. Riggin is lucky. A few more inches over, and he wouldn't be here with us. We were able to remove the bullet, but it was complicated. To control the situation, we had to put him in a medically induced coma. Until he comes out of it, he'll be in ICU, so only one of you can go back and see him at a time."

I grabbed my purse, knowing Ahmad would be the one to sit with him. But to my surprise, I heard him say, "She's going to go back with him and keep the rest of us updated."

I looked at him, my heart racing. "You sure?" I asked, a mix of gratitude and anxiety flooding me.

"Yeah, I'm sure. There's no one else he'd rather see when he wakes up," he said with conviction.

"Umm, okay," I replied, my voice shaky.

I followed the staff back to his room, and as I walked in and saw him hooked up to all those machines, it felt like my knees might give out. The sight of him lying there, so vulnerable, made my stomach churn. I wasn't sure if it was the overwhelming emotions or the hospital smell, but suddenly, my mouth went dry, and nausea washed over me. "I need a bathroom," I told the nurse, who quickly guided me away.

I lost track of time in that small, sterile room, trying to calm my racing heart. When I finally emerged, the nurse was waiting for me. "I wasn't sure if you wanted to get comfortable since you're all dressed up, but I put a set of scrubs in the room for you," she said kindly.

"Thank you," I murmured as she left me alone with Armand. I changed my clothes and pulled a chair close to his bedside, needing to feel connected to him, even if he was still unconscious.

Time stretched on, and I stayed right by Armand's side. He hadn't woken yet, but at least he was off the machines and breathing on his own. I found myself in and out of the bathroom, throwing up more than I could count. I didn't know why; the stress was overwhelming. When I stepped out again, the nurse was there, checking his vitals.

"Are you okay?" she asked, concern etched on her face.

"Yeah, I'm just not sure what's going on. I've been sick since I got here. I think it's the nerves—just wanting to know he's okay," I replied, trying to mask my anxiety.

"You know, I found out I was pregnant while sitting in a hospital room just like this after my husband was shot," she said, her tone light but with a hint of understanding.

"Well, I know I'm not that," I said quickly, trying to brush off the thought.

"I said the same thing," she laughed gently. "But my grandma told me, if you've been fucking, you could be pregnant."

We shared a laugh, but it didn't fully ease my mind.

"Well, let me know if you need anything," she said as she exited the room.

As I sat there, my thoughts spiraled. Armand and I had been reckless, no protection used more times than I could count. There was no way I could be pregnant—especially with his actual wife already pregnant. Just the thought of it sent my mind into a tailspin.

Suddenly, my phone rang, pulling me from my thoughts. "Hello?" I answered, my heart racing.

"How is he?" Ahmad's voice came through, tense and anxious.

"He's off the machines but still hasn't woken up," I told him, my voice shaking.

"This shit is crazy," he replied. "How's Armani?"

"He'll be okay," he answered. There was a heavy silence, then I ventured, "Have you seen her?"

"Nah, she's hiding, but she can't stay that way for long. We'll find her," he said firmly. "In the meantime, keep me updated on what they're saying about my baby bro. And be careful—if that bitch comes up there, call me ASAP."

"Okay, I will," I promised, hanging up. The moment the call ended, I rushed back to the bathroom, feeling the bile rising again.

I couldn't take it anymore. I needed to know for sure, so I decided to take a test. The thought of being pregnant consumed me, and I knew I had to find out.

When I came out of the bathroom, I rang for the nurse, and the same one returned. "Yes?" she asked, her smile warm.

"Can I get a test?" I asked, my voice steady despite my racing heart.

"Sure, let me go find one, and I'll bring it back," she said, disappearing down the corridor.

I sat back in the chair, anxiety twisting in my stomach, waiting for the answer that could change everything. The sterile smell of the hospital mixed with the tension in the air made it feel like I was suffocating under the weight of uncertainty.

The nurse returned, placing a pee cup and a test in front of me. "Sorry it took so long. I had to run to the gas station to grab this. You can pee in this cup, and I'll get my girl downstairs in the lab to run it," she explained, her tone casual but kind.

I nodded, barely processing her words. Once she walked out, I stared at the test for a moment, my heart racing. I grabbed the cup and rushed to the bathroom, every step heavy with dread. I peed in the cup and dipped the test into it, sealing it before I could second-guess myself. Standing there, I felt like I was holding my breath, waiting to see what the little stick would reveal.

When the positive sign appeared, I covered my mouth in shock, the realization hitting me like a freight train. I snapped a quick picture, wrapped the test in tissue, and tossed it in the trash, as if getting rid of the evidence could somehow change the reality of it all. I stepped back into the room and called for the nurse.

When she saw the cup, she quickly put on gloves and took it from me. "Once I run this, I'll bring the results back to you," she assured me.

Waiting for her to return felt like an eternity. When she finally stepped in, she handed me an envelope. My hands trembled as I opened it, and there it was, clear as day:

Pregnant. I took another picture and sent both results to Destiny. Within seconds, my phone started ringing.

I hurried back to the bathroom for some privacy. "Hello?"

"Who's pregnant?" Destiny asked, her voice sharp with curiosity.

"Me," I confessed, feeling the weight of the words as they left my lips.

"Bitch, I know you lying," she replied, incredulous.

"I'm so serious."

"Oh my god, friend, you're pregnant!" she exclaimed, excitement pouring through the phone.

"Yes," I confirmed, my heart racing.

"You've got to tell Armand, 'cause I know it's his," she insisted.

"How do you know?" I challenged her.

"Because Sergio's dick ain't that good to be making babies," she said, laughter bubbling up.

"Well, I can't tell Armand," I told her, my voice dropping.

"Girl, you better get over that mad shit and tell that man," Destiny urged.

"I'm not even mad! His wife shot him! I've been here in the hospital since it happened, just waiting for him to wake up," I replied, frustration creeping in.

"Damn," was all Destiny could say.

We chatted for a little longer, Destiny doing her best to encourage me. When we hung up, I looked in the mirror, the gravity of the situation crashing down on me. "God, you've got to let him pull through—for the sake of me and this baby," I whispered to my reflection, feeling a mix of hope and dread.

Another day passed, and I longed to hear Armand's voice. I sat holding his hand, reminiscing about all the moments we'd shared. "Armand, you are amazing. You're so much more than what you've been through. You are strong, an incredible man, a protector, and a lover. You've put me first time and time again. I didn't say it enough, but I love you. You can't leave me. I need you here with me. You've got to pull through this. I'm so sorry for pushing you away. I mishandled you, and now I see that. If you just wake up, I'd give us another chance," I cried, tears spilling down my cheeks.

"Do you promise?" I suddenly heard a weak voice say, sending a jolt of shock through me.

"Armand!" I jumped up, my heart soaring.

"Hey," he said, trying to muster a smile despite the pain.

I quickly pressed the call button, my heart racing as I waited for the nurse. Her face lit up when she saw he was awake, and she hurried to call for the doctors. After a series of tests and a conversation with Ahmad on speakerphone, Armand was moved to a normal room.

I sat in the chair across from him, just soaking in the sight of him, until he broke the silence. "Did you mean what you said?" he asked, his gaze locking onto mine.

"Huh?" I responded, momentarily lost.

"About giving it another chance."

I looked at him, processing his words. "Don't tell me that was just an opinion because you thought I was dying," he said, a hint of desperation in his voice.

"I will give this another chance, but… we have to take it slow," I said firmly.

"Okay, so as soon as they let me out of here, we're going on a trip," he declared, determination shining in his eyes.

"Armand, I said take it slow. We need to be somewhere it's just me and you, where we can fully focus on each other," he replied.

"Okay, but not until they give you the okay to be on a plane," he insisted.

"I'm getting on one with or without their okay. All I need is you and some painkillers, and I'll be fine," he said, a

Hall Pass

teasing smile breaking through the seriousness of the moment.

I couldn't help but smile back, feeling the warmth of hope flooding back into my heart.

TWENTY-SIX

Armand

After what felt like an eternity in the hospital, the plane rumbled gently through the clouds, a silver bird slicing through the vast expanse of blue sky and giving peace to my mind. It was a peaceful sight, despite the fact that the doctor had strongly disagreed with my decision to travel. But I wasn't about to waste another second waiting to fix things with Dior. I sat next to her, my fingers drumming nervously against the armrest, each tap echoing the frantic rhythm of my heart. With everything that had happened, instead of being furious with Shanny for her betrayal, I chose to see it as a second chance. I had Dior here with me, and that was all that mattered.

I had even told Ahmad and Armani to let Shanny be, even though she had gone MIA since the shooting. There was no point in adding more chaos to an already tumultuous situation. But I wasn't naive; I made it a priority to get the divorce papers filed. The relief that came with that decision was almost intoxicating—I was finally free.

Hall Pass

The hum of the engines filled the silence between us, but it was nothing compared to the weight of the words I needed to say to Dior. This trip had been meticulously planned—even from my hospital bed, every detail crafted with the hope that a change of scenery would help mend the fractures in our love.

Dior gazed out the window, her expression unreadable, lost in thoughts I could only guess at. The sun cast a golden glow on her skin, illuminating the high cheekbones that had once made my heart race. She was breathtaking, and I couldn't shake the prayer that everything would go as planned on this trip. I found myself lost in memories of our late-night conversations, the way her laughter danced through the air, how her eyes sparkled when she spoke of her dreams, and the warmth that enveloped us when we cuddled. But that was before the truth had shattered our fragile world.

"Dior," I began, my voice barely above a whisper. She turned to me, her eyes narrowing slightly, a mix of curiosity and caution that sent my stomach into a tight knot. "I know this trip was… unexpected."

"Unexpected is an understatement, Armand," she replied, a hint of sarcasm lacing her words. "Just promise me you'll keep an open mind. Enjoy yourself on my dime."

"Okay," she said back, her tone dry but with an edge of vulnerability that tugged at my heart.

I swallowed hard, the memory of the bullet that had nearly taken my life still fresh in my mind, a brutal wake-up call that forced me to confront my demons. "Dior, I know I messed up. This trip is just the beginning of me trying to fix things. I swear I'll spend the rest of my life making it right for you."

As I spoke, the weight of my promise hung in the air—heavy and real. The clouds parted slightly, allowing a beam of sunlight to stream through, illuminating the space between us. In that moment, I clung to the hope that this trip could be the fresh start we so desperately needed.

Dior's gaze dropped to her lap, a silent acknowledgment of the pain I had caused. "You put me in a position where I had to question everything I thought I knew about you and myself. I can't just forget that," she said, her voice trembling with emotion.

"And I'm not asking you to," I replied, my heart racing. "I'm asking you to let me work towards earning your trust and love again." The look in her eyes told me she was fighting back a storm of words and tears, and it broke me a little more.

We were headed to a small coastal town, a place I had googled obsessively, always saying I'd go when I had the time. It was a paradise where the sands were soft and the waves whispered secrets to the shore. I had chosen it for its beauty, hoping it would soften Dior's heart. But I knew that beauty alone wouldn't mend the fractures between us; I had real work to do.

When we landed, the warm sun enveloped us, and I took a deep breath, letting the salty air fill my lungs. This was the ultimate recovery—way better than being cooped up in a depressing house with my mind racing. I glanced over at Dior, adjusting her sunglasses, her posture still a fortress of guarded emotions. Reaching for her hand felt monumental, but I had to try. "Can we just… take this one step at a time? I want to show you how serious I am about making things right."

She hesitated, her eyes flickering with uncertainty. "Fine. But don't think this means I trust you again."

As we got into the car and headed to the house I had rented, anticipation buzzed in the air. Everything should have been ready for our arrival. When we pulled up to the gate, I was taken aback by the sight of the house. I had booked it based on the pictures and ratings, but none of that did it justice. The place was stunning, complete with a full staff, housekeeping, and even a personal chef.

As we stepped inside, I couldn't help but point out, "I had your own room set up."

"Yes, sir! We can take you to the rooms now," one of the bellboys chimed in, breaking the moment.

We followed them as they led us to the rooms. Dior's room was first, and they had followed my instructions to a T. There were flowers everywhere, and a balcony that opened up to breathtaking views of the water. They even had her bath water ready, steaming and inviting. "You like?" I asked, a hopeful smile on my face.

"It's beautiful," she replied, her voice softer than before. "Well, unwind. I've got the chef preparing dinner for us at 6 PM," I said, making sure she felt comfortable before the bellboys led me to my room.

I took a short nap, but before I knew it, it was time to get dressed. I had planned a candlelit dinner in the backyard, something special to set the tone for our fresh start. I pulled out the all-black outfit I had packed and called to make sure they'd delivered the all-black dress I had chosen for Dior.

When she finally emerged, my breath hitched in my throat. The dress hugged her in all the right places, accentuating her curves perfectly, but nothing could compare to the way her face glowed with a renewed freshness.

I stood up, pulling out her chair with a flourish. She sat down, rolling her eyes playfully. "Don't overwork yourself," she said reminding me of my injury.

"I'm good," I replied, grinning. Dinner was a quiet affair at first as we savored each course the chef brought out, the tension between us palpable. Finally, I decided it was time to clear the air. "So, I really want us both to enjoy this trip, so I want to talk that way you can have all the time you need to think while we are here.

"Okay, put it all on the table." she said, her tone cautious.

"I married Shanny a few years back after my mom passed. Her dad was my cellmate in jail, and when some guys tried to jump me, he saved my life. He taught me more than I ever thought possible during my bid. I felt like I owed him something. So when he asked me to marry his daughter—the high school dropout with dreams but not much else—I hesitated but eventually said yes. I never thought I'd run into you again or have the chance to fall in love like this."

"Why didn't you tell me this in the beginning?" she asked, her brow furrowing, a mix of confusion and hurt in her eyes.

"Because I was already seeking a way out. I had moved out of the house and into the hotel," I admitted, each word heavy on my tongue.

"The hotel you own?" she interjected, disbelief coloring her tone, her eyes widening in surprise.

"Yes. I didn't mention the hotel or my money because I had a wife who was a gold digger. I wanted our relationship to be genuine, no strings attached," I explained, my heart racing as I hoped she'd understand.

"I'm not a gold digger! I was with you when you had nothing," she shot back, her passion igniting the air between us.

"I'm not saying you are. I just wanted a pure relationship without any baggage. I knew you didn't need me then, and you still don't," I said, trying to clarify, my voice softening.

"And what about Renee?" she pressed, her tone sharp.

"She just wanted some dick, and I was being childish. I was so mad about you being there with Sergio," I confessed, the weight of my past mistakes crashing down on me.

"Yeah, and you almost got yourself and her fucked up," she said, shaking her head, disbelief mingling with concern.

"Baby, at the end of the day, I'm sorry. I want to start fresh, no secrets between us. So here," I said, sliding a folder across the table, my heart pounding.

"What's this?" she asked, opening it, her curiosity piqued.

"I'm now legally divorced," I told her, holding my breath, dreading her reaction.

"But I'm not," she replied, a whirlwind of emotions crossing her face.

"And I'll wait for you, no matter how long it takes," I assured her. She nodded, reaching into her purse and pulling out a small envelope, sliding it across to me.

I opened it, my heart racing. "How are you going to handle me and her being pregnant?" My face lit up as I stared at the paperwork from the doctor. I jumped up from my seat, lifting Dior out of hers and spinning her around, forgetting all about my injury in my excitement.

"Bae, you can't be lifting me!" she laughed, a mix of surprise and joy in her voice.

"You're having my baby!" I exclaimed, unable to contain my excitement, the reality washing over us like a wave.

"Yes! That's why you had to pull through in that hospital," she said, her eyes sparkling with happiness. But her smile quickly faded. "What's wrong?" I asked, sensing her shift.

"This shit is going to be so ghetto—me and your ex wife pregnant at the same damn time," she said, a hint of worry creeping into her tone.

"Don't worry about that," I reassured her, though I could see the concern etched on her face.

"How can I not? Our baby and his or her brother or sister are going to be born just weeks apart," she said, her voice rising, frustration bubbling beneath the surface.

"Baby, I don't even think Shanny's pregnant. I've been asking her for a test or documents from a doctor, and she won't give them to me. If she's pregnant, she'd have some type of belly because the last time I touched her was the morning after I ran into you and Destiny." A look of realization crossed Dior's face as she processed my words.

"There's something else I want to tell you," I said,

Hall Pass

steeling myself.

"Go ahead. I said put it all on the table," she urged, her eyes locked onto mine.

"I'm the reason why Sergio was in the hospital. I was so mad at how he treated you that I pulled up on him before he could go into work and beat his ass," I confessed, the weight of my actions hanging heavy in the air.

Dior's face was serious for a moment, then it broke into laughter. I was confused, caught off guard.

"That nigga got what he deserved. I should've let you beat his ass at the restaurant, but I was still mad at you," she said, her laughter infectious.

I joined in, a weight lifting off my chest. "Girl, you've got a hold on me. There's nothing I wouldn't do for you."

"How about to me?" she said with a smirk, mischief dancing in her eyes.

"Oh, we being nasty now?" I teased, my heart racing.

"Between the throwing up, this pregnancy's got me horny all the time," she admitted, her voice sultry.

I laughed, the tension between us crackling. "Well, baby, you know damn well I aim to please when it comes to you. You could lay across this table right now, and I'd eat you up," I told her, my desire bubbling to the surface.

"Well, shit, fuck this food. Let's go back to my room," she said, her eyes sparkling with mischief.

"Nah," I replied, and she looked at me, confusion washing over her. "I don't want to rush into anything on the first night. I want you to be able to take in everything I've told you and think about it without distractions."

I could tell she didn't like that, but she nodded, a reluctant acceptance in her eyes.

In that moment, everything felt right. The past didn't disappear, but it was a new beginning, and I was ready to embrace it all—together.

We spent the rest of the night talking, laughter filling the spaces where silence once lingered. I couldn't wipe the smile off my face, even as we danced to slow music, lost in each other. I admired her, thinking about how amazing it was that we were about to have a kid.

As I walked Dior back to her room, I kissed her forehead softly. She held on to my hand for a moment with the door open, her eyes sparkling, looking like she wanted to pull me in. But she finally let me go, and I felt the weight of the night settle around us, promising more to come.

The next day, I wanted to sleep in, but Dior knocked on my door, her energy infectious. She wanted to spend the day exploring the vibrant streets. So, I got up and dressed, ready to dive into the city with her.

We wandered through colorful murals and bustling markets that pulsed with life. I pointed out the little things I loved about the town—how the sun set over the water, how the local café served the best pastries. I wanted her to see the man I could be, not the one who had hurt her.

As evening approached, we found ourselves at a beachside restaurant, the golden hues of sunset painting the sky in breathtaking swirls. The atmosphere was electric, laughter and music mingling in the air like a living thing. I watched Dior, and it was like she was glowing to me, her smile lighting up the space around us, reminding me of everything I'd missed.

"Do you remember our first date?" I asked, a hint of nostalgia creeping into my voice, ready to weave our past into this beautiful present.

She raised an eyebrow, a playful smirk tugging at her lips. "How could I forget? You were late because your little car broke down."

"But I made it up to you with those terrible tacos," I chuckled, recalling the memory of those nasty street tacos we devoured because we were too late to catch the movie we'd been dying to see.

Dior laughed then, a sound that sent warmth flooding through me. "Those were awful. I still can't believe you thought random food truck tacos were going to be good!"

"Hey, I was young and reckless," I replied, leaning in slightly, letting the warmth of the moment wrap around us. "I didn't know anything about good food back then."

As the sun dipped below the horizon, casting a warm glow over the sea, we finished our food, and I asked Dior if she wanted to join me for a walk on the beach. Holding her hand felt electric as we strolled along the shoreline. I turned to her, my heart pounding. "Dior, I need you to know that I'm committed to being better. I messed up, but I want to be the man you deserve."

Hall Pass

Her eyes searched mine for sincerity, piercing through the walls I had built around myself. "Being better isn't enough, Armand. You need to show me that you mean it. Actions speak louder than words. We have a baby on the way—what kind of example will we be setting?"

I nodded, the weight of her statement settling deep in my chest. "I know. I will. Just… give me a chance."

We walked barefoot along the beach, the waves lapping at our feet, and I felt a surge of determination. I picked up a shell, smooth and iridescent, and handed it to her. "For you," I said, watching her face light up as she examined it, her fingers tracing the delicate patterns.

"You always did have a knack for finding the pretty things," she said, a hint of warmth creeping into her voice, and for a moment, it felt like we were back to the beginning—two kids lost in the magic of the moment.

We walked in silence, the moon now casting a silver path across the water. I felt the enormity of the moment, the delicate balance of our past and what could still be. I took a deep breath, steeling myself for the next step.

"Dior," I said, stopping to face her, the cool breeze

swirling around us. "I'm not asking for everything to be fixed right now. But I want to be part of your life again. I want our child to see their momma and daddy in love, just like you saw your parents. I want to provide, protect, and be a husband and father. I bought this a while ago, and I wasn't sure if the time would ever come. I know this isn't ideal and you have to handle Sergio, but will you marry me?" I said, kneeling in the sand and pulling the four-karat ring from my pocket, the diamond glinting in the moonlight.

She studied me, her expression softening, tears welling in her eyes. "Well..." I held my breath, waiting for her answer. She started to nod her head. "Yes. Yes, I will!" she said, pulling off her ring from Sergio and tossing it into the waves, as if shedding the past.

"I'm willing to wait; we don't have to rush into a marriage. But you putting on this ring lets me know that we are a family," I said, my voice steady as I spun her around. We kissed, and in that moment, I felt like this second chance God gave me was nothing short of a blessing.

As we stood there, the waves crashing softly against the shore, I knew this trip was just the beginning. I would fight for her—not just with words, but with every action I took. The journey ahead would be long and fraught with challenges, but for the first time in ages, I felt like I could see a path forward.

We made our way back to the house. I dropped Dior off

at her room. "Come in," she told me, her voice laced with an invitation.

"No, I still don't want to rush into sex," I told her, sensing the disappointment on her face. I wanted to show my love for her without jumping into bed, but I couldn't lie—I was craving her like crazy. I leaned in, giving her a kiss, our lips locking together, igniting a fire that made my body stand at attention. I had to stop myself.

"Goodnight," I murmured, reluctantly pulling away and heading to my room. I quickly jumped in the shower, trying to wash away the tension and relax. As I lay in bed, the weight of the day settled over me.

Then I heard a soft knock on the door, and my heart raced. Dior had always had that effect on me—a mere sound made by her could send my thoughts spiraling. I opened the door, and there she stood in a black silk gown that hugged her curves, framed by the soft glow of the hallway light. Her eyes sparkled with seduction.

"Can I come in?" she asked, not really looking for an answer, because she walked in before I could respond.

As she entered, I couldn't help but notice how the room seemed to come alive with her presence. The quiet intimacy of the space wrapped around us like an embrace. I closed the door behind us, the click echoing in the charged atmosphere.

"Armand," she began, her voice low and sultry. "Yes?" I replied, my pulse quickening.

"I want you. I'm not asking you. I'm telling you. I know you've been trying to be a gentleman, and that's all nice, but I need to feel you inside me. Even if that means I have to do all the work due to you being hurt."

I stepped closer, feeling the magnetic pull between us. "Do you really?" I said, teasingly licking my lips, watching her reaction.

"Yes," she moaned, her breath hitching as she untied my towel, revealing the desire that simmered just beneath the surface.

"Damn," was all I could let out, the sensation overwhelming as I felt the heat radiating between us, igniting something primal deep within.

Our eyes locked, and the air thickened with unspoken words, heavy with desire.

"I'm gonna be gentle with you tonight, I promise," she said, her voice low and sultry as she began to stroke my manhood. "Damn," was all I could manage, the pleasure coursing through me.

I reached out, taking her hand in mine, feeling the warmth of her skin send a rush of electricity through my body. She pushed me back on the bed, and I laid there, watching her as she leaned down, ready to give me head. "Good girl. Look at me," I murmured, moving her hair aside to fully appreciate her beautiful face.

Pregnancy had unleashed a freak in Dior; her skills were on a whole different level tonight, or maybe she just really missed me. Either way, I was sure I could last more than five minutes. She smirked as she swallowed my juices, and my heart raced.

"On my face now," I commanded, my voice firm.

"Baby, you gotta relax," she replied, her eyes sparkling with mischief.

"I wasn't asking; I'm telling you. On my face now. Either you're gonna sit on it willingly, or I'm gonna put you on it myself," I said, my words dripping with lust. She bit her lip, a clear sign that I had her turned on.

I got comfortable on the bed, and she climbed on top, making my face her seat. She moaned as she rode me, rocking her hips in perfect rhythm. She tasted like the best dessert I had ever had—sweet and intoxicating. Each time I slid my tongue into her, she responded with a soft gasp, her warmth enveloping me. "Oh my God, baby," she said, grabbing the headboard for support.

I held her hips, anchoring her in place, not wanting her to move until my throat and face were coated with her juices. When I was finally done with her, she was shaking, trying to get down.

"You done?" I asked, my breath heavy.

She nodded, but the fire in her eyes told me she wasn't finished. "Use your words, baby. Tell me exactly what you want."

"I want you to make me release like a waterfall," she said, her voice a mix of desperation and need.

I spread her legs and rubbed her clit, teasing her sensitive spot, knowing just how to push her buttons. "Baby," she moaned, her body arching toward me.

"You want it?" I asked, my voice low.

"Yes," she replied breathlessly.

"Beg for it," I commanded, leaning closer.

"Baby, please give it to me," she pleaded, and with that, I slid in, starting slow and gentle, but going deeper and harder with every thrust as she begged for more. I could feel her body tensing, her walls tightening around me.

"Let it all out," I encouraged.

"Not yet. I'm waiting on you," she said, her eyes locked onto mine.

"Give it to me. Cover me with it. I'm ready," I told her, feeling the tension build between us. Within minutes, we both reached our peaks, our bodies shuddering in unison. We went a few more rounds, even sneaking into the shower, the hot water cascading down our bodies, amplifying the pleasure.

When we finally tapped out, she laid in bed, and I held her close, rubbing her belly, both of us basking in the afterglow.

The rest of the trip was filled with smiles, love-making, and making memories that felt like a dream. But soon, it was time to return home. We got off our flight and headed straight to Dior's house. I honestly couldn't wait to help her move out of that place. Every time we were here, I felt the weight of her sharing this house with Sergio.

We came in and went straight to the bedroom to take a nap after that long flight. But when we opened the door, I couldn't believe what I was seeing. "Shanny!" I screamed out, shock coursing through me.

Shanny turned around, her eyes wide, with Sergio underneath her.

Dior's expression twisted into anger as she turned to look at me. "Is your ex-wife fucking my still-husband in my damn bed?" she demanded, disbelief and fury radiating from her.

I couldn't even figure out what to say. "Well, I just figured you had my husband, so I should sample yours. And girl, now I know why you wanted mine," Shanny said, smiling as if this were all a game.

"Dior, let me explain," Sergio said, looking stupid and

desperate.

"Both of you get out of my house!" Dior yelled, her voice shaking with rage.

"Baby, relax. Think about the baby," I urged, trying to keep her calm despite the chaos surrounding us. I didn't want her to get too angry, but my heart raced at the situation.

"Baby?" Shanny scoffed, disbelief dripping from her voice.

"Yes, she's having my baby," I said, locking eyes with Shanny, daring her to say anything else.

"Bitch," Shanny hissed as she started to move toward Dior, looking like she wanted to fight.

I stepped in front of Dior, my protective instincts kicking in. "I wish you would. I will break your fucking face," I warned her, my voice low and dangerous.

"I already shot you once," she shot back, a smirk on her lips.

"And there won't be a next time," I countered, my gaze unwavering.

"Dior, you're having his baby?" Sergio asked, his voice incredulous.

"I am," she answered, her voice steady despite the storm around us.

All hell broke loose in that room, and before I knew it, the sound of a gunshot rang out, slicing through the chaos like a knife.

.

Hall Pass

Coming soon

Purchase the next book in the Hall Pass Series

https://authorbreannaj.com/collections/frontpage/produ cts/hall-pass-2

Breanna J

CHECK OUT OTHER BOOKS BY AUTHOR BREANNA J.

- In the Name of Love
- In the Name of Love 2
- The Cost of Love
- No more secrets
- Feelings
- Pleasurable Desires
- The Entanglement
- Unexpected
- Still Unexpected
- Pleasurable Desires 2

Breanna J

Author Breanna J ORDER FORM
www.authorbreannaj.com

Book Title	Price	Check to order
In the name of love	$10.99	
In the name of Love 2	$11.99	
The Cost of Love	$14.50	
No More secrets	$9.95	
Feeling	$10.50	
Pleasurable Desire	$14.50	
The Entanglement	$19.50	
Unexpected	$20.00	
Still Unexpected	$22.00	
Pleasurable Desires 2	20.00	
Hall Pass	$22.00	
Total		

CUSTOMER'S NAME_____
ADDRESS:_____

Hall Pass

CITY/STATE: _____
CONTACT/EMAIL: _____
Shipping [ ]   Drop off [ ] Pick up [ ]
Please Allow 8-10 Business Days Before Shipping NOTE: Due to COVID-19 Some Orders May Take Up To 3 Weeks Before They Ship. We are NOT responsible for lost of damaged packages NO RETURNS and NO REFUNDS
Payment Methods
Cash app:$authorbreannaj [ ] Paypal:@authorbreanna [ ] Venmo:@author-Breanna [ ]

Breanna J